HOW TO TAME A *Wild* FIREMAN

A BACHELOR FIREMEN NOVEL

Jennifer Bernard

D0001965

AVON

An Imprint of HarperCollins*Publishers*

This book is a work of fiction. References to real people, events, establishments, organizations, or locales are intended only to provide a sense of authenticity, and are used fictitiously. All other characters, and all incidents and dialogue, are drawn from the author's imagination and are not to be construed as real.

AVON BOOKS
An Imprint of HarperCollins*Publishers*
10 East 53rd Street
New York, New York 10022-5299

Copyright © 2013 by Jennifer Bernard
ISBN 978-0-06-227365-9
www.avonromance.com

First Avon Books mass market printing: October 2013

Avon Trademark Reg. U.S. Pat. Off. and in Other Countries, Marca Registrada, Hecho en U.S.A.
HarperCollins® is a registered trademark of HarperCollins Publishers.

Printed in the U.S.A.

10 9 8 7 6 5 4 3 2 1

To my family, in the widest sense of the word

Acknowledgments

I'd like to thank wildland firefighters John LeClair and Kristin Dunlap, along with Captain Rick Godinez of the Los Angeles Fire Department, for sharing their knowledge of firefighting. Any mistakes are mine, not theirs. Many thanks to Jenny Bartholomew for her insights into special needs children. To my critique partners, Lizbeth Selvig and Tam Linsey, what would I do without you? And finally, grateful thanks to my editor, Tessa Woodward, the entire Avon team, and my agent extraordinaire, Alexandra Machinist.

HOW TO
TAME A
Wild
FIREMAN

Chapter One

Ten years ago

There are tattoo *parlors* and then there are tattoo *studios*. The Rusty Needle was definitely the former, thought Lara Nelson as she dismounted from the back of her friend Liam's dirt bike. Liam's brother Patrick had already parked his motorcycle and was staring at the grungy back-alley hole in the wall, which looked even dingier at this late hour. Sailors would love this place; hipsters not so much. Its curb appeal consisted of a broken neon sign and a skull and crossbones decal on the front door. She hadn't even known the place existed in Loveless, Nevada.

"I'm not getting an infection just because you want to impress your Princeton friends," she grumbled as she caught up with Patrick. Liam glanced her way, and she quickly signed the same sentiment to him.

Seamlessly, they all switched to signing.

"I don't give a crap about Princeton," said Patrick. "This is for my brother. So he doesn't forget me when I turn into an Ivy League dickhead."

"You're only a dickhead sometimes," signed Liam, who didn't understand sarcasm. Lara laughed, giddy after a night spent driving aimlessly around Loveless. There weren't many night spots to choose from in their town.

"This is for you too, Lara," Patrick said out loud, which he did when he wanted to tease Lara without upsetting Liam. "A souvenir of Loveless to take to college with you."

"There's got to be a better souvenir than an infection," she said dubiously. She stared at the daunting sign in which half the letters flickered sickly. "The Rusty Needle?"

"There's a T in front of Rusty. It's the Trusty Needle. Perfectly safe."

Squinting, she peered more closely. "I don't see any T."

"It fell off, then. Seriously, who would name a tattoo parlor the Rusty Needle? Anyway, this is the only one that's open. And we haven't even gone inside yet. Grow some balls, Lulu."

"What would I do with those?" she snapped back. She refused, absolutely refused, to protest the nickname. He knew she hated it, but she wouldn't let him get to her.

Patrick, the older brother and most annoying guy in town, if you asked Lara, was the usual instigator of mayhem. Lara's role was to make sure her best friend, Liam, didn't get steamrolled into doing something he didn't want.

She stood between the two brothers and quickly signed to Liam. "You don't have to do this, Liam. We can hang out while Patrick gets his tattoo, then laugh when he cries like a baby."

"I want one," he signed back, seriously. "If we make sure it's well-sterilized, I want to get 'wild thing' tattooed on my butt."

She bit back a smile. Liam was not a wild thing. He was the dreamy one, the offbeat one, always lost in his own world.

Patrick Callahan, on the other hand . . .

"I want a freaking ball of flames streaking across my chest." Patrick cackled gleefully, his bright blue eyes glinting in the neon light.

"Subtle."

"Maybe you should get little bunny fou-fou hopping across your shoulder blade," he mocked, touching the back of her shoulder.

Fiercely, she tamped down the quick shiver that went through her. This was new, this weird, totally unwelcome attraction that had sprung up since Patrick had come back from college for Christmas break. She didn't even like Patrick. He was too crazy, too reckless, too . . . unnerving. She always felt on edge around him. But Liam idolized him. Since she and Liam had bonded as fellow misfits the first day she walked into Loveless Middle School, she was stuck with his older brother too.

"Screw that," she retorted, adjusting her ripped black tunic top, which she'd layered over a black tube top. Black was her favorite color, the only color that made her feel safe. She'd even dyed her blond hair black. "If I'm doing it, I'm getting something weird and different."

"Dragon?" he mocked. "Chicks love dragons."

"No. Nothing girlie. Something like . . . I don't know. A jellyfish."

"A *jellyfish*?"

"Okay, maybe a squid. Squid. Ink. Get it?"

He shook his head. "Why don't you at least *try* to be sexy, now that you're getting out of Loveless? You might be able to pull it off."

God, she hated him. And of course she wouldn't try to be sexy. That was the last thing she wanted, being who she was, living where she did. But Patrick wouldn't understand. He would never get how it felt to be an outcast, the way she and Liam did.

Liam broke into their conversation. "No fights. Are we going to get the tattoos?"

"That's a hell yes," signed Patrick, with a quick, challenging glance at Lara. "I'm in. No fear. Seize the day. We'll never forget this moment, the three of us getting jabbed with needles and spilling blood together."

Lara realized things were spiraling out of control, which happened a lot with Patrick around. "I didn't bring enough cash."

"It's on me. Do or die. Together forever." Patrick put one arm around each of them and shepherded them toward the door of the Rusty, and hopefully Trusty, Needle.

By the time they stumbled out, it was sometime around four in the morning. Night hung still and clear around them. Stars glimmered overhead. Pain throbbed in their various body parts. Only Liam had backed out, unable to get past his fear of germs. He'd watched the tattoo artist like a hawk the entire time to make sure everything was properly sterilized. The smell of rubbing alcohol surrounded them like a toxic cloud. Their eyes were bleary, their senses stunned.

Patrick looked exhilarated. "Whooo-hoooo!" He howled into the night sky. "Now that's what I'm talking about! Yeah, baby!" He vaulted onto his bike. "Hell if I can sleep after that. Anyone want to head out to the cliffs?"

"No!" Lara folded her arms across her chest, although every movement of her left arm felt uncomfortable. She didn't even want to think about the ridiculous goldfish on her upper arm. It was the closest design to a squid the tattoo artist knew how to do. "I'm going home."

Liam signed. "Do you need a ride?"

"Nope. You know how the Haven feels about motor vehicles. I'd rather walk. I need the fresh air." Her Aunt Tam, head of the Haven for Sexual and Spiritual Healing, tried to maintain a tranquil atmosphere free from engine noise. Exceptions were made, of course, but not at four in the morning. "But . . . uh, yeah. It's been real. Drive safe."

"Safe?" Patrick started his bike. The drone of its engine echoed through the empty, down-at-heels street. "What kind of boring-ass word is 'safe'? I want to live on the edge! Be wild! Go crazy! Right, Liam?"

He signed the gist of his manifesto to Liam, who gave a worried shake of his head. Lara knew he was fretting about the lateness, even though Friday night was the Callahan brothers' designated late night out. Lara's heart ached for her friend. Oh, Liam, with his quiet manner and guileless blue eyes. Always in Patrick's shadow, though he never seemed to mind. Then again, it could be hard to tell what he minded, since social interactions were challenging for him.

"Whatever," she signed, flapping her hands against each other. "I'm out. See you whenever."

Liam gave her an awkward wave. Then he carefully

climbed onto his bike. Patrick offered a soldier's salute. "We who are about to face our father's wrath salute you."

She waved good-bye and turned toward the empty street that would take her home. The last she heard of Liam and Patrick was the receding roar of their two bikes and the occasional war whoop from Patrick.

She had no idea everything would change— forever—fifteen minutes later.

Ten years later

News spread fast in San Gabriel Fire Station 1. In the apparatus bay, Fred the "Stud" abandoned Engine 1 mid-chrome-polishing and raced to the training room. From the workout room, Vader saw him run past and tossed his fifty-pound free weight aside. Double D nearly tripped over it, but in his eagerness to see what was happening, managed to leap high in the air, agile as a gazelle.

"What's going on?" asked a bewildered Sabina Jones as firefighters streamed past.

"It's Psycho," someone panted. "He's gone crazy."

"Always a relative term when it comes to him," Sabina grumbled as she followed the general flow of movement.

Captain Brody stepped out of his office, where he'd been trying to distract himself from the imminent birth of his baby with a pile of paperwork. He took in the madness, a faint frown creasing his forehead. "What the hell is this all about?"

"Psycho's got an excavator!" Fred shouted. "He's in the backyard."

The captain looked at Sabina, who shrugged. "You got me, Cap. I heard all the shouting and came running."

Vader picked up the intercom through which fire-fighters made general announcements about such things as dinner and handball matches. "Attention, everyone. If anyone's missing a sweet piece of heavy equipment, you might want to check the backyard. She weighs two tons, she's painted bright yellow, and she's a hot little piece of machinery."

"Get off that thing, Vader," snapped Captain Brody.

"For more updates, stay tuned to your local channel," Vader intoned, then quickly dropped the mic at a glare from Brody.

"Vader, go out there and find out what's going on." He'd go himself, but these days he liked to stay as close as possible to a phone—to two phones, in case his cell decided to drop reception.

"Jones, when's the last time you saw Psycho?"

Sabina rolled her turquoise eyes toward the ceiling. "To tell you the truth, Cap, I try to block it out when I see him. Anyway, he's off shift today."

He fixed her with a stern stare. "Anything I should know?" All his crew members knew what that meant. He liked to stay out of firehouse drama until his presence was absolutely necessary.

She shrugged. "It's a heat wave. Everyone's going a little nuts. And Psycho's Psycho. What more do you need to know?"

Brody groaned. The brass had begged him to fill in temporarily at his old position until they could settle on the perfect replacement. The authoritative and powerful Chief Roman had recently left, after becoming engaged to Sabina, and his shoes were hard to fill. Brody had warned them that he'd be taking paternity leave as soon as Melissa went into labor. But it wasn't happening yet, so Psycho's latest adventure would be his problem to solve.

"Stan," he muttered to the firehouse mutt, a beagle mix who sat patiently by his right ankle. "What am I going to do with him? He's liable to blow this place up."

Stan gave him a wise look, but kept whatever insight he had to himself.

"Fine." Brody checked to make sure his cell phone was on, stuck it in his pocket, and strode out to the backyard to see what havoc Patrick Callahan IV was wreaking now.

In the cab of the excavator, Patrick took another long slug of vodka-spiked Arizona iced tea and sang the words to "Once, Twice, Three Times a Lady" as he lowered the bucket toward the crackling dry grass of the back lawn. He didn't ever drink on the job, but he happened to be off shift at the moment, as he'd switched with Brent on the A shift.

Alcohol wasn't permitted on the premises, but then again, he wasn't technically *on* the premises. The way he looked at it, he was a couple yards *over* the premises.

And the premises weren't much to speak of. It hadn't rained in eight months and temperatures had been stuck over 100 for the past two weeks. The grass was probably dead. For sure, no one would miss it.

"She's once . . . twice . . ." He hooted at the top of his lungs. Why couldn't he remember more than that one line? He scowled at the bottle of iced tea. Too much poison. He really had to straighten out one of these days. As soon as he got this thing dug, he'd do it.

New leaf. A new life. A clean, relaxed new life.

Vader appeared in front of the excavator, waving his arms over his head.

Patrick stomped on the brake and the machine lurched to a halt. He leaned out and shouted over the noise of the idling engine. "What's the rest of the words after 'Once, twice, three times a lady'?"

Vader cupped a hand behind his ear. "What?"

"Once. Twice. Three times a lady. What comes next?"

Vader's forehead creased in thought. He sang the tune, tracing the rise and fall of the notes in the air. "La la la la la . . ."

"There's gotta be more words," Patrick yelled.

But Vader apparently now remembered why he was blocking the excavator like some tree-hugging protester. "Captain wants to know what the fuck you're doing!"

"Tell him don't worry about it. He's going to love this."

"He said to find out what's going on. Right now it pretty much looks like you're digging up the backyard."

"Shhh." Since his shushing was hard to hear over the sound of the engine, Patrick put a finger to his lips to emphasize his point. "Don't tell anyone."

Vader gazed skeptically at the dent Patrick had already made in the lawn. "I think they're gonna notice."

"It's okay, 'ts okay," Patrick reassured him. "Everyone's gonna love this. Big hero, that's me. I figure we'll name it after me."

"Name *what* after you? The grave Captain Brody's going to bury you in?"

Patrick cracked up at that, bending over the controls, shaking with big heaves of laughter. "No," he gasped, when he finally got his breath back. "The Psycho Memorial Swimming Pool and Hot Tub. You're welcome."

The next morning Patrick stood in an at ease posture before an extremely serious Captain Brody. "At ease" didn't describe his mood one bit, but it was better than at attention. "At attention" would be hard to manage with a hangover this bad.

"If," said Brody, "and it's a big if, we decided the station ought to have a hot tub in the backyard, funds would have to be appropriated, bids submitted, contractors hired, so on and so forth."

Patrick nodded. It hurt. He didn't show it, of course. He prided himself on his ability to withstand pain.

"Of course, some might argue with the need for a hot tub, considering our current heat wave."

"It was supposed to be both," muttered Patrick, knowing it was the wrong direction to take.

"Excuse me?"

Patrick gritted his teeth. For all his faults, no one had ever accused him of lacking balls. "Both a swimming pool on hot days and a hot tub on cool days."

"Very ingenious." Captain Brody bared his teeth.

Patrick inclined his head. One didn't pass up a compliment from the captain even if it was sarcastically delivered. He decided to take the reins of this conversation—or at least attempt to. It had never worked with Brody in the past. Patrick didn't give a crap about most people's judgments, but the captain was different. It genuinely bothered him that Captain Brody didn't have a high opinion of him.

And this latest episode obviously hadn't helped anything.

"I'm very sorry for my actions, Captain Brody," he said stiffly. "They were very wrong. I've already apologized to Perini Construction for the temporary use of their excavator. I've replanted the sod I dug up. You have to water it every few hours, which I've been doing."

"I noticed. We now have one lone patch of green on our lawn."

"If you want, I can resod the rest of the yard." He

decided to reach even further into humility. "After all, station beautification was my original goal."

Brody's head snapped up, and Patrick knew he'd misstepped. Brody despised bullshit.

"I thought of that, but it's too easy. I have a better idea." Brody reached into the wastebasket, pulled out the morning paper, and plopped it on his desk.

Patrick stared at it. "You want me to write a letter to the editor? Apologize in writing?"

Brody glared at him. "The Waller Canyon Wildfire. Heard of it?"

Patrick looked again at the big color photo on the front page. It showed an SEAT—a single engine air tanker—dropping retardant on a forest of flaming trees. He swallowed hard. "Yes. I've heard of it." It was impossible to ignore, with Channel Six doing twenty-four-hour coverage of the massive and growing fire that was eating its way across bone-dry southwest hillsides. He'd been tracking its every move since it reached Nevada.

"Three states are now involved. Nearly four thousand firefighters are on the scene. They probably have room for one more."

Patrick froze. He couldn't be . . . was the captain getting rid of him . . . suspending him? He hadn't screwed up that badly.

"I'm sending you to Nevada," said the captain. "They're not in our GACC, but the fire's big enough so they're requesting help from outside the GACC."

GACC meant Geographical Area Coordination something, or so Patrick recalled. Sometimes it was hard to keep track of all the acronyms in the fire service.

"So, you're volunteering me?" he ventured.

"Yep. An old friend of mine's the incident commander out there. Seems they're in need of heli-rappellers. How long have you had your red card?"

"Six years." A red card certified that a firefighter had gone through enough training to tackle wildfires. Only a few of the San Gabriel crew had one, since they mostly dealt with structure fires, but Patrick was a glutton for training. "I worked on a rappel crew for a couple of years."

"I know that. I also know your certification is current. I'm not pulling this idea out of my ass. You seem a little . . . bored here in San Gabriel."

"I'm not bored, Captain, I was just letting off a little steam."

"Well, now you can let off steam in Nevada."

Patrick stared at him, his throat working. It wasn't just that he didn't want to go to Nevada. He *couldn't* go to Nevada. "Can't you just write me up?"

Brody's face tightened and his eyes narrowed. "You're passing up a chance to throw yourself out of a helicopter and hang out with the hotshots?"

Patrick stared stonily at his superior.

"Unless you can give me a good reason why not, you're going, Psycho. You're a good firefighter. Smart, on the ball, strong, extremely proficient technically. But you make me nervous."

"I've never fucked up on a fire."

"You've come close."

Patrick dropped his head. Yeah, he'd come close to the edge. That's where he liked it. He liked the high-wire act, the adrenaline, the death-defying thrill. But he knew the odds, and never went too far.

Of course, getting into a battle with Captain Brody carried no good odds at all.

"You have until next shift," said Brody.

Patrick wheeled around and stalked from the office. Everyone ignored him as he stormed through the training room and headed for the lockers. He passed Sabina and the battalion chief chatting near the TV, which, of course, was now tuned to the fire in question.

"Still trying to decide on lilies versus baby's breath?" he muttered, just to get under Sabina's skin. "Personally, I vote for tulips. They really make a statement." She shot him a glare, which didn't bother him one bit.

When he reached the lockers, an old school mini-cam loomed in his face.

"Inquiring minds want to know how it feels to have your ass handed to you," said Vader from behind the lens. "Here's Patrick Callahan with a full report."

"Fuck off."

"Nice, Psycho. You just gave me an R rating." Vader lowered the camera. "You don't look so good. What'd the captain say?"

"He said the station doesn't currently have a need for a hot tub, but if circumstances should change, he'll let me know."

Vader snorted. "Yeah right. What else?"

Patrick wanted to talk about it. He really did. And if he could talk about it with anyone, it would be Vader. They'd started hanging out after Sabina got together with the former chief, Roman. Vader liked having a buddy, and Patrick didn't mind. It was like having an eager puppy follow you around. A six-foot, 200-pound puppy who could bench-press you and your whole family.

Vader shrugged. "Interview's over, I guess."

The station's resident muscleman stashed his mini-cam back in its case, stuffed it into his locker, and extracted his helmet. He dropped a kiss on top of it and murmured, "You been good while I've been gone?"

Patrick smothered a smile. Besides his qualities as a friend, Vader was always entertaining. Something in him softened. He blurted out, "Why doesn't the captain like me?"

"Dude. Are you kidding? You just carjacked an excavator and tried to dig a hot tub behind the station."

"Before that."

"Before that you put superglue on the free weights in the workout room." Vader glared, a frown denting his strong forehead. "That hurt." His brow cleared. "ER nurses were cute, though."

"Before that."

"Before that you put soap suds on the floor of the handball court. And 'borrowed' a news chopper to convince the weather girl to go out with you."

"That was my first year here. I don't do that crazy shit any more. Not as much," he added quickly. "I work my ass off. I pick the hardest jobs. I always come through. I volunteer for extra shifts. When I'm not here, I'm training. Or signing up for some charity event. You know I bring in more money for charity than anyone else at this station. Hell, in this city."

Vader shrugged. "Brody thinks you're a loose cannon."

Patrick slammed his fist into his locker. Who was he kidding? Vader was right. The all-seeing captain knew the truth about him. Maybe Brody had magic powers and saw right to the bottom of his no-good soul. He slowly banged his head against the strip of metal separating the lockers.

Fuck it. Only one thing to do. Get through the shift. Do the job. Go back to his apartment and catch up on his sleep. Not that it was much of an apartment. Mattress on the floor. A couch, a TV he never watched, a refrigerator stocked with Red Bulls, protein drinks, and not much else. Truth was, he avoided going home as much as possible. He preferred to stay busy. But he'd just finished a triathlon a few days ago, and his next rock climbing trip wasn't until next month. The thought of his empty apartment was, quite frankly, depressing. It still didn't feel like "home," even though he'd lived in San Gabriel for the past four years. Home was . . .

He forced back a wave of nausea. No more drinking for a while. He'd focus on getting ready for the climbing trip. That would keep him busy. That would keep him from thinking about the Callahan Ranch in the crosshairs of a wildfire. About his family forced to evacuate, or worse, refusing to evacuate. Did they still have horses? What about the chickens? Who was taking care of things there?

Hell. He slammed a fist against his locker, making the entire row rattle. Vader held his helmet protectively and glared at him.

"Gotta talk to the captain," Patrick muttered. He hurried back toward Brody's office. Stan blocked his way, as he'd recently gotten in the habit of doing—like some kind of toll keeper. Patrick dug in his pocket for a treat and came up with a mint slightly furred with lint.

Stan didn't mind. He jumped for it, gulped it down, and removed himself from Patrick's path.

Brody looked up as Patrick walked in. "Think it over?"

"The thing is," said Patrick, "my family's from Nevada."

"I know."

"My father was even governor when I was a kid."

"I know."

"I haven't been back in ten years."

"I know."

Patrick didn't bother to ask how the hell Brody knew all that shit. Brody knew everything. "The fire's getting close to Loveless, which is where the Callahan Ranch is. The Incident Command Post is actually located on the outskirts of Loveless."

"I know."

Patrick took a deep breath and launched himself into the kicker. "When I was nineteen, my father kicked me out and told me never to come back to Loveless. He had a pretty good reason." Nearly getting your little brother killed definitely qualified as a good reason, but the hell if he'd explain it to the captain.

This time Brody was silent. Finally, he'd surprised the captain. A sort of stillness settled around them. From outside the office came the low murmur of the TV reporters talking about the Waller Canyon Fire, the shouts of the guys as they gave Truck 1 its morning hose-off, the snuffling of Stan as he wolfed down another treat. The familiar, beloved sounds of Fire Station 1.

"Well, I guess you have a choice to make," said Brody eventually.

Patrick stared at him, taken aback. He'd been expecting condemnation, as if he'd just confirmed all of Brody's worst suspicions. Instead, he caught the captain's level, measuring glance.

"And you're the one who has to make it. A man's got to do what a man's got to do," Brody finished cryptically.

But for some reason, in that mysterious way the captain had, his words made perfect sense to Patrick.

He nodded once, twice, making up his mind. "I'll go."

"You want to go to Nevada?"

"Yes. I want to go." It was the last thing he wanted to do, and yet, suddenly, the *only* thing he wanted to do. "I'll do it on my own time. You don't have to pay me."

Brody raised an eyebrow. "No need for that."

"Yes there is. I mean it, Cap." He managed a smile, though the thought of going back to Loveless was already making him tense. "In the words of the master, a man's got to do what a man's got to do."

Chapter Two

*O*utside Room 1176 of the pediatric ward of San Diego Hospital, Lara checked the corridors for signs of the chief resident, attending physician, or the nurse who hated her guts. Her heart pounded so loudly it drowned out the murmur of voices at the nurse's station and the constant ring of the phone. Breaking hospital rules could not only get her in major trouble, but it was definitely not her style.

The coast was clear. Slipping into the room, she gave ten-year-old Naomi Bly a thumbs-up. The girl dropped her book, her face lighting up like Christmas in September.

"Dr. Nelson! You got her?" she whispered.

"I got her. But she can't make a peep. And you only have a few moments." She hurried toward Naomi's bed. The poor girl, who had a flair for the dramatic, was going through the worst week of her life, as she'd announced to the entire staff. After a week of tests she'd finally been diagnosed with a blood disorder so rare, it didn't even have a real name. The only thing that could possibly provide even the remotest, smallest tidbit of comfort, she claimed, was Gigi le FouFou.

Who was at this moment scrambling out of the tote bag in which Lara had stashed her.

The tiny, raggedy mop of a bichon frise scampered across the covers into Naomi's arms, where she proceeded to lick every inch of the girl's face she could reach. Lara winced, even though she'd insisted that Naomi's mom wash her thoroughly before bringing her to the hospital. The prospect of breaking the rule against animals in the hospital had made her stomach cramp with anxiety, but the blissful look on Naomi's face made it worth every stress-filled moment.

"Thank you, Dr. B. You're the bestest ever. Isn't she, Gigi? Oh yes, she is." Naomi buried her face in the dog's fur. Gigi yipped and squealed. Even from a few steps away Lara could see the tiny dog vibrating.

"Shhh." She put a finger to her lips. "Don't get her too excited."

"She's never been away from me for a whole week before. Come here, pet her head, right here on top. She's so soft. Doesn't she smell like watermelon? My signature scent is watermelon, you know. My mom must have given her a bath with my shampoo." She inhaled blissfully. Gigi gave a sharp, happy bark.

Lara groaned. How soundproof were the walls? What would she say if she got busted? *I'm as surprised as you are. That dog must have scaled the walls and climbed in the fourth floor window.*

"Naomi, please keep her quiet. Someone's bound to hear, and if it's—"

"Me, for instance?" A dry voice behind her made her spin around. Adam Dennison, Chief Resident, stood in the open doorway, along with a man in a business suit Lara had never seen before.

"Um . . ." Lara shifted to block their view of the bed. "Naomi and I were just . . . um . . ."

Adam pinned her with one of his devastating, skeptical raised-eyebrow looks. A brilliant chief resident, he was also a bit on the neurotic side. He'd earned the nickname Dr. OCD for a reason. He and Lara had always gotten along well—she had a soft spot for offbeat people—but lately he'd tried to ask her out a few times. So far she'd managed to dodge the question.

"We'll talk about this later, Dr. Nelson." Adam gestured to the man still standing quietly behind him. "This is Mr. Standish. He's a lawyer and he says he's been trying to reach you for a few days now. You can use my office."

Lara's gaze slid to the other man. In his late fifties, he wore a gray suit and gave off a definite undertaker vibe. She suddenly realized who he must be. "No." She shook her head. "I can't. I'm busy. I have three patients waiting and—"

"Please," said the man, adjusting his horn-rimmed glasses. He cleared his throat. "Don't you owe it to your aunt?"

He'd said the magic words. Not only were they true, but she didn't want him spilling any more details about her outrageous, recently departed aunt in front of Adam Dennison. Or Naomi, for that matter.

"Fine," she said faintly. "But I should take care of this . . . um, situation." She stepped aside to reveal Naomi huddling with Gigi le FouFou as if the Secret Service was about to tear them apart.

"I've already called Mrs. Bly," said Adam. "Give her one last hug, Naomi."

Lara couldn't bear the tragic look on Naomi's face. She brushed past Adam on her way out the door.

"Come see me as soon as you're done," Adam called after her.

Mr. Standish wasted no time. As soon as Lara had closed the door of the chief resident's office, he whipped out a laptop and placed it on the desk. "Ms. Tamera Baumgartner made a video intended for you. I barely managed to dissuade her from putting it on YouTube, but it's my job to make sure you watch it."

Lara mustered a smile. "Fine. I haven't been avoiding your calls, I promise. I've just been busy."

The lawyer waved away her explanation and pressed the Play button. Lara watched the screen as the clip loaded. Her heart jumped into her throat as her aunt appeared, a vibrant splash of color against the gray institutional background of a hospital in Guatemala. Her short hair was Kool-Aid purple, her lipstick bright fuchsia, and she wore a gold lamé cloak over her hospital gown. "Hello there down on planet Earth, this is your Aunt Tam Baumgartner coming at you from the Great Beyond. How's tricks, Lulu?" She laughed, the great, hearty sound filled with a phlegmy rattle. "By the time you see this, I'll be dead, but don't you worry, I'll still look fabulous."

Lara let out a hysterical bubble of laughter. "You really do, Aunt Tam, I have to hand it to you . . ."

Aunt Tam was ignoring her, which was her prerogative, since she'd died a few days ago. "I've had a marvelous time roaming the world searching for a cure. But you can't run from that bastard known as karma, toots. And you've been much on my mind, little Lulu. I know I put you in some awkward, maybe even mortifying situations while you lived with me. I want to make it up to you, my pumpkin seed, if it's the last thing I do. And what do you know—it is!"

The dying woman threw her head back with a delighted laugh that rippled through the dreary, textbook-lined office like a breeze through a set of chimes. Eyes blurring, Lara fisted her hands against her thighs, determined not to cry in front of the lawyer.

Then Aunt Tam dropped her bombshell.

Lara was still sitting on the floor of Adam's office, alone and shell-shocked, when Adam appeared. He took off his scrubs coat, loosened his tie, and sank into his ergonomic chair. Adam prided himself on the tidiness of his desk, and now he made a microadjustment to a small pile of paperwork. "I really ought to report your little stunt."

Lara shook herself out of the stupor caused by Aunt Tam's announcement. Just because her life had just been thrown a major curveball didn't mean she could neglect her patients. "How's Naomi?"

Adam ignored her question. "What were you thinking, Lara? This is so unlike you." Two vertical lines of judgment appeared between his eyebrows. Had the man never bent the rules in his life?

"Come on, Adam. She needed her puppy, that's all. Service animals are allowed. Gigi provided a service. She didn't come into contact with anyone else on the ward and I made sure she was clean."

"Gigi?" Adam snorted. "Let me guess. The parents let the kid name the dog. Rules are rules, Lara. Not even third-years get to break them at will."

Her sense of annoyance increased. "Save it, Adam. If you want to report me, go ahead. Just tell me how Naomi's doing."

"Sure. But first why don't you tell me what the lawyer wanted."

Lara gritted her teeth. If she hadn't been so gobsmacked by her conversation with the lawyer, maybe she would have had a little more patience for Adam's power games. "You really want to know?"

"Of course."

"He wanted to inform me that my aunt left me some property."

Brightening, Adam leaned forward and propped his elbows on the desk. "So you're an heiress of sorts. That's great news. What sort of property is it?"

"Well, Adam, it's not something you would understand. It's probably better if we don't discuss it." Considering that she'd spent the last few years not discussing anything about her past, this seemed the best policy. Especially because at the moment she was very much afraid that discussing Aunt Tam would make her burst into tears and ruin her reputation as the resident who never lost her cool.

"Lara, Lara. I think I know you well enough that nothing is going to change my opinion of you. Is that what you're worried about?"

She bit the inside of her mouth to keep her sarcastic comeback to herself—it would have been something along the lines of: *Of course, because your good opinion is the only thing in the world that matters to me.*

"Thanks, Adam, but—"

"I thought you wanted to know about your patient and her little bundle of allergens?"

Lara scrambled to her feet. "Do you have to be such a dick?" She clapped her hand over her mouth, just as shocked by her words as Adam was. His jaw dropped and his chair nearly tipped over backward.

"What is going on with you, Lara?" he asked when he'd stabilized his chair. "You're not acting like yourself at all."

She shifted her hand away from her mouth enough to say, "I'm sorry."

"Apology accepted. I'm going to assume it's the grief talking."

The grief. True, the grief was there, lurking in her chest like a wildcat she didn't want to let out. Especially not in front of Dr. OCD.

"Maybe you should just tell me the rest of it, get it off your chest," he said soothingly. "I aced my psychiatry rotation."

"Of course you did," she murmured. What else would an obsessive compulsive do?

Adam got to his feet and walked around the desk to stand next to her. He put a hand on her shoulder and lowered his voice intimately. "You should give me a chance to be there for you. A sign of things to come, you might say."

A shudder went through her, and she fought the urge to step back. The thought of being close to Adam held no appeal. But that was her problem, not his. Brilliant and ambitious, highly eligible Adam had no trouble attracting women, despite his quirks.

She remembered something Aunt Tam had always preached: true intimacy kept no secrets. Maybe that was the key. Maybe if she shared something personal with Adam she'd be more interested in him.

"Okay," she said slowly, fixing her gaze on the gray tile of the floor. "My aunt was Dr. Tam Baumgartner. She used to have a radio show about . . . well, sex. The show was called *Ask the Sex Guru*." She didn't dare look at Adam yet, but felt him stiffen in surprise. "She ran a sort of center, a counseling center. Like a retreat. It was called . . . is called . . . the Haven for Sexual and Spiritual Healing. She left it to me. I used to live there, you see, after my parents died in a car accident."

She squeezed her eyes shut. Now that she'd started, she couldn't shut up.

"She left me the Haven, with the recommendation that I sell it to pay off my med school bills. She knew how much the place embarrassed me."

"I can see why." He squeezed her shoulder sympathetically.

That comment made her bristle. "She also asked me to make sure the Goddesses are taken care of first."

"Excuse me?"

"They're not really goddesses, of course, they're her workshop leaders. She called them Goddesses to encourage participants to connect with their inner divine nature. She hired all of them except Janey, who came with the place when she bought it. It used to be a brothel, you see. In Nevada. Loveless, Nevada."

Finally the flow of words trailed off. Adam's hand seemed to be frozen in place on her shoulder. She raised an eyebrow at him. He was staring at her as if she'd suddenly turned into a bichon frise.

"You used to live in a brothel with your aunt the sex guru? *You?*"

"Well, it wasn't a brothel when I lived there, it was a . . . what do you mean, *me*?"

"No offense, but even though you're very attractive, you're on the uptight side. Conservative. Focused."

Lara flinched. Those words shouldn't hurt, since she'd worked so hard to fit that description. She should be glad Adam saw her that way.

Maybe it was even true, after all this time.

She cleared her throat. "I'm going to take some va-

cation time and go back to Loveless. I have a clinic rotation coming up, so it shouldn't be a problem."

"You're going back to the brothel?"

She could swear she heard a snicker in his voice.
Pressing her lips together, she spun toward the door.
"Yes, and I have a million things to do before I go."
First on the list, check on Naomi.

But then a hand on her arm stopped her. She turned
to meet Adam's contrite gaze. "I'm sorry, Lara. I
shouldn't be teasing you at a time like this. Can I help?
Do you need someone to go with you?"

"No, thanks," she said politely, although the
thought of meticulous Dr. Adam Dennison showing
up in tumbledown Loveless made her want to laugh
out loud. "I'll be fine."

"Naomi's sleeping, by the way," he said gently. "I let
the dog stay until her mother came. It was a nice thing
you did, though completely against the rules, not to
mention out of character. I'll let it go this time."

"Thanks, Adam." She gave him a wobbly smile. If
he was going to be nice, she might lose her battle with
the tears. "I'll call you from Loveless."

He made a jerky motion toward her, as if he weren't
sure whether a hug would be welcome. The gesture
made her soften, and she stepped forward. The citrusy
scent of his aftershave surrounded her, along with an
overlay of antiseptic. She pressed a quick kiss on his
cheek.

Mistake. As soon as she pulled away, she spotted
that look on his face. *That look* was a hypocritical mixture of disapproval and lascivious speculation. She'd
seen it a thousand times in Loveless as soon as people
figured out whose niece she was and where she lived.

With barely a wave good-bye, she fled to the wom-
en's locker room, which was empty at the moment—

her first stroke of good luck that day. As she dialed the combination of her lock, she cursed her moment of weakness. Why had she told Adam all that stuff? *Why?* Things would never be the same between them. And she hadn't even told him to keep it to himself. It might be all over the hospital by morning.

She dug through the overstuffed tote bag she'd crammed into her locker that morning. Her personal iPhone was in there somewhere, and she had to start making a list. *Talk to the chief of staff about vacation time. Call Mrs. Hannigan about Britney's prescription. Call clinic to rearrange interview. Tell Emily I can't watch her cat this week after all. Book flight to Elko. Book rental car.*

There was nothing like a list to calm you down and make you feel on top of things. Lists contained practical, concrete steps instead of embarrassing, vaguely spiritual preachings. That's why she loved the medical field. It was based on facts, not intuition. If they talked about penises, it was in a medical context, not sexual, and they didn't call them lotus roots.

A memory flashed through her mind—a quarrel. Herself at fifteen, fingers stuffed in her ears.

"Can you please postpone the penis talk until I leave for school? Or at least until after breakfast?"

"But it's completely natural, Lulu. You don't have to be afraid of sex."

"I'm not afraid! I just don't want to think about it first thing in the morning!"

"I see your inner goddess is quite disturbed about this."

Lara had stuffed her fingers deeper. "Whatever."

"Fine, since you're still in your pubescent squeamish phase, we'll call them lotus roots instead."

Lara couldn't stop a burble of laughter. Aunt Tam might have been . . . unique . . . but she'd had the biggest heart in the Northern Hemisphere. And, Lara reflected, she wasn't fifteen anymore. She didn't have to allow the Haven's crazy atmosphere to upset her. She could apply her academic training to the Haven and sort everything out with rational common sense.

Lara stripped off her scrubs and pulled on teal seersucker capris and a white blouse. She owed her aunt so much. She *loved* her. She even owed this outfit to Aunt Tam, who'd warned her no one would trust a doctor who wore black. A sudden attack of sadness made her lean her head against her locker. What a terrible niece she was. She'd dragged her feet about going back to Loveless, even when she knew Aunt Tam was sick. The least she could do now was honor her last request.

At least she didn't have to worry about a memorial service. Tam hadn't wanted one, although no doubt the Goddesses had held some sort of ceremony. They'd probably held a drum circle and danced until dawn. Naked.

After her parents died, Aunt Tam had swept into Lara's life like some kind of rare comet. She'd always approached life as a weird, amazing, fabulous adventure. Maybe Lara should try to approach her trip back to Loveless in the same way.

It was guaranteed to be weird anyway.

Chapter Three

On top of everything else, it was wildfire season in eastern Nevada. The sky was a yellowish-pink, as if the sun was held captive in some hellish otherworld. As she drove into Loveless in her rented white Aveo, Lara's throat prickled from the smoke that hung in the air. An old frontier town, Loveless had retained its ramshackle roots. A wooden boardwalk wound its way past the storefronts of the downtown business center. A banner strung across Main Street read, THANK YOU, FIREFIGHTERS! She spotted a few people walking around wearing bandannas over their mouths, but most Nevadans took the yearly onslaught of brushfires in stride.

Loveless had a *High Noon* feel; cowboys were a common sight. Real ones, not the expensive snakeskin-boot cowboys she occasionally saw in San Diego. These guys were tough as rawhide and could drink all night and sleep it off on horseback.

The grief that had lurked in Lara's heart since she'd first gotten the call about Aunt Tam bloomed into full-fledged sorrow as she passed all the familiar landmarks of Loveless. The family-run, one-screen movie theater where Aunt Tam had taken her to every single movie that ever came to town. The Loveless Pharmacy, where Lara had bought her black hair dye. Loveless High School, where she'd spent some of the most miserable years of her life—except for Liam.

But lately her contact with him had been via text message only.

And there, at the edge of town, stood the Haven for Sexual and Spiritual Healing, squatting like a fat, overdressed, confused opera singer stranded by the side of a dusty highway. In its first lifetime it had actually been an opera house, adorned with ornate, elaborate curlicues and even a gargoyle—anything that might look hoity-toity. Then it had become a brothel. The owner had painted it pink, chopped it up into rooms, added some frescoes and canopied bedchambers, and named it the Pink Swan. The brothel did well, until a recession hit. That's when Aunt Tam had swooped in. She'd decided she needed a base where she could help people in a more hands-on manner, in addition to her radio show. And thus the Haven for Sexual and Spiritual Healing was born.

The inspirational sayings attached to the fence posts that lined the driveway set the tone.

SMILE. YOU ARE DIVINE. RELEASE YOUR FEARS. SURRENDER TO BLISS.

Lara could practically hear her aunt repeating the slogans to eager couples. She'd always hidden in her room playing loud music during workshops, but she caught enough to know she wanted nothing to do with the sexual self-actualization business.

But that didn't mean she didn't appreciate the God-desses. When the front door, with its carvings of Greek nymphs, opened and four women hurried out, a huge smile spread over her face. She jumped out of the car and into their welcoming group hug.

"Lara!. . . . Look at you, all grown and luscious . . . I told you she always had good bones . . . never mind her bones, look at that skin . . . We're so sad about Tam, we're just lost without her . . . come inside, this smoke is terrible for your skin . . . I heard on the news it's like smoking a pack a day . . . but my oh my, you should see some of the firemen who've shown up to fight this thing . . ."

Lara let them bundle her inside the building. It was like being carried down a river of fragrant bath suds. It had always been like that; the Haven often felt like a cross between a dysfunctional family and a hippie sorority, with maybe a dash of burlesque show thrown in. The "Goddesses" had always been there for her. They'd helped her with homework, makeup advice, and boy trouble.

Janey, the most senior Goddess, who had to be in her mid-fifties by now, still looked spectacular with cocoa-dark skin and magenta-striped hair piled on her head in an unruly heap. She led the way into the "Be Loved and Welcomed Room," which was filled with a motley collection of love seats, fainting couches, and velvet armchairs. Inside the Haven you could easily forget there was another world outside. Everything was either gold or deep burgundy, left over from the brothel days, or a newly added shade of white called "sea breeze." Lara had mockingly referred to it as "lo-botomy white" as a teenager.

"How you holding up, dollbaby?" Janey asked, when they'd all settled in and Annabella had left to fetch refreshments. Janey was the intellectual of the group, and took a scientific approach to sex. She'd once warned Lara not to date a new guy while taking birth control pills because they'd mess with her ability to chemically sense if he was a good genetic match.

"I'm doing okay. I just never thought Aunt Tam would actually . . . I mean, I figured she'd beat the odds. Find some shaman in Peru or somewhere who'd chant her back to health."

"I'd have put money on her outlasting us all," said Dynah Steel. Six feet tall, her wheat-gold hair tucked into a ponytail, she wore a ribbed white cotton tank over a skirt decorated with OM symbols. Bright purple cowboy boots completed the look; Dynah had always refused to be a cliché. She'd joined the Haven while Lara was in college.

"My heart weeps for you, Lara, even though I've only heard about you from Miz Tam," said a delicate-looking blonde, whose hair was pinned in dozens of little knots, and whose violet eyes were rimmed in tragic-looking charcoal.

"You must be Romaine," said Lara, remembering Aunt Tam's mention of a fragile new runaway she'd taken in. Lara still didn't understand why Romaine had named herself after lettuce, but there was a lot she didn't understand about the sex industry. And the self-help industry.

"Your aunt saved my life," she answered dramatically. "I'll hold her close forever."

Annabella came back into the room carrying a red enamel tray. It held a pitcher of cucumber-scented water, glasses, and date-almond cookies. Annabella, who came from Brazil, was a fount of oddball beauty tips. She'd taught Lara not to wash her hair every day to preserve the oils—and how to shop for hair products at the hardware store. "Diatemaceous earth, *querida*. I can barely pronounce it, but I swear by it."

Lara took a glass and sipped. It was heaven on her throat, which was already feeling the effects of the smoke in the air.

"I might as well tell you right up front that Tam's passing has raised some issues for the business," Janey said. "Not that it matters to you, since you've always kept your distance from the Haven."

"Actually—"

"It's my fault. I'm no good at the workshops," interrupted Romaine, who looked to be on the edge of tears. Or maybe her eye makeup always made her look that way.

"I'm sure that's not true," said Lara uncomfortably.

"It is." Janey was never one to dance around the truth. "Romaine still hasn't connected with her inner power. But she's working on it."

"The problem is," said Dynah, "the wildfire's been terrible for business. No couple wants to deepen their relationship while they're hacking their lungs out. I say we need to get back to basics. The old in-and-out, wham bam thank you ma'am, see you same time next week."

Lara winced. So this was her legacy. "I don't know if that's—"

"Silly us," said Annabella, nestling into a love seat and curling her legs under her like a cat. "As if you care about our little problems. It will all work out. It always does. We want to hear about you, *querida*."

"Well, as a matter of fact—"

"It's not going to just magically work out," said Dynah, legs crossed, one purple cowboy boot bouncing restlessly. "I need to make me some money, honey. I have a horse ranch all picked out back in Kentucky, just waiting for my down payment. And right now the money's disappearing faster'n my virginity on prom night."

"That's not true," said Janey, perching a pair of wire rims on her eyes and pulling out a ledger. "Business was up ten percent last week."

"Yeah, from zero."

"Tam always told us that focusing on the negative solves nothing," said Janey, her brown eyes firing sparks behind her glasses.

"Negative income solves nothing either. We're in the sex business. All the other stuff is woo-woo. The workshops, the spiritual babbling, the perfume."

"Aromatherapy," said Annabella, toying with the dark hair that flowed over her shoulders like lava. "And it's not woo-woo. It's transformative."

"No one came here for aromatherapy, I'll tell you that. And now no one's coming much at all."

"Hang on." Lara waved a hand in the air for attention. "I'm still confused. Business is down, is that it? The market for sex has collapsed?" She winced. That hadn't come out right.

Annabella clucked her tongue reproachfully. "It's not only about sex. We tend to people's deepest needs. Now we are also tending to other needs."

Puzzled, Lara frowned. "I'm almost afraid to ask, but what other needs?"

"Neuromuscular. Myofascial. That sort of thing."

Lara blinked. For the first time in her life Annabella was actually speaking *her* language. Anatomical terms—the soothing lingo of the medical world.

"*Sí, querida!* We've been practicing our massage on some of the firefighters and they really seem to appreciate it. Romaine and I have been working our little fingers to the bones on those handsome men." Annabella winked. "Tough job, no? You should come along with us, Lulu. We're leaving as soon as—"

"Focus, ladies, focus," Janey broke in. "Fact is, our clients are getting older. They're starting to be more concerned about their spines than their inner selves. It's distracting from our mission. Besides, your Aunt Tam was the heart and soul of the workshops. She was like the Deepak Chopra of sex. Without her, it's just—"

"Sex," said Dynah. "Nothing wrong with that."

"One thought—Dynah's—is to go back to our roots, and revive the Pink Swan," Janey explained.

Lara glanced around the Be Loved and Welcomed Room. It wouldn't take much to turn it back into a brothel. Take away the jade sculpture of Kuan-Yin and the Tibetan "tongka" tapestry, and maybe the placard that read, RELEASE YOUR MIND AND THE REST WILL FOLLOW. Which, she was pretty sure, her aunt had stolen from Salt-n-Pepa.

She shook herself back to attention. What was she thinking? She wasn't here to help rescue the Haven. She was here to break the news to the Goddesses. "Actually, I came to tell you guys something."

"Or . . ." said Janey, scanning the ledger. "Another idea is to turn the place into a spa and continue to offer massage and maybe mani-pedis. We might have to remodel, which would take a bite out of our reserves, such as they are."

"The Pink Swan Healing Spa." Annabella wrote the name with her finger in the air. Both she and Romaine gazed at it as if they could actually see it. Dynah rolled her eyes and snorted scornfully.

"Tam didn't leave so much as a note with instructions about what she wanted to do with the Haven. We're not even sure who owns it now. Unless . . ."

Slowly, all of them turned their gazes on Lara, who

felt herself turn pink. Somehow she'd lost control of the conversation. Scratch that—she'd never had control. She never did at the Haven. And now she had to tell them that all their ideas for the Haven were pointless. The place had to be sold.

"Aunt Tam left the Haven to me."

Somewhere in the back of her mind, she could swear she heard her aunt's rippling laughter.

And then a cacophony of voices broke out.

After assuring the Goddesses that she'd think about their ideas before making any final decisions, Lara escaped to the room where she'd lived from the age of twelve. Aunt Tam had completely redecorated it, banishing everything black and goth—everything Lara—and turning it into a pink cotton candy nest.

Tears collected at the corners of her eyes as she cursed herself once again for not coming back in time to see her aunt. Being in this pink room—bedspread a deep rose, curtains a pale sunrise pink, rug a delicate mauve—was like being pulled into one of her aunt's famous rosewater-scented hugs. Her aunt welcomed everyone, never judged, never rejected. Aunt Tam had never lost faith in her through all her rocky, sarcastic, morose, grieving growing-up years.

And now she trusted her to take care of the business she'd left behind—the business that had mortified Lara nearly to death as a teenager.

She set down her suitcase and stretched her arms overhead, feeling her muscles sigh in relief. As a resident, she was so busy she sometimes forgot she had a body that needed attention: food, water, sleep. She liked it that way, liked focusing her whole self on her quest to become a doctor, liked putting lots of distance between her present and her past. Living in Loveless, as the niece of the local wacko, had been excruciating. She'd wanted nothing to do with the place.

But she owed Aunt Tam.

Quickly, she changed into her grungiest clothes—cutoffs and a tank top—as advised by the Goddesses, who claimed they always came back from the fire stinking of sweat and smoke.

On her way out the door her old corkboard caught her eye. She went closer to look at the photos and scraps of old poems and band flyers pinned to the board. Most of the photos were of her and Liam Callahan. He always wore that lopsided, dreamy grin; she was always making some sort of funny face. She probably wouldn't have smiled once during her entire high school years if Liam hadn't made her.

Liam had been her lifeline.

Another smile caught her eye. Patrick, side by side with Liam during their infamous "stand on one leg" competition, in which Patrick's tenacity had almost beaten Liam's single-minded focus. In the moment when he conceded to his brother, Patrick had aimed that vivid smile at the camera. His eyes, even in the old photo, nearly jumped off the corkboard with that piercing, vibrant blue.

Patrick Callahan. What had ever happened to him after the accident? He'd been banished from the family, cut off from the Callahan money. No more Princeton. She'd been so wrapped up with Liam's recovery that she hadn't spared a thought for Patrick, except to curse at him like everyone else—though for her own reasons.

But now, looking at the photo, the look on Liam's face tugged at her heart. Liam had idolized Patrick, and Patrick, for all his wildness, had been really good with Liam. Patient, affectionate, protective, yet always daring Liam to test his limits. She knew from Liam that none of the family had been in touch with his older brother for years.

What *had* ever happened to Patrick?

Patrick drove his steel-gray 1986 Dodge Ramcharger to Nevada. The high-clearance, four-wheel-drive old-school sport utility vehicle, from which he'd removed the backseats to make a sleeping space, served as his home-away-from-home on the road. The damn thing was so tough and rugged, he'd nicknamed it the Hulk. As he neared the fire-affected zone, he had the highway virtually to himself. The other vehicles were heading away from the fire, not toward it. Gas stations and convenience stores were empty, as if aliens had landed and snatched everyone up, leaving nothing but smoke smudging the sky and hot blasts of wind.

Vast stretches of Nevada and its neighboring states were burning, and from the dry look of the vegetation, what wasn't yet on fire soon would be.

Brody had shown a glimmer of respect for his decision to go to Nevada. That meant a lot. But he hadn't told Brody that he had no intention of letting his family know he was here, not even Liam or his little sister Megan. The last time he'd seen them all was in the hospital, with Liam unconscious in the next room, his father out of his mind with rage, yelling at him to get out of town and never come back. He'd meant it too. The private security guards had proved that. His mother had told him it would be better if he left, and even Megan was afraid to talk to him.

The worst of it was, he didn't even remember the details of the accident. It didn't matter. He was the big brother. Liam was deaf and mildly autistic. Whatever had happened, it must have been Patrick's fault.

The familiar tension grabbed at his neck. He rubbed the tendons with one hand. He was going back to Loveless out of principle, nothing more. He might be the disinherited black sheep, but he wasn't going to let his family's property be destroyed if he could help it. And he wasn't going to let "Governor Blowhard" keep him out of his own hometown.

The winds were out of the southeast, a steady thirty mile an hour breeze that was pushing the fire in a determined march across the state. The town of Loveless should be safe enough, since it was to the east of the fire. But Callahan Ranch was closer to the edge of the flames. Hopefully his father had hired people to clear the brush from around the structures. But since he'd been banished from his father's sight, he couldn't exactly go and check on it.

Instead, he was heading to the Incident Command Post that had been set up at a fairgrounds about fifteen miles outside of Loveless. Patrick was to report to the incident commander, a man named Morton Deitch. Brody said he was a straight-up guy, and he'd even put in a good word for Patrick.

Patrick didn't want to admit it, but he'd repeated those good words to himself a few times. Helluva firefighter. *Strong, smart, a lot of initiative.* No "keep an eye on him" or "watch your back," as he might have expected.

He took a long glug from a gallon jug of water he'd picked up along the way. In this heat, hydration was incredibly important, so much so that Brody had reminded him to start hydrating before he even got to the scene. Not something they had to worry about when fighting structure fires in San Gabriel.

The rolling, rocky hills, an ominous shade of cardboard brown, shimmered on either side of the car. This area hadn't had rain in months. It was hard to believe that anything had ever been green here. Now that he was a trained firefighter, he looked at the landscape with a more experienced eye. That wasn't just pretty vegetation, it was fuel. Sagebrush with a grass understory, and P.J., as it was called. Pinyon and juniper, a highly flammable combination of resinous evergreens.

Wind buffeted the Hulk, or would have if it hadn't been built like a Mack truck. He had all his firefighting gear stowed in the bed, along with a tent, sleeping bag, blankets, jugs of water, even a food stash. If he got stranded by the fire, he could survive for weeks, as long as he didn't burn to death.

And then he saw it. A huge, horizon-long, rolling, roiling mass of dark flame edged into view. *"Holy Mother of God,"* he whispered to himself. That was one big-ass fire. It hunched like a hungry dragon over the subdivisions scattered on the vulnerable hillsides below. He'd heard that thousands of people had been evacuated. Jesus. No wonder there was hardly anyone on the road.

For one second he was tempted to turn around and do the sane thing, for once in his life. But that thought quickly fled. Sanity was overrated. Besides, the moment he first saw the fire on the news, he knew he'd end up here. This fire was . . . personal.

The Loveless Fairgrounds, a ramshackle conglomeration of dusty old shacks, had been transformed into a tent city swarming with busy firefighters and support staff. Big tan canvas Weatherport tents shuddered in the stiff breeze whipping through the camp. Patrick identified the Air Ops tent, Ground Operation, Safety, and finally located the Incident Command tent and the incident commander himself.

Battalion Chief Mort Deitch looked and talked like

a cowboy in slow-mo, but from the respect people showed him, he was sharp as an ice pick. He was over six feet tall, even taller with the cowboy hat he wore. He took time to shake Patrick's hand and show him where the ground logistics people were, so he could stash his gear and set up his tent.

"Brody said you just got recertified in heli-rappelling."

"Yes, sir."

"But you're out of San Gabriel, right?" Meaning he made his living fighting structure fires rather than on a hotshot crew.

"I worked on rappel crews before I decided to try staying in one place. But I've thought about joining a hotshot team."

"Thrill junkie?"

Under that slow, shrewd gaze, Patrick couldn't lie. "That's a fair statement."

Deitch nodded, seemingly unworried. It went with the territory, after all. "One of my rappellers got himself injured during a landing. Busted his ankle. Can you go up today?"

"Why not?"

Patrick shifted his shoulders under his rucksack, from which his boots dangled. These were different from his regular fire boots. Known as "whites," they were big black logger heel boots with heavy Vibram soles, and uppers that went halfway up his calves. They added about six pounds to his backpack, but they were worth every ounce.

"Go stash your stuff and get geared up. We've got a R.A.W.S. station the feds are all hyped up about. Need you to do the prep on it. Thousands of dollars at stake, yadda yadda."

"Got it." Remote Automated Weather Stations contained critical weather monitoring equipment that generally cost a bundle.

"You've been hydrating?"

"I'm kissing cousin to a water balloon right about now."

Deitch chuckled, and turned back to the array of laptops and laminated maps laid out on a folding table. "Don't forget to take a whiz before you go topside."

"Yes, sir."

"And grab some chocolate chip cookies. The townspeople are knocking themselves out for us."

Townspeople. That would be the town of Loveless. The town inhabited by Callahans. He couldn't get in that chopper fast enough; the last thing he wanted to do was run into someone who knew him.

"We even have some ladies offering up free massages." Deitch gestured toward the Med Unit tent. Just outside of it sat two massage chairs occupied by firefighters, their faces buried in a kind of doughnut brace, while two women kneaded their backs. The masseuses were both attractive, but for some reason he looked right past them to another woman inside the med tent. She knelt on the ground, bandaging some poor sap's foot with quick, efficient movements.

Something about her looked familiar. Her blond hair, which was fastened on top of her head in a careless knot, shone like a sunflower in the smoky air. Lush but compact, she wore knee-length cutoff denims that revealed pale, shapely calves. Her bare arms were equally firm, causing a man to wonder what the rest of her looked like. And there, on the back of her shoulder, wasn't that a little tattoo?

Then the woman turned her head sideways, calling out for more gauze.

And that voice, smoky, intelligent, often mocking

(when addressing him), nearly knocked him off his feet.

Lara Nelson?

He started in her direction, but the equipment manager arrived and began steering him toward the supply cache.

He twisted around for one more look. It couldn't possibly be Lara. Lara dyed her hair and wore nothing but black. She wasn't overtly sexy like this woman. Lara had never wanted to be sexy; she'd always said so—in that throaty voice that made him want to roll her onto the nearest flat surface.

Lara—or the woman who sounded just like her— had turned back to her task and was now speaking earnestly to the firefighter with the injured foot. Patrick noticed a flush of pink across the nape of her neck. She was getting sunburned. He should warn her. Liam would want him to say something. It was exactly the sort of thing that bothered Liam . . .

The stab of sheer pain that always accompanied thoughts of Liam nearly made him stagger. No time for this now. *Forget Liam. Forget Lara. It probably isn't even her.*

He didn't have a spare second to investigate further. After a quick stop at the supply cache, he changed into his "yellows and greens"—fire resistant Nomex shirt and pants. He pulled on socks and his fire boots. It had been a couple years since he'd worn this style of boot, but they still hugged his feet perfectly.

Once he reached the heli-spot, where a Bell 205 waited, he fastened on the climbing harness and checked the Sky Genie. Since the rope that wound through the Genie offered the only way to slow or stop a descent, he liked to double check it himself. He slung his P.G. bag, which held his personal gear, over his back. It contained a fire shelter, underwear, extra clothing and enough food and water for three days. When you went rappelling, you never knew how long you might be out there.

He shook hands with the other firefighter he'd be rappelling with, who introduced himself as Dan McInnies from Jamberoo, Australia. He nodded to the spotter and the pilot, then pulled on his flight helmet. He climbed into the chopper, pulled down one of the seats and fastened himself in.

No need for breathers—those were reserved for structure fires. For this mission his tools would be chainsaw, fusees, and hand tools. The chopper was already loaded with the let-down boxes filled with everything they would need. These would be sent down after the rappellers; for some strange reason, rappelling while loaded with sharp things wasn't allowed.

"A tanker just dropped a load of retardant, so be careful out there. No more scheduled for now," shouted the spotter.

Retardant was nasty stuff, a mixture of water and sludge so heavy it could break your bones if it fell on you. "Too bad," shouted Patrick. "I love the smell of retardant in the morning."

Dan laughed. Already Patrick liked him.

The chopper blades began to whir, slapping at the air. Its nose dipped forward a bit, and they rose off the heli-spot. Patrick watched the crowded fairgrounds disappear below them, the black ants of people scurrying around, then the bare expanse of ranchland slipping past—everything from cattle to llamas to ostriches were raised around here—then, disturbingly quickly, they were flying over the heart of the beast.

Storms of black smoke churned beneath them, making the chopper sway from side to side. Fire created its own weather, its own eighty mile an hour winds, its own hurricanes and twisters of smoke. Flames lurked behind the veil of all that black destruction, as if they were hiding until they could leap out and strike the unwary.

Patrick's heart raced and his mouth went dry. The Waller Canyon Fire was a magnificent, terrifying, awe-inspiring, gut-churning sight. And he was supposed to drop into the middle of it, like a piece of dandelion fluff landing on a volcano.

"Holy Mother Mary," he breathed out loud. He saw Dan cross himself. A guy could definitely find religion moments before rappelling into a wildfire.

He focused on the gear check the spotter was performing. Harness, check. Rope, check. Gloves, check. *Death wish, check.*

"There's your spot," said the pilot into their headsets. "See that building down there?"

He pointed, and Patrick saw it well enough. The edge of the fire was a couple miles out but heading in that direction. If they could clear a wide enough area around it in a speedy enough manner, the weather station should survive.

If.

Staring at the massive, maniacal fire, it seemed like a big if to Patrick.

The chopper maneuvered over the clearing and hovered. "I'll wait if I can, but don't be surprised to see me bail," said the pilot over the comm. "They've been keeping me busy."

"Got it."

"Ready?"

"Ten-four."

The spotter opened the door on Patrick's side of the chopper. Hot wind battered his face. The spotter worked the rope through the Sky Genie on Patrick's harness and fastened it off. Patrick got into position, facing the inside of the chopper, his back to the great beyond, while the spotter went through the same routine for Dan on the other side.

"Good to go!" he said over the helmet comm. "Have a good ride, guys. See you on the other side."

Patrick took a deep breath and dropped backward, ass first, into emptiness. He felt a moment of weightlessness until the harness jerked against the rope. It held, cradling him securely in the crazed, hot wind swirling around the chopper. Rope whizzed through the Sky Genie as he lowered himself at a controlled pace toward the ground. The rope wavered, swinging in the open air, then settled under his weight. He slid down, gloved hands gripping the rope, his heart racing a mile a minute, toward that tiny, vulnerable building—a bull's-eye in a target of flame.

Chapter Four

If Lara blocked out the faraway roar of the fire, the barked orders and tense teasing among the firefighters, not to mention the unrelenting heat and the sweat running down her sides, she could almost imagine she was back in the relative peace of San Diego Hospital.

For the first time since coming back, she actually felt comfortable.

When she'd first shown up with Annabella and Romaine and offered to help the medical staff, it had been an entirely different story.

"No," Bill Donnell, the head of the Med Unit, told her, barely glancing her way, and clearly lumping her in with the ladies. "We already contacted all the local medical resources in the area. Massage doesn't count as a medical resource."

"The firemen adore our massages," Annabella protested.

"Massage away. But no medical treatment." And

he'd brushed past them on his way to a firefighter who'd just been brought in via helicopter with a gash on his leg. Someone had applied a clumsy tourniquet. Donnell used scissors to cut through his filthy pants.

Stung, Lara followed. "I'm not here to give massages. I have a medical degree from Stanford."

"The good Lord spare me from med students."

"I'm not a student, I'm finishing up my residency at San Diego Hospital."

"I hear they have a topnotch plastic surgery department."

"Mine's in family medicine."

"See any kids around here? Didn't think so."

He stalked away from her, but she chased after him again, followed by Annabella and Romaine. "I've done some emergency fieldwork too. Family medicine involves all age groups."

"Yeah? What was your last case?"

Lara winced, but couldn't lie. "I delivered a baby on a city bus."

The medic swung around, his hard gaze raking her.

She stood her ground and barreled on. "Do you have any idea how unsanitary conditions are on a bus? I've done ER rotations and treated burns and broken legs."

"You're not going to give up, are you?"

She shook her head.

"Fine. Take this one." He gestured to the gurney where his newest patient lay clutching his thigh. "If he loses a leg it's on you."

Romaine gasped. "Why do you have to be so mean, Mr. Fireman?"

He spared her a glance of disbelief, then turned his attention back to Lara. After all her time in med school and in the hospital, it would take more than a few harsh words to knock her off-stride. She welcomed the challenge. Besides, she realized as soon as she bent over the injured firefighter, the poor guy was in no danger of losing his leg. It was a shallow flesh wound, no more. Someone out in the field had panicked and applied a completely unnecessary tourniquet.

She quickly snapped on some gloves and examined the gash. "We can lose the tourniquet, it's not helping anything. I'll clean it, use some steri-strips to keep the wound closed, and he's good to go. He may not even need stitches."

"I told Mort he was a freaking idiot!" The firefighter sat up, looking better already. "I always bleed like a stuck pig. Can you get this thing off me now?"

Donnell gave Lara a wary nod. "He's all yours. If you don't kill him, we'll try you out on another. But I gotta warn you, it's not glamorous work. Mostly, you'll be dealing with blisters. Now get busy, another crew just hiked in."

As she began dismantling the tourniquet, she caught the admiring gazes of Annabella and Romaine.

"I offered him some shiatsu on the first day we were here and he nearly bit my head off," whispered Romaine.

Annabella merely put her palms together and bowed to her. Earning their respect was surprisingly gratifying.

From then on the Goddesses brought her cookies and water bottles as she worked. A steady stream of injured firefighters limped to her corner of the medical tent. The work was not at all what she'd expected. Very few of the injuries were burns. As Donnell had warned her, the injuries mostly had to do with feet. Blisters were a big one. She spent a lot of time setting firefighters up with bowls to soak their feet in, nearly gagging from the stench as they removed their socks. She saw a few rolled ankles thanks to the rocky terrain they were working in. Dehydration was the other big culprit, causing heat exhaustion and stress. For this she handed out mineral supplements, glucose tablets, and lots of bottles of water. If the case was severe, she called for a Medevac.

The other big surprise was how much the firefighters stank. Didn't anyone take showers? Noticing her scrunched nose, Donnell explained that many firefighters were reluctant to shower in a stall where a thousand other filthy guys had already showered. After the fire was out, a lot of them booked a hotel room just to get clean.

"You're done," she told her current patient, though the word "patient" didn't fit the utter lack of patience with which he watched her work. He was in his late twenties, his face streaked with grime and soot, his muscular body straining to get back into action. He'd cut his thumb on a branch; she swabbed and bandaged it and now he was raring to go. Showing no respect for her careful bandage, he swiped it across his forehead.

"Hey! I worked hard on that."

"Gotta break it in." He winked at her. "Nice work, Doc." He bounded out of the chair.

"I think you should rest a little before you go back out there," she called, futilely. He waved her off as he reported to the incident commander. "At least hydrate!"

"You should take your own advice," said Annabella, who was working the kinks out of an exhausted firefighter's shoulders a few yards away. "And you should put on sunscreen too. You're starting to burn. Did you notice that gorgeous fireman who was staring at you?"

"No."

"He had the bluest eyes I've ever seen. Very . . . what's the word . . . charismatic. Fiery. *Fabuloso* ass."

"Shh." She glanced around at the bustling scene. "Don't talk like that here. People might get ideas."

"I might not mind those ideas. Especially with someone like him."

Annabella's description filtered into her mind. *Blue eyes. Charismatic.* Of all the people she'd known in her life, one boy fit those words perfectly.

No. It wasn't possible. Just because *she* was back in Loveless didn't mean Patrick Callahan was. And why would the exiled son of the former governor be fighting a wildfire?

"He was looking at you as if he recognized you."

The firefighter she was massaging lifted his head. "I have blue eyes. And women tell me I have a nice ass."

"And so you do, *querido*," said Annabella soothingly. "I noticed right away."

Lara plunged back into her work, pushing aside the uneasy feeling Annabella had inspired. It would be too weird a coincidence if she and Patrick were both back in Loveless. Both helping out at the same wildfire. At the thought of seeing him again after all this time, a shivery thrill tightened her stomach. Love him or hate him, Patrick wasn't the kind of guy you ever forgot. Not that she loved him. Or hated him—too much. No, she was neutral on the subject of Patrick Callahan IV. Totally neutral.

Patrick and Dan worked like dogs, clearing away the vegetation around the squat little concrete building bristling with electronic monitoring devices. In the distance, they heard the fire beating at the air like demented angel's wings. The chopper didn't wait around long, clearing out about ten minutes after they started the prep. Neither of them worried about it. Either someone else would pick them up or they'd hike out to a road.

First they got the chainsaws going and cleared away the bigger brush. Then they went after the understory with Pulaskis, trying to get it all the way down to dirt. Their goal was a cleared perimeter of at least a hundred feet.

They hacked at the brush, muscles straining, sweat drenching their yellows. Patrick's feet weren't yet used to the brutally rocky terrain. It felt as if they were burning up inside his boots. He kept an ear tuned to the steady roar of the fire. It sounded like the thunder of an otherwordly, enormous herd of stampeding mustangs, coming closer, closer . . .

When they'd gotten about three-quarters of the job done, a voice crackled over the tactical channel.

"Fire's picked up speed. Chopper's unavailable, but according to the map there's a two-track vehicle trail about a mile to your east. We'll send ground crew out with a four-wheel drive. Can you make it?"

"Ten-four. I know where it is," answered Patrick. If he wasn't mistaken, he and Liam used to ride their dirt bikes down that road.

"Let's light some fusees and get the hell out," he told Dan.

"Man with a plan. I like it."

They pulled the long red fusees from their packs. They looked like firecrackers but smelled much worse. As Patrick cracked the fuse on the end, the stench of sulfur made his eyes burn and tear up.

"Bet you don't do that much during a structure fire, mate," called Dan.

"Nope. I'm the topman. Give me an axe and I'm home."

Blinking through the smoke, he touched off little fires at regular intervals along the rest of the perimeter. The dry grass crackled and burned nearly instantly.

"What is this stuff?" Patrick called to Dan.

"I heard it called cheatgrass. They planted it to restore burn areas. It kind of took over. Very dry and flammable."

Patrick gave a harsh snort. "Are they trying to keep us employed?"

"Doing a bloody good job."

"I hear that."

When the understory had burned to the dirt, they stamped out the last remaining sparks with their boots, then gathered up the chainsaws, remaining fuel, and Pulaskis. Dan took a long draw on his water bottle. Patrick followed suit, angry with himself for forgetting such a crucial detail of wildland firefighting. Dehydration could kill you out here.

When he was done, Patrick stowed the bottle with the rest of his line gear and heaved his PG bag onto his back. "Let's book. I don't like the sound of that fire."

"Lead the way, Yank. Unless there's a wallaby around, I'm lost."

Patrick set off toward the east. Even though both of them had worked hard, he set a quick pace out of respect for the insistent bellow of the oncoming fire.

"Sounds like a monster," he called to Dan as they trotted through the pinyon.

"They're saying she's a record-setter."

They hurried across the rocky, treacherous landscape, in which steep hills and loose dirt threatened to twist their ankles and bake their feet. Patrick blotted out the pain and focused on moving forward, paying attention to every footfall. The last thing he wanted to do was get injured on his first day out here.

At the thought, he remembered the girl in the med tent, the one who looked so much like Lara. At the same time, it occurred to him that the two-track road where they were headed dead-ended at Goldpan Canyon.

Goldpan Canyon.

A memory rushed back—the last time he had gone there with Liam and Lara, during the summer after his freshman year in college. He'd had a fight with his father and needed to run, or howl, or beat someone up—or something. The devil in him had chosen to tease Lara.

"All I'm saying is, if I lived with all those women, I'd try to pick up a few pointers." Patrick had waited until Liam's attention was elsewhere, so he could keep the conversation between Lara and him.

Lara, as always, gave as good as she got. "So you need pointers? And I thought you were God's gift to sorority girls."

"Nothing wrong with honing my skills. Come on, sneak me in, just once, so I can listen at a keyhole."

"What's in it for me?"

"I have some ideas. Fun ones." He winked, loving the way she flushed under his teasing. None of the more sophisticated girls he knew at Princeton were as fun to rile as Lara. And when she got mad, her eyes glowed like amber in firelight and her lush lips tightened.

So did his cock. He couldn't let Liam know how much his best friend turned him on.

"Unless your ideas involve you jumping off a cliff, they won't be fun for me," she retorted.

He laughed. "You know you shouldn't tempt me like that." And as soon as he said the word "tempt," he found he couldn't drag his eyes away from her. She lay on her side, propped on one elbow, her black hair brushed away from her face, black makeup smudged around her eyes, making them even more dramatic. Everything about her contradicted itself. The harsh ink-black of her hair didn't match the fine texture of her skin. Her goth-girl clothes masked the beckoning curves of her body. His hands itched to tear that long gloomy dress off her body and find out what she really had going on underneath. What was it about her that got under his skin like that?

With a huge effort, he made himself look away, shading his eyes to check the sun.

"It's getting late," he signed, after tapping his brother on the shoulder. "We have fifteen minutes until Liam has to cut up apples for the horses' bedtime snack." They all knew how much Liam hated being late for anything in his orderly routine.

Liam got an anxious look. "Lara can't help me tonight. She has a date."

"Oh really?" Patrick swung his gaze back to her. Her cheeks turned an endearing rose-pink. "I thought you didn't date Loveless boys." Although he tried to make a joke of it, it came out more serious than he'd intended. Lara never went on dates. The local boys were all too scared of her. He was pretty sure he didn't like the idea of her on a date.

"The key word is 'boy,'" she said, tossing her head. The movement made her breasts stir under her shroud-like dress. And suddenly he didn't care if she dressed like a ghoul, if she lived in a whorehouse, or even if she despised him. He had to touch her, had to see what she felt like under him. In a flash he was on top of her, rolling her onto her back and stretching her arms to either side. Her eyes went wide with shock, her breath came hot against his face.

"What are you doing?"

"Proving I'm not a boy." The words sounded like the growl of a wild animal. Her eyes flicked sideways to Liam, who was staring at them in alarm.

"Stop," she said in a low voice. "You're scaring him."

He didn't release her, not yet. She felt too good under him, firm and curvaceous and yielding. "But not you? I don't scare you?"

For a long moment she stared up at him with eyes that looked like smoky gold in the late afternoon sun. He felt the beat of her heart, the flutter of her pulse. She smelled like roses and sweat, utterly lickable. "No," she said. "I know you don't want me. You're just playing games, like you always do."

He bit his tongue to keep from telling her just how wrong she was. He wanted her so badly he was afraid to move his lower body in case she felt the physical evidence.

"Get off me." She wrenched her hands out of his grip and pushed against his chest. From the catch in her voice, he knew he'd thrown her off balance. Good. He liked having Lara's complete attention. He rolled off her, then farther down the slope, toward the edge of the cliff. He vaguely heard Lara and Liam shouting behind him.

Good. They should be scared. Because inside he was a fireball about to detonate, and if no one understood that . . .

He stopped himself at the very edge, digging his hands into the scrubby grass. Liam stumbled to his knees and grabbed onto him. His brother's terrified expression made Patrick curse himself. When Liam got overwhelmed, it took a while to calm him down.

"Don't worry, I've got pinpoint control," he signed as he sat up. He rhythmically squeezed his brother's arms, starting near his shoulders and moving down to his wrists. The pressure usually helped calm him.

Lara, white with fury, burst out, "We ought to just push you over," turned in a whirl of funereal skirts and stormed back up the slope.

Patrick tugged his attention back to the rocky ridge he was currently climbing. No time for reminiscing out here. When he got to the top, he looked back. From that elevation he could see the leading edge of the flames. They looked like a towering, spitting orange demon in a cloak of black smoke.

"I see the road," shouted Dan. He sprinted toward the narrow, overgrown trail on the far side of the ridge. Patrick didn't move. The mighty presence of the wildfire fascinated him; he couldn't look away.

"Come on," Dan shouted, his voice retreating into the distance. "Move your ass!"

"Coming." But still he stood rooted to the ground, riveted by the magnificent show, the Waller Canyon Fire's dance of the veils, performed only for him. Flame met flame in a sinuous, glowing tornado of gas, like an erotic, fiery lover.

He scrambled down the hillside and caught up with Dan, who had reached the two-track and was shading his eyes, looking for their ride. "Never seen anything like that," Patrick panted. "Wish I had my camera."

"You're a crazy bastard."

"That's why they call me Psycho. Hear that sound?"

"What, that little old campfire back there?"

"No. Listen."

A groaning *mwah* came from the other side of the road. "What is that?" asked Dan.

"Could be someone injured."

"No way. That's some kind of an animal. Probably

a sheep or something. Wildfires are hell on animals. Back in Jamberoo, I volunteer for wildlife rescue. That's why I signed up to help out there. I was on vacation before this fire broke out."

Patrick looked at Dan with new respect. He was obviously much more than the fun-loving Aussie he appeared to be. Then again, Patrick knew all about how misleading surface appearances could be. "I'm going to check it out. Keep an eye out for the vehicle?"

"Abso-bloody-lutely."

Patrick took off and scrambled up the hillside. His leg muscles burned from the jog through the woods, but physical pain never bothered him much. At the top of the rock-strewn hill, he lay on his stomach and peered over. He nearly jumped back in shock. A pair of terrified yellow eyes stared back at him in a white-furred, fluffy-bearded face.

"It's a freaking llama," he called down to Dan.

"Roast llama?"

"No. Lightly smoked." Patches of soot smudged the llama's face and trembling body. It lay on the hill, clearly exhausted by its attempt to climb to the top. The ranch next to the Callahan property had raised llamas; Patrick could tell that this creature was still a baby, and that she was female.

"Come on," he told her in a soft voice, extending his hand. "We gotta get you out of here. That fire might decide to head this way at any moment. You want to come with me and my friend?"

The baby llama sniffed his glove, recoiling from the rough, fusee-scented leather.

"Here, try this." Patrick pulled his glove off and let the llama sniff his hand. When the animal seemed comfortable with him, he carefully grabbed a handful of fur at her shoulder and urged her to the crest of the hill. She protested with a low humming sound, trying to dig her hoofs into the hillside. She even tried to spit, but she was so dehydrated she lacked the saliva. But Patrick persisted, pulling her onward until she gave in and stumbled after him.

"Oh shit, you're hurt," he murmured, seeing the blood on her foreleg. "I didn't realize. How's this?" He kneeled down, put both arms under her belly, then slung her over his shoulders, her legs sticking out in front of him. The hot skin of her belly pressed against his neck as he gingerly clambered down the hill toward Dan.

"Crikey," exclaimed Dan. "What if our ride doesn't come? We've got five miles back to the command post. You're going to do it wearing a llama?"

"Think of her as my fur stole," he said, though he knew Dan had a point. He was already breathing fast. But not as fast as the llama. He felt the pitter-patter of her heart and heard her panicked humming. He had to walk hunched over to keep her from sliding off. Blood dripped from the llama's leg onto his pants. He felt his already sore muscles flex and strain.

Didn't matter; no way was he going to leave the llama behind. Not once he'd looked into those scared, golden eyes. With any luck, their ride would show up at any minute. If not, he'd spend the five miles thinking up a good name for her.

"I'll switch off with you," Dan offered, confirming once and for all that he was Psycho's kind of guy.

"Deal. Think of it like a triathlon, except you're wearing your bike around your neck."

"You're a sandwich short of a picnic, mate."

"So they say."

Chapter Five

"**G**ood Goddess. What is that?" Annabella shaded her eyes and squinted into the sun. Lara finished stashing the bandage roll in her medical kit and stood up. An SUV, one of the fire vehicles, had pulled up outside the med tent. A strange figure was staggering away from it, silhouetted against the setting sun. It looked like a man, but with a weird animal's head, like some kind of creature from Greek mythology. Except the animal's head didn't seem to be correctly attached to its body. It was hanging to one side and making a panicky bleating sound. So maybe it was injured, and she'd have to treat its freakish, dislocated head, and how would that work? Family medicine didn't prepare one for treating mutant mythological creatures.

Can you feel your toes?

Baaaaa.

Follow this light.

Baaaaa.

She shook off the silly train of thought. She was tired, that was all. She and Annabella had been out here most of the day.

The monstrous creature was closing in on them. Now she could see that of course it wasn't one very bizarre being, but a firefighter carrying some sort of animal on his shoulders. Another firefighter strode next to him, carrying a gas can and some other gear. He pointed at the medical tent and the group veered toward Lara.

Now she could see blood all over the firefighter's front. Although she couldn't see his face, which was partially blocked by the animal, his body was breathtaking. His T-shirt was so drenched with sweat it showed every ripple of muscle in his powerful torso. He was about six feet tall, intensely powerful, with broad shoulders strong enough to carry a . . . whatever that was.

"Where's Donnell?" the second fireman asked her, in an Australian accent.

"He left me in charge. What is that?"

"Injured animal stranded by the wildfire."

The fireman came to a stop, bent down and set the creature on the ground. It staggered, nearly collapsing. Its frightened golden eyes flicked from one face to another, as if looking for its mother. Lara knelt next to it and gently reached for its injured leg, but it kicked feebly at her.

"Cheeky, isn't she?" said the Australian.

Out of the corner of her eye she saw the fireman straighten up and put his hands to his lower back.

"She's a llama," he said in a smoke-roughened voice. "I'm calling her Goldie Hawn. Anyone else notice the resemblance? It's the fluffy hair."

Lara sat back on her heels, nearly tumbling over

backward. She stabilized herself and glanced sharply up at the fireman. Intense blue eyes, the color of the deepest part of a flame, met hers.

"Patrick?"

"Hi, Lara. So it is you." He rolled his shoulders back to work out the kinks, while she tried mightily to ignore what that did to his rippling chest muscles. "I thought I spotted your goldfish."

"It's the guy I saw before, the one who was staring at you," Annabella whispered in her ear. "He's even sexier up close."

Lara ignored her. "What are *you* doing here?"

"I'm surprised to see you too. Are you still living in Loveless?" Patrick looked almost completely relaxed, as if there weren't a dangerous wildfire and an injured creature clamoring for his attention. But she knew him too well not to notice the wary look in his eyes. The last time she'd see him . . . well, she'd basically told him to rot in hell.

"As much as I would love to catch up over—I don't know, a glass of hemlock or something—I need to tend to this . . ."

"Llama," he said. "You can call her Goldie. She likes it. We practiced on the way here."

Lara swallowed and wrenched her gaze from his. It wasn't easy; Patrick had always been sort of . . . dazzling. Now, covered in grime and sweat, with new lines fanning from his eyes, a look of exhaustion creasing his face, he sent chills through her unprepared system.

She addressed the llama. "Hi Goldie. I'm not going to hurt you. I'm just going to look at your leg."

"She doesn't actually speak English," said Patrick, who seemed to be hiding a smile.

"What about Portuguese, German, or Thai?" Annabella widened her thickly lashed eyes and played with her ponytail. Patrick's gaze flicked over to her, then stayed. No wonder; Annabella was incredibly beautiful.

"She's a quick learner," he said with a smile that would fell an entire herd of llamas. "With the right teacher."

Lara rolled her eyes. No matter how much time passed, nothing ever changed. Of course Patrick still drew women like ants to spilled sugar. He was electricity in a bottle, adrenaline in a syringe.

Syringe . . . that gave her an idea.

Murmuring softly to the llama, she reached into her medical kit and found some Diazepam and a syringe. She'd used that sedative once on a cow; it should also cross over to camelids.

"How much would you estimate she weighs?" she asked, refusing to look up at Patrick and Annabella.

"It's not polite to speculate on a lady's weight. But I will say that she makes every ounce look good."

Lara glanced up in time to catch Patrick's wink at Annabella, who giggled. Yes, that worldly, sophisticated, sexually enlightened "Goddess" was responding to Patrick like a teenage girl.

"Not her," gritted Lara. "The llama."

"I'd say about ninety pounds," he said promptly. "About what I carry into a fire."

And he'd carried the animal how far? Lara shook her head. Patrick always did go for the fireworks, for the spectacular . . . even if it was a disaster.

Just being in his presence, feeling those familiar, unwelcome tingles, was a disaster.

"Maybe you should take a seat in that massage chair over there and let Annabella work on you while I deal with Goldie," she suggested sweetly. "Your shoulders must be killing you by now."

Patrick shot her a complicated look. Lara knew how much he'd always hated sitting still, even for something pleasurable. He liked fast cars, fast motorcycles, loud music, mile-a-minute action. He probably made love like a manic Energizer bunny—not that she wanted to picture that.

But instead of turning down the massage as she'd predicted, he blasted a killer smile at Annabella. "That'd be awesome, Miss . . ."

"Call me Annabella."

Annabella made it sound like some kind of sexual invitation, instead of simply her name.

"Annabella. I'm definitely feeling that hike. I could use a good rubdown, if you're really offering."

"Oh, I really am."

"Dan, mind if I take five?"

Lara started. Even though the Aussie firefighter was good-looking, with his hazel eyes and big cheeky grin, she'd forgotten he was even there.

"Take fifty. You earned it. I'm going to go grab a feed. Take it easy, Psycho." With a salute, the other firefighter jogged away.

Lara flicked the syringe to make sure it was completely filled. A drop of fluid flew into the air. The llama bleated nervously. Patrick patted her on the side of the neck and she subsided, rubbing her head against his hip.

"Where to, Annabella? Shirt on or shirt off?"

"Shirt off, most definitely. Do you mind essential oils or would you prefer . . ." Annabella's voice trailed away.

All set to plunge the syringe into the llama's vein, Lara couldn't help looking up to see why Annabella had stopped talking. Patrick was pulling off his sweat-soaked shirt, revealing a sight so sensational, he ought to sell tickets. Muscle after taut muscle was revealed, one by one, ridge after ridge of sheer male power marching up his torso. On top of all those muscles glowed a layer of vivid color, wild shapes in turquoise, crimson, and sapphire blue that resolved into a gargoyle, a horned demon, a sea monster, and there, on the right side of his rib cage . . . a fireball.

He drew the T-shirt over his head and balled it up. That motion made the sharply defined muscles on his upper arms flex. Biceps, she thought, half hysterically. And pecs and triceps and deltoids. That's all they were, anatomical parts like any others. They each had a medical name. *Pectoralis major, pectoralis minor, biceps brachii.* His shoulders were so *broad*. Had they always been like that?

Her gaze slid back to the fireball. After he'd gotten that fireball tattoo, everything went wrong. It blasted into their lives and changed everything. None of it would have happened if he hadn't insisted on that damn fireball.

Patrick was looking at her, she knew, even though she was still fumbling with the hypodermic and petting the llama. She felt the insistent weight of his gaze pulling hers like a magnet.

When she met his eyes, they held a stone-cold sober look, as if he knew exactly what she was thinking, and he agreed. *It was all his fault. Everything.* In that moment, he looked nothing like the wild boy she remembered.

He dropped his gaze and turned to follow Annabella to the massage chair. The llama gave a loud hum and tried to follow.

"No, Goldie," said Lara firmly. "You stay here with me." Since Goldie had turned her body in Patrick's direction, Lara poised the hypo over the animal's furry haunch. Panicked, the llama launched herself toward

Patrick. Her soft back hoof struck the side of Lara's head and everything went gray.

A moment later she found herself in the arms of a bare-chested, magnificent Patrick, being transported through the air. She was staring into the cobalt eyes of a stern-looking sea monster on the front of his shoulder. Her brain was still a little dazed; it must be, because she thought for a wild moment that maybe Patrick was going to make love to her right here and now. Annabella could give them some pointers.

She giggled helplessly, then winced at the ache in her head.

"If it's that much fun," he murmured, "maybe I should get Goldie to kick me in the head too."

A sunbeam of sanity stole through her haze. "Goldie. Don't forget," she mumbled. Poor llama. After being rescued by broad-shouldered, strong-armed Patrick, she was probably in love with him. But since she was a llama, Patrick would never look at her in that way.

Lara knew just how she felt.

"I won't forget," said Patrick. "I never forget the important things."

It was all too much. She closed her eyes until they reached the cot.

Patrick gently set down this new, disturbingly compelling, woozily sexy version of Lara Nelson.

"Good thing I'm a trained paramedic."

"She's got you beat. She's a doctor," said the gorgeous Annabella. It was kind of strange. What were all these beautiful women doing in the med tent? Didn't make sense. Nor did . . .

"Lara's a doctor?"

"She's extremely skilled and highly respected. She'll have her pick of jobs when she finishes her residency."

"Residency."

"In San Diego. We're extremely proud of her."

"I'm right here, you know," Lara mumbled.

"How does your head feel?" he asked. "Any nausea? Dizziness?"

"I know the symptoms of concussion. I don't have one," she said grumpily. "But yeah, my head hurts."

She put her hand to her head, which made her grubby white tank top rise up, revealing pale gold flesh. So that's what Lara's skin looked like. He'd wondered often enough back in high school. Now that she wasn't saturated in black, everything about her had a gold sheen. Even her eyelashes, which were mink-brown with bronze tips. And there on her shoulder was the infamous goldfish, just as he remembered from that horrible night. Her eyes, gold as whiskey lit by a sunbeam, made his breath hitch. When the fuck had Lara gotten so gorgeous?

She sat bolt upright, wincing. "What exactly happened?"

"I took my shirt off and you fainted," he told her, remembering how much fun it was to tease her. She gave him a look that was vintage, cut-the-crap Lara. "Don't be embarrassed. It's totally understandable."

She gave a loud sniff. "Yes, when you consider what you smell like right now." She pushed her tumbling blond hair off her face. "Like a gas leak at a petting zoo. There are showers out back, you know."

So she still gave as good as she got. And she still remembered things about him, like the fact that he didn't enjoy touchy-feely crap like massages. Make that, didn't *used* to enjoy them. Working as a firefighter made you appreciate anything that took away the soreness. He'd even gotten interested in acupuncture.

But Lara didn't need to know all that. If she wanted

to despise him, he wasn't going to stop her. He deserved it.

"Let me call Romaine to pick us up," said Annabella.

"No. I'm fine," Lara said. "Headache, that's all. Get me some Tylenol and I'll be good to go." She put her hand to the side of her head. "Where's the llama?"

"Out cold," Patrick told her. "We're not sure what to do with her next, but Donnell is back. He can handle it."

"No! That llama is *my* patient." Lara tried to get up, but Annabella stopped her with a hand on her shoulder.

"Don't be compulsive now, *querida*. Goldie's in good hands. You can stay and flirt with the handsome fireman."

A slow wave of pink traveled up Lara's face. Something about that endearing, telltale flush, which he knew she had always hated, gave him a funny, almost nostalgic feeling. It made him think of the times he'd ditched his own friends to goof around with Liam. They'd pick up Lara, grab Cokes, and hike out to the canyon, him acting the fool to make his brother laugh, while Lara rolled her eyes at the silly boys. He could practically smell the dust on the road, the wild daisies dotting the fields.

It made him remember everything he'd lost that long-ago night.

"I should go," he said abruptly. "Check in with the I.C. Let's catch up later, Lara." He needed to get back to work. He'd drink some water, fuel up, and get back to the fire lines, where he knew what he was doing.

"But you need to rest," Annabella called after him. "And what about the massage? I can help you."

He raised a hand in a gesture he hoped she'd interpret as "Thanks but later," and kept going. Give him a new T-shirt, maybe scrub off some of the stench, and he'd be good to go. The one thing he couldn't possibly do was stay and chat with Lara and Annabella right now. Maybe later he could put on a good front and find out what she'd been up to since she left Loveless and turned into a knockout.

He poked his head into the Incident Command tent and spotted Deitch shaking his head at his laptop.

"Got another mission for me, Chief?"

Deitch barely looked up. "This somabitch ain't following any rules, I'll tell you what. Every time we try to calculate the rate of spread, it blows our numbers right out of the water. It's just too damn dry around here."

"It is that," agreed Patrick. "Dry and hot as hell. I forgot what Nevada was like this time of year."

Deitch grunted. "All the choppers are out right now. Besides, you need a break."

"I had a break."

"Not long enough, boy. You look like you're one strong breeze away from a coma. You're grounded for the night. It'll be getting dark soon anyway. I ain't sending any more choppers out."

"Send me out on a ground crew, then. I didn't come all the way here from California to sit on my ass."

"I don't care why you came. You get some rest or you won't be going out tomorrow either. Now git."

Patrick ground his teeth. Were all fire chiefs the same? Did they all have to order you around like a kid?

He ran his hand through his short-cropped hair, laughing at himself. Of course they ordered people around. That was their job. It made sense, unlike being ordered around by a dictatorial, full-of-himself blowhard like his father.

He squinted up at the sun, which was quickly dropping behind the scrubby pinyons at the edge of the fairgrounds. Okay, so Deitch had a point. No heli-rappelling would be happening tonight. And he had to admit his muscles ached, not to mention his feet. "Psycho" didn't mean superhuman. He'd be a liability out there. He'd hold his nose and grab a long, hot shower, ignoring the reek of a thousand stinky fire-fighters who'd showered before him. Then he'd sack out in his tent, get a good rest so he could kick the Waller Canyon Fire's ass in the morning. And whatever they were cooking up in the food trailers smelled pretty darn good to him. He'd make a stop there after he cleaned up.

Heading across the dusty fairgrounds, he glanced over at the medical tent. A small throng of people clustered around something on the floor—Goldie, he saw, as two firemen shifted places. Poor Goldie would be terrified when she woke up and found herself sur-rounded.

Not his problem. He'd done his part. Dragged her away from the path of the fire. She'd be fine now. None-theless, his steps slowed as he passed the tent. Lara's blond head was bent over the llama's leg. It looked like she was sewing.

Fuck. She was stitching up Goldie. Drawing a needle and thread through the llama's flesh. A wave of dizziness passed over him. Damn, why'd he have to picture that? A tattoo needle was one thing. It just jabbed at you, over and over, like a drill. But a freaking needle punctured the skin and the thread passed right through the hole.

Oh hell, he was going down. All the tension and ex-haustion of the day, the strain of the hike, plus the nau-seating thought of those stitches, combined into one whirlwind knockout. It was either go down willingly or fall on his face.

Surrendering, he bent over, hands on knees. Staring at the gravel under his feet, he drew in one deep breath, then exhaled. Then he drew in another, held it, and exhaled. Finally his head started to clear.

Thank the sweet Lord. If he lost consciousness anywhere near Lara Nelson—especially after she'd gotten knocked out by a llama—he'd never hear the end of it.

He was just about to straighten up when a soft voice, a familiar, wistful voice he hadn't heard in ten years, spoke next him. "Patrick? Is that really you? Are you okay?"

The ground came up and swallowed him.

Chapter Six

*P*atrick awoke to the sight of Lara looking unbearably smug. She was leaning over him, waving something under his nose. It smelled horrible and made his eyes water. Even so, part of him—a completely inappropriate part—responded to her nearness. From this angle, he could see right down her top to the soft shadow between her full breasts.

He'd always suspected she was stacked underneath those funeral outfits she used to wear.

Then his gaze drifted to the girl hovering anxiously behind Lara.

"Meggie," he said weakly, struggling to sit up. Lara pushed him firmly back down. She had some strong muscles in those nicely rounded arms.

"I didn't mean to make you pass out," his little sister said, her freckled face twisted with remorse. Little sister—after ten years, she wasn't so little anymore. She must be twenty-four or so by now. Wire-rimmed glasses perched on her nose, hiding worried blue eyes.

"That's okay," he croaked. "Not your fault."

"Of course it's not your fault, Megan," said Lara. "He's exhausted and probably dehydrated. Do you know what happens when you get dehydrated in this kind of heat? Your kidneys can shut down. Deitch was telling me about a girl in Alaska who had to get both legs amputated because she didn't drink enough water."

In his opinion, she related that story a little too gleefully. "I've been drinking like a fish," he protested.

"You have to keep your glucose intake up too. If you don't have enough fuel, all the water in the world won't help." She held up a brownie as if it were a club she wanted to brain him with. "Your sister made these. Open wide."

He grabbed her wrist before she could stuff it in his mouth. "I can feed myself, Dr. Bossypants."

Her pulse sped up, fluttering against his palm. So she reacted to him. Good. Not that it put a dent in her sass.

"Pretend it's a peeled grape and I'm one of your groupies," she said with a sweet smile.

"What makes you think I have groupies?"

"I said this was pretend, didn't I?"

He laughed, and before he knew it the brownie was lodged in his mouth. Nice move, he had to admit. He took a huge bite, nearly scraping her fingers with his teeth.

"Cute," she said, snatching her hand away and leaving him in sole possession of the dessert. "You must be feeling better. Of course, anything's better than unconscious."

He chewed thoughtfully. "I'd have to say that depends."

Meggie cleared her throat. Despite the ten years that had gone by, she could still have passed for a teenager. Her wispy ginger-brown hair was pulled back in a ponytail, with a blue paisley bandanna keeping the flyaway strands off her face. He remembered her as a sweet, vivacious girl who loved to ride horses almost as much as she loved her family. When Liam had gone deaf at the age of eleven, she'd learned to sign faster than anyone except for Soledad, their housekeeper. Their impatient father had relied on her to translate for him. He remembered her as a giggly sort of girl, but now she didn't look as though she smiled much.

"Why didn't you tell us you would be here?" she asked in a hurt tone of voice.

He deflected the question. Megan was an innocent bystander in the war that constituted the Callahan family. "Were you out here by coincidence or were you looking for me?"

She flushed a bright red. "Of course I wasn't looking for *you*. I didn't even know you were coming."

Ah. So she'd been looking for someone else. He wondered which of the lucky firefighters here had caught her attention.

"But I knew you were a firefighter. I saw a picture of you in that *People* magazine article on the Bachelor Firemen."

"Wait a second. The *what*?" Gleeful laughter quivered at the corners of Lara's luscious mouth. Fan-tastic. Patrick braced himself for an onslaught of mockery, but instead Megan looked curiously from one to the other of them.

"So you both just got back to Loveless?"

Lara lifted one shoulder. A smudge of soot on her cheek caught Patrick's eye. How inappropriate would it be to wipe it off? He clenched his hands against the impulse. No need to stir up trouble.

"I just got in today," said Lara.

"I was sorry to hear about your aunt," Megan told her.

Patrick gave Lara a curious look, but she turned her head away, busying herself with her medical kit. She probably wanted a change of subject; anything connected to the Haven had always made her uncomfortable.

"I just got here too." He sat up, strong enough now to push Lara's hand away. "I bet you never thought you'd find me facedown in the dirt. No comment, Lara." He threw up a hand to stop her inevitable jab.

"While you were passed out, I heard some of the other firefighters talking." Megan's eyes lit up, so she finally looked like the excitable girl he remembered. "They said you drove here all the way from California, then went right onto a helicopter, rappelled into the fire, then hiked out with that llama on your shoulders. Is that true?"

"Pretty much."

Lara snorted. "Pretty stupid."

"That's why they call me Psycho."

"Excuse me?"

"Firehouse nickname. So . . ." He finished the brownie, dusting the last crumbs off his hands. "Any more commands from the doctor? And how's my llama doing?"

"Sleeping off the sedative. She'll be fine. And yes, I do have orders. Take Megan to the dining tent. Let her fuss over you. Get out of my hair."

Her mention of hair made his eyes stray back to the thick, buttery gold strands stuck to her damp neck. What would it look like released from the clip that secured it on top of her head? What if that sweat was from a bout of all-day lovemaking instead of a fire scene? What would she look like under him, flushed from his kisses, wearing nothing but her hair, like a sensual Rapunzel?

His eyes dropped to her mouth. Even in her teenage angst years, she'd never been able to disguise the shape of her mouth, which managed to be both erotic and ironic, lush and mocking. Of all things, a dimple sometimes appeared on the lower curve of her cheek when she was especially amused by something. It was a very distracting mouth.

His cock seemed to think so too. Annoyingly, it stirred to life. Time to get some distance from Dr. Lara Nelson. "Yeah, sure," he said. "Let's go, sis. You might have to carry me, though."

"I think I can spare a shoulder," she said with a smile. If you asked him, her smile looked a little rusty.

Leaving Megan behind had been the hardest part of walking away from Loveless—other than the even worse part, leaving Liam in the hospital. But he hadn't had a choice about that.

Meggie had been his father's pet, so he'd known she'd be fine. And she was fine—thinner and more anxious than he would like, but still cute as a daisy. As she walked beside him, holding tight to his arm, she drew interested glances from the various exhausted firefighters milling around.

"So which is he?" he asked her as they approached the catering trailers.

"Excuse me?"

"The guy you came out here to see. You brought brownies to the command post. They weren't for me, since you didn't even know I was here. Great brownies, by the way. Were those walnuts?"

"Pecans. He's . . . some people might be allergic to walnuts."

"So your mystery man has an allergy. The plot thickens." He slipped into the old teasing pattern as if it were a favorite bathrobe.

"Maybe I was just being nice."

"I'm sure you were. You're a sweetheart."

"How would you know?" she murmured, before clapping a hand over her mouth. "Forget I said that."

Good grief. Had she always been this tentative, this unsure of herself?

"It's okay. I deserve it. But I knew you for the first fourteen years of your life. I doubt you've changed that much." They reached the catering trucks, two huge tractor trailers set up in an el-shaped pattern. "Do you want to wait for me in the tent? I don't think they let family members eat here. It's about twenty-five bucks a meal and is practically guaranteed to include some kind of pork product." The fire service had a saying: when fires break out, pigs die.

"That's okay, I don't want to eat. I'll just tag along with you."

A line of firefighters was moving briskly past the hand-washing station. Patrick joined them, followed by Megan.

"Maybe I have changed," she said. "Maybe you have too."

Patrick pumped hand soap onto his blackened, filthy hands and scrubbed thoroughly.

"Let's not delve into any emotional stuff, okay? It's too early."

"It's dinnertime."

"Then it's too late."

With his hands washed and dried, he stepped up

to the window, where the server handed him a plate filled with pork chops and mashed potatoes.

"Requiem for a dead pig," he told the guy next to him, who laughed. With Megan tagging along, he stopped at the salad bar table and loaded up with greens and sliced cucumbers and carrots. The two attendants, one from the federal government, one from the catering company, clicked their counters.

Long banquet tables and exhausted firefighters filled the big white dining tent.

Megan took in the scene, scanning the firefighters seated at the tables, shoveling food into their mouths. "He's not here."

"Sorry. What's his name, in case I run into him?"

"And what, tell him I *like* him, the way you told Jimmy Hong?"

"That wasn't me. That was Liam. He didn't know any better."

And as soon as his brother's name slipped out, everything changed. Her face went wary as a trapped rabbit's. *Crap.* Already he'd upset her. He grabbed the nearest folding chair and sank into it, desperately wishing he could undo the last half minute.

Megan stood over him, worrying at her lower lip. He noticed that her nails were bitten down to nubs. His little sister had grown into a worrier.

"Liam's gone," she said abruptly, dropping into the seat next to him with a soft whoosh. "He left about six months ago."

"*Left?* What do you mean, left? Where is he?"

"I don't know."

"*What?*" For a second Patrick thought he might pass out again. The thought of Liam out on his own, wandering by himself—his naïve, socially challenged self—made him want to rip something to shreds.

Not his poor sister, however, who was looking at him with big, wary eyes. "So you don't know either?"

"How would I know where he is? I was banned from his presence. The hospital literally wouldn't let me back in. Dad hired security guards to keep me away." It occurred to him that she'd only been fourteen at the time of the accident. "You know all this, right?"

"I know the gist. I was there." She lifted her chin stubbornly. "Lara and I both told Dad it wasn't right, but we probably just made things worse. Why would he listen to a kid and someone from the Haven?"

He hadn't known about any of that. "Well . . . thanks for standing up for me." For a brief, humiliating moment his throat closed up. He hadn't paid much attention to Megan during that terrible time.

She shrugged one thin shoulder. "I'm not sure Dad even heard me. Like, literally heard me. I said it kind of softly. I wasn't as brave as Lara."

"It's the thought that counts. But Liam, when did he leave? How? *Why?*"

"I don't know. He left in the middle of the night with some money and all his favorite things packed into a suitcase. I know he was angry with Big Dog because he kept firing all the servants. You know how he is about doing things correctly."

Patrick remembered Liam's obsession with rules all too well. He used to wonder if Liam became his shadow to make sure he followed them—which he rarely did.

"But he's deaf, not to mention mildly autistic. He needs help."

"Maybe not as much as we thought. You should have seen him during his rehab. He took it really seriously. The therapists were kind of slacking off, like hey, it's just this deaf guy, what difference does it make? But he was totally dedicated. You know how he can get. He just blocks everything out and goes."

Patrick grimaced against the pain of hearing so many details about Liam. It was like hearing about a limb that had gone missing. *Oh, I saw your leg crossing Main Street the other day. It looks pretty good.*

"He always could surprise you," he muttered. "Shocked the hell out of me a bunch of times. Does anyone know where he is? Did they try to find him?"

"Big Dog refuses to talk about him. But I think he might know something." She dipped her head, drawing circles on the table with an abandoned paper cup of water.

He eyed her, so pretty, so anxious. "You still live there? At the ranch?"

She nodded. "I take care of the animals, collect eggs, that sort of thing. Most of the servants are gone now. Big Dog fired everyone, but he can't fire his family."

A self-conscious look came over her face. The knowledge hung between them that Big Dog had, in effect, fired his eldest son.

Energized by a sudden, fierce need to change the subject, Patrick jumped to his feet. "Come on, let's see what they've got for dessert."

"Wait, Patrick."

Her pleading tone filled him with dread. She wanted something from him, something he wouldn't want to give, and he'd have to disappoint her, had already disappointed her a million times over, so how could he possibly do it again . . .

"Come to dinner."

And there it was.

He groaned and grabbed his head. "You've got to be kidding."

"I'm not. Really. Please come."

"Is this an authorized invitation? Did you get it approved by Big Dog, or did he ball it up and feed it to the chickens?"

"Stop."

"Megan, you can't invite me to Big Dog's house without his permission. He threw me out and told me never to come back. You don't mess with the former Governor Callahan. Remember the profile that called him a one-man mafia?"

Megan was shaking her head like a scolding schoolteacher, as if he were in the wrong. "It's different now. He won't mind. Well, he might mind, but I'll make sure it's okay."

Patrick felt his eyebrows climb toward his forehead. "*You'll* make it okay. Have you forgotten how much he hates me? Has he forgotten?"

"He doesn't hate . . . well, anyway, please, please come."

Stubbornly, he shook his head. "I'm not here for a family reunion. I'm here to fight a fire. I won't have time for one of those cozy Callahan dinners in which I get verbally eviscerated. I need to keep my strength up."

"After the fire's out. Before you go back to . . . California, is it?"

"Yes."

"Yes, you'll come?"

"What are you, a politician's daughter? Yes, I live in California."

He scowled, hoping to forestall more questions.

"But will you come?"

God, he wanted to say no. But there was that hopeful look in her eyes. He'd seen that same look in the eyes of a girl when he'd used the Jaws of Life to extract her from a wrecked Miata. *You'll save me, right? I'm not stuck here forever. My life isn't destroyed because of someone else's wrong turn.*

Besides, he'd come here, to Loveless, Nevada. In the back of his mind hadn't he imagined seeing the ranch again? Maybe even his family?

"I'll think about it. But only after we get the fire contained. And anyone at my firehouse can tell you I take a lot of crazy risks, so don't count on anything."

She went pale. "That's not funny."

It wasn't. Of course it wasn't. He'd forgotten how to talk to normal people, non-firefighting, non-death-defying people. "Sorry."

She got up and gave him a little shove on the shoulder. "Just for that, you owe me dinner."

As he watched, jaw agape, she stuck her tongue out at him and walked away.

Had his little sister just played him? Man, he was out of practice.

He spent the next day with about twenty ground pounders in the heart of the Loveless National Forest, hacking at scrub until his shoulders burned and his hands blistered. He ran through three cans of fuel for his chainsaw. The three others on his crew had been spending the nights on the line, so he decided to do the same. He hadn't had time to track down Goldie's owners, and no reports of missing baby llamas, apparently known as crias, had come through. Feeling responsible for the poor animal, he'd asked the Haven "Goddesses" to keep an eye on her in between massages.

When it got dark he set up his fire shelter in the black—the already charred, safe zone—and slept under the stars. It was so hot he didn't even need a sleeping bag.

He tried not to think about the disturbing news that

his brother Liam had left the nest. How could his parents have let Liam just walk away, as if there weren't a million things that could hurt someone like him? Patrick had always been Liam's self-designated protector, but he knew he'd failed horribly that night. He'd let Liam get hurt; the guilt, as much as his father's orders, had chased him out of Loveless. He'd assumed that Liam was better off without him, better off in the care of his parents.

But what if he'd been wrong?

Of course, he had no right to criticize. He'd been off in San Gabriel. Fighting fires, jumping off helicopters, getting more ink, living on the borderline between crazy and stupid.

If he hadn't found a career in firefighting, he'd either be dead or a criminal by now. Firefighting had saved his sorry ass. It gave him a sense of doing something important. Something that mattered. But did he need the adrenaline even more than the sense of purpose? And was it all just a way to make himself feel better about what he'd done?

If he saved a million lives, it wouldn't make up for how he'd let Liam down. But all he knew how to do was keep trying.

The next day was more of the same. Chainsaw work, clearing scrub, lighting fusees, hacking at dirt with Pulaskis. From the tactical channel, they knew the wind had changed direction and was nudging the fire closer to them. They didn't have much time before they had to hike out.

The chopper dropped off a new guy, Gary, some gas cans, a sack of water bottles and MREs, and some news.

"One of the choppers landed wrong and started to roll off the cliff. Just crumbled away beneath it," shouted Gary over the whine of chainsaws and the thunder of the flames in the near distance. "They tied it off, but now they have to divert another chopper to help out. Deitch was pissed as hell. We need to head that way when we're done here."

"Wouldn't want to be that pilot."

"Hell, no. Or the pilot who took a wrong turn while he was dropping retardant. Saw that pink shit coming through the air, never hit the ground so fast in my life."

"Anyone get hurt?"

"Gonzalez. I think he was faking it to get to the hot doctor babe."

Patrick felt his hackles rise. "No kidding."

"Have you seen her? Blond, with a body like Scarlett Johanssen. Hot stuff, man. Next time I'm at the I.C., I'm asking her out. Hey, watch that chainsaw."

"Oops." Patrick's lip curled as he yanked the chainsaw back so it didn't spit wood chips in Gary's face.

"Yup, beer, burgers, and a hot blonde. Just gotta put this little fire out first. They say it should be ten percent contained by tomorrow."

Ten percent contained. That meant that before long he probably wouldn't be needed. His presence at dinner would be requested by his persistent little sister. And there would be no way out.

But—maybe he could make an excruciating family encounter a little more bearable with the addition of a certain blond doctor babe.

Chapter Seven

It was two days before Lara saw Patrick again. But she heard about him, in his new identity of "Psycho." Apparently his legend had preceded him. Everyone agreed that he was an unpredictable, death-defying madman who never met a risk he wouldn't take.

But that didn't appear to bother his sister, who still seemed to adore him.

"Make him say yes," Megan pleaded over the phone as Lara spread ointment over a nasty burn on a fireman's forearm. "I can't reach him at all."

"That's because he's at the fire line. The cell service is very unreliable out there."

"He's got to come back sometime. If you see him, pounce on him and make him say yes."

"Pouncing is not my style. I'm not a wildcat. Besides, why would he care what I say? Psycho—I mean, Patrick—always did his own thing. He never listens to anyone."

She had to admit, his new nickname suited him.

"Please, just . . . try, okay? It's really important."

Lara thought helping the men and women injured while battling the fire trying to incinerate Nevada rated higher in importance. And when that was done, she had an embarrassing family legacy to deal with. She heaved a sigh and pulled her cell phone away from her ear.

"Keep soaking for the next fifteen minutes," she told the firefighter, a young kid who looked about twenty, with the worst blisters she'd ever seen. She could relate, since she herself had developed blisters after her first day out here. After that she'd switched to rubber-soled hiking boots and felt much more comfortable.

"These firefighters are awfully cute," she told Megan, after she moved out of earshot.

Silence, then a nearly inaudible sigh.

Lara refused to pry. She'd fought tooth and nail for her privacy growing up, and she hated intruding on other people's.

"I have to go, Meggie. If I see Psycho, I'll remind him about the invitation."

"Do you really have to call him that?"

She laughed. "If the shoe fits . . ."

Stuffing her phone back in her pocket, she heard the whirring of a helicopter's blades. She straightened up, feeling her lower back complain. This was the chopper that had gone to help the helicopter that got stuck. The original mission had been to pick up an injured medic, who was still out there. As the "medium"—she'd heard it called that—hovered over the heli-spot, she saw Donnell and a couple other guys rushing toward it with a gurney.

It must be something serious, which meant it was something they wouldn't let her assist on. They passed the minor wounds on to her, claiming the big stuff—broken limbs, head injuries—for themselves. It made sense, since she didn't work for the fire service. But her competitive nature didn't like getting relegated to the background.

Just then Donnell, who was in deep consultation with the pilot, beckoned her over. She ran to join them.

"Mind being deputized?"

"What does that mean?"

"Means we temporarily hire you. You're covered by our insurance so we can stuff you in a chopper and fly you into the flames."

Her jaw dropped. She'd had to sign a waiver when she first arrived, but this was even more involved.

"I've been watching you. You do a good job. We got a broken chopper and an injured medic out there. He needs to get checked before we load him into the chopper. Right now I got no one else besides you."

Desperation. That explained it. She pushed her sweat-drenched hair behind her ears. "Of course I'll go. What'll I need?"

"Everything's on the bird already. Sign here. Social security number there. X on that line. After that, we have to get your PPE on. Personal protective equipment. You got boots? . . . Good, we can set you up with everything else."

And just like that, she found herself employed by the United States Forest Service. She hadn't even asked about pay or benefits. Did they offer much vacation time?

Wait a minute, this *was* her vacation. Just what she'd always wanted to do on her off-time, fly into fires and take over sexual healing centers.

At the supply cache, someone found her an olive drab flight suit. They asked if she was wearing cotton.

She had to check the labels, but her Bermuda shorts and T-shirt did turn out to be cotton. Apparently that was enough to pass the regulations, as they told her to put the flight suit on over her clothes.

Then she ran back toward the heli-spot, where Donnell waited with another firefighter, who was putting a white flight helmet on his head, his expression unreadable. He handed her a similar helmet.

"This fellow here is going to take you out there. Name's Grant. Let him help you. He's a trained paramedic."

She nodded to Grant and took the helmet. Donnell hurried off, with a final, "Stay safe." Nervous, she fumbled with the helmet until finally Grant reached over and settled it on her head. "You sure you're ready for this?"

Hell, no. "Absolutely."

"Let's go, then," he said.

Following his lead, she climbed into the chopper, as she'd watched so many of the firefighters do, and entered an utterly male world of equipment, gear, and sweat. An empty gurney took up a corridor down the middle of the chopper. Grant pulled two seats down from the wall and sat in one. She gingerly settled into the other and buckled herself in.

"Before we take off, I have to give you the safety briefing," Grant said. "Ready?"

At her nod, he launched into a rapid-fire explanation of what type of helicopter it was, where the fire extinguishers were located, how the doors operated, where the first aid kit was, and the fact that the ELT was in the nose of the aircraft. He finished with "Briefing done, let's move," which was obviously aimed at the pilot, not her. She was still wrestling with the ELT thing. Weren't those the black boxes that were supposed to survive a crash and explain what happened?

Somehow, the safety briefing didn't make her feel any safer.

"What's the patient's condition?" she asked into the helmet mic as the chopper lurched into the air. Out the window the grubby tents of the command post were replaced by the rustling leaves of treetops, then a carpet of gray-brown vegetation interspersed with vast stretches of scorched black fields.

"Broken bones, for sure. A tree fell on him. Some dude carried him on his back up the cliff to the crashed chopper. Crazy, but he saved his life."

A sneaking suspicion filtered into Lara's thoughts.

"What are their names?"

The pilot shook his head. "We didn't get that far. I had to transport the other injured. No room for anyone else. There's the fire."

He pointed ahead. Lara twisted around to peer out the front of the chopper. A churning, flickering mass of destruction stretched ahead. Even though she knew the fire didn't have an individual identity, it sure looked like it meant business, creeping across the landscape, devouring every tree, every blade of grass, every home it encountered. Surely it would get full at some point and slink back to its cave like a satisfied monster?

Then she sucked in a breath as she spotted the disabled chopper. It lay on top of a rise at the edge of a sandstone cliff. The fire was licking at it, as if trying to leap up the cliff. The chopper sprawled sideways at an improbable angle, like a broken child's toy. Amazing that it hadn't tumbled off the cliff by now; they must have done a good job tying it off.

"Looks like we got here just in time," said Grant.

She squinted, peering closer, and spotted two small figures near the chopper. One lay on the ground, the other waved his arms at the chopper.

"I estimate we'll have about six minutes to land, assess the patient, and get him on board."

"What? I can't do that. What if he has a broken neck? Moving him could . . ." She trailed off. Not moving him would almost definitely kill him. She'd just have to do her best.

"Hang on," said the pilot abruptly. "Lots of air currents from those flames."

So that's what was making the chopper wobble back and forth. Lara squeezed her eyes shut as they tilted to one side then the other, as if they were trapped inside a drunken elevator going down. But the darkness made her too nervous, so she opened her eyes and stared at the floor of the chopper as it lurched violently back and forth.

Don't get sick, don't get sick. Don't throw up all over a Fire Service helicopter and an unfriendly firefighter.

She managed to get a grip on her queasiness as the chopper settled onto the flat surface of the cliff.

Thank God.

But she didn't have much time for prayers of gratitude. The chopper door opened, hot air rushed around her like ten thousand blow dryers, and Patrick, wild blue eyes blazing from a face nearly black with soot and grime, reached into the chopper to help her out.

"You stalking me?" he yelled over the steady beat of the chopper blades.

"Screw you," she shouted back, in no mood to banter. "Where's the patient?"

He grabbed her arm and ran, ducking under the blades, toward the man lying on the ground. "I've been checking his pulse, it fluctuates between eighty and ninety."

"Has he regained consciousness at all?"

"Nope."

"You carried an unconscious man up this hill?"

He grinned at her. "You want me, don't you?"

She made a face at him and set to work. The injured medic was older than she'd expected, and looked vaguely familiar. The tree must have struck his upper body. His breathing was shallow, his face pale. Shock. She quickly located a fractured left arm, three broken ribs, and swelling around his neck. With Patrick hovering over her, she gingerly felt the vertebrae on the back of his neck. Nothing seemed obviously out of place, but even a hairline fracture could be trouble.

Grant had already brought the gurney from the chopper and waited impatiently for instructions.

"Grab me the C collar," she told him. "We're just going to have to go for it." Grant hurried back to the chopper.

"The ride's going to be brutal," said Patrick.

"No kidding." She winced just thinking about it. "It couldn't be worse than being carried on your back, though. If there's damage, it's probably already done."

"Now there's optimism."

Grant returned with the C collar. "Pilot says we have one minute or he's going to leave without us."

"Can you lift his head while I put on the collar? Very, very carefully?"

Grant nodded and knelt on the other side of the fallen medic. Together they maneuvered the injured man's limp head into the stabilizing collar.

"Let's get him on the gurney. On two," she said. "One, two." Gently the three of them rolled the patient onto the stretcher.

"Hurry," yelled Patrick. "I think the chopper's about to light up." He grabbed the handles at the foot of the gurney and Lara hurried to the patient's head. "Careful now."

As fast as they could, without bobbling the man too much, they trotted toward the chopper. Grant climbed in first, while Patrick and Lara helped guide the loaded stretcher after him. Grant immediately set to work securing the patient. Patrick jumped in after him, then put out a hand to help Lara board. As soon as she grabbed it, his grip switched to her wrist.

"Gotta go!" The pilot yelled.

"Go! Go!" Patrick yelled back at him. "We're good!"

"What?" She was certainly not good, seeing as she was half in, half out of the chopper. She scrambled to get both legs on board. Something metal scraped her shin. The chopper began to lift into the air.

"I'm not letting go of you," Patrick said calmly, his fist still wrapped around her wrist. She could practically feel the bruises forming. "Take your time. Get one leg in, then the other."

She heaved one leg onto the floor of the helicopter. A rush of heat tried to gobble up her other leg. She yelped. Had she just been burned?

"You're okay," urged Patrick. "If you panic I'll kick your ass. Now the other leg. That's right. I gotta say, I like this angle, Lulu."

"You're a pig!"

"Nice move, insulting the guy holding you above a raging wildfire." He laughed maniacally. He was enjoying this, the jerk. Loving every second. He really was "Psycho."

"Come on," he yelled. "You can do it. You're flexible. Didn't you do all that tantric yoga with the Goddesses? Yeah, I admit, I spied once or twice."

"*What?*" Fury carried her the rest of the way into the belly of the chopper. As she rolled onto the steel floor, warm from the flames still only a few yards beneath the helicopter, Patrick reached over and pulled the door shut.

Immediately the terrible roar of the wind and flames lessened. Lara lay panting on the floor until Patrick hauled her into one of the pull-down seats. "I hate you, Patrick Callahan IV."

"If I had a nickel for every time I heard that from a woman whose life I just saved, I'd . . . well, I'd have a nickel. Most women want to kiss me."

"You didn't save my life," she ground out. She checked the gash on her shin. Sure enough, blood dripped onto her boots.

From the chair next to her, Patrick fixed his vivid blue gaze on her.

"Fine. Thanks for that part," she said grudgingly. "But I'm really pissed about the rest of it. You had no right to come onto Haven property and—"

He shrugged, grabbing two water bottles and tossing one to her. "I couldn't have if I wanted to. Your aunt was pretty strict with her security."

"You mean . . ." She gaped at him. The water bottle felt cool in her hands. She pressed it against her hot cheek.

"I lied. I was trying to piss you off. You always moved faster when you were fired up."

He gave her a diabolical wink. God, she wanted to rip his head off. Smash his face in. Scratch his eyes out. It took her right back to her teenage years, before she'd claimed her life as a rational med student.

"Congratulations," she gritted. "I didn't think I could hate you more, but I do."

"What's that they say about the thin line?" He

toasted her with his water bottle, then glugged from it. She watched his Adam's apple move under the stubbly, tanned, filthy skin of his neck. Dirt and sweat shouldn't be this sexy, should it? Her gaze traveled to the other side of the chopper, where Grant sat opposite them, head tilted back, eyes shut. Even though he too was handsome—and almost as dirty as Patrick—he didn't have a fraction of Patrick's impact on her.

"In this case, that thin line is the size of a super-highway," she told him.

"Then I think it's time for you to cross to the other side. In return for saving your life—for which I have yet to receive a decent thank-you—you're going to do something for me."

"Dream on."

"Can you deny that you owe me?"

"Don't I get any thanks for risking my life in the first place? I'm not a firefighter. Someone owes me!"

He jerked his head toward the injured man. "On his behalf, thank you. He'll be your love slave as soon as he wakes up."

Lara ground her teeth.

"Come on, it's not that hard. All you have to do is go to dinner with me."

A weird dizziness made her head spin. Was Patrick asking her out? After all the long-ago nights she'd spent alternating between dreams of kissing him and smashing his face in, was one of those idiotic fantasies about to come true? "You mean, like a . . . date?" She presented the word as if it were a piece of spinach stuck between her teeth.

"Sure. The kind where you meet the future in-laws and realize the hell you're about to suffer until you die or divorce, whichever comes first."

Reality came crashing down. "You want me to have dinner with your family?"

"And me."

"Right. You and the rest of the Callahans, who think of me as 'that hippie chick.'"

"They hate me more, if it makes you feel any better."

Something flickered in Patrick's eyes. Something, dare it be said, serious and—good Lord almighty—genuine. For the first time, she looked at him, really looked at him, noticing the set of his jaw, the sober cast of his lips. She realized that he must have gone through a lot in the past ten years. And that coming back wasn't easy on him.

"I get it," she finally said, trying to keep it light. "The mighty 'Psycho' doesn't mind jumping out of a helicopter, but he wants someone to hold his hand when he sees his family."

He didn't take offense, as she'd predicted, as he would have in the old days. Didn't get defensive or mock her. Instead he gave her a slow smile, unsettling in its sweetness, and said, "Please, will you hold my hand, Lara Nelson? I'd be grateful."

Chapter Eight

When they got back to the command post, an ambulance was waiting for the injured firefighter. Patrick watched as Lara briefed the paramedics on his condition. Lara Nelson, a doctor. A *good* doctor. Not that he was surprised. She'd always been smart. But he supposed, now that he thought about it, that he'd never expected to see her again. After the accident, he'd put her into the mental black vault where he kept all thoughts of Loveless.

When she finished with the paramedics, he helped her take off her helmet. He wasn't quite ready to let her go, he realized.

"I'll take your gear back to the supply cache," he offered.

"Thanks." She unzipped her flight suit and peeled it off her body. His throat tightened as each inch of her pale gold skin was revealed, as if she were a Christmas present that had been hidden in a closet for ten years.

Her damp T-shirt hugged her full breasts; he could see the faint outline of her bra underneath. Even in grubby shorts, her long, bare legs had more effect on him than a stripper's. He stood like an idiot as she added the suit to the pile of gear in his arms. *Say something, jerk.*

When he spoke, his voice sounded like a rusty hinge. "So . . ." He cleared his throat. "What are you doing back in Loveless?"

She shot him a suspicious look. "Why do you ask? Shouldn't you get back to work? Don't you have more reckless heroic deeds to perform?"

"Nah, I've already passed my daily limit."

"So you admit you have limits. That's new."

"A lot of things are new." He couldn't help running a quick glance up and down her body. "Megan said your aunt died. Is that why you came back?"

"Sort of." She headed toward the med tent, and he fell into step beside her. "She left me the Haven. I'm trying to figure out what to do with it. As quickly as possible, so I can go back to San Diego."

"That's where you live?" All this time, she'd been in California, just like him. San Diego was only a few hours from San Gabriel. What were the chances?

"Yes. I'm hoping to get a position at the hospital clinic there. I think my chances are pretty good."

"I bet they are."

Another suspicious look. "Is there supposed to be an insulting double entendre in there?"

"Of course not. Why would there be? I meant that you're obviously a great doctor. You just got on a chopper and pulled a downed firefighter out of a wildfire. That makes you a hero in my book."

Those whiskey-and-caramel eyes fixed on his face. "You're being sincere."

"It's been known to happen. Just don't tell the guys."

"The guys?"

"My crew back at the firehouse. I have a reputation to maintain. I'm the resident troublemaker."

She snorted. "That shouldn't be too hard for you."

Before he could point out that a lot of things could have changed in ten years and she shouldn't jump to conclusions, something crashed against his leg. "What the—" He looked down to find Goldie rubbing her fuzzy white head against his thigh. "Oh, it's you." He bent down so the baby llama could bump her head against his cheek, making the cutest little bleating sounds. "Talk about a troublemaker."

"She really has a thing for you." Laughter rippled through Lara's husky voice. From this angle, he was uncomfortably close to her bare legs. How would the sweet knobby curve of her kneecap taste? What about her sleek inner thigh where it disappeared under her shorts?

"At least someone does." He pulled a mock-pitiful face. Still gazing down at him, she smiled, the first spontaneous, genuine, unguarded smile he'd seen from her yet. And *wham*. A spike of electric attraction nearly knocked him into the dirt. He saw it in her expression too—along with shock and alarm. For a long, loaded moment raw awareness hovered between them.

She looked like she might run. No matter what, he couldn't let that happen.

He rose to his feet, still holding his armload of gear. "I'd better take this to the supply cache and find Goldie some food. But when you come to dinner, I want to hear all about the Haven and what you're trying to do. And your medical career. And everything else." Was she seeing anyone? Maybe she was married. He glanced at her left hand but saw no wedding ring. But that didn't mean much. Many firemen didn't wear them either; rings and firefighting could be a bad combination.

"I don't know . . ." Wariness was written all over her dirt-streaked face.

"Come on. You want to let Goldie down?" As if on cue, Goldie tilted her head toward Lara and adorably blinked her yellow eyes. Patrick reminded himself to give her some extra alfalfa.

"I'll try. I have to meet with some realtors, though. And I don't intend to be here more than a few days."

"Neither do I. See? We have so much in common." And there it was again, that zap of electricity. This time it kept him rooted to the ground as she muttered a good-bye and hurried to the med tent.

Damn. His instincts were screaming the same way they did when he was about to jump out of a chopper or dive off a cliff. If he was smart, he'd rethink the dinner invitation. But screw "smart." Life was all about the risks. Especially a risk as tempting as Lara Nelson, all grown up.

Loveless had five realtors, only one of whom had time on his schedule to meet with the new owner of the infamous Haven for Sexual and Spiritual Healing. How quickly she had slipped back into the familiar feeling of being an outcast. As she sat in the waiting room of Horvath and Associates, she caught a few surreptitious glances from the young, fresh-faced receptionist.

When the realtor appeared, tall, beer-bellied, and familiar, her heart sank even further. "Dean," she said, without enthusiasm. "How are you?"

"Fantastic. Couldn't be better. Come in, come in." The former quarterback of the Loveless High School football team ushered Lara into his office. She took a seat in the comfortable chair facing his desk.

"I couldn't believe it when I saw your name on my schedule," said Dean, kicking his boots up on his desk. "I thought you left town years ago."

"I did. But my aunt died and, uh, left me some property. I'm looking into selling it."

"Some property . . ." Dean tilted his head back and gazed up at the ceiling. "Now let me see. That would be . . ."

Lara clenched her jaw. Dean always had been a bully. "The Haven for Sexual and Spiritual Healing."

"Right, right. I remember something about the place."

Lara met his pale blue eyes. They contrasted very unfavorably with the electric blue of Patrick's, which had been haunting her ever since the chopper rescue. "I'm sure you do."

The friendly, utterly fake smile dropped from his face. "Not a happy memory for me, I gotta say."

It hadn't been her finest moment, she had to admit. "You were being cruel to Liam. I had to do something."

"You did something, all right."

She'd confronted him in the cafeteria and told him if he didn't leave Liam alone, she'd reveal the fact that his parents had taken the Opening Your Energy Channels to Multiple Orgasm workshop at the Haven.

Unfortunately, one of his football team members overheard, and Dean had been the laughingstock of the school for a week. Granted, it was a nice break for her—and no one dared mess with her or Liam after that—but she hadn't intended to humiliate him.

Her temples throbbed, and this time it wasn't from constantly inhaling the smoky air at the command post. The fire had been mostly contained. The firefighters were heading home. If only she could do the same.

She cleared her throat. "Be that as it may, property is

property. A sale is a sale. Commission is commission. And high school is ancient history, don't you think?"

He gave her a nasty look. The gold wedding ring on his left hand caught her eye. She racked her brain for the name of the tennis-playing country club type he used to date.

"Did you get married to Patty? You guys were such a cute couple."

He ignored her feeble attempt at peacemaking. "I don't know anyone around here who wants to buy that old eyesore."

"Okay, well, the buyer doesn't have to be local. Maybe someone wants to start a ranch, or a school or something. It has twenty acres of land attached."

"A twenty-acre ranch?" He snorted. "You've been away from Nevada too long."

"Not long enough," she muttered. "Fine. Tell me what I'd have to do to make the property more enticing to a buyer. Subdivide it? Tear down the building?" She hated the thought, but she had to consider all possibilities.

He looked at her stonily and played with a gold pen on his desk. Maybe she needed to do more damage control.

"Dean, look. I never meant anyone to hear what I said that day. I'm sorry it got out of control like that. I only wanted to protect Liam, I didn't mean to hurt you."

If possible, his expression became even more unyielding. "You're apologizing thirteen years after the fact?"

"Since you've apparently held a grudge for thirteen years, yes," she snapped. "Didn't I try to tell you how to handle it? Didn't I tell you to ignore it and it would go away?"

Instead, he'd beaten up half the school and gotten suspended for a week.

He pulled his booted feet off the desk and planted them on the ground. She braced herself for an ignominious flight out the door. "Okay, Lara Nelson, apology accepted. In exchange, here's my real estate tip. Only one family in this town might be interested in buying your property. Didn't Callahan try to buy it once before? Didn't he hate having a hippie free-love commune in town?"

"It was never a hippie commune," she protested, as if it mattered at this point.

"Whatever you call it, he wanted it shut down. Maybe he'll buy it now, just to get rid of it once and for all."

Lara gripped her leather tote bag, the one that had shocked poor Romaine by being made from actual cowhide. "I'm not interested in doing business with the Callahans."

"Well, that's all I got for you. Good luck." He stood, his body language clearly screaming get-the-hell-out. "Welcome back to Loveless. Too bad you can't come over for dinner, but Patty never did like you much."

She stood too. "Grow up, Dean. Honestly." She searched her memory for a workshop catchphrase. "Holding onto anger is like swallowing rat poison. Focus on the positive, release the negative."

When he looked like he'd toss her out the window if she stayed any longer, she lifted her chin and swept out of his office.

Out on the dusty sidewalk, she took a shallow breath of still murky air. The hint of smoke made her think of Patrick. Then again, most things had been making her think of him. Just like that long-ago Christmas, when all of a sudden she'd felt that irritating, uncontrollable attraction to him. This new Patrick had an even more disturbing effect on her. Maybe it was his fireman's physique, or the strength that radiated from him, or hell, maybe it was the llama. Whatever it was, she didn't know what to do with it.

She could run. Back out of dinner at the Callahans and hide out at the Haven. That would make the most sense. Or she could spend more time with him. Surely she'd find some flaw to take the edge off his appeal. But what if that didn't happen? What if he got even more attractive? Was that even possible? A little butterfly storm of anticipation fluttered in her belly.

Even as she picked up the phone, she had no idea what she was going to say to Patrick.

"I'm running late," Lara said on the phone. "The realtor kept me waiting half an hour. Then he told me he doesn't like me. It was almost as fun as dangling from a helicopter."

"You're not getting out of this," Patrick told her sternly. "You promised." She'd done no such thing. He waited for her to protest, but she didn't. He pressed his advantage. "I'll see you at the ranch whenever you get there. I'll have a nice cold drink waiting for you. A virgin daiquiri or something." Lara had never been a drinker. She had been a virgin. But what about now? . . . Sternly, he ordered his unruly mind to stay away from that line of thought. "I'll rub your feet." That direction wasn't any better. "We'll stick pins in a realtor doll, how's that?"

"Now you're talking." She laughed. Lara had the sexiest laugh, like magic fingers up and down his spine.

"I'll see you in a few minutes." He hung up before she could argue. The tight knot of anxiety in his chest loosened a bit. Yes, he was about to see his family. But Lara would be there; she wasn't going to back out. For some reason, he thought everything would be okay if she showed up. Maybe it was because she was a link to Liam. Or maybe it was because when Lara looked at him, she didn't see a walk on the wild side, the way most girls did. Granted, she saw someone who got under her skin and pissed her off. But he didn't mind that. It even made him a little nostalgic.

Besides, she'd grown into one hellaciously sexy woman, and that fascinated him. At the very least, he'd get to see her one more time before he left.

His gear was already packed into the back of the Hulk. A long hot shower at a hotel had cleaned every last speck of soot and dirt off his body. The only loose end he hadn't quite figured out was what to do with Goldie. The llama's affection for him had only grown while he'd been in the field. She kept trotting after him, nudging him with her nose and making snuffling sounds.

How were you supposed to break up with a llama?

He asked a few of the local guys if they wanted a new pet, but everyone was too exhausted to give poor Goldie a thought. Loveless had a couple veterinarians, but no animal shelters. The nearest shelter was in Durgin, the next big town over.

In the end he made a makeshift box for Goldie in the back of the Hulk and decided he'd drop her off at the shelter on the way back to California.

The gates of the Callahan Ranch stood open, which would never happen at a still-working ranch. His father, Patrick Callahan III, known as Big Dog Callahan to everyone except his wife, who called him Cal, had given up raising cattle when he'd become governor. When he was voted out of office after one excru-

ciating term, he got into real estate investment. They'd
kept a small herd of mustangs, which Big Dog Callahan considered his mascot. Patrick grew up riding
mustangs; he'd been trying to recreate the wild joy of
it ever since. Dirt bikes came close. So did helicopters.

Llamas, on the other hand . . .

Goldie gazed out the window with her flat yellow
eyes and munched on the grass he'd given her as a
road snack.

"If you get carsick, tell me and I'll pull over," he told
her.

Her jaws shifted side to side as she chewed.

"If I don't find a home for you here, how'd you feel
about bunking with Stan at the firehouse? You don't
hear about too many stations with their own llamas.
We'd have to call you the Bachelorette Llama of San
Gabriel." He chuckled, filling with warmth at the
thought of Station 1. He'd be home soon enough, back
in Truck 1 where he belonged.

Patrick's gut tightened as he made the familiar drive
down the winding gravel driveway. Something wasn't
right here in Callahanland. It looked as if no one had
been tending the grounds for a while. The grasses had
grown taller than he was. The way they swayed in the
dry breeze made him shudder. *Fire hazard.* How had
the ranch avoided catching fire? One spark from the
wildfire and it would have gone up like a pile of sticks.
It still could.

He'd have to tell his father to do something about
that. Not that his father had ever listened to anything
he said, but now that he was a trained and experienced
firefighter, maybe things would be different.

The sight of the ranch house shocked him even more.
The sprawling structure was completely overgrown
with shrubs and tall grasses; everything looked dan-

gerously dry. The outbuildings—guesthouse, bunk-house, barn, stables, well house, garden shed, chicken coop—were just as bad. What was going on here?

Megan and his mother waited on the wide porch that wrapped around the front of the house. Megan was practically bouncing up and down with excite-ment, but Candy Callahan looked . . . well, worried. Externally, she hadn't changed much, still slim and straight, but when Patrick bent down to kiss her on the cheek, he noticed new frown lines under the gardenia-scented powder. A former beauty queen and kinder-garten teacher—before Big Dog Callahan had swept her off her feet—she was still gorgeous, with her chin-length auburn bob and bright blue eyes. Patrick had never understood how she put up with someone as impossible as his father.

"Hi, Mom," he murmured in her ear.

"Patrick, honey." She stood on tiptoe to wrap her arms around his neck. "I can't believe Megan talked you into this."

"Is it a bad idea?" He straightened up with a laugh.

"You never know. That man, he's liable to make me scream more often than not these days."

Megan shot him a nervous look and adjusted the glasses on her nose. She wore a denim skirt dotted with daisies and a dainty white blouse.

"And that's different how?" Patrick winked at Megan.

"Oh, you troublemaker. Megan and I told him we'd both eat at Denny's tonight if he made any fuss. But you know how he is."

"Not big on the listening, you mean."

"Promise you'll be nice?" His mother fixed a strand of hair displaced during their hug.

"Have I ever been nice, Mom?"

"Patrick . . ." That warning tone still had the ability to make him back down.

"I'll be nice. Hey, I have a llama in my rig. Should I take her to the stables?"

Megan's face lit up. "Goldie's here?"

"She wouldn't have missed this for the world." His mother and sister followed him back to his truck, where Goldie was now fast asleep, her fluffy white beard nestled on her front hooves. Candy and Megan cooed over her until Patrick shushed them.

"Don't wake her up, she hasn't been sleeping well since the fire," he whispered with a wink.

Which reminded him . . .

"I'm expecting a guest," he told his mother as they all strolled back to the porch. "Remember Liam's friend Lara Nelson?"

Candy frowned. "She's not coming here, is she?"

For the first time, Patrick wondered if his old rebellious impulses were leading him astray again. "She was Liam's best friend. Why not?"

Candy pressed her lips together, then shrugged.

Megan glared at him as they trooped into the house. "You did not have permission to bring Lara," she hissed as he stepped across the threshold. "It was hard enough getting him to agree to you."

"Thanks, I needed that," said Patrick dryly.

"Oh, you know what I mean. Will you *please* be good? I promised Dad you would be."

But Patrick was busy dealing with the onslaught of emotions brought on by stepping foot inside his childhood home. As they passed through the living room, he saw that his cross-country trophies still lined the mantelpiece—except the one his father had thrown out the window in a rage.

Something about him landing in jail after the victory party that night had really ticked his father off.

Then there was the doorjamb where he and Liam had marked their heights as they grew up. A line high on the wood was gouged out and painted over, but Patrick remembered it perfectly. It had marked his father's height and was labeled "Governor Blowhard, March 1995." Yes, that had been his father's nickname among his opponents. But for some reason he hadn't liked seeing it written by his own eldest son.

Patrick had to admit he hadn't been the easiest child in the world.

In the dining room, his father was already seated at the head of the long table made from polished burl wood. Patrick Callahan III extracted himself from a thronelike chair and unfurled himself to his full height. Like Patrick, he wasn't particularly tall, but his physical presence made up for it. Burly-chested, his lion's mane of hair gone stark white, his face ruddy from the scotch he always drank before dinner, he was a man used to dominating every situation. As always, a cigar smoldered in a bison-skull ashtray next to his plate.

Intimidated despite himself, Patrick stopped a few feet from his father. "Hi, Dad. It's good to see you."

Those etiquette lessons at the governor's mansion didn't die easy.

His father stuck out his hand with the lopsided grin that had once charmed Nevada voters. Patrick breathed a silent sigh of relief. "Welcome back to the ranch, son. You've been in California, eh?"

"Yes. A little town called San Gabriel."

"Your sister saw you in the magazine. A 'Bachelor Fireman,' they said you were."

Patrick winced. Of all the things his father had to focus on, why that? "You know the media. Once they get started on something, you can't throw them off."

"Not unless you hire a good press agent and take them out for a steak dinner every week." His father rumbled with laughter. Patrick, glancing at his mother, who'd sat down in the chair at Big Dog's elbow, saw her face brighten. Maybe this wouldn't be an outright disaster.

"I'll mention that to Captain Brody." Patrick eyed the remaining seats at the table. A healthy distance from his father seemed best. He sat down at the far end and pulled out the chair next to him for Megan, who sat down gingerly. Parents at one end, children at the other. Callahan dinners had always been about battle lines. And armor. And weapons of mass destruction.

His father sat down and stuck his cigar back in his mouth. "You aren't the captain at your station? You an Indian or a chief? Can't be both, it's either one or the other."

Patrick gritted his teeth. "I'm the topman."

"Top man," said Megan quickly. "That sounds amazing. Even better than captain. Doesn't it, Mom?"

"Yes, honey, it does. It means you're the top man in your unit, right?"

Patrick tried hard, really hard, not to laugh, but didn't quite manage it. "Not at all. It means I go up on roofs and hack holes in them."

"Hack holes in them!" His mother looked appalled.

"That sounds like your kind of trouble," said his father. "I remember the time you tried to fly off the roof and took a bunch of shingles with you. Went splat, as I recall. Broke two bones in your arm."

Patrick counted to five before he spoke again. "When a house is involved in a fire, you have to create vent holes to let out the smoke. That's why we put holes in the roof."

"That sounds very brave," said Megan, trying desperately to get the conversation back on track. "Is it dangerous?"

"It's one of the more dangerous jobs, but firefighting is a dangerous profession in general. Luckily, we're highly trained and manage to avoid injury for the most part."

His father grunted. He'd looked happier when remembering Patrick's misdeeds. "Well, firefighting is a decent enough profession, I suppose. Meggie said you're helping out on our local wildfire."

"Was. It's mostly out now."

"Thanks to him," Megan pointed out. "He rappelled out of a helicopter *into* the fire."

His mother gasped in admiration, while his father puffed on his cigar.

"Still taking stupid risks, in other words," Big Dog grumbled.

Patrick clenched his fists, fighting to hang onto his manners. It had never taken longer than a few minutes for him and his father to start going at it. Why had he thought ten years would change things?

"Megan and I made beef stew and corn bread," said Candy, fidgeting with the rings on her fingers. "You boys always loved that."

"Sounds great."

"I'll get the stew." Megan jumped up and scurried from the room, leaving Patrick alone with his parents, who seemed just as uncomfortable as he was. Twice as uncomfortable, since there were two of them. Damn it, this was exactly why he'd wanted Lara here.

Instead, he was on his own. He reminded himself of all the fires he'd tackled and helicopters he'd jumped from, and took a deep breath.

"Speaking of me and Liam, Megan told me that he left. When's the last time you heard from him?"

A shocked silence gripped the room. Clearly he'd blundered his way into the wrong topic. Big Dog crushed his fist around a fork. "Why are you bringing him up? Trying to make trouble?"

"No, sir. I'd just like to know where he is."

His father pinned him with a harsh glare. "Not in the hospital anymore, no thanks to you."

Candy let out a gasp as Patrick bolted to his feet. "What the hell's that supposed to mean?"

"It means what it sounds like. And no swearing, boy."

"Cal, don't you dare!" Candy wailed. "You said you'd give him a chance. Do you want to drive all our children away?"

"Oh, so it's my fault again!" Callahan growled.

Candy was on her feet now too. "Maybe it is! You're the one in charge around here, as you've been telling me for the last thirty years! Why wouldn't it be your fault?"

Big Dog hauled himself out of his seat. He pointed a shaking finger at Patrick. "Only one person's to blame! He's the one who put Liam in the hospital. He's no different now, except he's got graffiti all over him!"

Patrick glanced down at himself. Sure enough, his T-shirt revealed a few tattoos, though not nearly the full extent of his ink. Maybe he should strip off his shirt and really give his father a shocker. But with Big Dog Callahan turning a disturbing shade of brick, he restrained himself.

"I'm going," he said instead, jaw tightly clenched. "I didn't come here to fight."

"If he goes, I go!" Candy's face now matched the red of her hair.

"No, Mom, you don't have to—"

Both his parents ignored him.

"Only say it if you mean it," roared Callahan.

"Oh, I mean it all right!" She planted both fists on her hips and fixed blazing blue eyes on her husband. "I'm tired of you running my children off. Now you apologize to Patrick!"

"I'd rather stick my cigar in my eye!"

Shocked, Patrick looked from one to the other. His parents had always stuck together, through four years in the governor's mansion, several fortunes won and lost, the infection that cost Liam his hearing. He'd never seen them turn on each other before. Should he do something? Step between them? Tackle his dad to the ground? What was he supposed to do?

It was one thing for his father to yell at him. But his parents fighting? He had no idea how to handle *that*.

His father wheeled on him. "See what you've done now, Patrick?"

There, that was better.

"Get out!" Big Dog thundered.

"Gee, that sounds familiar." Patrick finally found his voice. "Isn't that the last thing you said to me?"

"I still mean it!"

"Cal, you stop it, right now!"

"What's going on?" A wail from Megan cut through the clamor of shouting voices. She stood in the doorway, holding a heavy, steaming pot. Blinking madly behind her fogged-up glasses, she looked from one of them to the other. "What *happened?*"

No one wanted to explain. Patrick and his mother glanced at each other warily.

Into the silence, a throaty, tentative voice spoke. Patrick felt it on the back of his neck like a tickling caress.

"Sorry I'm late. I hope I haven't missed too much."

Chapter Nine

Lara, her buttery hair loose to her shoulders, peered from behind Megan. "Oh good, you haven't even sat down yet."

Patrick tried to catch her eye. He shook his head, then drew a finger across his throat—the universal symbol for "stop before you step into a shit storm."

But she was looking at his parents, smiling brightly. "Mr. and Mrs. Callahan, so nice to see you again. I'm Lara Nelson, in case you don't remember. Liam was a good friend of mine back in high school. I came to visit him a few times after the accident . . ." Finally she seemed to become aware of the tension paralyzing the room. Callahan swung his head toward her like a bull spotting a red cape. Her eyes went wide.

"Is . . . uh . . . maybe this is a bad time. I probably have the wrong house. Did I say Callahan? I meant . . . Candygram. No one here ordered a Candygram, did they? Didn't think so. I should really go."

Patrick had to give her points for creativity.

She took a step backward.

"I know you," growled Callahan. "The hippie girl. From that candy-ass peace-and-love commune down the road."

"Definitely a bad time," said Lara. "I'll be going now. But someone should really help Megan with this pot. I think she's about to drop it, and the poor girl can't see a thing."

Patrick hurried forward and took the stew pot from Megan's hands. "Don't leave," he muttered urgently to Lara.

"I'd rather jump from a helicopter than stay here another second," she hissed back. "Sorry, Megan."

"It's okay." Megan wiped the steam off her glasses and planted them back on her face. "This is all Patrick's fault anyway."

"*What?*"

"Why did you invite Lara? You knew it would rile Dad up even more."

And in fact an earthquake seemed to be erupting across the room. Callahan slammed a fist onto the table, making the silverware jump and the glass in the windows rattle. "Don't I get a say in what goes on in my own house anymore?"

"Uh-oh," said Megan. "You'd better go, Lara."

Lara nodded and whirled around, her hair fanning behind her.

"Wait for me outside," Patrick told her. "I'm right behind you."

Big Dog roared. "This is donkey's balls! The last thing we need around here is free love hippie riffraff wandering around like they own the place!"

Candy slapped her hands over her ears. Patrick hurried to the table, put down the pot of stew, and gave his mother a quick kiss on the cheek. "This smells great, by the way," he muttered.

He could have sworn he felt the hot blast of air from his father's end of the table.

"Going again?" Callahan shouted. "Don't come back unless you're invited."

Patrick took a deep breath. It took everything in him to hold back the angry retorts that tumbled through his mind. *I wouldn't come back if you got on your knees and begged me. Kiss my ass, Governor Blowhard.* Either he'd matured or he was out of practice. But instead of blasting his father right back, the way he would have in the old days, he headed for the door.

"You have my cell now, Meggie. Don't be a stranger."

Her pretty face crumpled, and that was the hardest part of all.

"I'll call you," he promised. "Maybe you can visit me in California."

She nodded, clearly holding back tears. He loped out of the house, hoping Lara hadn't left yet. Even though the evening light had gone dark gold, the blast furnace heat hadn't lessened. It thickened the air like honey, setting Lara's hair ablaze with light. She leaned against a white Chevy Aveo. She was playing with the keys, jingling them rapidly from one hand to the other. His swift survey told him she looked extra sexy in a pair of jeans that kissed her curves, and a silky tie-at-the-waist top in a shade of beige that ought to look boring but didn't. Not at all.

He should have paid more attention to her mood than her looks. As soon as he reached her side, she hauled off and punched him in the shoulder—hard.

"What the hell?" Grimacing, he put a hand to his shoulder.

"You did that on purpose," she said in a low, furious voice.

"What?"

"You wanted to upset your dad. So you invited me. He's *always* hated me."

"I swear, Lara, that's not why –"

She cut him off. "Why else would you invite me?"

"Because I wanted you here. With me. I wanted to see you again." Even to him, that sounded weak. He tried again. "I thought if you were here, at least one good thing would come out of it."

"Good thing? What good thing?"

"You." He gave her a cautious look, hoping she'd understand. "We used to be friends, right? Now you're . . ." he searched for the right words. " . . . on my mind. A lot. I didn't want to leave without seeing you again."

Seeing her was just part of it. All his senses were homed in on her, capturing the faint scent of sandal-wood rising from her skin, the rapid skittering of her heartbeat. A clear bead of sweat pearled at the base of her throat. His mouth watered. Was he the only one feeling this intense attraction?

Maybe he was, because she was looking at him as if he was crazy. "You saw what just happened in there."

"So I miscalculated. He had no call to treat you like that."

Her eyes flashed whiskey-dark, the way they used to when he'd teased her as a kid. "I don't care what he says about me." She raised her chin, firmed her gen-erously curved lips. And suddenly he saw what he'd never understood before: her hurt, her bravado, her courage.

He stepped forward and brushed his thumb over her cheek. "I'm sorry, Lara. I'm really sorry."

This close to her, he had a giddy sense of entering a new country, one whose fascinating terrain begged to be explored. He saw her lips tremble, watched her pupils dilate, whiskey turning to dark desire. Sudden lust hung thick between them. Her skin felt so lush under his thumb—like the petals of some kind of tropical flower.

He bent his head and brushed his lips against hers with the softest, slightest possible contact, which nevertheless shocked him with a third-rail current of electricity. Every single hair on his body stood on end. And it wasn't just him. She drew in a quick gasp, her mouth softening, luring him in. She tasted like the sunset sky, like wild honey, like that moment of weightlessness on the edge of a rappel. Desire rocked him, made his hand, still framing her face, shake.

Then something hard was jabbing him in the chest. Lara's emphatic index finger. He took a step back, the taste of her still vibrating on his lips. She looked just as shaken as he was, but also mad as hell.

"No, Patrick. Have you forgotten I've known you since you were *fourteen*?"

He scrubbed a hand through his hair, trying like hell to pull his wits together.

"The whole time, you were fighting with your father. Making trouble. Playing the rebel. You *wanted* him to react. Wanted to make him yell and scream. Liam always hated it. But you didn't care. You did it anyway. And you're *still* doing it. That's why you invited me. You *used* me to get to him. It's mean and childish and just plain idiotic." Lara shook her head, raking him from head to toe with scornful, blazing eyes. "He's all fired up now, thanks to you. Mission accomplished, *Psycho*. You haven't changed a bit. I hope you're proud of yourself."

She got into her Aveo and drove off without a backward glance. Patrick spun around and slammed his fist against the tanklike door of the Hulk. *Damn it to hell.* He'd fucked everything up once again. His parents were at each other's throats and Lara despised him.

He should have stayed in freaking San Gabriel.

He opened the tailgate and found Goldie trying to clamber to her feet. Her golden eyes skittered in a nervous sideways back and forth pattern. "Oh for the love of . . . sorry, Goldie. I didn't mean to scare you. Better hop out. Potty break. You won't find a better place to take a crap than right here."

Goldie crept to the tailgate, then peered out. "It's okay," he murmured to her. "I understand why you're scared, but no one here has anything against llamas. You're perfectly safe." When she still hesitated, he reached in and lifted her out. Setting her on the ground, he patted her gently. "Good girl, pretty girl. Poopy-time now."

He led her to a thick clump of grass at the edge of the circular drive. The place was one giant fire hazard. And he'd never even gotten a chance to mention that to crazy old Big Dog.

"Patrick." He almost jumped at the sound of Megan's voice right behind him. He turned to find her facing him, arms across her chest, chin stuck out, glasses speckled with salt, the way they always got when she'd been crying.

He would have ripped his own face off if that would fix anything. "Aw, Meggie, don't cry. I'm sorry."

"No." She shook her head vigorously. "It's not you. He's gotten worse. Don't you think? I mean, look at this place."

Patrick looked uneasily around the property, which

was more unkempt than he'd ever seen it. "Are they short on money? I can send some."

"No, it's not that. I don't know what it is." She shoved her hands in the pockets of her skirt. "Thanks for coming, even if it was a complete disaster. At least Mom and I got to see you."

He studied her, feeling like the biggest loser on the face of the earth. "I can't be here. I make it worse."

"I suppose." But she chewed her bottom lip, looking unconvinced.

"Will you tell Dad that he needs to get the brush cleared away from the house? The outbuildings too. The more the better."

"He knows. Some firefighters came by here and warned us about it." An adorable hint of pink appeared in her cheeks. "One of them said he'd do it, but Dad didn't want him here."

"Why? Did he ask you out?"

"*Patrick.*" Then she smiled suddenly. "Not exactly. But sort of."

"He'd be a lucky, lucky guy if you said yes," he said softly, brushing her cheek with his thumb. "Hey, I have an idea. Could you take care of Goldie for me?"

It was either a terrible idea or a stroke of brilliance. Was his newfound pet safe with Big Dog Callahan?

As soon as Meggie's face lit up, he decided it was genius.

"I'd love to!" She clapped her hands together and bounced on her toes. "I have the perfect spot for Goldie in the stables! I bet she'll get along great with Angelbaby. We only have three horses left, so Goldie can have her own stall, and in the daytime I can take her out to different fields and she can eat the grass down. She can clear our brush for us."

"She's just the girl for the job." He handed her the rope he'd tied to Goldie's temporary collar.

"And you'll come back and check on her?" The hope in Megan's face made him want to drown himself in a bucket of ice water.

"I'll write. Goldie will appreciate that. She's always saying how much she regrets the passing of the old epistolary days."

Megan giggled. Patrick gave Goldie a rough pat on the neck and grabbed her blanket from the back of the truck. One last hug for Megan and he got in, made a tight, high-speed reverse turn that mowed down some shrubs at the edge of the drive, and roared toward the front gate.

Hey, he had to leave his mark.

And he kept leaving it, from Loveless to California, starting with tequila shooters at the Ride 'Em Hard Bar and Grill, which he fled with three bikers in hot pursuit. They caught up with him in Henderson, where they all mutually decided to settle matters with a high-stakes pool game. That's how he became the proud owner of a Harley. The Harley got dumped around mile 85, when he needed more room because somehow he'd picked up a family of traveling Mormons who kept lecturing him about his immortal soul.

By the time he reached San Gabriel, he'd left a trail of empty bottles, angry citizens, and big tips for hot cocktail waitresses in his wake. He'd spent more hours drunk than sober, but at least only the sober ones were spent on the road, thanks to his new drink invention—espresso mixed with Red Bull with a dash of ginseng. He'd outwitted two Highway Patrol officers, half a biker gang, and a kamikaze porcupine determined to become roadkill.

But he still hadn't forgotten the scornful look in Lara's eyes when she'd told him what she thought of him.

Chapter Ten

The firehouse welcomed Patrick back with a few claps on the shoulder, some razzing about the TV footage of him carrying Goldie on his shoulders, and an invitation to a cake-tasting at Chief Roman's restaurant.

"What's a cake-tasting?" he asked Sabina blankly.

She was busy checking the pressure on her oxygen tank. "Pretty much what it sounds like," she muttered. "Feel free to skip it. Roman told me to invite you."

Normally her attitude toward him wouldn't bother him, but right now it reminded him a little too much of Lara Nelson's. "What is it you have against me, Two?" He asked. "Seems like ever since I started here you've had a chip on your shoulder about me."

"You're imagining it." She stowed the oxygen tank and began checking her breathing apparatus for air leaks.

"I don't think so. Did I do something to piss you off? I mean, besides the usual checklist?"

"What do you care? I didn't know you were such a sensitive soul."

"Well . . ." Of course he wasn't sensitive. Was he? Nah. That didn't mean he didn't have feelings, though. Lots of them. "Maybe you don't know that much about me."

"Maybe I don't." She squinted to make sure the "O" ring was in place on the regulator. "Maybe that's the problem. Who are you, Psycho? I mean, deep down inside. What drives you? What moves you? What makes you want to cry like a baby?"

His mouth dropped open.

"And if you answer that, I'll throw up on your boots." She stood up, eyes glinting turquoise.

For a moment he'd gotten totally sucked in and nearly bared his soul. "See, that's what I'm talking about. That sort of thing."

She snorted. "What sort of thing? You tease me, I tease you. That's the way the firehouse crumbles." She strode off with that lithe, athletic grace of hers.

Patrick scuffed his Adidas on the concrete floor of the apparatus bay. Nothing she'd said answered his question, and yet he had the feeling the truth was in there somewhere.

"You know me, right, Vader?" He asked the big guy as they lifted weights in the workout room.

Vader grunted. "Yeah. You're the craziest bastard in the San Gabriel fire department."

"But besides that."

"Besides that, you're a pain in my ass."

Patrick couldn't argue with that. "True."

"I know you," yelled Fred from the treadmill. "About as much as I want to, anyway."

Fred exchanged high fives with Ace, the rookie, who was on the next treadmill over. Patrick shot the kid an evil glare, which made him drop the grin and focus on not falling off. "Conversation over," he said through gritted teeth.

"What's up with you, dude?" Vader asked as he clenched one powerful bicep in a vein-popping curl. "You've been weird ever since you got back from Nevada."

"Nothing."

"Breathe too much retardant?" He cackled.

"Probably misses his llama!" called Fred.

"Llama-llama-ding-dong," sang Ace in a surprisingly good tenor.

The general laughter was interrupted by a loud tone that sent everyone into instant alertness. "Reported traffic accident for Engine 1, Truck 1, Paramedic Squad 3. Highway 30 at the Old Courthouse exit. Passengers trapped with four vehicles involved. Incident 429, time of alarm 2:42."

They all scrambled to their feet and ran into the apparatus bay to don their gear. Captain Brody was the last to gear up, which was very unusual.

"Melissa okay?" Double D yelled as he hoisted himself into the engineer's seat.

"No news," said Brody curtly.

As Patrick settled himself into Truck 1, he realized that Brody was the only guy at the station who knew anything about his history. Only Brody knew he was the son of a former governor of Nevada. Only Brody knew he'd been kicked out of Loveless. Only Brody knew he'd decided to go back anyway.

He'd throw himself into the flames for any single one of his brother firefighters. Their friendship, their loyalty, their bond as fellow warriors on the frontlines meant everything to him. And yet to them, "Psycho" was the beginning and end of Patrick Callahan. Wild man, loose cannon, crazy asshole.

Highway 30 was a mess. The backup stretched for a mile, and the California Highway Patrol was already on the scene, working to divert traffic and clear a lane in time for rush hour. Two of the vehicles, a little white Camry and an SUV, lay on their sides, halfway off the shoulder, billows of smoke rising from their engine compartments. The other two were dented and mangled, but the passengers were already talking to the CHP.

Truck 1 pulled onto the shoulder and the crew jumped out. Patrick grabbed the Jaws of Life from its compartment on the side of the truck, then followed the others to the overturned cars. The engine crew was already blasting the smoking cars with water.

Captain Brody spoke over the tactical channel. "Two female victims trapped inside the white Camry. One may be conscious. Truck 1, you got extraction."

Patrick ran to the uptilted side of the Camry. The underside would be far too dangerous to approach until the car was secured. Waving the smoke out of his eyes, he peered in. In the driver's seat, a woman was slumped over the wheel, blood trickling from a gash on her face. Closer to him, a young girl, maybe ten years old, looked back at him with dazed, terrified eyes. She was completely pinned against the passenger side door, which had been crushed by its collision with one of the other vehicles.

Fred appeared next to him. "I'll get the jaws set up," yelled Patrick. "You assess her condition." When people were trapped inside cars, it could be a terrifying experience to have the Jaws of Life cutting into the steel around you. Fred was the go-to guy for talking to victims. He had a friendly manner about him that put people at ease during traumatic situations—the perfect man to talk a young girl through the extraction.

Patrick pulled back to set up the jaws. A sudden hazy memory of the night of the accident flashed into his mind. A wall of metal slamming into his face. The starlit landscape tumbling around him. As usual, the memory ended there. The next thing he remembered was firefighters swarming the scene, and headlights slashing across the motor home that he and Liam had slammed into.

He'd struggled against the paramedic testing his pulse, frantic to get to Liam, but the guy was too strong for him. He could only watch while the firefighters got Liam out of the twisted metal of his bike and into an ambulance. They did it so efficiently and he was so woozy, he thought he was hallucinating. They'd seemed like gods.

Sometimes he wondered if that's why he'd become a firefighter. That exact night, that moment . . . if he could just make it right . . .

He shook off the memory, focusing on his task.

"Psycho, something's wrong," called Fred. "She's not answering me. I don't think she understands me."

"Did you try Spanish?"

"Yup. Nothing."

The girl wasn't Asian, which ruled out three of the other languages—Korean, Cambodian, and Hmong—commonly found in San Gabriel. Patrick lugged the jaws to the door and looked at the girl again. Tears were flowing down her cheeks. She kept wiping them away with her fingers but they didn't stop. One of her hands was bloody but she didn't seem to realize it. With every swipe across her face, she left a streak of blood.

"Don't do that," said Patrick, shaking his head. Her

gaze landed on him, then veered off into the distance.

"Where are you hurt?" he asked, more loudly. Maybe she was in such a state of shock that she couldn't hear him over all the noise—firefighters shouting, horns honking, engines running.

He said it again, even louder. Staring into nowhere, she didn't respond at all. He stared at her, frustrated, then gave up and turned away. One unconscious victim and one unresponsive one. What the hell. They'd just have to start up the jaws and hope for the best.

Then it struck him. She'd looked at him when he shook his head but not when he'd spoken.

A chill shot through him and his throat went tight. The girl was deaf.

"Hang on," he muttered to Fred, shouldered him out of the way and waved his hand in front of the window. He ripped off his padded firefighter gloves. When her gaze fluttered back to meet his, he pointed to her and made the sign for "hurt"—his two index fingers jabbing into each other.

A spark of interest lit up her eyes. She lifted one hand and signed back. "A little. Is my Mom going to be okay?"

His ASL was rusty after ten years, but it came back pretty quickly. He signed back rapidly: "We have to get into the car so we can help her. We have to use a special piece of equipment." He lifted it to show her. "It's going to cut through the metal. It makes a loud, horrible noise."

She smiled. Her amused grin lit up her face and made his stomach clench from emotion. "No problem for me."

"That's right," he signed back. He clapped a hand on Fred's shoulder. "This man will run the jaws. I'll keep signing with you the whole time."

He turned to Fred, whose jaw looked as if it were about to hit the ground. "Are you okay with that?" he asked him. Remembering that he'd signed the whole conversation with the girl, he explained, "You take the jaws, I'll keep talking to her."

"You know *sign language*?"

"My brother's deaf."

"You have a *brother*?"

"Yeah, I have a brother. He's mildly autistic and never mentioned that his ears were hurting and so he went deaf. Now can we get this girl out of there?"

Fred was still staring at him as if he'd grown a dick on his head. "He's *autistic*?"

"Stud, I swear to God . . ."

"Okay, okay . . ."

Fred maneuvered the jaws into position. Patrick positioned himself so he could still communicate with the girl while staying out of Fred's way.

"What's your name?" he signed.

"Isabelle." She spelled it out, then gave him her signing name too. "Jump rope girl. What's your name?"

Patrick hesitated. Maybe Psycho wasn't the best name to offer a traumatized deaf girl who'd just been in an accident. He'd been "Psycho" since he joined the San Gabriel Fire Department. But he couldn't go backward. Didn't want to.

He shrugged, and signed. "My name is Patrick."

The story of Psycho and the deaf girl reached the station before Truck 1 did. The other firefighters clustered around him as they stripped off their gear.

"Can you read lips too?"

"What's the sign for 'I gotta pee like a sonofabitch'?"

"How do say 'MILF' in sign language?" That was Vader, holding his helmet under one arm.

Patrick scowled at him. "Why do you want to know that?"

"Personal reasons."

Captain Brody's calm voice cut through the chatter. "Psycho, come see me in my office when you're done."

"Yes, sir."

An ominous quiet descended after Brody left.

"What'd you do now?" asked Vader. "You saved that girl."

As Patrick put his turnouts back onto the rig, arranging the pants around the boots next to Truck 1, try as he might he couldn't think of a single thing that would have angered Brody. Ever since he'd gotten back from Loveless he'd been on his best behavior. Not on purpose, but because he was licking the wounds Lara had left on his ego—and because he'd been hung over the first few days.

Until Lara had ripped into him, he hadn't realized how much respect he had for her. He'd always known she was a good person—a brave person—who had stood by Liam when everyone else thought he was weird. He'd always appreciated what a loyal friend she was to his brother. But it had never occurred to him that her good opinion might matter to him.

Turned out, it did. A lot.

He pictured her at the command post, all blond and bare-legged, kneeling to bandage a guy's arm . . . dangling from the helicopter, yelling at him the whole time . . . A smile twitched the corners of his mouth. She'd become a helluva woman. And all he'd done was poke at her, tease her, and drag her into the worst family dinner in Callahan history—which was saying a lot.

He was a fucking idiot.

When all his gear was squared away, he strode

down the corridor that led to the training room, the kitchen, and Brody's office. He caught a few more curious glances from passing firefighters and a suspicious, narrow-eyed stare from Sabina. He blocked her path and squared off with her.

"Yeah, so I kept a few secrets from the crew. Sound familiar?"

For years, Sabina had hidden the fact that she used to be a famous child actress. She could hardly criticize him for a similar secretiveness. But Sabina raised her chin and stood her ground. "Just tell me you're not ashamed of your deaf autistic brother and we're cool."

Rage swept Patrick, so deep and sudden it felt like a plunge into a red whirlpool. If Sabina hadn't been a woman, he would have grabbed her by the throat. Instead he balled his hands into fists and fought the fury, his body shaking from the epic struggle.

"My brother, Liam," he said in a low, fierce voice he nearly didn't recognize, "was my best friend. I'm proud to be his brother. *Proud.* And fucking lucky. No one ever loved me the way he did. And if you ever say that again . . ." Emotion grabbed him by the throat, strangling the words.

"All right, all right," said Sabina softly. "I hear you. I shouldn't have said it. This is a new side of you, that's all. I'm trying to put it all together."

He stood, shaking like a caged tiger, as she gave him a friendly pat on the shoulder. "You're a good guy, Psycho. I never would have believed it. Shows what I know." She gave him a quick flash of a wink and moved on down the corridor.

It took him a number of deep breaths and a head-whack to get a grip on himself. Must be the aftermath of the highway accident, he thought. Crashes always gave him the heebie-jeebies, and seeing that girl, so vulnerable and alone in her silent bubble, shook him up hard. It was the same with Liam; he'd always been his younger brother's connection to the outside world. Lara had been Liam's safety net, but he was the one who dared his brother to run and ride, to get tattoos and race dirt bikes. He couldn't stand seeing Liam isolated and left to himself. And Liam had loved following after Patrick as he climbed the tallest trees and rode the wildest horses, making sure no rules were broken in the process.

Until it had all gone wrong. And it was his fault. Completely his fault.

Shaking it off, he made his way to Brody's office. His captain looked up, apparently irritated by any interruption of him staring at his cell phone. The cell was now placed squarely in the center of his desk.

"Nothing yet?" Patrick asked.

"No, damn it all. Not so much as a Braxton-Hicks contraction."

Patrick held up a hand in protest. "Really don't need the details."

Brody didn't seem to hear him. "Now she's got some hot lead on a story and she's talking about going out of town to interview someone. I tried to put my foot down, but she says she's still barely one centimeter dilated and—"

"I'd like to take a short leave of absence," interrupted Patrick, without thinking. He snapped his mouth shut in the aftermath of that unexpected statement. Where the fuck had that come from?

"Is my childbirth talk driving you off?"

Patrick snorted. "No. But I mostly get along better with babies *after* they're born."

"I brought you in here to talk about how we can make use of your signing skills. They really came in handy out there today. Good job on that."

"Thanks."

"I was thinking you could train the rest of us in some basic signs. Things we need all the time, like 'anyone inside?' and 'where'd the fire start?'"

"Yeah. Sure."

"But now you want to take a leave?"

Patrick shifted from one foot to the other. When he'd gone back to fight the wildfire, it had been under duress. And it turned out to be just as god-awful as he'd feared. His father had ripped him a new one, he'd screwed things up with Lara, he'd behaved like an asshole.

But . . . he'd seen Megan, his little sister, all grown up. He'd kissed his mother's cheek. Those things stood out more than his father's ranting. Besides, he couldn't let Lara have the last word—words—especially when those words made him out to be a dick. And what about Goldie . . . Goldie, that sweet baby llama, she didn't deserve to be abandoned.

"The thing is, they're still on red alert out there. The drought's nowhere near over, they've got extreme high temperatures, and my father hasn't cleared one square inch of brush on the property. All the structures are potential bonfires. He needs someone to get that place fire-ready. But he won't let anyone do it. Throws them off the premises. He already threw me out, so I'm used to it."

"What you're saying is, you're the only one as hard-headed as he is?"

"Exactly. I have to go, Captain."

After one of his patented, long, measuring looks, the captain nodded. "I guess you do. Good luck."

And with that, for the first time Patrick could remember Captain Brody stood up, reached across the desk, and shook his hand.

Chapter Eleven

A rare silence ruled the Haven for Sexual and Spiritual—and possibly Neuromuscular—Healing. All the Goddesses were at the movie theater, watching the new James Bond. But Lara had been so exhausted by the long days at the wildfire and the blowup at the Callahan Ranch—not to mention the kiss from Patrick—that she slept for twenty hours straight. She'd surfaced briefly, let Romaine feed her a kale-carrot-ginger smoothie, and gone back to sleep.

It had now been over a week since her arrival in Loveless, three days since her meeting with Dean, and she needed to take care of business. She sat on the cushions of the Room of Soul Harmony, the ledger books spread open on the gold-painted floor, the tinkle of the fountain the only thing breaking the silence.

So no one in Loveless would want to buy the Haven, according to Dean, except the Callahans. The Goddesses would be happy to hear that, and she certainly couldn't do business with the Callahans since Big Dog despised her and Patrick probably did too, now that she'd been so rude to him.

She still winced every time she remembered the things she'd said. *Mean and childish and just plain idiotic.* Was that really what you were supposed to say to a firefighter who'd worked his very sexy butt off on the fire threatening your hometown? The other people in the town had brought cookies and blankets and coupons for every business in town. Anyone who'd fought the fire was entitled to a free dinner for two at the Fourth Street Diner, a free bag of potpourri at the Crafts 'n Kitsch, and a free dog-grooming session at Love Your Pup.

She wondered if llama-grooming was included in that offer.

Closing the ledger, she slowly banged her head against its hard cover.

Patrick had fought a fire and rescued a baby llama, and all he'd gotten from her was a rude lecture. What was wrong with her?

No. She opened the ledger again and stared at the blurry entries. The problem wasn't with her. It was *Patrick's* fault. He always brought out the worst in her. With Liam, she'd been patient and kind and *fun*. The ultimate good friend. With Patrick, she'd always been awkward and snarky and irritable. Clearly the blame was his.

The cheerful tinkle of the fountain pulled her attention away from her righteous indignation. Did it have to be so goddamn *soothing*? She didn't want to be soothed. She wanted to get a grip on herself, figure out what to do about the Haven, and go home to San Diego.

Focus, focus. She flipped the pages of the ledger to

the list of workshops held during the past year and how much money they'd brought in. In retrospect, the trouble signs were obvious. The Multiple Orgasm workshop had not multiplied—it had subtracted. The Shine Your Heavenly Body nude dancing weekend had been a disaster, with only two participants, who must have been staring at each other in utter embarrassment. The Seven Chakra Challenge still did well, probably because it mostly involved sitting. However, costs had gone up because the Haven had invested in some comfy armchairs.

No question about it, the Haven was showing signs of age. Aunt Tam never would have allowed it if she hadn't been traveling through South America consulting shamans.

Maybe she should take the Goddesses' request to keep the Haven open more seriously. Maybe they should do some workshops on aging. She squinted up at the cupid-adorned ceiling, imagining the new curriculum. Getting It On in Your Golden Years. The Kama Sutra for Seniors, and its companion workshop, the Seven Chiropractor Challenge. She couldn't help giggling, until she imagined herself trying to teach such a workshop.

Noooo! She was absolutely not going to get stuck here in Hopeless, Nevada, teaching sex workshops to the elderly. Or to anyone. Hell, she didn't even know that much about sex, not really. That is, she *knew* about it. She'd known all the basics since she'd come to live with Aunt Tam. At age fifteen she'd accidentally overheard a snippet of Annabella's workshop on "Nurturing the Lotus Root," often referred to as "blowjob class." Once she'd opened the silverware drawer and found a misplaced vibrator.

Sex was everywhere at the Haven. The Goddesses

were always talking about how people shouldn't be so "uptight" about sex, that it was no big deal. *If it was no big deal,* she'd asked, *why are you always talking about it?* In self-defense, she'd done the equivalent of putting her fingers in her ears and saying "lalalala." She had adopted black as her signature color since hippies didn't wear it. And she'd somehow managed to scare off all the boys. They all thought she must be ultra-experienced since she lived at the Haven. They'd never guessed that while she knew about the *mechanics* of sex, she still didn't understand what the fuss was all about.

But then that kiss with Patrick had happened. Or was it a kiss? Maybe his face had just accidentally gotten too close to hers. Maybe he had no idea how much that brief meeting of lips had affected her. That one shiver of contact felt as if it had changed the chemical composition of her body, turned it from an ordinary lump of flesh to something fiery and magical. As if he were some kind of alchemist.

Abandoning the ledger, Lara lay back on a pile of Indian print pillows decorated with glinting sequins. It felt decadent to relax like this. She never relaxed anymore, not since she'd started med school. Her eyes drifted shut, lulled by the fountain. Again the look in Patrick's eyes as he'd cradled her face flashed across her vision, bringing a flush of heat.

Aunt Tam had always told her that her sexual side would awaken one day.

"So then I'll finally get it?" she'd asked. "I'll know why all these people get so obsessed and spend all this money to improve their sex lives?"

"Exactly, Lulu," Tam had said. "Until then, don't worry about it. Just enjoy where you are."

But until now it hadn't happened, even though she

tried sex in college, then again with a fellow med student, then again with a guy in her condo complex, just to make sure. She'd even tried kissing a girl, but hadn't gotten very far with that. As a medically trained professional who followed scientific principles, the conclusion seemed obvious: she just didn't like sex.

But then . . . that kiss. She thought about Patrick's piercing blue eyes, his muscled chest, and the way he moved in his snug, worn jeans, with that hip-swaying, hypnotic half swagger. A bolt of desire struck her midsection with such power that her eyes flew open and she sat upright.

She looked wildly around the room, as if something had actually slammed into her. What was going on? Why couldn't she put one little maybe-kiss with one annoying former friend out of her mind?

The Buddha of Compassion and the goddess Kuan-Yin were no help with their peaceful, blank expressions. The fountain chimed in, of course; it had something soothing to say in water language. Lara put her hand to her lower belly, which still tingled. Now she remembered; she'd felt this before. That Christmas, when Patrick had changed from Liam's older brother to . . . fascinating guy who made her body parts tingle. Oh, crap. Now the attraction was back, stronger than ever.

And she'd driven him away. Where were the Goddesses when she needed them?

Half an hour later, having completely given up on the idea of sorting out the Haven's problems, Lara drove her rental car into town. Often the Goddesses hit the local pubs after the movies. As Janey put it, "We need to work off the extra testosterone."

She pulled up outside the Love 'Em and Leave 'Em

Saloon but saw no sign of the old maroon Cadillac the Goddesses used for group outings. The movie probably hadn't ended yet. She hesitated. Did she dare walk into a Loveless bar by herself? How many old high school acquaintances would she run into? Would they all be as nasty to her as Dean had been?

Hey, she could take it. She'd lived through it in high school, and nothing could be worse than that.

Steeling her nerve, she stepped into the still-hot night, clicked the lock on her rental car, and marched into the tavern. Darkness, sprinkled with a few flashes of neon, greeted her. She paused just inside the door, waiting until her eyes adjusted to the lack of light. What she could see, once things came into focus, wasn't exactly reassuring. The place was packed, customers three deep at the bar and all the small round tables filled. An unnerving number of faces turned in her direction.

Surreptitiously, she checked her outfit. Jeans and a scoop-necked white T-shirt that she'd always thought flattered her curves, along with an amber necklace that made her eyes sparkle, or so Aunt Tam had told her. Modest by the standards before her; the prevailing skirt length seemed to be a half inch away from porn. Maybe she was overdressed?

She sighed. Nothing changed. She'd never manage to get it right in Loveless. Soldiering forward, she made her way toward the bar. Was it her imagination or were people parting before her, clearing her a path? No, it was definitely true. By the time she got to the bar, an empty stool was waiting for her. What was going on? Casting a suspicious glance at the nearby customers, she picked up no clues from their blank expressions. She looked at the stool, checking for sticky stuff or whoopee cushions, then scolded herself. This wasn't third grade.

Even though she wasn't normally much of a drinker, she could use one right about now. Sliding onto the bar stool, she looked defiantly at the bartender, a leathery, weather-beaten man in his sixties.

"Vodka on the rocks," she told him. "With lots of lime." At least she'd get some vitamin C along with her alcohol.

Without expression, he poured the drink with quick, practiced movements, slapped a coaster on the scratched surface of the bar, and slid the drink to her. She reached for her purse, but he shook his head.

"On the house."

It had to be some kind of trick. "What do you mean?"

"We're real grateful for what you did out there on the fire. You saved Doc Sanderson's life."

A murmur of assent rippled through the bar crowd.

"I did?" Dr. Sanderson, she vaguely remembered, was the popular and beloved town vet.

"He'd volunteered himself for fire duty. Member of the National Guard and all. He got some bones broken when a tree fell on him. Heard you helped get him out."

"Oh. Well, I didn't do that much, really."

The bartender pushed the drink closer to her. "I doubt you'll be paying for a drink in this town for the next year."

Still uncomprehending, she glanced at the people around her, now spotting friendly smiles and even a few familiar faces. There was Mr. Tremaine, her tenth grade biology teacher and coach of the track team. He winked at her, just as he'd always done with his favorite runners.

And was that Amy Mulligan, standing and lifting her glass? Amy had given her the nickname Lusty Lara, which wasn't particularly clever but still managed to ruin junior year. The worst part was that she'd voted for Amy for student body president.

Apparently Amy still had leadership qualities. "To Lara Nelson. Thanks, hon, for helping us out," she called over the crowd.

"Hear, hear," came a rumble of voices from all corners of the bar.

"We're proud of you," said someone she didn't recognize.

Had she stepped into some bizarre alternate universe time warp? Not only high school enemies but total strangers were saying nice things to her? It didn't compute.

Only one thing for it. She lifted her glass of vodka, tilted it to the crowd, and downed it.

Patrick cruised into Loveless around midnight. Too late to show up at the ranch, especially since no one knew he was coming. He figured the news would go over better if it was a done deal. No giving his father time to post guards at the gates, the way he'd done after the accident. No giving his mother a chance to talk him out of it. He'd sleep in the Hulk, as he had plenty of times before, and in the morning show up on his family's doorstep, give Goldie a snuggle, and get to work.

But tonight he needed to relax after the long drive. A game of darts at the Love 'Em and Leave 'Em would do it. He found a parking spot around the corner from Loveless's most popular night spot and strolled down the boardwalk until he reached the familiar door of the bar where he'd spent many a night ruining the Callahan family reputation.

The Love 'Em and Leave 'Em was the water cooler of Loveless. If you wanted to know the town gossip, you'd hear it here first. If you wanted to make a statement, you came here. From old cowboys to young manicurists, everyone drank at the Love 'Em. Unless the town had turned against you, in which case you'd be tossed out on your ass.

No one paid attention to him as he pushed the door open and stepped inside. At the bar, he noticed a knot of men clustered around one particular stool. Maybe a celebrity had dropped in for a cold one. A local rodeo star might be paying a visit, or Matthew McConaughey could have returned for another round after that epic night back in the nineties.

He craned his neck, but all he made out was a long, curvy, jeans-clad leg hooked onto the rung of the stool. So a woman was causing this stir. She wore little bronze sandals that showed off tidy, unpainted toenails. Sexy, but unusual; the women of Loveless went through a lot of nail polish, as he recalled. So maybe this woman wasn't a local. Increasingly curious, he wound his way through the tables to get closer.

Then, through the interwoven hum of the crowd, the throaty strand of the mystery woman's voice shone through. He felt the impact at the base of his spine, in his cock. Holy fuck, was it Lara? What was she doing here? She didn't drink, let alone socialize with the citizens of Loveless. In a hurry now, he bobbed his head this way and that, aiming for a clear visual.

And there she was, a white T-shirted goddess gracing a Loveless dive with her presence. Her thick blond hair tumbled down her back in a freewheeling riot. She perched on the edge of the stool, one hand carelessly clutching a glass, the other flinging gestures into the air like confetti. Her eyes glowed like flaming whiskey; she looked like a lioness in tight jeans. No one could look away.

Lara Nelson, lit as a pinball machine?

Patrick shook his head, blinked, checked again. This time she was leaning forward to listen to an older man who was holding a beer bottle. Patrick conceived an instant dislike for the guy, who had to be at least forty and had no business talking to a hot babe like Lara. As the man leaned in to touch Lara on the arm, Patrick strode forward and blocked the move.

"Hands off, mister. Don't you think she's a little young for you?"

The man gaped at him, but Patrick ignored him, paying attention only to Lara. Her eyes darkened and her mouth fell open as she took him in. That mouth . . . he gazed at it hungrily, following the generous curves that promised so much.

"No, I don't," said the man.

"What?" Patrick had already forgotten what they were talking about.

"I don't think she's too young. She's a doctor. She just told me how she helped a woman with hyperemesis something."

"Gravidarum," said Lara solemnly. "Hyperemesis gravidarum. It's a severe form of morning sickness that . . ."

Was he doomed to hear about pregnancy wherever he went? "Just how buzzed are you, Lara?"

The man shouldered his way back into the conversation. "And who the hell are you, anyway?"

"Yeah," said Lara, slightly slurred. "Who the hell are you?"

"So you don't know this bozo?" the man asked her.

She shook her head in strong denial. "Oh no. I know him inside out. Upside down and all around."

Patrick's cock stirred, damn that pesky organ. It was her voice that did it to him, that sexy, sultry, velvet glove of a voice. "You're drunk."

"No. I *have* drunk. But I am not drunk. And I *will* drink."

Amused, he put his hands on his hips. "Do you always parse verbs when you drink?"

"Look, son, I don't think she wants you here."

"Too bad. I am here. And I'm not budging."

"If Lara wants you gone, you're gone."

Patrick glared at the other man. He could take him, no problem. But an uneasy glance around the rest of the crowd told him he'd have to battle them all. He lowered his voice. "Lara, let's get out of here. You've had enough. I'll take you home."

"Why," she swayed toward him and poked him in the chest, "should I go home with you? And what are you doing here anyway? Didn't you go back to San Gabrehel? San Gariel? San Gabie-ell?"

Man, she was really toasted. "I'll tell you later. Right now, let's get some air."

"I don't want air."

"Okay, then maybe some water."

"Don't want water."

"What do you want? Whatever you want, we'll get it." He tried to keep his voice low, for her ears only. If he could just coax her out of the Love 'Em and Leave 'Em, he could sober her up enough to get her home. The Goddesses probably had some homeopathic hangover cure they could give her.

Lara grabbed a handful of his T-shirt and dragged him in closer, so her mouth, that luscious, sex fantasy mouth, was whispering in his ear. "Wanna know what I want?"

With a hand on her upper back to keep her from

sliding off the stool, he nodded. The movement made her lips brush against his ear. He went hard as a rock.

"I want *you*," she said in a husky murmur. "I want your hot, hard, thick, throbbing . . ."

Oh God, he was going to come in his pants, right here in the Love 'Em.

" . . . lotus root."

Chapter Twelve

*H*oly crackerjack, Lara was drunk. Nothing else could make her use Haven language, which she'd always mocked in high school. Patrick hooked his arm around her waist and slid her off the stool.

"Let's go, honey," he said, for the benefit of the on-lookers.

"Yes, let's go." She'd forgotten about whispering, and was in fact yelling over the sound of vintage Olivia Newton John blasting from the jukebox. "Take me to bed and show me what all the fuss is about."

Someone snorted.

"Y'all can take me too," said a girl in a skintight tube top, winking.

"Where's the party headed?" a guy in a cowboy hat asked.

Patrick put his arm around Lara in a gesture of pure possessiveness, just to get the point across. "The party's staying right here. We're going home."

"Aren't you the Callahan kid?" someone asked as he guided Lara toward the exit. He recognized the voice as belonging to a mechanic in town. Patrick knew, from personal experience, that he liked to pick fights in bars, especially with college kids.

"Yeah," said his drinking buddy. Patrick knew him too; he owed him a split lip from the night he turned eighteen. "That's the one who nearly killed his little brother."

"There was somethin' weird about that kid anyway," someone else chimed in.

Lara twisted out of Patrick's grip and stomped toward the two customers. "Liam's not weird," she said, hands on hips. "Who said that? Who? I'll take you down, right here, right now."

"Whoa, whoa, whoa." Patrick dove after her, snagging the waistband of her jeans before she launched herself at the little knot of men. They put their hands up in a *What'd I say?* gesture. He gave them a long warning look, which he hoped they'd interpret as "I'd kick your ass if I didn't have to get this drunk girl out of here."

He wrapped his arm around Lara and steered her in the direction of the front door.

"They're talking trash about Liam," she insisted, squirming in his grasp. He tried not to think about how warm and womanly she felt, all curves and heat and satin-soft skin.

"Who cares? They're drunks at a bar, trying to get something going. Ignore them."

"You aren't the boss of me."

He bent down and growled in her ear. Only a few more steps and they'd be out the door. "Right now, I *am* the boss of you. And you'd better not forget it."

She drew in a long, wondering breath and looked

up at him, her golden eyes going wide. "Patrick! That's so . . . politically incorrect."

"Oops." Not that he cared.

"No, I like it. It's . . . rawr . . ." She made a gesture like a cheetah clawing the air. " . . . very hot."

Now that was more like it. Not that he was going to follow up on it, given the amount of alcohol in her system. "How many drinks have you had, Lulu?"

"See, there you go!" She tore herself away from his grasp and faced him, hands back on hips.

Patrick sighed, glancing longingly at the door, only a few feet away. So close, yet so far. "You sure get feisty with a few drinks in you. I had no clue."

"You," she poked him in the chest, "have no clue about a lot of things. Like that I don't like the name Lulu."

"You don't?" He was genuinely astonished. "You never told me that."

"So you're blaming me now?"

"No, but if you'd told me . . ."

"Oh, because you're so sensitive and care so much about my feelings."

He drew back. "Why wouldn't I care about your feelings?"

"You only cared about your own feelings. Not Liam's, not mine, not your mother's, not your father's . . ." The list showed every sign of continuing for an indefinite amount of time, but another customer, Patty from the craft store, apparently decided the conversation ought to become general. She stepped between them, brandishing her glass of red wine.

"This here is a learning moment, y'all. If I'd known about learning moments earlier, I might never have split with my ex. He was a monster in bed, and now all I've got is my vibrator, and—"

"We're not in a relationship," Patrick interrupted.

"Ugh, no way," Lara agreed. "Never."

He took advantage of the change in subject to grab her arm again. One step, two steps. Finally, they were going to make it out the door. He could practically touch it. But he had to clear one thing up first. He looked down at her, capturing her hazy gold gaze, noticing the flush on her cheeks. "What do you mean, never? I thought you wanted me to show you what all the fuss is about. I thought you wanted my hard, throbbing—"

She flung herself at him. Suddenly she was pressed against his chest, her body molding against him, warm and soft and ridiculously tempting. He staggered and grabbed onto her upper arms to stabilize them both. And then her mouth was on his, and oh Lord almighty, full contact was just as insanely arousing as that barely-a-kiss at the ranch had been. No, more so.

He slid his tongue across her lips because he simply had to taste those rich, generous curves. That sizzling moment at the ranch had been just a tease, and now that her lips were touching his again, the need for more consumed him. She moaned into his mouth, parting her lips so his tongue slipped between them, into the intimate haven beyond. Excitement, thick and urgent, stirred his cock.

He breathed in her scent, which was both familiar and exotic, with that trace of sandalwood he associated with the Haven. As if they had a mind of their own, his hands slid down her back, finding the curve of her waist, the flare of her hip, the arch of her back. He groaned.

"You're killing me, Lu . . . Lara," he mumbled against her mouth. "We can't do this."

And yet somehow his hands were on her ass, and

he was absolutely sure he'd never felt anything that good in his life. Full and firm and sensual, her ass fit perfectly into his spread hands, exactly in the right spot to yank her closer against his groin.

Fuck, that felt good.

She tightened her arms around his neck. "You said my name right," she murmured happily. "You do care!" Kisses peppered his neck and jaw, sending sweet fire straight to his cock.

Oh Lord. They had to stop. And he, as the more sober one, had to be the one to do it. He dragged his hands off her ass and glanced over his shoulder at the crowd. Everyone was goggling at them. Was someone taking a picture with their camera phone?

He grabbed her hand. "Come on," he growled. He swung open the door, pulled her outside and dragged her behind him toward his rig.

"There's my car," she sang happily as they passed a white Aveo.

"We can get it tomorrow. You can't drive tonight."

"Okay, boss."

When he looked at her, she winked provocatively. That one tiny gesture acted like a bolt of lightning to his overexcited system.

"Stop that right now."

"Stop what?"

"No coming on to me, Lara. I can't take it. You're too damn sexy, and I'm not a freaking monk." Reaching the Hulk, he found his keys and opened the door with such violence it nearly came off its hinges.

She laughed as if he'd said the funniest thing ever. Then she pulled her hand from his and did a little runway dance right there on the sidewalk. "I'm too sexy for my fireman . . . too sexy for my fireman . . . so sexy . . . it hurts."

Patrick gritted his teeth, unable to look away, even though every little thrust of her pelvis made his vision haze over. "Get. In."

"Okay, boss."

This time he managed to look away when she winked. He waited, envisioning himself as a big, unfeeling boulder as she settled herself into the passenger seat. When she was safely inside, he closed the door, locked it—because who knew what she'd do next—and jumped into the driver's seat.

"Fasten your seat belt," he said, but her head was already lolling against the back of the seat.

"Shit," he muttered, and reached over to pull the seat belt across her, which turned out to be impossible to do without touching her. He clenched his jaw against the rush of heat that accompanied every brush of his hand across her flesh.

"Hey, you," she murmured, her eyes slitting open. "Are you coming onto me?"

"No," he said roughly.

"That's mean."

"Don't think I wouldn't, babe. I'd be all over you like pink on cotton candy if you weren't buzzed out of your mind."

"I'm not as drunk as all that," she protested, suddenly sounding almost sober.

"You're drunk enough." A muscle twitched in his jaw as he turned the key in the ignition. "You're staying at the Haven?"

She heaved a sigh. "Yes."

"Drink this while I drive." He handed her a bottle of water. As soon as she put it to her mouth, he looked away, telling himself it was best to concentrate on driving rather than the way her lips wrapped around a long object.

A long silence followed as the mostly empty streets of Loveless slipped past, giving way to the road that headed out of town toward the Haven. Patrick figured Lara was probably dozing off, but he kept his focus on the road.

When they'd almost reached the town limits, she finally spoke. "Would you really?"

"What?"

"Would you really come on to me?"

Hell. She probably wouldn't remember much about tonight anyway. "Yes."

"You really think I'm sexy?"

"Hell yes."

More silence. When he finally looked over at her, she was looking back with a mystified expression on her face.

"Patrick . . ."

"Yeah?"

"What are you doing here? The fire's out."

"How about I explain it sometime when you'll remember?" He pulled up to the crazy, nymph-adorned front entrance of the Haven.

"You think I'm going to forget?"

He stepped out of the truck and walked around to the passenger door. When he opened it, Lara was giving him a funny, frowning look, as if he were a math problem she was trying to solve.

"What are you doing?"

"Memorizing," she said softly. "I don't want to forget."

His breath stopped. He felt like some kind of butterfly pinned by the golden intensity of her gaze. No one had ever looked at him so comprehensively, as if he was someone worth a thorough examination. While he stood there, paralyzed, she stepped out of the truck. At first he thought she might plaster herself against him again; his whole body tensed in aroused anticipation. But instead she brushed past him. "Thanks, Patrick. I really hope I don't forget. Anything."

And she stepped, mostly in a straight line, toward the Haven's gold-painted door. He watched her from the truck, not trusting himself to accompany her, but needing to make sure she made it okay.

When she finally disappeared inside, he drove away, trying to remember the last time he'd been this rattled, and failing.

To say the Callahan family was surprised to see him would be like calling a backdraft a pleasant breeze. His father stomped around, roaring at the top of his lungs, while Patrick planted himself in the living room, arms crossed over his chest, letting the rant flow past him. Megan was at work, which meant there was no one to hold back Big Dog's fury.

When his father had finally tapered off, Patrick laid out his intentions and reasons for being there.

"Someone's got to get this place fire-safe. The vegetation needs to be cleared back a hundred and fifty feet from each structure, or this could all burn. The whole enchilada. Think about your legacy, Callahan. Do you want to leave Megan and Liam with nothing?"

"What's it to you?"

"Megan is my little sister. You think I want her out on the street?"

That did it; Big Dog never could stand for anything bad to happen to Megan. " 'Dozer's broken," he grunted, which Patrick took as a statement of surrender.

"I'll see about fixing it."

His mother, who had come into the room, clapped her hands together. "You'll stay in the guesthouse."

"I can sleep in my truck, Mom," Patrick protested. "I don't mind."

"Don't make me mad," she said. "Come along, I'll get you settled in." She led him outside, where he took a deep breath of air. It held a tinge of smoke, but anything was better than the stench of hostility inside the house.

The guesthouse was a small, cozy wooden structure that squatted between the barn and the big house. It used to be the well house of the original ranch, and had been converted to a tidy little cabin with its own kitchenette and tiny bathroom.

"Not bad," he said, surveying the hardwood floors and cowhide-upholstered furniture. It put his own apartment to shame.

"Well, we fixed it up for Liam's physical therapist," his mother said, avoiding his glance. "When she left, after he was recovered enough, he moved in here."

Patrick went still. Liam was the last person to occupy this space? He tried to picture his brother living here, but in his memory his brother was still a kid. "Did he cook for himself and everything?"

"He did. It was strange, Patrick. In some ways, the accident made him a lot more mature. He had to grow up quickly, I guess."

That familiar lump formed, the one that kept him from talking about Liam. He nodded.

"Well, anyway, I don't know when he's coming back, so you can rearrange things however you like."

"Shouldn't we try to find him, Mom? What if he's in trouble?"

She fiddled with her bracelets. "He sends us a message now and then. He's all right. But please don't talk about him around Cal. It'll just make him furious."

So Liam wasn't completely out of touch. That was

good to know. But Patrick still didn't like the idea of him wandering around by himself.

Candy patted him on the cheek. "Make yourself at home, honey. Oh, except for the barn. Your father has turned it into his private clubhouse, no guests allowed."

The rules were coming fast and furious. No Liam talk, no going in the barn. Patrick gave a wry smile. "I'm here to do a job, that's all, Mom. Think of me as a fireman for hire."

"Well, I'll try, but you'll at least be eating dinner with us, right?"

Because the last one had gone so well. "I plan to work until I drop. And I have plans tonight."

"You do?"

He didn't. But he *planned* to have plans.

"Mind if I ask with whom?"

He gazed levelly back at her until she nervously tucked a lock of auburn hair behind her ear. "I have to check on a friend."

He deliberately left out Lara's name. From now on he wasn't going to put her in any line of fire from his family. As soon as his mother left, he checked his watch. Still only ten in the morning. Too early to bother her. She'd probably be sleeping it off until at least noon.

He changed into work clothes—worn jeans, a T-shirt, sturdy boots—and headed to the toolshed. Later he'd see about fixing the 'dozer—a workhorse D-6 Caterpillar—but frankly, the fire line around the property wasn't his first priority. Protecting the house and other structures came first. Which worked out well, since it was hard manual labor and he needed to work off some energy. He found a machete that looked relatively sharp, a weed-whacker, and a chainsaw. He took the chainsaw outside and yanked on the starter. Nothing. Eyeballing the chain, he saw black gunk built up between the teeth. It set his own teeth on edge. All good firefighters knew you had to keep your equipment in top condition. What was his father thinking, neglecting his tools like this?

Tomorrow he'd take the chainsaw into town. But today, damn it, he wanted to get some work done. He grabbed the gas-powered weed-whacker, but got the same result as with the chainsaw. He hefted the machete. Somehow the thought of slicing through his father's overgrown shrubs was quite satisfying. Forget the power tools, he'd use the machete.

But first he swung by the stables, which sat just beyond the barn. Remembering his mother's warning, he gave the big red barn a wide berth. The three remaining horses greeted him with soft whinnies. He spent a moment with each, letting them learn his scent. As soon as he walked into Goldie's stall, which smelled of hay and manure, Goldie trotted up to him and butted her head against his hip.

"Hiya, Goldie," he murmured, running his hands down her snowy neck. "Miss me?"

She made a sound that he chose to interpret as yes.

"Want to clear some brush? You can eat it, I'll hack at it." He unchained her from her tether and led her outside. In the sunshine, she gave a little caper that made his heart melt.

"You sure are a cutie, aren't you? Well, come on, then. I hope you're hungry."

With Goldie following close behind, he took the machete to the back of the house, where the bushes and grass were the most overgrown. He swung the machete, loving the way it glided smoothly through the air, biting into the thorny vegetation. After a few more cuts a small space had been cleared, and a heap of dry, tangled branches lay on the ground. Goldie did her part, chomping away as if she hadn't eaten in days. With more time, Goldie and several of her friends could probably make a serious dent in this brush.

For the next two hours he swung and chopped and dragged the debris into piles. It felt good, even with the hot sun burning down on him. Sweat poured off him in waves. He didn't mind that either. He'd always loved a good sweat, whether during a fire, a bareback gallop, or some crazy-ass triathlon. Or something even more interesting . . .

When he finally took a break, it was close to one in the afternoon. Lara would probably be awake by now.

He pulled out his cell phone and dialed the Haven's number. A sultry voice answered. "Haven. Answers for all your sexual and spiritual needs."

He had a brief vision of Lara's dark whiskey eyes penetrating to the bottom of his soul, and wondered if that greeting might actually be accurate. "I'm calling for Lara Nelson. Is she there?"

"One moment."

The sultry voice was replaced by a scratchy one. "Hello?"

"Lara, it's Patrick. How are you doing?"

She groaned. "Ask me later. I may have a more optimistic answer then."

He wouldn't get a better opportunity than that. "Fine. Pick you up at six? You can tell me all about it."

A startled silence, then a hesitant, "Sure."

"Cool."

He was about to hang up when she spoke again,

this time with a mortified note in her voice. "But Patrick, just so you know, I remember everything. In case you want to change your mind."

A thrill shot through him. So she remembered. The kiss. The chemistry, the way their bodies felt together, the things she'd said, the things *he'd* said.

"Nope. I'll see you at six."

Chapter Thirteen

"And my crystal ball says," said Annabella, "that was the fire hottie."

Lara groaned and searched through her medical bag for some aspirin. "Hottie is not part of the approved Haven vocabulary."

"I'm Brazilian. Haven is not my first language. What is that, a painkiller? I can do better than that." Annabelle floated over to the kitchen counter, where she tossed ingredients into a blender.

Lara surreptitiously downed her aspirin. Nothing wrong with a Haven smoothie, but she'd take all the help she could get. She wasn't used to drinking. And to have Patrick witness the whole thing, or at least the most embarrassing moments . . .

But try as she might, she couldn't summon much of a feeling of humiliation. He'd been there for her when she needed it; any more alcohol and things could have gotten out of hand. Not only that, he'd told her she was sexy and he kissed her. Well, she'd kissed him, but he definitely kissed her back, in a way that still made her head spin when she thought about it.

She'd been doing almost nothing else since she woke up.

"Here, try this." Annabella handed her a glass full of a yellowish-green concoction the color of baby vomit, if that baby had been gorging on mustard and spinach.

"That doesn't look like something I should put in my body."

"Don't be a child. It has turmeric, ginger, and kale. You'll survive. Drink up."

Lara drank, trying to block out the taste, the smell, the color and texture of the drink. To be fair, she couldn't imagine anything tasting very good at the moment.

"Not bad," she told Annabella when she'd finished. "Thanks." She put the glass in the sink and leaned against the counter, propping her head on her elbow. Going back to bed sounded like a good idea, but bed was so far away.

"Are you really going out with the fireman?"

"I don't know if it counts as 'going out.'" He hadn't phrased it that way.

"Be careful with him." Annabella looked mysterious as she rinsed out the blender. She was dressed in full Goddess regalia, a long white skirt with a fitted Indian top that bared her stomach.

"What do you mean?"

Annabella lit a stick of incense and waved it around Lara's head. Lara sneezed. "This will help clear your heavy hangover energy. That kind of man, he's very full of testosterone. He has an ambivalent connection to his feminine energy."

Lara waved fragrant smoke away from her face. "His feminine energy? Are we back to speaking Haven? I'm not afraid of testosterone, Annabella." Actually, she liked it. A lot, if last night was any indication.

"That's not what I'm saying. The testosterone makes him very attractive, but it isn't what makes him dangerous. It's the other part of him. The part that took care of the llama. That part could steal your heart while you aren't even looking."

Lara stared at the other woman, arrested. As much as she liked to laugh at the silly sayings and jargon of the Goddesses, she knew how perceptive they could be. And Annabella was absolutely right. If Patrick hadn't rescued the llama, and then worried about her afterward, she wouldn't find him half so appealing. Or if he hadn't watched out for her last night. Or if he hadn't always loved his little brother . . .

Annabella was right. Patrick was dangerous.

"Oh no," she said out loud.

"Oh, yes."

"You think I shouldn't see him?"

"Of course I don't think that. He's probably a magnificent bed partner."

Lara buried her face in her hands, a million moments of oversharing from her childhood flashing through her mind. "Please don't," she murmured.

"Lara, *meu filha*, when will you stop seeing sex as something to be embarrassed about?"

"I'm not embarrassed, and sex isn't on the agenda. I'm just not used to thinking about him in that way." Okay, that wasn't exactly the truth. She'd been thinking that way pretty much since she'd seen him rescue Goldie.

Annabella raised one slim, skeptical eyebrow. "I suggest you begin, then. He wants you, and you want him."

Lara touched her burning cheeks, sure her face was about to catch fire. "How do you know these things?"

"It's my business." Annabella shrugged. "But if you like, we can change the topic. Have you given any more thought to our situation here?"

A pang of guilt made Lara bite her lip. She hadn't told the Goddesses about her efforts to find a buyer for the Haven. Other than that, she'd been busy with the fire and hadn't come up with any other brilliant plans.

"Let's talk about it later, okay, Annabella?"

She gave the older woman a kiss on the cheek and wandered off to the meditation garden, where pink stone benches surrounded a shimmering copper gong, and herbs were planted in the shape of a karmic wheel. As a kid she'd always found the mingled scents of lavender, rosemary, and thyme incredibly soothing. Maybe the same magic would still hold.

Lara sat on a bench, plopped a straw hat on her head, and inhaled the deliciously fragrant air.

The way she saw it, she had three choices when it came to Patrick. She could blame it all on the free drinks and the fact that she wasn't used to alcohol. She could claim she'd been temporarily possessed by a supernatural being—maybe a Goddess—at the Love 'Em and Leave 'Em, and therefore wasn't responsible for her behavior.

Or—most frightening and intriguing of all—she could admit that she found Patrick terribly attractive and give in to her desire to satisfy her curiosity.

But she'd have to make it crystal clear that this was only a sort of scientific experiment. She knew what sex was like. Underwhelming, in her experience. What happened when you included toe-curling, spine-tingling attraction? The scientist in her wanted to know. And assuming Patrick wasn't averse to the experiment, why shouldn't she find out?

They both knew it wouldn't lead anywhere. Neither of them lived in Loveless, and whatever Patrick was doing here, he probably wouldn't stay for long. Plus, they had too much history. A *Callahan*, for Pete's sake. His family despised her. She didn't think much of them either, except for Megan. And Liam, of course. And Candy Callahan might have her moments. And now Patrick was turning out to be not exactly what she'd thought.

A bee hummed in a lazy circle around her head.

Who was she kidding? Only the third option held any appeal at all. Annabella's warning filtered through her mind. But she didn't need to worry. Patrick Callahan IV wouldn't steal her heart. She wouldn't allow anything like that to happen.

When Patrick roared up the drive in his gray, tanklike Dodge truck, Lara skipped out the front door before the Goddesses could descend on him. She'd allowed Dynah to help her dress, since they were about the same size. A hip-hugging, gold-threaded skirt with a slit up to her thigh moved sensuously with each step. A corset-style top with a demure eyelet pattern left no room for a bra.

"I feel so aware of my body," she'd told Dynah.

"Exactly the point. And you won't be the only one, I guar-on-tee. Here, take these."

Dynah had handed over high-heeled silvery sandals. As a doctor, Lara knew all the ways that heels could cause damage. But she took them without protest. Sometimes a girl had to do what a girl had to do. That included leaving her hair long but fluffing it out with some hair product, and adding a spritz of perfume that she hoped would mask the persistent Haven scent of sandalwood.

She wasn't going for hippie. She was going for hypnotic.

By the time she ran out to meet Patrick, she felt more feminine than she had in a very long time. Perhaps ever. His reaction made all the fussing worthwhile.

Halfway around his truck, he stopped in his tracks and shoved his hands in his pockets. His bright blue eyes traveled up and down her body as he gave a slow whistle.

"You look incredible," he finally said.

"What, you didn't know I had it in me?"

"I didn't say that. Don't put words in my mouth."

The word "mouth" made her look at his, which brought her back to the previous night when that mouth had claimed hers with such fierce, primitive command. She swallowed hard. Maybe Patrick was too dangerous for her. She was so inexperienced compared to him, no matter how many Goddesses had helped raise her.

Then she saw his expression, the nearly slack-jawed lust and awe, and she squared her shoulders. Of course she could do this. This was Patrick. She'd known him since the age of twelve. What was she so afraid of?

She moved forward, the high heels giving her stride an extra sway, which Patrick registered immediately, judging by the clenching of his jaw and narrowing of his eyes.

Hey, this was kind of fun.

He scrambled to open the door for her, which she allowed him to do, though it seemed a little retro to her. She climbed onto the seat, arranging the slit in her skirt so she didn't flash him.

Then again, maybe a little flashing wasn't out of the

question. As he hurried around to the driver's side, she adjusted the panels of her skirt so the skin of her thigh showed. Not a lot, just enough to put *that* expression on his face, that determined, don't-distract-me, let-me-steal-another-peek look.

Of course, he was well worth looking at himself. He wore a pair of dark blue jeans and a crisp white shirt with the sleeves rolled up to show his forearms. He smelled like he'd just stepped out of a shower, and she noticed that his hair was still damp behind his ears. The back of his neck was a dark tan. She wanted to run her finger across it.

"Have you been out in the sun?"

"All day. I'm clearing brush from the property."

"Oh." Suddenly it all made sense. "That's why you came back?"

"Partly." He gave her a sidelong look but didn't elaborate. She frowned, still perplexed by the whole thing.

"I thought you and your parents were on the outs."

"We are. But I'm not going to let Megan and Liam's inheritance burn down, not if I can help it."

She saw his hands clench on the wheel as he steered his truck down the road toward town. "Megan and Liam's? Not yours?"

"He cut me off after the accident. Big Dog doesn't change his mind about stuff like that. About anything."

"So . . . what you're saying is you left your life in San Gabriel to come back and save something that doesn't belong to you."

He shot her an odd look. With the setting sun turning the hills behind him pink, his eyes looked extraordinarily, almost unnaturally blue. "You didn't think I had it in me?"

She flushed. "I didn't say that."

"Yeah, you did. I remember it exactly. You were wearing a pretty peachy sort of top and a denim skirt and you had this look in your eyes that said I was no better than a slug."

"I'm sorry," she stammered. "I didn't mean it that way, I—"

"It's okay. You were pissed, and you had a right to be. I'm not saying you were wrong."

She shook her head in confusion. This man had a way of surprising her every time she turned around. "Then what are you saying?"

He tilted his head, as if listening to someone whispering in his ear. She noticed the lines fanning from the corners of his eyes and the brackets next to his mouth. They changed his looks, made him into someone more mature, more intimidating.

"I want another chance," he finally said. "I want to prove I'm not the things you said. Not *only* those things."

"Patrick, you don't have to prove anything to me. What does it matter what I think?"

Again he looked at her sideways. "I'm not sure," he said simply. "All I know is, I'm not leaving Loveless until you look at me with something else besides scorn."

An embarrassed snort escaped her. "I don't think scorn was on the agenda last night."

"Yeah, about that . . ."

But they were pulling up outside the Loveless Bistro, known for its backyard terrace and intimate atmosphere. This time Lara opened the passenger door before Patrick could reach it. She stepped out and closed the door behind her. A queer, disappointed feeling made her hug her arms around her middle. Patrick didn't want the pleasure of her company. He wanted to prove something. *Win* something. Typical Patrick.

When he appeared, offering his hand, she slowly shook her head. "So you're going to wine me and dine me and prove what a nice guy you are?"

He stopped dead and rubbed his hand across the back of his neck—the exact spot she'd wanted to touch. "That doesn't sound good, when you put it that way."

"Let's stipulate that I think you *can be* a nice guy, when you want to. And let's also agree that even if I *was* filled with scorn and maybe a little pent-up rage after that dinner at your parents—not that I ever got to eat—I'd definitely gotten past it by last night."

"Okaaaay," he said slowly. "What then?"

"That's my question. Do we still have any reason to go out tonight? Or should I just sign on the dotted line, 'I hereby admit Patrick's a nice guy,' and call it a night?"

"Wow," he said. He looked down at his shoes—worn cowboy boots—then off into the distance. "I'm thinking I ought to be offended."

She swallowed. Was she being rude? Couldn't she be like a normal girl and go out to dinner with a cute, sexy hero fireman without lecturing? Not to mention that she'd just taken a jackhammer to her idea of sleeping with him. He'd never want her now.

She aimed a wistful glance at the Loveless Bistro. First the Callahan family dinner, now this. Patrick's invitations never seemed to lead to actual food. She should have brought a snack.

Deflated, she reached for the door handle.

Patrick stopped her with a hand on her arm. The touch made her wobble just a bit and clutch at the door frame. "But I'm not offended. Because you're making some good points." He narrowed his vivid blue eyes at her. "How do you do that?"

"Do what?"

"See through me like I'm frickin' cellophane."

"I don't know. I don't mean to." She ought to pull her arm away from his grip, since it was inspiring all sorts of naughty longings that weren't going to get satisfied now. But she didn't. In fact, she let him draw her closer. He leaned in, so she felt the heat of his body. All her female nerve endings responded to his pure, unadulterated maleness. Pheromones, that's all it was, she thought frantically. Hormones, endorphins, serotonins, other mysterious chemicals.

He cupped her jaw, rubbed a thumb across her cheekbone. His eyes were pure blue fire and they reached down inside her and roiled everything up like a tornado.

"Listen to me, Lara Nelson. Maybe I do have some mixed-up idea that I need your good opinion. If that bugs you, I'm sorry. But mostly . . ." He ran his thumb across her lower lip, and she nearly staggered. "I want to talk to you. Have dinner with you. Touch you. And maybe kiss you some more, if you'll let me. What do you say?"

Chapter Fourteen

In high school a date with Patrick Callahan had turned any girl into an instant object of envy. Not only was he a Callahan and good looking, but he had that wild, rebellious edge that acted like catnip on the girls of Loveless—all of Elko County, really. Lara had never gone out with him on anything resembling a date, and so far it wasn't at all what she expected.

After they ordered—juicy steaks, recommended by Patrick as the perfect hangover food—he turned those killer blue eyes on her, folded his arms on the table and asked her how she wound up becoming a doctor.

She eyed him uneasily. Such a simple question, but he might not like the answer. "Because of Liam," she finally said. "I'd been thinking about it a little before, but after the accident, that's when I decided."

Her answer made him flinch, as if he was absorbing a body blow. He toyed with the silverware, his strong hands very brown against the white tablecloth. "No one ever told me about what happened after the accident. All I knew was they wouldn't let me in and no one would talk to me."

"Not even Megan?"

"I hated putting her in the middle. She kept bursting into tears every time I called her. The whole thing made me crazy. Sometimes I was afraid I'd lose it and get violent with someone."

The waiter brought them big glasses of ice water; neither of them wanted drinks, after last night. Lara took in the strain on his face. After the accident, she'd been so angry at Patrick. She'd never thought about what he must be going through. "Sounds like it was pretty rough," she said slowly.

He gave an impatient shake of his head. "If it was, I deserved it." He took a long breath. "So tell me about Liam in the hospital."

"Are you sure?"

He nodded, pressing his lips together. Good lips, she noticed. Just the right amount of fullness, a slight stubble developing above and below. Character and humor, that's what his lips revealed.

"I'm not sure I'm the right person to ask, but I'll tell you what I know. He was in a coma for a few weeks. He had a broken pelvis and some nerve damage. They had to do a few surgeries. When he finally healed enough, he had to relearn how to walk. Everything was harder because of the autism and his deafness. Your father couldn't deal at all. It was kind of the last straw for him. I wanted to help more but he didn't want me around because I'd been there that night. Big Dog hired a bunch of therapists and it seemed like Liam was always busy. I applied to an accelerated premed program soon after and left Loveless. I hardly saw him after that."

Patrick listened as though she were peppering him with buckshot instead of information. She had to give him credit, though; he took in every word and didn't ask her to stop. "Did you keep in touch with him?"

"For a while," Lara answered warily. This was dangerous territory. She knew Liam didn't want to be found. He trusted her to keep his whereabouts private. But if Patrick posed a direct question, she wouldn't lie. Both Lara and Liam were sticklers about honesty. Time to change the subject. "What about you? What did you do after you left Loveless? I wondered."

His eyes lifted to hers. She shifted in annoyance; would that lance of blue flame always have such an impact on her? "You did?"

"Occasionally. When I wasn't cursing you out." She smiled to take away the sting.

"You know the basics. I went to California. Became a firefighter. I guess we have that in common."

"What?"

"I decided to become a fireman after the accident."

The waiter arrived with their steaks. She shook her head as she cut into the thick cut of prime rib. "Funny how one night changed everything. I decided to become a doctor. You decided to become a fireman."

"Yeah. I'm not sorry about that part. I would have gone back to Princeton and, I don't know, gone to law school or something. Maybe I'd be running for Congress by now."

Lara lifted her eyes to the ceiling. "Lord save us."

"Making fun of me? Didn't you know that's what Big Dog wanted? That's why the accident pissed him off so much. I ruined three futures in one stroke. Mine, Liam's, and his."

Lara put down her fork. Under a surface layer of lightness, she heard the pain in his voice. And something about what he'd said bothered her. She wanted to correct it, but wasn't sure exactly how. She spoke carefully, as if walking on ice about to crack. "Why do you say that?"

He looked genuinely confused. "What do you mean?"

"You sound like you blame yourself for the whole thing. Like it was all your fault."

"Of course it was. Everyone knows that."

She frowned. "How do you know?"

Patrick stared at Lara as if she was questioning whether the earth was round. "I know because I know. That's why Big Dog kicked me out. That's why Mom couldn't even look at me. Why Megan cried every time I called her. And you. You said you kept cursing me out."

"Yeah. But not because of the accident. That was an *accident*. Big Dog blamed you because he had to blame someone. I was mad because you left."

He gripped the edge of the table. "Because I *left*?"

"You left Liam when he needed you. He didn't have anyone to fight for him. They treated him like a child, even after he got through surgery. You wouldn't have let them do that. You walked out on him, Patrick. Callahans aren't supposed to do that."

He bolted to his feet. If an earthquake had struck the bistro at that moment, he wouldn't have noticed. The entire world was already rocking beneath him. *"They wouldn't let me in the fucking hospital.* I figured he'd be better off without me."

Lara tilted her head up, the soft overhead lighting giving her eyes a fierce golden glow. She spoke with soft, devastating emphasis. "I don't agree."

Patrick ran a hand through his hair, feeling his head might literally explode. "What the fuck, Lara."

"Everyone's staring at us, you know."

He sank down in his seat. Sitting was better. Now he felt less at sea. He shook his head. This was all too much; he could only deal with one thing at a time. "Why don't you think the accident was my fault?"

She lifted her shoulders in a shrug. "Well, was it? You were there, I wasn't."

"I don't remember much about it. I remember shouting something to Liam, but of course he couldn't hear, then waking up with a bunch of paramedics around me. I tried to shove them away and to find Liam, but they were already strapping him on a stretcher." Even talking about it made his chest tight.

Lara pushed her plate away, as if the memories stole her appetite. "Look, whatever happened, I'm sure it was an accident. Big Dog blamed you because that's the way he is. I never believed it was your fault, but no one cared what I thought. Why should we all have to go along with what Big Dog believes?"

Abruptly, she leaned forward, putting her hand on his. A spark leaped between them. "Have you ever thought about talking to the firefighters who were there that night?"

He stared at her. It had never occurred to him to do such a thing. But the fact that she cared enough to suggest it made him want to pull her into his arms and bury himself in her softness. She was so beautiful, all creamy and golden, her expression so earnest and determined.

"I'm sure at least some of them are still here in town. You should go by the station and . . ."

She tapered off, clearly picking up on his sudden emotion. Silence fell between them. A charged, vibrating silence.

"What? What'd I say?" she asked.

"I want you," he said, his voice thick with the lust he couldn't hide. "You have no idea how much, Lara."

He watched her throat move as she swallowed. His cock stiffened. God, couldn't he have phrased it with a little more finesse? She must think he was some kind of beast. He opened his mouth to apologize, but before he could speak, she opened hers too.

"I want you too," she whispered, pink creeping up her cheeks.

Finding that irresistibly adorable, he cupped his hand around her face. "You're not still mad at me?"

She appeared to deliberate, which, since it involved running her tongue across her lips and catching the lower one between her teeth, he enjoyed enormously. "No," she said finally. "You were young and you did what seemed like the best thing. Besides, I can't be mad at you. You're too sexy." She winked, her gold-tipped eyelashes dipping down.

Lara Nelson, winking at him. God, he couldn't take this. His cock pushed against the fabric of his jeans.

"Can we get out of here now?" he asked in a growl.

She nodded. That delicious color kept coming and going in her cheeks, and her eyes were the color of dark honey. If he didn't get her in his bed soon he swore he'd die.

They raced through the formalities of paying and tried not to look like crazed teenagers as they hurried out of the restaurant. Patrick drove with one hand on the wheel, the other holding Lara's. Touching her felt so unbelievably good. He felt drunk. Who needed alcohol when Lara Nelson was around?

By the time they reached the Callahan Ranch, the lights were out. He parked and they ran across the yard to the guesthouse. Neither said a word until they were inside and Patrick had locked the door behind him. Then they faced each other in the subdued darkness of the moonlit living room as though seeing each other for the first time.

"We've been naked before," Patrick pointed out, clearing his throat.

"Skinny-dipping in Mrs. Jenkins's pool, you mean? Doesn't count. I stayed on the other side of the pool from you the entire time."

"You did that on purpose?"

Her eyes widened with a silvery gleam. "You noticed?"

"How could I not notice? I was dying to see what you were hiding under your goth girl nun outfits."

"Goth girl nun?" Indignant, she gave his chest a teasing push. He caught her wrist and lassoed her against his body.

"Goth girl nun," he repeated against her ear, while she giggled softly and squirmed. "I like the new look a hell of a lot better." He ran his hands down her back, greedily caressing the lush curves of her ass. With a quick move he hauled her against him so she could feel the hard bulge of his arousal.

She sucked in a breath.

"Can't you tell?" He loved the shiver that passed through her body. Her nipples hardened against his chest—thank God for thin tops. Unbearably aroused, he ran his hands up her lusciously curved sides. When he snuck his thumbs between their bodies to lightly flick her nipples, she gave a low moan deep in her throat.

"What are you saying, my old outfits didn't turn you on?"

"Actually, they did. You don't know how many stiffies I hid from you. Then again, I got a lot of stiffies back then."

He felt a hand cupping him, running down his hard length.

"Not as many now, though?"

"Now I know what to do with them," he growled. "And they last longer."

And with that, he lifted her up and slung her over his shoulder, caveman style. That damned slit in her skirt, the one that had been distracting him all night, rode up to her ass. He shoved the skirt out of his way and clamped one hand on her upper thigh.

"Hey," she said in a choked voice.

"Something wrong?" He shifted his hand onto her butt, feeling the heat of her sex through her silky panties.

"No," she answered with a squeak that made him smile with deep male satisfaction. He couldn't wait to get her naked. He strode toward the bedroom he hadn't slept in even once. Good thing it had a bed in it; he hadn't even checked. But it was big and looked clean, and that was enough for him.

He set her down at the foot of the bed and raked her up and down with hungry eyes. That corset top—that was hot. But the skirt had to go. He slid his hands under the waistband and tugged it over her hips. She shimmied, helping him, her hands on his shoulders. When it was in a little puddle at her feet, she stepped out and kicked off her shoes.

Moonlight clung to her long firm legs, as if the moon was just as entranced by her as he was. He dropped to his knees and ran his tongue across the smooth expanse of her thighs. So soft, like licking whipped cream. He reached her inner thigh and surprised her with a tender bite.

She gasped, and he felt a tremor shoot through her. He clamped his hands on her ass and nudged her legs open. He wanted to breathe in the warm scent that seemed to float from the core of her. When he brushed his face across the mound swelling beneath her panties, she made a strangled sound.

His cock strained at the fly of his jeans.

Not too fast, he told himself. *You've been waiting a long time for this, and you didn't even know it. Take your time.*

He wanted to strip off her underwear and taste her with his tongue, but instead opened his mouth and fastened it over her sex, sending his hot breath through the thin fabric.

"*Jesus,*" she hissed.

He did it again, exhaling a long stream of heat against her clit. She squirmed in his grasp. When he ran a thumb across her underpants, he found them damp with arousal. Her hand dug into his shoulders, her body shook.

Not yet, not yet. He mouthed the words against her sex, which made her tremble even more.

He rose to his feet and turned her around. Holy fuck, the way her ass looked framed by her corset top. He closed his eyes for a second, afraid he'd go off before he'd so much as seen her naked. Clamping down on his need, he undid the hooks at the top of her corset to loosen it. Then he turned her around, loving the wildness in her eyes and the fast in-and-out of her breath.

"I've got to see you, Lara," he muttered, nearly out of his mind. She nodded, but when she moved to shrug off the corset, he stopped her. Utterly compelled by the enticing, moonlit curves of her flesh, he reached inside the top and drew out her breasts as if they were precious objects. With the way her skin glowed in the moonlight, maybe they were. Her breathing hitched as he ran his thumbs across their darkened peaks, then bent to kiss them. As he drew one pebbled nipple into his mouth, he pulled her toward him, bending her backward over his tensed arm. She tipped her head back, her hair tumbling over his hands.

He wanted to eat her alive.

Ravenous, he filled his mouth with lush flesh, swirling his tongue across her nipples, teasing, feasting, gorging on her until her breath was nothing but ragged panting. Then he stood back and looked at what he'd wrought: proud, wet nipples, her chest rising and falling, the corset erotically undone, her eyes frantic and wide.

Growling, he disposed of her top, practically ripping apart the rest of the hooks and tossing it aside. For one moment she stood in nothing but her panties, a pool of adoring moonlight at her feet, a goddess made of hairpin curves and marbled flesh.

And then she was on him, ripping at his shirt, fumbling at the fastening of his jeans. Together they flung off his clothes until he stood naked, his erection so full and hard it was nearly vertical. Her hands went all over him, up his chest, down his shoulders, along his cock, feeling, exploring, driving him into a maddened frenzy of lust.

They stared at each other, panting like two racehorses. He bent to his pants, pulled a condom from his pocket and ripped it open with clumsy hands. After sheathing himself, he lifted her in his arms, spun her around and tossed her on the bed. A half second later he was clawing her underpants down her body. A thick patch of gold curls glinted at the juncture of her thighs, an oasis beckoning him onward, pulling him in. He stretched himself over her body and pinned her arms to the bed. If she touched him too much, he knew he'd lose it.

He covered her body, every firm curve meeting his hardness, his cock probing at the mouth of her heated sex. In a minute he'd plunge in. But first he licked his way down her body, keeping her arms firmly pinned.

"Don't move," he growled after he'd moved down far enough so he couldn't reach her arms anymore. For a long, stunning moment she obeyed; he knew it was because it felt good and she trusted him. He found her clit with his tongue, stabbing delicately, swirling and dancing, then lapped the sweet juices from her tender folds.

That's when she lost it. A long cry rose over his head. Her hips rose up to meet his mouth, thrashing and crashing, her hands frantically scrabbling at his hair. He gripped her ass hard, the firm flesh giving beneath his touch. He held on tight, as if her orgasm was a roller-coaster ride, a dizzying, delirious, life-changing event. She tasted so sweet, like life and joy and hot, hot woman. It went on forever. His own cock throbbed with exquisite pain, but he didn't let her go until her spasms had nearly disappeared. Then he spread her apart, lifted his hips high over hers, and sank into her.

Home.

The sensation sang through his body. He was home, deep inside Lara's welcoming, velvety, pulsating body. With that incomprehensible revelation, he exploded.

Chapter Fifteen

Maybe this was how surviving a shipwreck felt, Lara thought, covering her face with one damp forearm. The kind of shipwreck in which you woke up with no idea where you were or how you'd gotten there. What had just happened? Patrick Callahan had flung her onto his bed and dismantled her entire world with his talented mouth and hard body.

So that's what the fuss was all about.

A secret smile stole across her face. Now she knew. No matter how much Annabella or the other Goddesses tried to explain, one night in bed with Patrick was all it took to make everything crystal clear. Sex was amazing. She didn't know how she'd missed it before. Maybe she'd just had bad luck the other times, or maybe the mood hadn't been right. She definitely owed Patrick for showing her how incredible the whole sex thing could be. And that's all it was, she told herself. Nothing more than sex. Amazing sex, yes. But that was all.

"You okay?" he murmured, rolling over on his side. She loved the roughened rasp of his voice. It told her she wasn't the only one whose world had been rocked.

"Yep. Thank you."

He laughed. She watched the muscles move under his tattoos. Even though she was already nearly bone-less from satisfaction, something stirred inside her at the sight. The sheer maleness of the man undid her.

"I'm serious," she said. "You helped me figure something out."

"What's that?" He trailed a finger along her rib cage. Little quicksilver tremors rippled across her skin.

She sighed. "If you must know, I never really got the whole sex thing before. It actually kind of irritated me. The Goddesses take it so seriously and everything has such a silly name in Haven language."

"Yeah? What are these called?" He circled his finger around one nipple.

"Flowers of femininity."

He gave a spurt of laughter. "You're joking, right?"

"Well, yes." She might be joking, but she was squirming nonetheless.

"What about this?" He cupped her sex. Her eyelids fluttered; she wanted to melt against him.

"Mound of Venus, of course."

"Of course. My lotus root sure enjoyed penetrating your Mound of Venus."

She giggled wildly. "No, *that* would be the Channel of Sensuality."

"The Channel of Sensuality? I'm not entirely clear." He slid a finger inside her, into the slick heat still pulsing from his lovemaking. Devilish blue eyes danced at her. "Is this what you mean?"

She took in a long, wavering breath. "Fine time for vocabulary lessons."

He probed deeper and found a spot that made her gasp. "What better time than the present? Isn't that what the sign says? 'The present moment is the true treasure of life'?" He used a deep voice that could have come from one of Aunt Tam's meditation tapes.

"Mmm-hmm," she choked out.

He pressed his finger against that one particular spot and used the heel of his hand on her clitoris. The hot pressure made her nearly jump off the bed. "What about this? What's this called?"

Her thoughts scattered like mice. "Which? What? Where?"

He smiled wickedly. "I'm not sure you were paying enough attention in class, Lara. You might need some remedial tutoring." He moved his palm against her sex in a slow, grinding groove.

"Just . . . don't stop . . . doing that," she gasped.

"Oh, I wouldn't think of it." He shifted closer to her, so he was growling in her ear. "It's too much fun watching you lose your mind. Do you have any idea how sexy you are? You're like some rich, buttery dessert. And that look in your eyes, like the cat who ate the cream. You make me absolutely crazy. I wish time would stop so I could watch you like this all day and all night. I'd keep you right here in bed and search out every place on your body until I know exactly what you like. I'd listen to every little sexy sound you make. My own personal Lara Nelson workshop. I'd call it, 'What Makes Lulu Scream?' and I'd study you until I know you better than you know yourself, and every time you want to come you'd find me and beg me—"

Her spiraling cry of release interrupted the hot flow of his words. She spun off into a wild world where all she knew was the hard hand between her legs, the low murmur of his words, and the brilliant starbursts behind her eyelids.

Good God, the man was magic.

When she could move again, she lifted her heavy eyelids. He was watching her with an expression she'd never seen on his face before—open, intimate, almost awed. "That was amazing," he murmured.

She shoved him away, embarrassed. "What are you talking about?"

"I just like seeing you come, that's all. It makes me happy."

Still trying to catch her breath, she dragged her tangled hair away from her face and studied him. His features were so familiar, but somehow new and different too. His intensely blue eyes looked too serious, his mouth too . . . vulnerable. Those lines she'd noticed before hinted at pain and endurance.

Where was the Patrick she knew, the wild, devil-may-care, in-your-face rebel? This Patrick touched something different in her, some tender place that . . . well, freaked her out. It was just sex, she reminded herself. Nothing more than sex.

She plastered a sexy, teasing smile on her face. "I guess the rumors were true all along."

He frowned. "Rumors?"

"All the girls used to say you must be a stud in bed."

Quick as a flash his face changed, closed off. "Did they now?"

She trailed a finger down his bare arm in what she hoped was a sophisticated gesture. "Don't be offended. I meant it as a compliment."

He rolled onto his back and stayed quiet for a long moment. "Thanks for the compliment, then."

But all the joy and fun had gone out of his voice.

After spending most of the day clearing around the ranch house, Patrick drove into town to pick up a part for the Cat. Something was wrong. Usually after a bout of sex he felt on top of the world. He couldn't put his finger on what had bothered him so much about his time with Lara. It wasn't the sex; that part had been fantastic, better than fantastic. But even thinking about Lara in those terms seemed wrong. It didn't fit what they were to each other. But what were they to each other? What was he to her? A stud?

For whatever reason, he didn't like the sound of that.

But another thing she'd said had definitely stuck with him. He headed into the heart of downtown, where Loveless Fire Station 5 was located. He remembered two names from that horrible night.

"I'm looking for Dan Farris or Simon Lavalle," he told the young guy in uniform, a good-looking Hispanic kid sitting behind the desk in the reception area.

The firefighter clicked the intercom and spoke in a deep, mock-official voice. "Firefighter Farris, please report to the front desk. The IRS is here." He winked. "Watch this."

Patrick grinned. You had to love firehouses. In a few moments an older man hurried in, wearing a look of alarm. Patrick remembered the short brown hair, grayer now, and the kind brown eyes. As soon as he saw Patrick, he hauled up.

"You're the Callahan kid."

"One of them. Nothing to do with the IRS. I'm a firefighter myself now, out of San Gabriel, California."

"Right. We heard you helped out on the Waller Canyon Fire."

The kid at the desk leaped to his feet. "Callahan? You're Patrick Callahan?" He stuck out his hand, looking nervous. "Honor to meet you."

All the attention made Patrick uncomfortable. Plus, the kid had turned a surprising shade of red. What was he missing?

"No big deal. We gotta help each other out, right?"

"Damn right." The younger fireman pumped his hand, then moved aside for Farris.

"What can I do for you?" Farris asked after they exchanged handshakes. Patrick, closely scanning his face, saw nothing resembling blame or criticism.

"I wanted to talk about . . ." He lowered his voice. " . . . back then. The accident. If you remember."

"Sure. Let's go into the captain's office. Let her know, would you?" he said to the kid, over his shoulder.

"Female captain?" Patrick asked when Farris had closed the door behind them.

"First in Nevada. Nice claim to fame. Does a helluva job too." He leaned one hip against the desk. "She lets us use the office for private conversation. So. Shoot."

Patrick shifted from one foot to the other. "I . . . uh . . . wondered if you remembered what happened that night."

Farris tilted his head. "You don't?"

"Only that I fucked things up pretty good."

Farris frowned. "I don't remember it that way. That RV shouldn't have been there. They'd run out of gas and hiked to the nearest town. Didn't even leave their hazards on. No one could have avoided it."

"But I was riding behind my brother. Liam hit it first. I should have stopped him. It should have been me." Bitterness clenched like a fist around his heart.

"Hard to say who hit first. But there wasn't anything either of you could have done, so just get that out of your head."

Patrick stared at him. *Get that out of your head.* Did it really work like that? "We were going too fast."

"Most kids on dirt bikes do. At least you were both wearing helmets. Would have been a whole different story without them."

A sudden remembrance surfaced. Liam's chin strap buckle had broken, which had freaked him out. Patrick had insisted they switch helmets. He'd pulled over before they hit the main road and refused to continue until they did so, even though the unfamiliar helmet was upsetting to Liam.

The memory felt like a beam of light in the murky darkness. Something shifted inside him. Maybe he didn't deserve all the guilt he'd been heaping on himself all these years. What a mind-blowing thought.

He took a long, exploratory breath, feeling as if a tight band around his chest had loosened just a bit.

"Appreciate your time," he told Farris. He wanted to say more, to give an inkling of what it meant to him. But the man seemed to get it without any embarrassing explanations.

"You got it." Farris gave him a soft punch on the shoulder, like a papa bear cuffing a cub. "Take care of yourself, Callahan."

The Goddesses called a group meeting over Clarity Smoothies and date-coconut bars. Lara, still floating in a wondrous sexual afterglow, wondered if they could tell that her whole world had changed drastically. She'd always had to battle for her privacy at the Haven. The last thing she wanted was to discuss what had happened between her and Patrick.

But they all seemed more concerned about the future of the Haven than her sex life.

"We've come up with a few ideas," said Janey, her glasses perched on her nose. "Number one, investors."

"What we need," said Annabella, looking directly at Lara, "is a decision." Lara shifted uncomfortably on her embroidered pillow. "What do you intend to do, Lara? I heard a nasty rumor in town the other day."

She gazed at the worried faces arrayed before her. With their wild hair and brightly colored clothes, they looked like characters from a performance of *Gypsy*. But they weren't characters, they were people who needed to figure out their futures. "What rumors?"

Annabella smoothed her dark hair over one bare shoulder. "I ran into Dean at the market. He said you'd met with him about selling the property."

The other Goddesses gasped.

"I had to look into all the options," she told them.

Dynah rose to her feet so she towered over them all, even more than she normally did. "Behind our backs? While we're racking our pretty little heads trying to figure out a way to save this joint?"

Lara winced. "It was a short conversation, and it didn't go far. He said no one would buy the place anyway."

Dynah planted her hands on her hips. "That potbellied weasel monkey. Why would he say a thing like that?"

"Because the town thinks we're weird, of course." Janey tapped a pencil on the ledger.

"Don't be ridiculous," said Annabella calmly. "It's the economy. This place needs so much work. You could sell it if you really wanted to, Lara. Hire a carpenter and fix the place up, you won't have any trouble. Don't listen to Dean. He's toxic."

Romaine's eyes, outlined in purple today, were wide with dismay. Or maybe purple eyeliner always conveyed dismay, whatever her actual mood. "Do you really want to sell it, Lara? This beautiful place?"

"It makes perfect sense," said Janey briskly. "She probably has lots of debt from medical school. And why would she want to get stuck with us? Annabella's right, dollbaby. If you want to sell, you should."

"Bull-freaking-crap," said Dynah. She'd never gotten on board with Haven jargon, now that Lara thought about it. "Where would that leave us? We've worked our patooties off here—sometimes *on* our patooties—and now she's going to leave us out in the cold? That ain't right, Lara."

Lara scrambled to her knees, slipped on her cushion, then kicked it aside so she could stand up. "Hang on, guys. I mean, Goddesses. I wasn't going to sell out and forget about you. Tam made me promise you'd be okay. I don't care about the money. I just don't know anything about running this place, and I don't want to learn."

"Let us buy it," said Annabella suddenly.

Dynah snorted. "With what, the money you send to your mother in Brazil? My horse ranch savings? Romaine's starter credit card with the five hundred dollar limit?"

"Janey has money," said Annabella.

"Janey's money was invested in the stock market." Janey avoided their stunned glances. "And you can spare me the lecture on the evils of capitalism. I got the point."

"You lost all your money?" Dynah dropped down next to her. "Oh, Janey."

Janey took off her glasses and swiped at her eyes. "I'm at peace with it. I consulted the pendulum, and apparently it's my karma to be broke. At least I have a home and work that means something to me. For the moment, anyway."

Lara gazed at the older woman, feeling about as low as the Turkish carpet under their feet. "Of course you have a home, Janey. Even if I sold . . ." She trailed off. Even finishing the sentence felt wrong. How could she sell the Haven? What would the Goddesses do? Dynah would be fine, but Romaine worried her. She was so fragile. And even Annabella—well, what were the job prospects for aging sex workers? She hadn't known that Annabella sent her money to Brazil, but it made sense. She never spent anything on herself.

"Never mind," she said. "Selling's not an option anyway. Dean was pretty confident no one would want it, except Big Dog Callahan, and I'd never let him get his hands on it."

All the Goddesses seemed to relax. Dynah tapped a finger against her cheek. "Then again, if that fireman son of his wanted to take over, I could think of a few things he could do around here."

Lara felt her face heat in slow but sure degrees. She pressed her hands against her cheeks. Annabella stood and pointed a dramatic finger at her. "You're blushing. You did it. You had sex with the fireman."

"Shhh," Lara said in a strangled voice.

Romaine crawled across the cushions, her purple eyes now wide with curiosity. "He's so wild and fierce. How did you handle so much masculine energy?"

"Errmm . . ." was all Lara could manage.

"I'm proud of you, Lulu," said Dynah, "not to mention just a teensy bit jealous."

Janey tapped her pencil on a nearby crystal lamp base. "Attention, everyone. Remember how Tam was always lecturing us about letting Lara have her privacy? And how one day she'd grow into her sexuality?"

Lara pulled a pillow over her flaming face. "Go away, everyone," she mumbled into it. When the questions kept coming, even through the muffling effect of cotton batting and silk, she pulled it away. "One more question and I'll sell this place," she told them with a scowl.

That shut everyone up. Into the ensuing stillness, she said, "Let's apply logic and common sense to the problem."

Right. Logic and common sense. The Haven had made her forget all about such concepts.

"The workshops aren't working because Aunt Tam isn't here to do them. You've just started the massage so it may take a while to catch on. Let's continue with the massage, maybe put some flyers around town to bring in more clients, and in the meantime we'll use the reserve fund to do some basic repairs."

The reserve fund lived in the hollow elephant statue in the corner. Janey strode to the statue and shook it, producing a pathetically tinny rattling sound. "I was afraid of that. The reserve fund is mostly gone. We've been running on empty for a while."

Of course it was gone.

"So we'll do the work ourselves," Lara said. "We're strong, enlightened women. Do we still have an account at Olson's Hardware?"

"Yes."

"Maybe he'll do a trade. He has a bad back, right? Massage in exchange for lumber."

Janey cocked her head. "Not a bad idea, Lara. Look at you, figurin' everything out. Maybe all that education was worth it."

She snorted. Not exactly what she'd had in mind

during "Introduction to Anatomy," but it would have to do. If only she'd taken a class in carpentry, she'd be all set. "Make a list of what we need to do. I'll talk to Ben Olson."

Patrick's cell phone vibrated while he was breaking in the new weed-whacker he'd bought in town. Sure it was Lara, he unearthed it from deep in his pocket. They had lots to talk about. He wanted to tell her what Farris had said, and ask her exactly what she'd meant by that "stud" comment. Normally he wouldn't mind being called a stud, but in this case it bothered him. He didn't even check the readout before he answered.

The throaty purr of her voice was like a cool drink of water on a hot day. "Hey there, Callahan."

Somehow it made all his worries scatter to the wind. "Dr. Nelson. How are my test results? Will I ever play the piano again?"

"Sure, if by play the piano you mean the kind of thing we did last night."

His cock went hard. Damn, this woman did something to him. "I'm in the mood for a little ivory-tickling right now."

"Hold that thought, hot stuff. I'm calling on Haven business."

"Trouble in Goddessland?"

"*Opportunity* in Goddessland. We need a man."

"Oh, really?" he drawled. "You came to the right cell phone."

"Not you, Callahan. You're busy. We need someone—actually, it doesn't have to be a man, but someone who's good at carpentry and stuff. We need to whip this place into shape. Do you know any carpenters in town?"

He didn't know anyone in town anymore. But he did know a guy who was a whiz with a chop saw, loved power tools, and was probably on the outs with his girlfriend. If he remembered the shift schedule correctly, he probably had four days off coming up.

"I'll make a call."

Chapter Sixteen

*P*atrick figured Vader needed some liquoring up before meeting the Goddesses, so they stopped in at the Love 'Em and Leave 'Em on their way back from the airport. They ordered beers and shots and tossed them back in quick order.

"How's the station?"

Vader shrugged his huge shoulders. "Same old. Cap's about to lose his mind. Melissa's working on some story, but he wants her to stay home. The guys put together a petition to finish that swimming pool you started and he nearly threw us across the room."

Patrick chuckled, a little embarrassed. It seemed about a million years ago that he'd commandeered the excavator.

"Sabina and Roman sent out their invites. Oh, here."

He dug a crumpled piece of formerly nice paper out of his pocket. Patrick peered at it. It had a few random-looking ink smears on it and a red lifesaver stuck to the back.

"What did you do to it?"

"Nothing. Told her I'd hand-deliver it. It's your invitation."

So Sabina had decided he was worthy of attending her wedding. Or maybe Roman had made the final call. Whatever the truth, Patrick was ridiculously pleased. Not that he cared about weddings, but he'd been left out of a few Callahan extended family gatherings, and it hadn't felt good. He examined the invitation, unable to find anything legible except the word "joined."

Which, for some reason, made him think of Lara. They'd joined. Hell, they'd joined up a storm. He'd never known joining could be so earth-shattering. But he had a feeling it had been a one-way street in that respect. Lara hadn't been earth-shattered. He'd satisfied her, but he hadn't blown her mind. Instead she'd made that crack about what other girls said about him. It had left a bad taste.

Maybe he needed to try harder. He liked that idea. He'd take her from moaning to screaming. Satisfied to ecstatic.

"Earth to Psycho." Vader was waving a hand in front of his face.

"Sorry," he muttered. "A lot on my mind."

"Chick shit?"

Patrick snorted. *"Chick shit?"* Where did Vader come up with this stuff?

"I know that look. Like you're trying to figure out where you left your balls. I've been there. There right now, in fact."

"Did Cherie dump you again?"

"Maybe. In girl code."

"Girl code?"

"She needs space. There's plenty of space between Cali and Nevada. You called at the right time, brother."

A smooth, slightly accented voice slipped between them. "Are you two manly men actually brothers, or is that simply a bonding term?"

Annabella and Romaine stood behind them, both loaded down with bags from Olson's Hardware. Vader's jaw dropped at the sight of a sultry brunette and an ethereal blonde who might have stepped from the pages of *Hippie Hustler.*

"Hey there, fine ladies," he said with a gallant bow of his head. He slid from his stool and gestured to it. "What's mine is yours. Please seat your lovelinesses down."

Patrick nearly burst out laughing. Vader loved women, all sorts of women, genuinely and sincerely, and you never knew what line he'd take.

"If what's yours is mine, I wouldn't mind a sip of that tequila." Annabella peered at Vader from under her eyelashes. Patrick wasn't sure why she was wasting her wiles on a sure bet like Vader.

But, as often happened, Vader surprised him. He signaled the bartender for another shot, then faced the two women. "I better make it clear from the get-go that my heart belongs to another. She doesn't know what to do with it yet, but that's okay. I'm in it for the long haul."

Patrick felt his eyebrows climb.

Romaine gazed at Vader with huge, misty eyes. Or maybe silver eye shadow always made her look misty. "That is so romantic," she breathed.

"And completely unnecessary," said Annabelle briskly. "We're not after your heart. Or your body." She ran her eyes over Vader's impressively bulging physique. "Except in the most practical way."

"If you're after the swimmers, they're saving themselves for my special someone."

Patrick hid his snort of laughter behind a cough. Annabella looked absolutely fascinated, as if she'd never encountered a specimen like Vader.

"Your reproductive faculties are safe as well. We have another sort of proposition."

"Oh hell no," said Vader. "Two chicks is one thing. Two dudes . . ."

Annabella wagged a scolding finger at him. "I never thought I'd say this, but this isn't about sex."

Patrick cleared his throat. "Annabella and Romaine, this is Vader. He came here from San Gabriel to help you ladies out at the Haven."

"The what?" Vader looked confused. Patrick hadn't given him any details other than that a friend needed a favor, he'd pay his airfare, and to bring his tool belt.

"Oh, you're our savior!" Annabella beamed at him, with a smile that would knock the space shuttle off orbit. "See, Lara had the crazy idea that we can take care of the repairs at the Haven by ourselves. We know nothing about that sort of thing. We can fix broken relationships, we can free up women's sexual energy and teach couples how to express their needs, but when it comes to hanging doors and fixing siding, we're a little lost."

Vader was hanging on her every word. "I have no idea what you're talking about, but I like that accent you say it with."

"Where's Lara?" Patrick asked, because it seemed to be the thing he wanted to know at all times.

"She's loading the wood into the Cadillac."

"So this is the friend I'm helping out?" Vader asked. "Friends?" He included Romaine, who smiled tentatively.

"Yes, I thought it would be a great opportunity for you. Did you hear what she said about broken relationships? These ladies are experts. That's what they do."

"It's our specialty." Romaine piped up. Patrick thought she must be the shyest Goddess in history. "Along with healing massage. We just want everyone to be happy and get along."

"I'll drink to that." Vader tossed down his shot, then stuck out his hand. "I'm your guy. You help me figure out Cherie, and I'll be your slave for the next four days. Now lead me to that lumber."

"Você é um amor." Annabella leaned in to kiss him on the cheek, then turned to Patrick. "And Patrick, you're more than welcome as well." She raised one eyebrow meaningfully.

What was she getting at? He certainly didn't need relationship help. He didn't even have a relationship. What he had was . . . an old friend. A friend with whom he'd had the best sex of his life. A friend who kept popping into his thoughts at the most random moments. None of that added up to a relationship. Not that he was an expert. His expertise lay more in avoidance of relationships.

He should probably sort this out with Lara before they went any further.

"Sorting" turned out to be even better than "joining." That night, after Patrick got Vader set up on the couch of the guesthouse, he went for a drive that just happened to take him past the Haven. His cell phone just happened to call Lara's—butt calls could be so inconvenient— and Lara, glowy and wild-eyed, just happened to skip out the Haven's front door and hop into the Hulk.

He drove a short distance to an empty moonlit field where he and Liam used to practice grass hump slalom with their dirt bikes. He'd barely spread a soft cotton blanket between two sheltering grass clumps when Lara jumped into his arms. Taken by surprise, he toppled over, still holding her tight, and she climbed on top of him. He buried his face in her warm neck and breathed deep. God, the smell of her, clean and spicy at the same time. The feel of her, tender-skinned but firm, each curve beckoning him on to the next. The neck led to the shoulder, which led to the upper curve of her breast, which—

She sat up and stripped off her top. It landed on top of the nearest grass tussock. He reached up to snag it.

"No need to let the cops know what's going on."

"We're in the middle of nowhere. I'm not worried." She unhooked her bra, and he stopped caring about anything but filling his hands with those glorious globes of flesh. The air was still warm from the brutal heat of the day, but there was just enough air current to make her nipples peak. Moonlight flooded the field, turning her skin to molten, living titanium.

"You're so freaking gorgeous like this," he murmured, catching her dark nipples between his fingers. She arched her back to push closer to his touch and tilted her head back, as if howling at the moon. The line of her throat was like a lark's song, clear and haunting and irresistible.

"I want you, stud," she said in a voice he almost didn't recognize, it was so thick with desire. Her hands went to the swelling front of his jeans. She undid the zipper, working it over the straining ridge of his erection. "Looks like it's mutual."

He answered with something incoherent. Of course it was mutual—wasn't it? Was there something he wanted to work out with her? He'd wanted to talk about something, hadn't he?

Then her cool, clever hand was on his cock and the rush of pleasure blotted out everything else. "Holy mother of God," he muttered.

Breathing hard, she worked his jeans down his hips just enough to free his erection. "Did you bring anything?"

"What?" For a blank moment he had no idea what she was talking about. "In the truck."

"Fuck that."

God, he loved it when she talked dirty. "I'm safe. Never go unprotected." Well, until now.

"Me neither. Well, I never really go at all. Until now. I guess I'm making up for lost time."

"No complaints here." Well, maybe he did have a complaint. But he couldn't quite remember what it was, since she was now running her hand up and down his shaft.

She lifted her skirt. *Damn.* She was naked underneath, all her feminine parts bare and moonstruck, her pale curls glinting silver. He touched her with a sense of awe, feeling the soft, damp flesh give beneath his fingers.

"Has anyone ever told you your hands are like magic?" She gave a soft gasp. "You probably hear that a lot."

"Stop talking, Lara."

"You mean, stop talking and get busy?" Teasingly, she lifted herself up on her knees and, still holding up her skirt, positioned herself over his cock.

"Shhht. Just shhht." If she kept going on like that, he'd have to start listening seriously. And he had a feeling he wouldn't like what he heard. He found the little nub begging for his attention and brushed his thumb back and forth across it.

She let out a loud moan. There, at least she wasn't

talking anymore, saying things that upset him. He ate up the sight of her, erotically poised over him, skirt raised for his pleasure.

"Touch yourself," he said.

"What?"

"I want to see you touch yourself."

"Why?"

"Because it's hot! What do you want, a workshop?"

She burst out laughing. He did too, through his turned-on haze. Patrick realized he'd never laughed so much during sex as with Lara. Maybe it was odd, but he liked it. It felt . . . real.

"Fine. As long as you promise to fuck me silly afterward."

There was that attitude again. To shut her up, he took her hand and pressed it against her sex, into her damp heat. Blood surged through his cock at the picture she made, her white hand working through her shining thatch of curls, a gleam of moisture peeking out.

When he heard her breath come fast, he grabbed the sides of her hips and thrust upward, into the hot welcome of her body. He groaned at the slick, clinging bliss of being inside her. She gasped and shuddered, then lifted herself up until he nearly slipped from her. Resting her hands next to his shoulders for leverage, she lowered herself back down, while he helped with shaking hands.

"Not too fast," he muttered. He wanted to draw this out as long as possible. Together they found a steady, toe-curling rhythm, corkscrewing their bodies together. He had to use every ounce of self-control to keep from simply exploding into the orgasm his body craved. But he wanted this to be good for her— more than good, he wanted to stroke her into a frenzy, change her world, blow her mind.

So he gritted his teeth, tightened his grip on her hips, and thrust, up and out, again and again, like a tidal surge or some other force of nature. With the warm, grass-scented air pressing around them, and the moon gracing them with its glow, that's how it felt, as if they were bound together in some fantastic natural phenomenon.

He felt her fight to go faster as she tightened around him. *Not yet, not yet.* He slipped his hand between their bodies, rubbing the spot he knew would make her crazy. She writhed and gasped, her long, moon-silvered hair falling in a curtain around them.

"Come on, Psycho," she gritted. "Show me how crazy you can get."

Everything in him sang with glee. *Time to let the wild dog off the leash.* He took command of those hips that were driving him nuts. One fierce thrust . . . *grunt* . . . and her body shook with tremors. Surrounded by her heat and softness, he lost his mind and all sense of where he was. Again and again he hammered into her until he felt the sharp pull of her release. Then he let himself go, soaring into fierce, primal sensation, holding tight to her body, an anchor in a wild storm.

When his mind stopped spinning, she was huddled on top of him, boneless and panting. He stroked her back, tangled his fingers in her hair. The sweat was already cooling on her body. He tried to say something but had to clear his throat first. "You okay?"

She shifted on top of his body.

Oh hell. Had he gone too far? Gotten too rough? For a moment he'd been in a different world. "Did I hurt you?"

She muttered something into his neck. He pulled her hair away from her face. "What'd you say? Something about a map?"

"Postcoital nap," she mumbled again. "Give me a second."

He smiled, a sense of contentment stealing over him. Sure, he'd had a great time, but it was almost more satisfying to see how she'd been affected. No, it *was* more satisfying. He could rest like this for a good long time, untangling the silky strands of her hair, feeling the gentle pulsing of her body, listening to the night sounds of the field, the occasional passing of a car on the faraway highway.

Finally she sat up, her eyes hazy in the soft, silvery light. "Okay, then."

He narrowed his eyes at her. Was that the most romantic thing she could find to say? "What does that mean?"

"Nothing. It's just a thing."

"A thing?"

"A thing to say."

He cocked an eyebrow at her. "And what's it supposed to mean?"

"I don't know. I guess it's open to interpretation. It might mean, do you want to get out of this field before we get trampled by a cow?"

"We've probably scared off all the cows, with those sounds you were making."

She giggled and tossed her hair over her shoulder. "Entirely your fault. I guess you bring out my wild side."

"Don't pin it all on me. You've been plenty wild all along. You just like to hide it behind black clothes and medical degrees."

"Hmmm. Maybe." She ran her finger across one of his tattoos—the gargoyle with the turquoise eyes and evil sneer. "Whereas some people wear their wildness right out in the open."

She shivered. He found her shirt and handed it to her. Her face disappeared behind soft cotton as she pulled it on, and when she emerged, she looked thoughtful. "Seriously, Patrick, I want to thank you."

"Don't start that—"

"I mean it. I never used to enjoy sex. I thought there might be something wrong with me. Do you know how good it feels to realize I'm just like everyone else?" She threw her arms open and howled up at the sky. "My sexual function is normal. I mean, I didn't think I was abnormal, but I did wonder why sex never seemed all that exciting. I have to hand it to you, Patrick. I don't know how you do what you do, but wow."

He scowled at her, all his reservations from earlier flooding back. "It takes two, you know."

"Yes, but you're the one who knows what he's doing. I just went along for the ride."

That wasn't how he remembered it. Hadn't she tackled him, straddled him, and driven him out of his mind?

"You have it all wrong, Lara. I don't have any special sex skills." Should he really be admitting that? Would he get kicked out of the man club?

"Well, whatever you do, it works for me. That's all I know."

He couldn't take it anymore, the way she was treating this thing. "Well, what I know is that it isn't always like this. Did you ever think it might be you and me, the way we click, the way we are together? Maybe that's why it's so good?"

She stared down at him, the skin between her eyebrows creasing in a puzzled frown. "Why are you trying to make more of this than it is? I thought guys liked things to be all about sex. Especially you."

At least she winced as she said that, but it still hit home.

Patrick hauled her off his body and set her on the blanket. He got to his feet and fastened his jeans. "You think you know me so well? Maybe you should open your eyes, Dr. Nelson. You can't put me in some little check box in your head."

She gazed up at him, mouth open, eyes wide, looking so adorable and tousled that he wanted to take her all over again.

No. Not this time.

"Come on, I'll take you home."

Chapter Seventeen

What had gone wrong? Lara kept asking the same question as she scraped paint off the door to the steam room, known in Haven language as the Energy Cleansing Room. One minute she and Patrick had been deep in sexual bliss, the next he'd practically tossed her over his shoulder and hauled her back to his truck. He'd barely said a word as he drove her back to the Haven. She'd jumped out as soon as they reached the front door and was hurrying inside when he called out to her.

"I volunteered to help out at the firefighters' charity barbecue this weekend. I want you to come."

But he'd said it almost grimly, as if he wanted her to come despite himself, or maybe as a challenge of some sort. And he hadn't said he wanted her to come *with him*. Just to come.

Oh, the man was simply too confusing. Things had been a lot easier when she'd been fifteen and simply hated him.

She dug the scraper against the soft wood. No, that wasn't quite right. She'd never hated Patrick, at least not without simultaneously being fascinated by him. He'd always been full of contradictions, the caring brother and the careless one, the wild one and the loyal one. Impossible, but impossible to forget.

"What are you doing to that poor doorjamb?" Romaine peered over her shoulder. "You're gouging big scratches in it."

Lara stared at her handiwork. Oops. "This wood is pretty rotten. Maybe we should replace it."

"I think we're going to have to. Let me ask Vader."

Right. And that was another thing. Patrick had magically materialized one of his big, brawny fireman buddies to help them with repairs. For free. Since when did Patrick care what happened to the Haven? She couldn't get a handle on him. He was always, annoyingly and inconveniently, showing a new side.

"Yup, I'd say that has to go," said a deep voice that seemed to come from miles over her head. She stood up and found the muscleman Vader, hands on hips, tool belt on pelvis, scanning the work she'd done. "Don't know what you've got against that door."

"She's probably transferring her emotions to inanimate objects," whispered Romaine.

"I'm not transferring anything, except paint from wood to floor." Lara tossed aside the scraper. "And apparently I've been wasting my time. All right, Vader, you're the boss. Tell me what to do."

"Oh baby." He winked. "I like the way you think."

Romaine prodded him in the side with the dull end of a screwdriver. "Zzzt. That's the kind of inappropriate innuendo we're talking about."

"Really? But I didn't mean anything by it. Lara knows it. It's harmless."

"What is this, more relationship therapy?" Lara rolled her eyes. The Goddesses had immediately taken to Vader and made him into their favorite new project. It reminded Lara of the one time she'd allowed them to give her a makeover.

"Don't knock it," said Vader. "I'm learning a lot. Romaine and I are going to dialogue later, right?" He curled his lip like Elvis.

Romaine poked him with the screwdriver. "Zzzt. Innuendo."

He groaned. "I can't help it. I'm a man. Maybe it would be easier if you cut my balls off."

When Romaine waved the screwdriver, he took a quick step back. "I wasn't serious."

"We don't believe in violence here at the Haven," she said sweetly. "And we don't want to neutralize your source of male potency. We merely want to bring it into harmony with the other elements of your being."

Lara nearly choked at the expression on Vader's face. "Romaine, why don't you start him off slow? Didn't you say you were going to teach him healing massage too?"

Vader looked as though he might fall at her feet from gratitude.

"We tried that. He wasn't able to deal with the feminine energy flooding his chakras. He might have to practice on another man. We thought your Patrick might be a good subject."

Now it was Vader's turn to choke. "Hell no. You have to give me another chance. I can handle the chick energy. Come on, let's go. I'll do it exactly how you showed me." He tugged at Romaine's wrist. When she didn't move immediately, he picked her up and flopped her over his shoulder. "Massage time. Let's git-'er-done."

"Vader, you can't just pick people up and haul them off," she said as Vader carried her down the hall. "Zzzt zzzt zzzzt!"

"If there was a fire, you'd be begging me to get you out of here."

Lara couldn't help laughing. She had to admit that having Vader around made things a lot more fun. And even though they all teased him, and he made fun of himself, everyone agreed he had tons of potential. Romaine came alive around him, and he and Dynah had already spent a night drinking at the Love 'Em and Leave 'Em.

The Haven was starting to shape up, although a daunting amount of work still remained to be done. She could probably beg another week of vacation from the hospital, but any more than that and she'd be in trouble. Her time in Loveless—and with Patrick—was running out.

Lara put a great deal of thought into what to wear to the barbecue. Vader was going too, as were all the Goddesses. They'd gotten to know the local firefighters well during the Waller Canyon Fire and had received a handwritten invitation from the fire chief. They were thrilled, even though only Dynah actually intended to eat anything resembling a rib.

Were cutoffs too casual? What about a denim miniskirt? She'd noticed that Patrick seemed to like her legs, though she saw nothing special about them herself. On the other hand, she wanted the people of Loveless to see her as a respected doctor. Ever since that night at the bar, she'd noticed more smiles when she went into town, more friendly waves and shouts of "Hey, Lara." If people here were finally starting to accept her, why jeopardize that?

Her standby, capris, would do. She chose a navy

blue pair with a pattern of daisies at the hem, then dug out a white halter top. Sandals, hair in a ponytail, and hopefully she looked just the proper degree of casual and unworried about impressing Patrick Callahan IV. This was her chosen personal style—whimsical and casual—nothing "Goth Nun" and nothing like the colorful Gypsy-wear the Goddesses wore.

In case she wanted to leave early, she drove her rental car to the park where the barbecue was being held. As soon as she pulled up to the building, excitement tightened her stomach. She hadn't seen Patrick in two days. What would he do when he saw her? Smile or scowl? Kiss her or ignore her?

She walked around the side of the building, following the flow of people. Mr. Olson from the hardware store waved to her, as did her old biology teacher. She smiled back, but she couldn't keep from scanning the grills where firemen were brandishing spatulas. Where was Patrick? She didn't see him anywhere; she felt his absence in the pit of her stomach. He was supposed to be working here. Had he stood her up?

She nearly tripped over a folding card table with a cash box on it and an alarmed girl behind it. "Oh, sorry."

"You should really pay more attention," said the girl with a sniff. She couldn't have been more than thirteen. "Five dollars, please."

"It's on me."

Shivers skittered up and down her spine at the sound of Patrick's voice. Awareness stroked the skin of her arms.

"That's not necessary," she said, turning to face him. He was smiling, that electric, blue-eyed smile that seemed to rearrange every atom in her body.

"I invited you."

He paid the girl, then took Lara's arm. She clenched her teeth to hide her embarrassing reaction, which was an all-body shiver of pleasure.

"Come on, you can help me with the ribs. You're good with a scalpel, right?"

"Actually, my surgical rotation was not my strong point."

"Good to know."

She darted sidelong looks at him as they headed toward a covered pavilion. He looked even tanner than he had two days ago, his short hair had picked up some blond streaks, and his biceps were straining his blue T-shirt more than usual. He'd probably been working out in the sun nonstop—instead of coming to see her. Maybe he'd flopped into his bed at the end of the day, worn-out from all that hard labor for his ungrateful family.

"What have you been up to?" she blurted. No reason not to ask, right?

"Working my ass off. I got most of the backyard cleared. Luckily, I've got my best helper on the job with me."

"Vader? But he's been with us . . ."

"Not Vader. He wouldn't be able to munch grass at nearly the same rate as Goldie can."

She laughed as he led her into the pavilion, where various brawny men were milling around in an atmosphere of cheerful, organized chaos.

He elbowed her and pointed toward one of the grills, where a boyish-looking Hispanic man was roasting ears of corn wrapped in foil. The smell made her stomach rumble. Megan Callahan was hovering nearby, darting nervous glances at her mother. Candy Callahan stood at the fringes of the crowd, watching the goings-on like a queen surveying the troops.

"I think I've finally figured out who Megan's crush is," Patrick whispered.

Judging by Megan's bright pink cheeks, Lara had to agree. "I know that guy. I treated him for a burn on his scalp. He's a sweetheart."

Patrick gave her a narrow-eyed glance. "Oh yeah?"

It took her a moment to recognize the look on his face. When she did, she couldn't hold back her broad smile. "Wow. You're jealous. Of a twenty-something."

"I'm not jealous. Just curious if I'm going to have to defend my sister's territory."

He stationed himself behind a foil pan filled with marinating ribs and picked up a knife, brandishing it with a move right out of *Psycho*, the movie.

"No, no," said Lara quickly. "He's all hers. And no wonder they call you Psycho."

Patrick laughed, spun the knife around and plunged it between two of the ribs. "Actually, don't tell anyone, but the nickname's because I was studying psychology at Princeton. Hey, are you thirsty? I got us some drink tickets too."

"I'm good." She watched him carve a swift line between two ribs, his hands sure and precise. A flush of desire flooded her. How did the man manage to make chopping short ribs sexy? "But I can get you something, since you're busy."

"No. Stay here. I want to talk to you."

She wasn't sure she liked the sound of that. "What about?"

"How'd you like med school?"

"Excuse me?"

"What's your favorite movie?"

She shook her head at him, completely confused. "What are you talking about?"

"It's just questions, Lara. A normal part of getting to know each other."

"You must have some kind of fever from working in the fields. Have you been hydrating enough? We've known each other forever."

"And yet . . . we don't really know each other at all, do we?"

Apparently not, since she could never predict what crazy tangent he'd take next.

"You could ask me some too. For instance, you could ask me what Farris told me about the night of the accident."

"You talked to the firemen?" A sense of pleasure bloomed somewhere in her middle. She'd suggested he do that, but never thought he'd listen.

"I did. Farris was there. Said it was completely the fault of the owner of the motor home. Never even thought to blame me. Or either of us. There was nothing we could have done to avoid it. Except not be out there in the first place, of course." He piled the ribs into a bowl, said, "Ribs up!" and another fireman came running to take them.

"Yes, but . . ."

Someone slid another pan of ribs in front of him. But before diving in, Patrick looked up at her, eyes bright as a bluejay's tail feathers. "But what?"

"But then you and Liam wouldn't have been you and Liam. You guys loved riding those bikes. It was your thing, your brotherly bond thing."

He looked down, then up again, with an expression that surprised her. Almost . . . tender. "You always did know him best. When's the last time you . . . ?"

She braced herself, waiting for the one question about Liam that she didn't want to answer. But just then the equivalent of a Gypsy circus flocked into the park. Or maybe a Roman emperor with a bevy of queens. Vader, arm in arm with Dynah and Janey, strolled in first, followed by Annabella and Romaine, who were carrying two big bowls of salad. They were dressed in a dazzling kaleidoscope of colors, from Romaine's pure white to Janey's royal purple. Vader wore tight jeans and a T-shirt with a leather vest over it. Heads turned, whispers rippled through the crowd.

Lara stepped farther behind the table, as if trying to hide, the way she had as a mortified teenager whenever she went anywhere with the Goddesses. She felt a warm hand on one shoulder, and turned blindly toward Patrick, ready to meet a glance of scorn or pity. Instead, she found sympathy brightening those vivid eyes.

He cupped the back of her neck and murmured, "Isn't it funny how something can take you back to your childhood as if no time had passed and you're still about ten years old?"

She let out a shaky laugh. "It's not that I don't love them. I do, even though they're completely wacky and I don't understand half the things they say. It's like I was a duck plopped down in a family of swans."

His hand left her neck and traveled down her back, nudging her closer to him. "I think you've outswanned them all."

She shifted closer, her body craving the feel of his. Ah, that felt better. Snuggled next to him, she let out a sigh. With the Goddesses snagging all the attention at the barbecue, she could finally do what she'd been longing to since she walked in. She turned her head into his side, into the clean cotton of his T-shirt, and inhaled deeply. Then she rose onto her tiptoes and pressed a kiss into the warm flesh of his neck. She felt muscles move under her lips as he swallowed.

"Lara . . ."

"No one's watching," she said, nibbling at the place where his neck joined his shoulder, where powerful tendons ran beneath salty skin.

"No." Firmly, he picked her up and put her aside. She stared at him, shocked. "Why do you think I invited you here?"

"Um . . . "

"I *invited* you here so we could hang out at a public event, so we could talk instead of just groping each other all afternoon."

She drew away, wounded. "I wasn't 'groping' you."

He snagged the sleeve of her T-shirt and tugged her back to his side. "I didn't mean it that way. I like the groping. I could grope you all day. I just mean that maybe we ought to mix in more talking. More getting to know each other."

She pushed his hand away. "You're not making any sense. We've known each other forever. What are you really trying to say?"

His eyes flared vivid blue. "Okay. I'm really trying to say that I'm not some 'stud.' That's insulting."

Horror-struck, she stared at him. Her "stud" comment came back to her in all its stupidity. She hadn't intended to hurt Patrick with those words, but she could see in his eyes that she had. "I'm sorry," she whispered.

Of course he wasn't just a stud. He was a glorious, complicated, fascinating man, one she couldn't stop thinking about. And that was the most terrifying thought of all.

"Sorry," she said again, louder.

Blindly, she spun around and pushed her way through the crowd, past people balancing paper plates loaded with ribs, potato salad, and corn. The heavy aroma of roasting meat made her stomach clench. Before she could make it out of the park, Annabella stepped in front of her.

"What's going on, *querida*? You can't leave yet. There's a drama taking place."

"A drama?" As if she needed more drama right now. Unless it came with a chaser of tequila, she'd skip the drama. She tried to tug herself away from Annabella, but the older women only held on tighter.

"Look over there."

Lara glanced in the direction Annabella was pointing and could barely believe her eyes. Tall Janey had one long arm wrapped around Candy Callahan. And Mrs. Callahan was . . . crying. Not polite, discreet tears, but big, heaving sobs. Megan hovered behind them, dancing from one foot to the other, wringing her hands.

"Did Janey say something to her?" Janey had a tough-love way about her that struck some people the wrong way.

"No. Mrs. Callahan drew her aside and asked to speak privately. I think they took computer classes together a couple of years ago. Janey went over there with her, and then . . ." Annabella gave a graceful wrist gesture. "This!"

Just then Janey released Candy, who turned into Megan's waiting embrace. Janey, determination written all over her face, strode toward Lara and Annabella. "We need to open up another bedroom. Candy's going to stay with us for a while."

Lara's mouth fell open. Her gaze flew back to Candy, who was now delicately wiping her tear-soaked face and talking, more calmly, to Megan and Patrick , who was now with his mother and sister. He looked up, meeting Lara's gaze, then put one hand to his ear in a "Call me" gesture, his eyes burning into hers.

Chapter Eighteen

*P*atrick pulled up in front of the Haven a few hours later. His mother, jaw set, eyes dried, immediately stepped out and began unloading her bags. "Your father's probably thrown the rest of my stuff in the fireplace by now."

"Megan's there. She'll talk some sense into him." He got out to help her, but she waved him off.

"If something like that was possible, don't you think I would have done it by now? No, instead I have to uproot myself from my home to make my point. Stubborn, impossible man." Irritated, Candy yanked out the handle of her roller bag. "Thanks for the ride, Patrick."

"Are you sure this is—"

"Am I sure? *Sure? You* haven't been here, Patrick! Until you've lived with that man, slept in his bed every night for thirty-five years and squeezed his babies out of your body, you have nothing to say about this."

That pretty much put him out of the running. "I get it, but what am I supposed to say to him?"

"I. Don't. Care." She stomped toward the Haven, then tossed over her shoulder, "Tell him I'm getting some sexual and spiritual healing, that'll show him. Oh look, there's a porter for my bags. Yoo-hoo!"

A grinning Vader was coming toward them. "That's not a porter, Mom, that's . . ."

But Vader was already picking up both Candy's bags and swinging them onto his flexing shoulders. "Mrs. Callahan, the Goddesses are waiting inside. We're happy to have you here at the Haven." He winked at Patrick.

Patrick watched in bemusement as his mother followed Vader to the nymph-adorned front door. "Need a ride, Vader?" he asked.

"Nah, I'm going to camp out here tonight. Got a lot of ground to cover before I leave tomorrow."

They disappeared inside the front door. For a moment Patrick longed to follow them in. What seemed more fun, the Goddesses, Vader, and Lara, or his father and an obsessed llama?

He sighed and turned the key in the ignition. Not that he begrudged his mother her show of independence, but she'd left him in an awkward position. The brush-clearing was almost done, but how could he leave Megan to deal with his enraged father all by herself? He'd have to stick around until the crisis passed. Worse still, he'd probably have to actually communicate with his father, something he'd managed to avoid so far.

On the bright side, this would give him more time to figure out what this strange thing was with Lara.

Back at the ranch, Goldie lurched to her feet as soon as he drove up and trotted to greet him with a flurry of head movements and bleats. He gave her some love, scratching her behind the ears and murmuring to her, then headed inside the big house. He found Megan, barefoot in cutoffs, in the kitchen, chopping carrots into the tiniest imaginable pieces.

"That's going to take you all day," he said, lifting the knife from her hands.

"Patrick! What are you doing here?"

"Came to see if the house was still standing." He set to work on the carrots. "Where's Big Dog?"

"He storms in and out now and then. He's been on the phone a lot. I don't know who he's talking to. Probably his lawyer." She sighed. "He can't disinherit Mom, can he?"

"Not likely. Don't worry about Mom, she's fine."

"He hates the fact that she's at that place. Why couldn't she just stay at a bed and breakfast or something?"

Patrick shrugged. "She said she wanted some sexual healing."

Megan put her hand to her mouth, then giggled. Then, surprising him so much he nearly dropped the knife, she gave him a big hug. "I'm so glad you're here. It makes all this so much more bearable."

"Don't say that," Patrick muttered. "Makes me feel like an ass." He didn't deserve her affection. Hadn't he abandoned her along with his brother?

"Megan!" Big Dog snapped from the doorway. "What are you doing?"

Megan jumped away from Patrick. "Nothing. Just hugging."

"You said you were going to cook dinner since your mother's run out on us."

"I am. Patrick's helping."

Patrick turned and leaned against the kitchen counter, folding his arms, daring his father to object. Big Dog looked terrible, as if he'd aged five years in one day. His white hair bristled from his head. His jaw stuck out as he met Patrick's gaze, but he said nothing. Just turned and left.

"So nice to have those father-son talks every now and then," said Patrick as he turned back to the cutting board. "What are we making, anyway?"

Megan stared at the carrots and burst out laughing. "I have no idea. I just came in here and started chopping. What can you make with teeny tiny bits of carrots?"

He slung an arm over her shoulder. "I'll figure it out. You want to go do something else? Nap? Listen to some music? Make a phone call?"

"No. I want to stay here with my big brother."

It was as if she'd reached inside his heart and plucked a deep, hidden chord. He made a face to hide his emotion. "Fine. Then you'll have to tell me all about Pedro the Fireman."

She instantly went pink. "Only if you tell me about you and Lara." She leaned both elbows on the kitchen counter next to him. "Because rumors are flying."

Patrick opened the refrigerator and took out a package of chicken breasts. "Lara and I are old friends getting to know each other again. That's all anyone needs to know."

Megan plucked at the frayed edges of her cutoffs. "Big Dog won't like it, you know. He hates that place, especially now. And he never liked Liam being friends with Lara. He wanted him to have male friends instead. He used to rant about how Lara was trying to worm her way into Liam's life so she could take his money or something. And if he finds out you're seeing her—"

Patrick slammed the package of chicken onto the counter. "That's it, Megan. Big Dog has nothing to say about what I do or don't do with Lara. Is he really so pigheaded he doesn't know that Lara was the best friend Liam ever had? She never wanted anything from him. She learned sign language so she could help him out in school. How dare he? Big Dog isn't fit to kiss her hand. If he says so much as one word to me against Lara, so help me I'll—"

He broke off. Megan was staring at him with wide eyes and parted lips. "Oh my," she sighed. "You *do* like her. I bet you're in *love* with her. Ohhhh." She drew in a long breath. "What would Liam say if he knew?"

The package of chicken suddenly felt clammy in his hands. He stared at it dumbly. *Liam*. Would Liam hate him for sleeping with Lara? For getting involved with his closest, most loyal friend? He swore under his breath. No matter what, he had to treat Lara right. With the respect she deserved. Not like a hook-up, or some casual thing between two people with incredible chemistry. No more screwing in open-air fields, or ripping her clothes off at the drop of a hat.

For Liam's sake, he'd behave himself.

And then a lightning bolt of sheer longing nearly brought him to his knees. Where was Liam? Where was his sweet little brother? What was he doing, all on his own out there?

He and Megan finished making dinner, then brought a tray up to Big Dog, who seemed to be deeply wrapped up in some kind of project on his computer. He barely grunted as he accepted the chicken pot pie Patrick had made.

"At least he's working," whispered Megan. "He doesn't work all that much anymore. Mostly he holes up in the barn and paces around."

Patrick stared for a long moment at his father's bent head, his white hair a bright punctuation mark in the dark-leather-appointed study. He'd never forget the many times he'd been dragged in here for a lecture, or the roof-raising shouting matches between them. From that desk, his father had continued to dabble in Nevada politics, had acquired properties, sold them, played the stock market, and badgered his oldest son.

With that many fingers on the levers of power, how could he have any trouble tracking down one wayward deaf son?

They closed the study door and headed back downstairs. "What did they do to find Liam?" Patrick asked softly, remembering the rule about not mentioning Liam around Big Dog.

Megan gave a nervous glance back up the staircase, as if their father might be listening through the door.

"I think they hired a detective. Mom was totally freaking, but Dad was mostly just mad."

"For a change."

She gave him a sly look. "He said that his sons kept kicking him in the balls."

"Okay, fine." Patrick was sick of Big Dog's crap, even secondhand. "Can you find the name of the detective?"

"Why? You want to find Liam?"

"Why not? He's our brother, and he's missing."

"Maybe he likes it that way. He's a grown man."

"Yeah well, I don't like it that way."

Megan skipped down the stairs ahead of him. "You didn't even know he was missing until you came back."

"I get it, okay?" he said, more sharply than he meant to. "I left. I haven't been part of the scene here. I'm an irresponsible brother and son. I'm going to rot in hell. But fuck it, Megan, I want to find Liam."

"Okay, okay." Megan waited for him at the bottom

of the stairs, her hands shoved in the back pockets of her cutoffs. "It won't be easy to get the name, but I'll do my best."

"Cool. Sorry."

She shrugged.

On his way out the door, he slammed the side of his fist against the doorjamb. Did he have to be such a goddamn ass? Megan hadn't done anything wrong, and here he was, yelling at her. Being home made him completely nuts.

Home? Loveless wasn't his home. Home was San Gabriel. Not this freaking ranch filled with family crap. He needed to get the fuck away from here. Hop on a motorcycle, jump in a car, or fucking *run* all the way back to San Gabriel. Six months ago he probably would have done exactly that.

But now . . .

He needed to see this through. Ripping off his shirt, he headed for the toolshed to grab a machete. Might as well take out his frustrations on some brush.

That night, under a blanket of crystalline stars, Lara tapped on the door of Patrick's guesthouse. She'd spent the evening scolding herself for being such a coward and practically fleeing the barbecue. He deserved better than a half-assed, whispered apology. He deserved a face-to-face explanation.

When he opened the door, he looked half asleep and knee-weakeningly sexy in boxers and nothing else. She steeled herself; she was on a mission, after all. "I didn't finish apologizing at the barbecue," she began, then stopped as he drew her into his arms.

He murmured into her hair. "Did I dream you? Because I swear you were in my head, right before you knocked on the door. Please tell me you're real."

"Real as you are. And I came to try to explain."

But he didn't seem to be listening as he ran his hands all over her body.

"What are you doing?" she asked, already breathless.

"Seducing you."

"But you said we should get to know each other and . . . well, I came here to apologize again . . . I shouldn't have said what I did. I don't see you that way, I promise. That was me being an idiot. It happens. Some might say it happens a lot."

"Shhh." He shaped her body to his, and she melted against him. "You're not an idiot. I'm glad you're here."

Little shivers of pleasure swam through her like fish riding the currents. A warning bell sounded in the back of her mind. This was a new side of Patrick, tender and sleepy and tousled, and, just like all the other sides she'd discovered, it was drawing her in, deeper and deeper.

"I need you," he breathed into her ear.

Oh God. "I need you too." And heaven help her, it was true.

He filled his hands with her flesh, pushing aside shirt, bra, anything in his way. She eagerly pressed into him, and then they stopped talking, except for a few words here and there. "Come," as he led her to his bed, "Beautiful" as he undressed her, "Oh God" as he spread apart her knees.

In his dark, starlit bedroom, she abandoned herself to his touch. Maybe he'd been right all along and it was a dream. The best dream ever, in which he stroked her, enflamed her, teased her until all the boundaries between them melted away. Everything disappeared but the moans and cries they stifled in each other's necks, and the suction of flesh on flesh, and the roaring of blood in ears.

He didn't let her up afterward, not that she made any effort to escape. With his heavy arm draped across her, securing her at his side, she drifted into a deep, utterly contented sleep.

Lara stole away from the guesthouse while it was still dark. The last thing she wanted was to run into Big Dog Callahan after a night of dreamlike sex with his son. She ran down the driveway to the outer gate, where she'd left her car. Somehow that encounter had gone all wrong. She'd intended to apologize. She'd intended to talk about favorite movies or worst med school experiences or whatever he wanted.

Instead, they'd ended up in bed. Again.

Damn the man. He managed to confuse her every single time.

The next night, he surprised her again. Sometime after midnight she heard a tapping at her window. She opened the casement to find him perched on top of an aluminum ladder leaning against the outer wall. Still blinking in confusion, she watched him drop lightly into her room. The wicked gleam in his eyes rivaled the starlight outside.

"My firefighting experience sure comes in handy sometimes. I always wanted to sneak into the Haven." He advanced toward her, lustful intent written in every line of his body. Her mouth went dry.

"What about the Goddesses . . . your mother . . . Vader . . ."

"The only Goddess I want is you."

He was on her now, nuzzling her neck as though looking for a place to make his mark. Her breath caught in her throat. "Are you sure about this?"

"Don't turn me away. I'm here to worship you. What's this you're wearing?"

"Pajamas." Silk pajamas, as a matter of fact, so filmy the heat of his touch transmitted instantly to her skin. His hands curved around her hips, then skimmed lower, sending enchanted sparkles everywhere they went. She closed her eyes as her body turned to stardust in his hands.

"Very sexy." His voice had dropped an entire octave, from teasing to incendiary. "Mind if we get rid of them?" With a swift motion, he stripped off her pajama top. He bent to her breasts, weighing them reverently in his palms, whispering against her nipple. "I haven't been able to get you out of my mind all day. Maybe longer."

She made an inarticulate sound, completely consumed by the quicksilver heat hurtling through her system like an express train.

He switched to her other nipple, where he alternated between licking and whispering. Both made her equally crazy. He pushed down her pajama pants until they pooled around her feet. "Turn around."

She stood still while he knelt at her feet and worshipped her body with his hands and his scorching mouth. The silky roughness of his hair brushing against her flesh gave her chills. His tongue glided across the divot behind her knee, up the back of her thigh. Along the way he scattered tender nips that made her gasp. She swallowed the sounds, but couldn't quiet her jagged breathing. Soon, she forgot to care who might be listening at this time of night.

The night was theirs, hers and her surreptitious lover's.

She was naked, visibly trembling, as he pulled her against his front, so her bare skin pressed against his clothes. The roughness of denim scraped against the back of her thighs, the heat of his chest radiated through his T-shirt. Her body clenched, already on the edge of orgasm.

"My wild goddess," he whispered in her ear. "I want you." One hand crushed her breasts together, the other clamped between her legs. She arched back against him, biting the inside of her cheek to keep from sobbing with pleasure. His hands felt so good on her body, they knew just how to move and find the spots that cried out for his touch.

Then he swung her around so she faced the window, the gardenia-scented night air kissing her nipples. He bent her over, placed her hands on the window-sill, then unzipped his jeans. The sharp sound of the zipper made her blood run fast. Oh, how she wanted him. Why had no one ever warned her she could crave someone this much? And then his hard length was inside her, his grip tight on her hips.

She fixed her gaze on the gleam of moonlight on the ladder, which turned to a blur as wild pleasure commanded her senses. The world around her lost its form, and became shadow and brilliance, texture and hardness, heat and yearning. Her body flowed with his, going where he wanted, where she needed to be, where the explosion beckoned. Her climax blindsided her, coming so quickly she let out a little cry before burying her face in the crook of her arm. Brilliant waves flashed through her and, it seemed, around her, incinerating the line between them, transforming her from the inside out.

Did he feel it too? He stiffened, his hips flexing hard against her rear, pushing her against the windowsill. She gave herself to his pleasure until his low groan filtered into the room, mingling with the murmur of cicadas outside.

"Lara," he murmured, as if it was all he could think

to say. He stood her up, then turned her so she nestled against his chest. As he rested his cheek on her head, she felt the racing beat of his heart, the heavy drape of his embracing arms. A deep tenderness swamped her—he'd needed her just as much as she'd needed him. They were in this together. A different sort of heat bloomed inside her, something warm and grateful and even humble.

To steady herself, she wrapped her arms around him, savoring his solid strength, the spent power still coiled inside him. No words seemed necessary, or even desired. The current that still flowed between them overruled any other form of communication.

They stood melded together for a long, silent, utterly satisfied moment. Slowly she became aware of the night sounds outside the window, the murmur of cicadas, the hum of her old computer.

Eventually, she drew away and murmured, "So, was the Haven all you expected?"

"Better than my wildest dreams." He lifted his head, as if noticing her room for the first time. "Since I'm here, want to show me the sights? It's like the Forbidden City in here."

"Really? You want to see the rest of the Haven?"

"Hell, yes. I spent enough time wondering about it as a kid."

So for the next hour or so they ran around the Haven in their underwear, giggling like little kids. She showed him the Be Loved and Welcomed Room, where they made a pillow fort out of meditation cushions. They snuck into the Energy Cleansing steam room, where they stripped, got as sweaty as they could stand, then ran outside into air that felt new born, fresh from the earth. They played naked tag in the meditation garden, Patrick vaulting over benches, Lara hiding behind the gong. When he struck poses imitating some of the sacred statues dotting the garden, she laughed so hard she nearly choked from the effort of keeping quiet.

If only she'd had *this* when she first came here. This lightheartedness, this goofy fun. Being with Patrick lightened all those dark nooks and crannies that still lurked in her heart. She didn't want it to ever end. They laughed and played and teased and kissed until the rising sun sent curious pink tendrils over the horizon.

Just before dawn, Patrick scooped up his clothes, gave her one last, deep kiss, and disappeared into the shadows beyond the house. The last thing she heard was a faint war whoop from the direction of the driveway. An eerie chill went through her as she remembered the last time she'd heard that sound from Patrick.

Chapter Nineteen

A couple hours later Lara awoke to banging overhead. And cursing. Then heavy footsteps, and a pounding on her door.

"Lara, are you up?" Vader called.

She rolled out of bed and, with a flush of hot memory, put her silk pajamas back on. "Do I have a choice?" she grumbled as she opened the door.

Covered in sawdust, Vader filled the doorway. "I'm leaving in a few, but I have to talk to you first. I won't have time to get the roof done. I got the tar paper down, but you're going to have to hire someone to finish it."

"Hire someone?" With what funds, exactly?

"I don't know when I can get back. I have stuff going on at home too."

"No, no, I totally understand," she said quickly. "You've been great. You've done more than enough, I can't tell you how much I appreciate it."

"I got something out of it too, you know. Cherie won't

know what hit her." He winced and hooked his thumbs in the belt loops of his jeans. "Figure of speech."

Lara pushed a tangle of hair out of her eyes, taking in the manly figure before her. Vader was strong, kind, and pretty good looking, now that she thought about it. "You know something, Vader?"

He gazed down at her with wary walnut-brown eyes. She leaned in closer and lowered her voice.

"I wouldn't pay too much attention to what the Goddesses told you. You're fine just the way you are. I bet Cherie thinks so too."

A muscle flickered in his jaw.

"Excuse me?" Annabella appeared behind him. "Did you really just tell him not to pay attention to our pearls of wisdom?"

"Eavesdropping?"

"No, just delivering bad news. I was going to, how do you say, sugar it, but somehow I no longer feel the need." Annabella raised one eyebrow in a magnificently disdainful manner.

Lara groaned. It was too early for drama. "What would another day in Loveless be without my morning dose of bad news? Go on, hit me."

"Olson's Hardware is cutting us off. No more trade for materials. He wants cash. No credit, just cash."

"Well, he's not the only hardware store in town. We'll work with someone else."

"I already tried Ace, Lowery's, and Shop and Save. They all say the same thing. Cash in hand. No trade. No credit."

Lara ran a hand through her hair, nearly getting it stuck in the thick tangles. A sprig of lavender caught in her fingers. She closed her fist around it before anyone could see it and question her. "Maybe we can get by with what we already have. Vader, can we?"

He shook his head. "No way. We still need shingles for the roof. Bunch of two by fours, one by sixes, not to mention screws, nails, hardware for the new windows—"

She held up a hand. "Okay, okay, I get it. We need tons more stuff and no way to purchase it."

All three fell silent.

"What shall we do, Lara?" Annabella asked.

Lara glanced longingly back at her bed. She knew what she *wanted* to do. Go back to bed. Better yet, go back to Patrick's bed. Better yet, go back to a time when she didn't have to worry about lumber and work trade and roofers.

She worried at her bottom lip. Something didn't sound right here. The last time she'd seen Mr. Olson—at the barbecue—he'd been perfectly friendly.

The barbecue. The same barbecue where Candy Callahan had decided to leave the ranch and stay at the Haven.

"Did Mr. Olson happen to mention why he didn't want to continue the trade?"

Annabella gave one of her gracefully nonchalant shrugs. "No, *querida.*"

"Fine. I'll make him tell me to my face." She marched to her closet, which still held all her old clothes. For this mission, she needed just the right outfit.

"What are you doing, Lara?"

"I'll tell you what I'm not doing." She yanked out a pair of black pants from her dresser, then found a black jacket with that extra dominatrix flair. "I'm not going to let Big Dog get away with this."

Suspicious confirmed. Lara roared up the Callahan driveway—well, as much as a fuel-efficient Aveo could roar. A plume of exhaust would have been so satisfying. Instead the little white car scooted down the circular drive, delivering her smoothly to the front door. She mounted the stairs, her rage rising the closer she got to the source of all her problems.

When several loud bangs on the door got no response, she opened it and called, "Megan? Patrick? Anyone here?"

Megan came hurrying in from the back somewhere, iPod buds dangling from her ears. "Sorry, Lara. Come on in."

"Is your father here?"

Megan looked wary. "In the barn, I think. Why?"

"I need to talk to him." She turned on her heel and clattered down the steps to the yard. Megan dashed after her.

"Why? Lara, stop. I don't think you should do that."

"This is between me and him, Megan. You can pretend you never even saw me if you want."

"Hey! I'm not that cowardly."

Lara dashed across the yard to the old barn, which looked like it needed some major repairs. The big double door was not only open, but off its hinges. With Megan at her heels, she stormed inside. Dust motes sparkled in the hazy light that filtered through the cracks in the roof. Old pieces of farm equipment shared space with bales of hay, coils of rope, and old barrels. After a quick scan, she spotted Patrick's father in a sort of den in the far corner of the barn. He lounged on a sway-backed couch, his feet propped on a bale of hay, a cigar smoldering in an ashtray on his lap.

Big Dog scowled at the sight of her. "What are you doing here? A man's home is his castle."

Lara got right to the point. "I talked to Mr. Olson. You threatened him so he'd stop selling us lumber."

A smug expression spread over Big Dog's face. "This old dog still has a few tricks up his sleeve, eh?"

Lara clenched her fists and sternly told herself to keep her cool and not go straight from zero to shouting match. She forced her voice to sound calm. "Why are you doing this? Because Candy's staying with us?"

"That's *Mrs. Callahan* to trash like you."

Lara felt her face go white. Big Dog had never wasted his charm on her, but he'd never been so blunt either. *Trash.* The word reverberated through her brain, throwing her off stride. "Your wife told me to call her Candy because she's a nice lady. Everyone at the Haven loves her."

Oops. Wrong move.

Big Dog snarled, literally snarled, like an actual dog. "Don't mention that place in here."

"Mr. Callahan." Lara took a deep breath. "I know you're upset about your wife . . . um, taking a little break. It's understandable. Anyone would be. They teach workshops about it at the Haven . . ." Noticing the ruddy color in his cheeks, she decided to drop that angle. "Maybe you should use this time to appreciate your wife and what she means to you."

Behind her, she heard Megan's strangled snort.

"I'm using this time exactly how I want to." Big Dog lumbered to his feet and loomed over her. "No hardware store in town will take your business. No roofer, no carpenter, no handyman, not even a Mexican day laborer will set foot on that piece of donkey-crap land you got over there."

Lara planted her feet as if she were leaning into a hurricane. That's how it felt—a blast of high-decibel hostility coming at her in waves. "You're trying to destroy the Haven, is that it? It won't work. We can survive without lumber. The Haven is about the people, not the place."

"You mean the whores!"

"Dad!" Megan gasped.

"They're not whores," said Lara through gritted teeth. *Don't argue, don't argue. He's just trying to piss you off. And it's working. Keep your cool. Stay logical.* "They help people. And right now they're helping your wife and you should be grateful."

Yikes. She was saying all the wrong things. She held her breath as Big Dog seemed to swell up like a rage-filled helium balloon. "If I may, Mr. Callahan, I hope you've gotten your blood pressure checked, because judging by the vascularization I see on your skin, you could damage your heart if you keep on like this."

He opened his mouth, snapped it shut, struggling with himself over something. Finally, the frightening scarlet tinge in his face subsided. He focused on her as if seeing her for the first time. "Who do you think you are, a doctor?"

"Well, yes. I am a doctor. I'm just finishing up my residency in the family medicine program at San Diego Hospital."

He walked to a barrel that sat in the corner and plucked a long-handled ladle off the wall. He lifted the lid and dipped the ladle inside. It came out filled with water, which he slurped. Lara squinted at the bits of hay floating on the surface. It didn't look sanitary to her, but Big Dog wouldn't appreciate her questioning *everything*.

"So you left that witch's coven and went and made something of yourself." He smacked his lips, sending a few drops of water flying.

"I wouldn't phrase it exactly like that."

He hung the ladle back on its hook, though it seemed to take him a few moments. "Then why don't you go back to wherever you live and leave things in

Loveless the way they are? You can start by leaving my sons alone."

Lara startled. "Your *sons*?"

"You know what I'm talking about. I see the phone bills. I wouldn't be surprised if you were seducing both of them."

Lara's mind reeled. Insult aside, this was important information. Big Dog was tracking Liam's text messages. She made a mental note to warn Liam.

Taking a deep breath, she fought to regain her calm. "We're getting off track here, Mr. Callahan. I came here to discuss the Haven, not my personal life."

"It's the same damn thing. They have my wife. You've got your claws into my son. I won't stand for it." Crimson flashed in his ruddy cheeks like a bullfighter's cape.

"No claws are involved, I promise, Mr. Callahan," Lara said, aiming for a soothing tone.

"Tell you what," he trumpeted. "Let's make a deal. Right here, right now. I'll buy that place over there if you stop banging my son. It'll be over soon no matter what. No Callahan would marry trash like you. Might as well get what you can before he gets rid of you."

Megan's sharply indrawn breath seemed to echo through the barn like a gunshot. It was a shot right through the heart, and Lara knew she'd feel the hurt later. For now, blood sang in her ears, and all caution fled like cobwebs before a broom.

Lara strode toward Big Dog until her nose was level with the buttons on his blue chambray shirt. "I wouldn't sell the Haven to you if I was down to my last penny. No wonder your entire family's bailing on you. First Patrick, then Liam . . ." Huge warning bells went off in her brain. *Stop. Stop now before you give away something about Liam.* "If you want to have any family members left, maybe you should try listening once in a while instead of blustering away like a big old whale."

That speech wasn't nearly satisfying enough. But tears were prickling the backs of her eyeballs, and she couldn't let Big Dog see them. *No weakness. Never let them see they got to you.* She whirled around, nearly bumping into Megan. "Sorry," she managed as she brushed past the girl and dashed out of the barn.

Trash like you. All the humiliation she'd suffered while growing up in Loveless rushed back. All the snickering in the school hallways, the snide comments in the girls' bathroom, the leers from idiotic boys who thought she might be "easy." The tight-mouthed looks of disapproval at the grocery store, the after-school jobs no one offered her. Everything she'd fled was still with her.

Trash like you.

It didn't matter if she'd become a doctor. It didn't matter if she hadn't been back to the Haven in ten years. In Big Dog's eyes she was . . . trash. And he didn't want her sleeping with his son.

All of a sudden she felt dirty for doing exactly that. By having sex with Patrick, she'd confirmed Big Dog's opinion of her. Why hadn't she stuck to her comfort zone, to her pleasant, sex-free existence? Getting involved with a Callahan had to be the worst mistake of her life.

But they weren't "involved." Not really. Nothing she couldn't fix before it went too far.

Somehow she found herself at her little Aveo, though she didn't remember her flight out of the barn. Hands trembling, she managed to open the door and slide into the driver's seat. Tears blurred her vision. As she started the car, an image of the Goddesses, sitting around the low table with their ginger tea and votive candles, brought a flood of warmth. The Goddesses never judged her. They'd always accepted her, even at her teenage moodiest. Even when she was trying to sell their home out from under them. They might be many crazy things, but they were unconditionally loving and kind.

"Home, James," she told her little rental car. And strangely enough, she kind of meant it.

Patrick caught no more than a flash of white as Lara's little car zoomed away from the ranch. He picked up his pace, jogging the rest of the way from the outer fields, where he'd been checking on the fire line along the road. Had Lara come to see him, then left when she couldn't find him? He checked his cell phone, but he hadn't missed any calls. Goldie trotted behind him, bleating in protest, as if to remind Patrick she wasn't a damn gazelle.

Inside, a strange, shell-shocked silence filled the house. His father was thumping around upstairs. Megan was nowhere to be seen.

Patrick dashed up the stairs. Without bothering to knock, he pushed open his father's study door. The untidy state of the room gave him a shock. Piles of paper cluttered the corners. He spotted a crumb-covered plate balanced on a windowsill. Red Sharpie markings dotted the map of Nevada that stretched across one wall.

Big Dog looked up from his desk, flashing his good-mood smile.

"Good. You're here. Ran off that hippie. Doubt she'll be back." He brushed his hands together.

"What are you talking about?"

"That Haven girl. Told her to stay away from my son. Whatever I said, it worked like a charm. She ran away like I set a fire hose on her. Not a bad idea, that."

"You bas—" Patrick stopped himself. "Big Dog, that was way out of line. My life is my business, not yours."

"Don't work that way, son. You're a Callahan until you die."

"Oh yeah? Unless you decide to cut me off and kick me out? You're full of shit."

"Don't speak to your father like that," Callahan roared so suddenly that Patrick took a step back. For the first time, he wondered if his father was really losing it.

"Look, Dad," he said in a placating voice. "Let's not fight now. Just tell me what you said to Lara."

"I told her the truth. I don't want someone like her around my family. Especially in my son's bed."

"I choose who's in my bed, not you."

"You shouldn't get to choose what to eat for dinner, boy. You want that hippie girl? You want to be a fireman? I aimed higher than that for you."

"Stop it now, Dad, I'm warning you."

"You're warning *me*? No, I'm warning you, son. Stay away from that place, unless it's to grab your mother and bring her back where she belongs. I've got plans for that sinkhole and they don't involve my son boinking that girl."

"Plans? What plans? What are you talking about?"

A strange, wary expression came over his father's face. He stepped away from the window and hobbled closer. Patrick noticed a speck of spittle on his father's cheek. He would have looked unhinged except for the determination in his eyes. "My plans are my business. But if you want things to come out okay for that girl, stay away from her. That's all I'm going to say."

"All you're going to say, huh?"

"That's it."

Patrick stepped forward, meeting his father in the middle of the room. It was one thing for his father to go after him, but he wouldn't let Lara get hurt. "Whatever you try to do to Lara or the Haven, I'll fight. You want a Callahan family feud to hit the news? Leave Lara alone or I'll start airing dirty laundry. No shortage of that."

They stood in a kind of standoff, Big Dog looming over him by a head. Patrick tried to interpret the flow of expressions across his father's face, but none of it was what he expected. Anger, surprise, fear . . . but mostly confusion.

"Get out," Big Dog finally said in a low voice. "Get out of my house."

Patrick didn't need to be told twice. It was a relief to be kicked out, once again. He held his father's gaze for one more moment, just to show he was leaving on his own terms, then headed for the door.

"All the structures are cleared to a hundred and fifty feet," he said over his shoulder. "This place is about as fire safe as it's going to get. I recommend you hire someone to tend to it on a regular basis. I was planning to rip off those old shingles on the barn roof and put up something more fire-resistant, but maybe you can hire someone for that too."

"Where are you going?" Big Dog shouted as Patrick jogged down the stairs.

Patrick didn't listen. Hadn't his father just kicked him out? He should get his story straight. The whole thing felt like the heart-of-darkness scene with the demented colonel in *Apocalypse Now*. Each step that took him farther away from Big Dog was a relief.

He was so eager to get out that he nearly barreled over Megan, who was waiting at the bottom of the stairs.

He steadied her before she could topple over. "Sorry, Meggie."

"What's going on?"

"I just got fired. Again." He kept moving, already making a mental list of the things he needed to do before he took off.

"What are you talking about?"

"He went too far. He insulted Lara, he's trying to manipulate and threaten me. The brush clearing is more or less done. Time for me to get the hell out. We both agree on that."

He pushed open the screen door and strode outside, where suffocating heat enveloped him. Goldie greeted him with an eager little hop.

Megan gave a soft gasp as she scurried after him. "You mean you're leaving?"

"Yep. My job's done. Managed to tick the old man off as a bonus, just for old times' sake."

He stalked across the yard to the guesthouse. Inside, he flung open the closet where he'd stashed his duffel bag. It was stuffed in the corner along with his Whites and other wildfire gear. He hauled everything out and thrust the boots into the bottom of the bag.

"This isn't a joke, Patrick." Megan sounded as if she were about to cry—or maybe she already was crying. He avoided her gaze, preferring to keep her as a hovering blur at the edge of his vision. He needed to focus on grabbing his things and heading out.

"Sorry. I always joke when I'm edgy. Keeps things from getting ugly." Duffel in hand, he strode into the bedroom, noticing that the sheets were still tangled from that fever dream of an encounter two nights ago.

Lara.

He had to see her. He'd make sure to clear things up with her before he left town. It wasn't as if they had a "relationship." Of course he'd miss her, miss her sandalwood scent, the way she cut through his crap, her down-to-the-bone kindness. He ruthlessly suppressed thoughts of everything else he'd miss, the heat between them, the laughter, the sense of rightness. Maybe they could see each other back in California. Yes, that might work.

With a huge sense of relief, he picked up an armful of sweaty T-shirts piled in the corner. "I'll have to hit a Laundromat on the way out of town."

"We have a washer-dryer right here. I'm doing laundry later today, I'll throw your stuff in too," said Megan.

"No biggie, honey. I do my own laundry at home all the time."

He tossed his duffel on the bed, then added his extra pair of jeans and a couple pairs of boxers.

"It's a good thing I travel light." He snapped his fingers. "Shaving kit."

He hurried into the bathroom. After stuffing his razor, shaving cream, toothbrush, and toothpaste in the bag, he glanced around the bathroom to see what was left. His gaze snagged on his own reflection in the mirror—his, and his sister's. There he was, scruffy and sweaty from his work in the fields. A bit red-eyed from squinting against the sun. Shadows under his eyes from two consecutive late, sex-drenched nights.

And there was his little sister right behind him, looking as if the sky was falling. Her mouth wobbled, her glasses had slipped down her nose. Little gingery tendrils of hair clung to her freckled face. "Don't do this," she whispered.

"Honey." Try as he might, he couldn't drag his eyes from her woebegone reflection in the mirror. "I'm done. In every sense. Besides, he told me to get out."

She bit her lip, looking tragic. "He doesn't always mean everything he says."

"He hates having me here. You'll be fine. Mom will come back. Everything will go back to normal."

Her eyebrows drew together in a soft, accusing line. "Normal? You mean the normal where you're not here?"

"I don't live here, remember?"

He couldn't take this. Shouldn't have to take this. Brushing past her, he left the bathroom, grabbed his duffel, stuffed everything inside and cinched it closed. "I'll do what I can from San Gabriel, okay? You can call me anytime."

At the front door, he pulled her in for a tight hug. She clung to him, shaking. *She's just upset,* he told himself. *She'll be fine.*

"Call me, okay? Every day if you want."

She nodded against his chest, then pulled away to swipe at her tears with the back of her hand. He noticed that she wouldn't meet his eyes.

"Love you, honey."

Still she wouldn't look at him.

To hell with it. He had to get going. Now that he'd decided to hit the road, he couldn't wait to get going. He flung open the front door.

Maaaah. Goldie stood right outside, the breeze ruffling her white fur. She wasn't afraid to meet his eyes. On the contrary, she fixed him with her devoted, golden gaze, her jaw moving back and forth, grass dangling from either side of her mouth.

"Goldie, this is it for a while." He patted her head and chucked her under the chin. Her eyes closed halfway and she made that affectionate rumbling sound he thought of as a purr.

The sound mingled with the sniffling behind him.

And the whisper of the wind in the tall grass near the barn—an area he hadn't tended to yet. But drowning out all those sounds was the chant of his own guilty conscience.

You can't leave, it told him. *They need you here.*

Where had that damn conscience come from? He'd been doing just fine without it.

Slowly, he dropped his duffel bag to the ground, then shoved his hands in his pockets. Goldie nuzzled the duffel with her head. He felt Megan's arms come around him from behind.

"Thank you thank you thank you," she said, her voice breaking. "You're the best brother ever."

That should have felt good. But instead it gave him an empty, hollow feeling. If he was such a great brother, why didn't he know where his little brother was?

Chapter Twenty

*P*atrick finally tracked Lara down at the Loveless city hall. She was arguing with a clerk behind the desk of the licensing department. She wore a conservative navy blazer that didn't quite manage to disguise her curves. As he approached, she threw up her hands, whirled around, and nearly slammed into him. He steadied her with a hand on each elbow.

"What's going on?"

She narrowed her eyes at him. "Hello, Callahan." Yanking her arms out of his grip, she stalked past him. He followed, lengthening his stride.

"Uh-oh. What'd Big Dog do?"

"Your father is a one-man wrecking ball. He doesn't want me to sell the place, he doesn't want us to fix it up, and now . . . he doesn't want us to be in business at all."

"Well, that's hardly a surprise. He campaigned against brothels in Nevada."

"No, that's not it." She slammed a sheaf of papers

against his chest. "He's trying to get our business license revoked because we *aren't* providing brothel-type services anymore. You'd think he'd be happy, right? Seriously, what does he want from us?"

"You're asking the wrong Callahan." He hurried to hold the front door open for her. She sailed through, barely noticing the gesture.

"You know what?" Her long hair flowed like a rebel flag behind her as she loped down the stairs. "This ticks me off so much I'm tempted to sell my body on the streets just so we can get our license back."

"Come on, Lara."

She didn't seem to hear him. "If I weren't so sexually repressed and uptight, maybe I would."

Sexually repressed? That wouldn't be his description of his wild nights with her. It was as if she'd forgotten them—as if the light of day had blotted them out.

"He's pulling every string he can think of," she continued, "and now he's trying to bury us in paperwork. Good thing Janey's a master at this stuff. Big Dog doesn't know who he's messing with."

The fluctuating flush in her cheeks gave him an uneasy feeling. Something was definitely up. He snagged her arm, stopping her headlong rush down Main Street. "Lara, can we talk? Cup of coffee or something?"

She wouldn't meet his eyes, instead shading hers to scan the street. "I don't have time. I need to get these forms to Janey. If only I could remember where I parked my car."

"I'll give you a ride. Look, I know you came to the house and talked to Big Dog today. I already told him to back off. He won't hurt you again, if I have anything to do with it. I just want to make sure you're okay."

"As you can see, I'm fine," she said briskly. "Oh, there's my car." She turned to him with a smile so forced it was more of a grimace. "You don't have to worry about me. I don't need help from a Callahan. I'm sure you'll be heading back to California soon anyway. It was really cool to get to know you again after all this time." She stuck out her hand.

He stared at it, dumbfounded. "What are you doing?"

"Shaking hands."

"Shaking hands?"

"Why not? I just thought, since we've been pretty intimate, all things considered . . ."

"Pretty intimate. All things considered." Though he realized he was repeating each outrageous phrase like a parrot, he couldn't seem to help himself.

She withdrew her hand. "Fine. No handshake, if you want to play it that way."

He grabbed her elbow and swung her up close against his body. "I'm not playing, Lara," he said fiercely. "You're the one that's playing. Mind telling me what the game is?"

Whiskey-gold eyes flashed at him. "You're manhandling me."

"And you're brushing me off." They stayed like that, gazes locked together, heat rising between them. He felt the race of her heart against his solar plexus, saw the pulse in her throat going wild. "At least tell me what's going on."

"Fine," she finally managed, in a choked voice. "I don't think we should be involved anymore. We'll still be friends, of course. I'm glad we got to know each other again. And I really appreciated the . . . well, having sex with you."

Patrick went still. He suddenly felt as if he were looking down at her from a great distance. Maybe he ought to be insulted or upset. Or angry. And maybe later he would be. But for now he saw the hurt lurking at the back of her eyes. "What exactly did Big Dog say to you?"

She wrenched herself away from him. Digging into the pocket of her blazer for her keys, she practically ran for her car. "I don't want to talk about it."

"For God's sake, Lara, you can't let him get to you. He's a jackass most of the time. Everyone in the frickin' state knows it."

"Maybe it's not about him." She opened the car door and stepped behind it as if it were some kind of shield. "Maybe it's about me and what kind of person I want to be."

"You mean the kind of person who runs when things get tough or someone says something nasty?"

She flinched. Then she raised her chin and tossed her hair over her shoulder. "Interesting comment, coming from you. I couldn't have a better role model, could I?"

Now that stung. The slam of her car door, as she slid inside, punctuated her insult with a bang. She rolled down the window with one long press of her finger. Two bright spots of color burned in her cheeks as she leaned out.

"Maybe I just don't want to be someone who has casual sex."

Unfair. Hadn't he been the one to suggest they get to know each other more? "That's a load of crap."

She lifted her nose in the air, looking so prim and superior he wanted to rip the fake-conservative blazer right off her. With another jab of her finger on the window control, glass rose between them.

Before he could protest that things between them had never been "casual," that this time he wasn't running, that he was sticking it out through all kinds of crap, she was driving down the street.

Well, *hell.*

Lara was still riding her self-righteous high when she walked into the Haven. She stopped dead at the sight of the Goddesses and Candy, all assembled in the Be Loved and Welcomed Room. "Did I miss a memo?"

Since the Haven didn't do "memos," preferring scrawled messages on the chalkboard, this was unlikely.

"We had some things to discuss without you," said Janey in her blunt way.

"Well." Lara fingered the paperwork from the city hall. While she'd been off fighting the municipal bureaucracy, they'd been meeting without her. It rankled, even though last month she would have screamed at the thought of having to attend a Haven meeting. "What's up?"

"Sit down, *querida,*" said Annabella, offering her a cushion.

"I'd rather stand. Pacing around nervously sounds good right now." She spared a glance for Candy. If Patrick's mother weren't there, she wouldn't mind venting about her frustrations with the male Callahans. Candy, looking serious, sipped from a mug painted with a yellow happy face.

Janey rang a meditation bell. "Focus, please. Let's bring our energy inward. We've important things to discuss."

Lara pressed her lips together. All the meditation bells in the world weren't going to make Big Dog Callahan leave them alone. She waited while the bell tone faded away. But the enforced moment of reflection brought only one thing to mind: the wounded look on Patrick's face when she'd lashed out at him.

"Lara, my dear," said Janey when the last vibration of the bell had died away. "We've come to a community decision that it's time for you to go back to San Diego."

"What?"

"Do you want to sit down now?" Romaine whispered.

Lara sank onto the cushion that suddenly appeared at her feet. "Why?"

"You've done all you can do here," said Janey. "You have a life in San Diego, and it involves things that are more important than our dramas."

"It's a close thing," said Dynah, "but I'd give saving lives the edge over the Haven horror show."

"But Aunt Tam—"

"Would not want your career completely upended by her death. She wanted to give you a gift, not force you to spend weeks or months whipping us into shape. We've decided you should sell the place."

Lara's jaw dropped. "But . . . but . . ."

"We'll be fine. We put our heads together and came up with a list of former clients who might be interested in buying the Haven. Mr. Callahan's influence doesn't go beyond the borders of the state."

"Or even the town," added Candy.

"Someone will want to buy it. If they want to run it as a sexual healing center, a spa, a brothel, or a cactus farm, that's up to them. Maybe we'll stay, maybe we won't. But there's life beyond the Haven. None of us needs to be tied to it forever, especially you, Lara."

Everything Janey said made so much sense. If she went back to San Diego, she wouldn't have to learn how to patch a roof. Or come up with workshop ideas for senior swingers. Or prostitute herself to qualify for a brothel license.

She winced as she remembered her empty threat and Patrick's face as she'd flung it at him. But that was an issue for another moment.

"I'll talk to the lawyer back in San Diego too," she said slowly. "Maybe he knows a realtor we can work with who isn't beholden to Big Dog."

"I bet I can rustle up a name or two," said Candy. "It would be my pleasure."

In San Diego she wouldn't have to deal with Big Dog's opinion of her ever again. She wouldn't have to remember her former outcast status every time she walked down Main Street. She could resume her life as a respected, well-educated, capable, skilled medical professional.

Best of all, she wouldn't even be letting the Goddesses down—they were telling her to go back, *urging* her, voting on it in her absence. What was she waiting for?

She nodded. "You're right." Funny how the words clogged in her throat. Of course they were right. Why wouldn't they be right?

"Let's face it, you never liked it here anyway, even as a little girl. I still remember the look on your face when you first saw Kuan-Yin." Annabella gestured to the statue behind her.

"Yes, but that was—" She broke off. The Goddesses were all smiling at her benevolently, just as they had when she'd arrived as a grief-stricken kid. She thought of the carob chip cookies Aunt Tam had baked for the occasion. Janey had made her a stuffed panda out of a pair of old pajamas. Annabella offered a prayer in Portuguese. They'd been so worried for her, and so kind. Suddenly, unexpected tears stung her eyes. She blinked madly, trying to beat them back.

"*Querida?* Are you all right?"

Blindly, she turned away. "It was never you guys. You were always so nice to me."

The soft fragrance of lavender mixed with sandalwood surrounded her as Annabella came to her side. "Then what, *amor*? Why do you cry?"

Lara shook her head fiercely. God, she hated crying. She was strong, she'd had to be, that's what got her through those tough times. But Annabella's hand on her back was so soothing, and the tinkling of the fountain so hypnotic. And all the emotion she'd shoved aside clamored to get out.

"I didn't want anyone . . . anyone taking the place of my parents," she choked out. "I didn't want another family. I wanted *them*. My mom and dad."

Then the tears came in earnest, deep, unstoppable sobs that shook her body like mini-earthquakes. And all the Goddesses were surrounding her with a cloud of sympathetic murmurs and soft hugs.

She stopped fighting and let the grief well up . . . for her parents, for Aunt Tam . . . for the wounded heart she'd kept locked up for so long.

For the next week, Patrick worked with the Cat on the fire line that ran along the road that bordered the ranch on two sides. He liked this project because it kept him away from the house and reduced the risk of another fight with his father. Big Dog hadn't seemed surprised to see him stay; maybe he forgot that he'd kicked him out. Who could tell what went on in that man's mind?

He'd gotten one brief phone message from Lara, explaining that she was going back to San Diego, wishing him well, and apologizing for her crack about being a bad role model.

He hadn't called her back. He wanted to. But he didn't trust himself to hang onto his manners if he reached her. What was the point, anyway? If she wanted to blow him off, pretend they had nothing between them besides sex and an old "friendship," well, maybe she was right. Women were the experts on things like that, right?

He'd spoken to his mother several times. At first he'd intended to beg her to come back. But as soon as he heard the cheerfulness in her voice, he changed his mind. Instead, he promised her he wouldn't upset Big Dog and that he wouldn't let Megan do all the work.

Keeping that promise was another matter. Big Dog lurched around the house, often with his Bluetooth clamped to his ear, his voice a low rumble of complaint. When Patrick asked who he was talking to, he always answered, "Old buddy from the administration."

He spent much of his time closeted in his study, and the rest in the barn or roaming the property.

"You did a good job on the clearing," he told Patrick after one of these long walks.

Patrick had been so bowled over, he barely remembered to say thank you. So maybe his father wasn't *always* a jerk. He'd had his decent moments even during Patrick's rebellious years. Those moments just seemed fewer and further between.

But Big Dog's softening only went so far. One day, when he was lounging in the TV room with a beer, smiling over the fact that his name had come up in a TV report about colorful politicians, Patrick pulled up a stool and asked him about the detective he'd hired to look for Liam.

Big Dog's broad smile disappeared at the speed of Road Runner in fast forward. "You dare to ask me about your brother?"

"Yes. I dare. I want to find him. What if he's in trouble?"

"It's not your problem."

Patrick stared at him. "Do you know where he is?"

Big Dog wouldn't answer. Red crept up his face in that ominous way they all dreaded.

Patrick kept his voice as even as possible, though everything in him wanted to scream at his father. "I just want to see him. That's all."

"Mind your own business," growled Big Dog.

Fuck. Patrick kicked over the stool and flung himself out of the room before he lost it and upset his father, as he'd promised his mother he wouldn't do. Outside, he strode toward the ancient dirt bike he'd resurrected—his very first, acquired at the age of thirteen. He launched himself onto it and savagely hit the kick-starter with his heel. The comforting grind of engine cogs filled the air, drowning out the fury in his soul.

Why did his father have to be so stubborn? So impossible? He zoomed down the driveway, onto the main road, then zigzagged down empty back roads. What was he doing here, spinning his wheels, trying to take care of an old man who didn't respect him? Maybe even hated him?

He skidded through a sharp curve, then righted himself, his nerves screaming with adrenaline. Damn, it felt good to dance on that edge again. He took the next few turns at a gravity-defying slant, whooping with glee. When he passed the field where he and Lara had made love, he opened the throttle even further.

See if I care, Lara Nelson. See if I think about you anymore. See if I dream about you every other night and spend half the day thinking of all the things I should have said when you were kicking us to the curb.

He passed a tractor, a girl on a bicycle, a cement truck. Heads whipped around as he zoomed by, accompanied by a few angry shouts and brandished fists. By the time he got back to the ranch, he felt a million times better.

Megan was waiting at the stables, where he kept the dirt bike. She sat cross-legged on a bale of hay. The orange-striped barn cat had his chin draped over her thigh as she gently scratched the nape of his neck. She watched Patrick walk in, her expression unusually serious.

Sweaty and exhilarated, he took off his helmet. "No lectures, sis."

"You underestimate me."

"You may have a point there." He propped his bike against the wall. "If I do it again, hit me."

"I have some information for you."

Instantly he sobered. "You got the detective's name from Big Dog?"

"No. He won't say anything about that, and he's been locking his office at night so I can't even snoop."

Patrick's shoulders dropped. Hell. At this rate he'd never see his only brother again, thanks to his ornery father. "Well, whaddya got, then?"

"I think Lara knows where he is."

He spun around to face her. *"What?"*

"When Dad was yelling at her about you, he said something about Liam's phone bill. It made me think she's probably in touch with him."

He stood for a long moment, battling a storm of emotion. "Megan—"

"You have to go. I know. It's okay."

"You sure?"

"I want to find Liam too." She smiled at him wistfully. "I can handle a dose of undiluted Dad for a little while."

He scooped her into a bear hug. "You're the best sister in the world."

Chapter Twenty-One

Lara slid back the curtain and stepped next to the bed where Mr. Kline lay, eyes closed. He was eighty-nine years old, in good health except for late phase dementia, and now suffering from injuries sustained from his latest unsupervised exploration of the neighborhood—including a badly placed skateboard.

"How's he doing?" she asked his daughter, Ruth, a harried-looking woman who had Lara's deepest sympathy.

"Not bad, I suppose. He doesn't complain about the pain. He does think my son is stealing his mail, though."

"Don't talk about me like I'm not here," grumbled Mr. Kline.

"I'm sorry about that," Lara told him. "I thought you might be sleeping. How are you feeling?"

"Wouldn't you like to know?" He winked.

Lara gestured to the stethoscope around her neck. "Do you mind?"

"Pretty woman wants to test my heart? Twist my arm."

She smiled at Ruth, who rolled her eyes slightly, and checked his heart rate. "You're sounding pretty good, there, for an old guy."

Mr. Kline's answering laugh was a chorus of gurgling hacks, thanks to his history of cigarette consumption. This was the third time he'd been admitted, and each time the Klines had requested her.

She finished the examination, checked his bandages, and wrote out another painkiller prescription. Afterward, Ruth followed her outside the examination room and lowered her voice. "Dr. Nelson, we're starting to talk about . . . you know." She glanced toward the closed door. "Of course, it would be easier if we didn't have to have the same conversation over and over."

"It's tough, I know," Lara said. "Have you called any of those numbers I gave you?" Last time, she had loaded Ruth up with numbers of support groups and agencies that dealt with the elderly.

"It's hard to find the time, but I went to one meeting. It made me realize how lucky I am. He's still so sweet-natured, you know? Maybe even more than he used to be. The stories some people tell . . ." She shook her head. "I'm lucky, that's all. And I like having him with us. If it weren't for the paranoia and the wandering, I wouldn't think twice about keeping him. But . . ." Her eyes filled with tears.

Lara put a sympathetic hand on her arm. "Keep thinking about it. You don't have to do anything until you're ready."

"Thanks. I really do appreciate it. You've been great."

Lara smiled at her and hurried on, carrying with

her that glow only a satisfying interaction with a patient could give. *This* was what she was meant to do; she felt it in her bones. When she put on that white doctor's coat and slung the stethoscope around her neck, everything fell into place. Even though practicing family medicine had plenty of chaos and uncertainty, everything else made up for it. She loved being a rock for people at their most frightened. She loved feeling her way toward a correct diagnosis. She loved knowing that her hard work and knowledge made a difference for someone. She loved helping people.

And right now she loved the Goddesses for sending her back.

Although she did miss all the sleep she'd been getting back in Loveless. Not to mention the sex. And she shouldn't have left Patrick that way, with those harsh words inspired by Big Dog. It wasn't Patrick's fault his father was an ass. He was completely different from his father, brave, caring, exciting . . .

Stop that. For the thousandth time she shoved aside the memory of the time she'd spent with Patrick. Now that she was back to her regular life, it was all starting to seem like a weird dream. It was all so unlikely. Her and Patrick Callahan, making love in a moonlit field?

Yeah, right. Maybe the whole thing had been a hallucination inspired by years of sexual repression. She should probably go see a psychiatrist.

At midday, in line at the cafeteria, she eyed her usual cheese and pastrami sandwich. If the Goddesses were here, they'd be making everyone beet and ginger smoothies. They'd be shocked by what she and the other doctors usually ate. With a surprising pang of homesickness—make that Haven sickness—she grabbed a banana and a yogurt instead.

"Good to have you back, Dr. Nelson," said the chief

of staff, pausing next to her table. He was a burly, imposing man who somewhat reminded her of Big Dog Callahan.

"Good to be back."

"You look . . . different."

Must be all the sex, she almost said. "I finally caught up on my sleep."

He chuckled. "I'm still working on that. Have you decided what you're doing next year? I hear there's an opening at the clinic."

"Yes, I have an interview set up for next week." The job would be perfect for her. The clinic was always looking for good family practitioners. She knew the staff and respected them. She wouldn't have to leave San Diego. And the pay, while not spectacular, would help put a dent in her medical school debt.

But . . .

She didn't even understand why there was a "but." But there was.

"Good luck with it," said the chief of staff, moving on. "We like to keep the good ones close."

Warmed by the compliment, she finished her lunch. Then, deciding it was a little too healthy for a resident—they might laugh her out of the hospital—she grabbed a couple of Kit-Kat bars for dessert. This was her Friday, and she might as well celebrate with chocolate since nothing more interesting was likely to appear.

The only incident of note during her shift, other than a spate of stomach flu cases, was the arrival of a boy who'd been trapped in a burning tree house. She'd gone down to the ER to borrow one of their ultrasounds when the double doors burst open. A firefighter in full turnout gear strode in, a young boy in his arms. The sight was so dramatic—usually paramedics brought people in on gurneys—that everyone stopped and stared.

And she, Lord help her, felt a shock all the way to her toes. The fireman's face was streaked with grime, but his blue eyes glittered past the dirt. It wasn't Patrick—of course not—but Patrick would have looked just like this if he'd just pulled a boy from a fire. Which he'd probably done, many times.

She turned away, grabbed the ultrasound and wheeled it toward the elevator. As she and the machine rose toward the third floor, she ordered her heart rate to return to its normal pace. *Nothing's changed because you saw a fireman*, she scolded herself. You're going to see them on a regular basis. If you get all woozy every time, we're going to have a problem.

She fixed her gaze on the institutional gray of the service elevator wall. It looked a little more drab than it had a few minutes ago. She took her second Kit-Kat bar from her pocket and peeled back a corner of the wrapper. Yep, this chocolate didn't taste quite as good as the first one had. In fact, her whole life, now that she thought about it, seemed a little more boring.

Her cell phone rang. It was Adam Dennison. "I had a brain wave. How about if I come over and make you dinner tonight?"

"Make me *dinner*?"

He lowered his voice. "I've been thinking about us, Lara. I missed you while you were gone. I want to do something special for you to welcome you back. A 'purple feast.' I got the idea from a magazine."

"Excuse me?"

"The magazine said it's a new trend. Nothing but purple food. Eggplant, grapes, port wine cheese, and whatever else I see at the grocery store in the indigo to fuchsia range. I bought a color wheel to help me coordinate."

A headache niggled at Lara's temple. "You really don't need to do that, Adam."

"I want to. I want to show you another side of me. You see me only as the dedicated doctor. But I can enjoy myself too."

Lara closed her eyes, scrambling for a way out. "I might be working late."

"That won't be a problem. I rented some Colin Firth movies too. You can't turn down Colin Firth."

Lara frowned at the phone; nothing coming out of it seemed to make any sense. "Adam, what's going on here? Have you suddenly turned into a chick flick fan?"

His voice went oddly vulnerable. "Give me a chance, Lara. That's all I'm asking."

The elevator door opened and Lara wheeled out the ultrasound machine while balancing the phone on her shoulder. What was holding her back? Adam Dennison was probably a much more appropriate choice than Patrick Callahan. He was one of the most sought-after doctors at the hospital. Brilliant, good-looking, ambitious . . . compulsive.

She closed her eyes and tried to imagine getting wild with Dr. OCD in an empty field. He'd carefully spread out a sheet of plastic, then maybe a comfortable foam pad. Or maybe he'd put up a tent. He'd probably spray the perimeter for bugs and use a lint roller to remove every speck of grass from his clothes.

But then, she knew she would have been the same way—cautious and safe—until Patrick came along.

She couldn't get involved with Adam. Not after Patrick. Even if she never saw Patrick again, he'd ruined her for someone like Dr. Adam Dennison.

"It's not a good idea," she finally said. "I mean, we're coworkers. It would be horrible if things got awkward."

"I don't know what you mean. Haven't we been headed in this direction all along?"

They had? Had she somehow managed to give him the wrong impression? "Well, I thought we were good friends—"

"Exactly. We're friends with the potential for much more. As long as we're honest and keep the lines of communication open, we'll be fine."

She really had to find out what magazine he'd been reading. He'd never mentioned "lines of communication" or purple feasts before in her memory. Still, he had a good point. Communication was important. She should probably communicate a huge, testosterone-drenched detail by the name of Patrick Callahan. She opened her mouth, but he spoke first.

"I'll be there at seven. Your key's still under the mat, right?"

Damn him and his OCD memory. He must have remembered that detail from the time he'd driven her home after a bad reaction to a flu shot. But maybe it was for the best. Tonight she could explain in person that they weren't headed for any kind of a future together.

"Thanks for the offer, Adam. It's really very sweet. I'll see you tonight. I have to go now. I've got a patient." She patted the ultrasound machine as if it were human and hung up.

As she tended to her last two patients, the conversation with Adam kept running through her mind. Everything he said sounded so *reasonable*. They were grown-ups. They didn't do drama. In fact, in that way they were perfect for each other. That's why they'd always worked well together at the hospital. They liked things orderly and consistent and logical. No chaos. No . . . *intensity*. No excitement.

So why couldn't she even think about kissing Adam without flinching, whereas thoughts of kissing Patrick kept waking her up at night?

Darn him.

On the way home she took a call from Mr. Standish, her aunt's lawyer. Cars whizzed past her on the dark freeway as she listened to the rat-a-tat voice on her speaker phone. "I found a realtor who knows eastern Nevada like the back of his hand. He says he can sell the property in a fruit fly's heartbeat, as long as you don't care what happens to it."

"Well, I do kind of care. I mean, I don't want to sell to just anyone."

"What if they want to tear down the existing structure?"

The existing structure? Was that real estate code for her childhood home? "Absolutely not."

"Okay, then what if they want to add on . . . say, make it a dude ranch operation? Add cabins and horse manure? Maybe a few cowboys and girls?"

She wrinkled her forehead, trying to picture it. Dynah might like that. "I guess, maybe."

"Well, he's going to call you. You can work it out with him. But never fear, we'll get this thing sold and get you a tidy little profit."

"To be shared with the Goddesses."

"You can share it with God, your janitor, a pet shelter, whatever you want."

Luckily, he hung up before catching her involuntary burst of giggles. She'd forgotten that most people didn't refer to other people as "Goddesses."

Oh, Aunt Tam. Your legacy lives on. Even though it may become a dude ranch.

By the time she turned the key in the door of her condo, she was bone-tired. Which was why her first thought was that she had to be hallucinating.

Patrick Callahan IV sat in her one good piece of furniture, an armchair upholstered in sleek lipstick red. Dressed in his usual jeans and T-shirt, this one black with the white outline of a lizard, he sat with one ankle crossed over the opposite knee. Adam must have insisted he take off his shoes, because on his feet were blue athletic socks with holes worn in the heels. Dark stubble dotted his jaw; he looked as though he'd driven all night to get here.

The entire room vibrated with his blue-eyed, red-blooded, utterly masculine energy.

Adam sat on the couch, wearing an apron with the words, LAUGHTER ISN'T THE BEST MEDICINE. ATIVAN IS. He was watching Patrick as if he were an unpredictable zoo specimen. Lara couldn't tell if he looked horrified or fascinated. The holes in Patrick's socks had probably given Adam a heart attack. On the other hand, there was no ignoring Patrick's incredible, potent charisma. Just sitting there, he made the entire room tilt in his direction. It was nearly impossible for Lara to drag her gaze away to meet Adam's.

Patrick jumped to his feet. "Lara. I have to talk to you."

Adam got to his feet too. "Should I have warned you, Lara? He said he was a friend from Loveless."

Patrick gave Adam a hard look. "I am a friend from Loveless."

"He is," agreed Lara. "Psycho."

Adam frowned, looking highly offended.

"I don't mean you're psycho. He's Psycho."

Now Adam took a step back.

"I don't mean that he's crazy, although I wouldn't rule it out. Psycho's his nickname. For obvious reasons, if you know anything about him. But let's stick with Patrick for now. Patrick, have you met Adam? He's the chief resident in the Family Medicine program."

Now why had she thrown that in? Was the exact nature of her relationship with Adam any business of Patrick's?

Adam apparently thought it was. "Well, I'd say our relationship is a bit more than professional," he sniffed.

Lara directed a full-throttle smile his way. "How's the purple feast coming?"

"Very well. It's only enough for two, though." He sniffed again and eyed Patrick, who now had his arms crossed over his chest and his feet braced apart.

"Patrick won't be staying. But can I have a minute alone with him?"

Adam, after darting a triumphant look at Patrick, headed into the kitchen.

When they were alone, she caught Patrick's puzzled look. "Purple feast?"

"All the food's going to be purple."

"Yeah? I had a grape Slurpee on the way here."

She laughed, then wiped the smile from her face. "What are you doing here?"

Patrick tilted his head. "For some reason, you don't seem too happy to see me."

"Well, I've had a long day. You could have called and let me know you were coming. It wouldn't have been such a shock that way and—"

"Where's Liam?"

The blunt words dropped into the stream of conversation like twin boulders. She stalled. "What do you mean?"

"Don't play games with me, Lara. This is too important to me. If you don't know, fine. I'll leave you alone. It's a simple question. *Do you know where he is?*"

Throat constricting, she gazed at him helplessly. She didn't want to lie. In fact, she'd told Liam that she wouldn't lie. "Don't put me in this position," she whispered.

Patrick's eyes flared, as if he were a tiger sighting its prey. "You *do* know. Damn it, Lara." He shoved his hands in his jeans pockets, no doubt to keep himself from strangling her. "Tell me where he is. Please."

"Why?"

"Why? Because I'm his brother. Because I want to make sure he's okay."

"He's okay." There. If there had been any doubt about her involvement, she'd just blown it out of the water. "And anyway, that's not enough."

He whirled on her. "Not enough? What the fuck does that mean?" The force of his intensity might have been enough to make her flee, but this was about Liam. She'd go pretty damn far for her old friend.

"He wants to be left alone, unless someone has a really good reason to find him. So I want to know your reason."

"You're the one with the keys to the gate? Saint Peter of getting to see Liam?"

She lifted her chin and folded her arms across her chest, trying to quell her nerves. Hell, if things got really ugly, she could call on Adam. He could come out and throw purple food at Patrick. "He's a grown man, Patrick. This is how he wants it."

A muscle in his jaw jumped, and a grim expression settled over his face. He looked infinitely older than the boy she'd once known. "Fine," he finally said. "I want to see him because I want to see him."

Before she could protest that it was the lamest reason ever, he continued in a low voice that vibrated, raw and powerful, through the room. "I want to see him because my eyes hurt from not seeing him. My heart hurts from it. He's my brother. I love him. He knows how much I love him. I bet he wants to see me too. And I want to . . . tell him I'm sorry. I shouldn't have left him, like you said."

Damn it. He had to go and say the perfect thing. Her throat tightened with emotion. That wary, vulnerable look on Patrick's stubbly face made her want to hold him and kiss him and . . .

"Okay. But if you're going to see him, I'm coming with you. I don't think it would be a good idea to surprise him, and it's not always easy to get ahold of him. And it might be better to have a third person there. And I'll want to explain why I ratted him out."

Patrick let out a long breath. "Fair enough. Is it far? Can we go tonight? It's kind of late to be showing up on someone's doorstep. Maybe tomorrow? How long will it take to get there?"

"Patrick. Take a breath. It's going to take at least a day to get there."

"A day?" He ran one hand through his short-cropped hair. "Where the fuck is he?"

"He's in Mexico."

Chapter Twenty-Two

Since Lara hadn't yet unpacked from her trip to Loveless, she was ready to go in just a few minutes. While Patrick cleared space in the Hulk, she explained the situation to Adam, who was meticulously slicing eggplant. Why oh why had she let him come over? She felt like the biggest jerk in the world, telling him she'd have to skip out on the purple feast.

"I'm really sorry, Adam. Can you invite someone else?"

Adam set down the extremely expensive ceramic knife he must have brought over; it certainly didn't belong to her. "You're going to go away with this guy the second he snaps his fingers?"

"It's not like that. He wants to see his brother. It's a long story."

"One you've never even mentioned to me."

"Well . . . that's because . . ." Because why? Because

their friendship hadn't included such basic information as her life before her residency.

"Have you slept with him?"

"That's sort of a personal question."

He shot her a sour look. "I didn't realize those were off-limits. I thought we were friends. Is there a reason you can't tell me the truth?"

Lara shifted the strap of her overnight bag from one shoulder to the other. It would certainly be easier to tell him the truth if he weren't currently making her dinner. "Yes, I did sleep with him. It just, you know, happened."

"The way it's never happened with us."

Lara chewed at the inside of her mouth. "I guess you could say that. But other things happened with us. Good things. Friend and coworker sort of things."

"I could have any woman at the hospital, you know."

That might have been a slight exaggeration, but she wasn't going to quibble. "I know. You're great, Adam. But don't you think if something was going to happen between us, it would have by now? Maybe we're better off as friends."

She put her hand on his shoulder. The muscles of his upper arm felt firm and solid under her palm. Adam worked out, after all. But tingling electricity didn't race through her body the way it did when she came into contact with Patrick.

Stop comparing them, she told herself. *It's not fair.*

But Adam was apparently thinking along the same lines. "You'd better quit that," he murmured. "Something tells me your Psycho guy wouldn't like seeing us like this, and he isn't nearly as polite as I am."

She snatched her hand away. "He doesn't own me."

"I saw the way he lit up when you came into the room."

"Yeah right. He's not that type."

"And you lit up when you saw him. The two of you were like a couple of lightbulbs."

"I have to say that you're taking this really well, Adam."

He shrugged and turned away. "Like I said, I'm not exactly hurting for company. I told you we'd be friends as long as we were honest. You've been honest."

A lump formed in her throat. Obviously, she'd underestimated Adam. Maybe he truly could be her friend.

"I'll lock up here," he continued. "Good luck with that maniac. See you on Monday."

As she skipped down the stairs, she thought about the fact that she and Patrick had never defined what was going on between them. They'd left things—well, she'd left—in a completely unsettled state. And now they were about to drive to Mexico together. This could be trouble.

Patrick was still in the back of his Dodge, moving things around. Wrinkling her nose, she went to the tailgate and handed him her bag. "Why does it smell like a zoo?"

"I had Goldie in here for a while, and it's never recovered, no matter how much air freshener I spray. But it's clean." He put her bag at the head of a pile of blankets he'd spread out on the vehicle bed. "I've got a sleeping bag and three blankets here, and the top one just came out of the laundry. It's fleece, it's soft as a baby bunny, and smells like Megan's lavender detergent. Do you want to lie down? You look pretty wiped out."

"I don't think that's a good idea. We haven't even talked about how we left things, and—"

"I didn't say have sex, I said sleep," he said shortly.

"I'd like to cross the border tonight. You can sleep while I drive."

Lara blessed the darkness for hiding her fierce blush. "Right. Well, that's okay. It looks comfy, but the border guards might think you're trying to smuggle someone into Mexico. Don't we have to get some kind of permit to cross the border?"

"We can get it there."

Even in the scant light cast by the street lamp, she noticed the dark smudges under his eyes, which matched the shadow darkening his jaw. "How long have you been driving?"

"I left around two. What is it now, about nine?"

"Patrick! You need to sleep."

"I'm a firefighter. I'm used to going without sleep."

"Are you sure you don't want to stay here and leave first thing in the morning? It's not exactly safe to drive all night on no sleep. They say it's just as bad as driving drunk."

"No." It came out as more of a bullet than a word. "I'm a perfectly safe driver. And I'm not staying anywhere near that guy."

The jealous tone in his voice gave her a sneaky thrill. "Adam? Why? He's a nice guy."

"Glad to hear it." His voice was muffled as he jammed old cardboard cups and fast food wrappers into a plastic grocery bag. "I'll sleep in the Hulk if you want to stay here at your place."

Sure. She could do that. But that would require parting ways with Patrick for the night, and that thought had zero appeal. "We could stay at a motel. You could get some sleep and we could leave when we wake up."

He went still. She held her breath. He found one more stray wrapper, stuffed it into the trash bag, then crawled out of the truck. He closed the tailgate—the entire vehicle shook as he did so—and confronted her. Resting one hand on the back of the truck, he leaned close, his eyes fierce points of light in the ambient dimness of the street.

"It will be really hard for me to keep my hands off you if we're sharing a motel room. Or the back of the Hulk. Or anywhere, for that matter. No sleep would be happening, that's for sure."

She swallowed hard, and didn't answer. But that seemed to be enough of an answer for Patrick.

"Any other helpful suggestions?"

She shook her head.

"Let's load up, then."

For a while they said little as Lara gave him directions to the Mexican border. She sat with one leg under the other, angled toward him as she pointed him toward the I-5 freeway, which would end at the crossing. A feeling of warmth and inevitability spread through her. Had she really thought she'd seen the last of Patrick Callahan? She must have been delusional.

"Where do we go after we cross the border?" He took a long swig from a can of Red Bull that sat in his cup holder.

"Baja," she answered, deciding that she'd make him pull over at some point and shut his eyes. Red Bull only went so far.

After they crossed into Mexico, the busy freeways of San Diego County gave way to a long, nearly empty highway that took them into the warm, sage-scented night. It unfurled hypnotically before them, interrupted only occasionally by signs that said things like DESPACIO and CURVA PELIGROSA. Her thoughts drifted. Everyone in Mexico must be sleeping, since it was way past midnight. They must be snuggled up in bed, cozy and relaxed . . .

And just like that, her eyes fell shut.

She came partly awake again when they pulled onto a scenic outlook that might have been carved from the top of a cliff. It overlooked a rugged canyon filled with shadows. When he turned the headlights off, deep night closed in around them. She murmured a question.

"Shhh," Patrick said as he slid out of the driver's seat. "I'm going to take a short catnap in the back. Are you okay here? The doors will be locked. You can have the whole seat to yourself."

She shook her head, still too sleepy to form words. But she knew she didn't want to be separated from him.

"You're coming with me, then." She heard the tailgate clang open, then felt a rush of fresh air. Then she was being lifted in his arms like a baby and carried around to the back. It felt sinfully good. She wrapped her arms around his neck and snuggled her face into his chest.

"Don't drop me," she murmured.

"Oh no." The tenderness in his voice gave her a shiver. "I'm never going to drop you. And one of these days you'll start trusting me."

She wanted to protest that statement. It wasn't that she didn't trust him. She didn't trust herself, or maybe herself with him, or him the way he had been, or something like that . . . the thought was simply too tangled to emerge. Instead she let him settle her onto the nest of blankets. When he lay down next to her, she cuddled close, with a sense of regret that they weren't naked. After one long, luxurious exhale, she fell back asleep.

She woke up with something tickling her cheek. Soft puffs of air warmed one side of her face. The dust-coated window was a block of cobalt, shading to glowing amethyst at the bottom. It must be close to dawn. She tilted sideways and saw Patrick, deeply asleep, his mouth open just enough to let out little snuffling noises. For a moment she simply took in the sight of him at rest. Normally he had such a vibrant, alive presence. It was hard to take her eyes off him. It was just as hard now, with his face relaxed into peaceful lines, his eyelashes fanned across his cheeks. He looked almost absurdly handsome.

She traced the line of his jaw, feeling the roughness of his whiskers. He must be going on a couple days without shaving. His scruff abraded her fingers and sent a pleasant wake-up call to her nervous system. When she reached the corner of his mouth, she felt it twitch. She froze. She hadn't intended to wake him up, just to . . . fondle him. Without his knowing.

Not cool, now that she thought about it. She started to draw her hand away, then yelped as she found her index finger enveloped in warm wetness.

"Where do you think you're going," he murmured thickly, his words blocked by her finger.

"I didn't mean to wake you up." She tugged her finger free.

"Then you'll have to pay the price," he growled. He rolled to his side and raised himself on one elbow. "I did warn you, after all."

"Yes, but—"

"No buts. I've got you right where I want you. In the back of my truck in the middle of a foreign country." His eyes glittered like chips of blue quartz. With his zero dark thirty shadow and general air of disrepute, he looked downright dangerous. Something thrilled deep in her belly.

"So you planned it this way," she said breathlessly.

"Yes. My master plan is working perfectly. Prepare . . ." He nipped at the corner of her jawbone, where it met her neck. " . . . to surrender."

"Really? Surrender? What about, ah, negotiation?"

"I'm open to negotiation." He grabbed the edge of the blanket between his teeth and yanked it aside. Her heart skipped into double time. "What are you offering?"

"Well, I could, um, give you a kiss." She pressed her lips against his strong throat in a quick, darting kiss.

"Ah, the famous throat kiss. An intriguing opening gambit. One might say it's a low-ball offer. Especially compared to, say, this." With a dramatic gesture, he unzipped her sweatshirt. She wore a thin tank top underneath; the sudden rush of air made her nipples tighten. "And now you're upping the ante, I see." He homed in on her chest with a focus that made her nipples peak even further.

She lay, heart pounding, blood racing, as he took her in, inch by slow inch. "God, I missed you, Lara."

With that, he pushed her tank top above her breasts, flicked her bra aside—thank goodness for front clasps—and descended on her like a wildfire on kindling. Taking her breast into an open-mouthed kiss, he drew an instant response, a low cry that made her bite her lip.

"Don't hold back, sweetheart. I love your sounds." He lifted his head, leaving her aroused nipple burning for more. "I love the way you say what you want. Tell me right now. What do you want? I'm open to negotiation, remember."

"More," she ground out.

"More of what. This?" He slicked his tongue across the upper curve of her breast, barely brushing the edge of her nipple. It was like being singed by a lighter;

every nerve ending stood up and clamored for attention.

"That. And the other one."

"Now you're talking." He plumped her breasts, one in each hand, while he feasted on the sensitive peaks.

"Oh Patrick," she cried, feeling waves of bright electricity flash through her body. The echo of her voice against the truck walls reminded her of where they were. "We can't do this. Not here. Someone might see."

"No one's passed by here all night." He twirled his tongue across flesh that screamed for more, no matter what her common sense said. "We'd hear if a car drove up." He suckled deeply at one nipple. "The doors are locked." He left her breasts and trailed a wet path down her stomach. "We're totally safe." Her body arched as she fisted her hands in the blankets. "But if you're really nervous about it, we can drive until we reach the next village." He unzipped her shorts. "We can find something that passes for a hotel." He reached under her waistband and pushed aside her panties. "We can wait until they open and book ourselves a room." He cupped her sex in his strong hand. "Of course, I don't know how long that will take, and considering that you're already this wet, it might be a little frustrating just sitting around, twiddling our thumbs."

He wiggled his thumb against the little bundle of nerves that craved his touch.

"What are you doing to me?" She moaned. "I can't think straight when you do that."

He did it again, brushing her sweetest spot with firm back-and-forth movements.

She gave a strangled cry and squeezed her legs together, trapping his hand—so strong, so hard, so just where she needed it. He pressed more firmly against her and whispered hot words in her ear.

"I'm going to flip you over. Then I'm going to get so deep inside you your head will spin. Here we go, honey."

In a swift move, he turned her onto her stomach. She moaned at the feel of the fleece blanket on her skin. God, it was soft, like an angel's cloud, and it smelled clean and lovely and . . . there went her pants. And then came a hot hand shaping her ass, curving around the cheeks with voracious appreciation.

"I want you so bad, Lara Nelson. I've never felt this way, and it's kind of flipping me out, but I don't give a crap right now. I just want to be inside you before I lose my mind. That all right with you?"

She answered with a slow undulation of her body—showing worked so much better than telling. She grabbed his hand and guided it back to her sex, where he'd been doing such delicious things a few moments ago. His muscled arm came under her; she pressed against his wrist in an agony of need.

"Hang on, sweetheart. Gotta do this right." His hand disappeared for a moment while he put on a condom. She squeezed her eyes shut. She wanted time to freeze just where it was, with Patrick's harsh pants and fumbled movements filling the silence. If only she could live in this moment, right here, right now, forever.

Then he was back, his hot hand cupping her sex, his hard body settling over her, his knee parting her legs from behind. Slowly, he pushed his erection—a velvety soft, insistently rigid shaft—into the give of her passage. Inch by inch he penetrated her. He seemed so much more enormous at this angle. She lifted her hips to accommodate him, and felt his hand grasp her with even more firmness. His palm moved against her sex in a deceptively slow-motion grind. White-hot need jackhammered through her.

"Holy mother of . . ." She gasped. "Don't . . . frickin' . . . stop . . ."

"Hell no." His hot breath against her neck fueled the feeling of madness. She felt impaled, spread open, helpless and yet intensely powerful. "But I don't think I can last long."

"This isn't a damn marathon," she snapped, nearly out of her mind with desire. He gave a strained laugh and canted his hips forward, sliding all the way inside her, taking up all the space—no room for restraint, for doubt, for fear.

"Now," he growled, and the world exploded into bright colliding shapes and colors. She flew high, so high, twirling and spinning as giddy ecstasy racked her body and soul. Again and again, as if tumbled by an upsurging fountain, she soared skyward, leaving gravity far behind.

If only she never had to go back.

Chapter Twenty-Three

Patrick eased himself off Lara's still-trembling body. He felt gutted, as if someone had reached inside him and turned everything upside down. He lay on his back, one hand settled on Lara's hip. She curled into the shape of an unfurling fern, her body a lovely arc.

How had she become so important to him, in such a short amount of time? Now that he thought about it, maybe she'd always been important to him. She was Liam's only real friend. The only other person he trusted to treat Liam right.

And he'd taken her in the back of the Hulk without a second thought.

Slinging one arm over his eyes, he fought a confusing onslaught of emotions. He shouldn't have done it. *But it had been phenomenal—for both of them.* It wasn't fair to Liam. *What did Liam have to do with it?* He should talk to Liam before he went any further with Lara. *But how would he avoid her until then?* Was he

such a beast that he couldn't control himself around
a woman?

Not just any woman. Lara.

And a terrifying revelation dawned. *It was Lara.*
Whatever he felt about Lara, he'd never felt it before.
He didn't know what the next step was, he didn't
know where it was going, what he should say or do; he
didn't know shit.

Except that she'd somehow become completely inte-
gral to his existence.

"You look like your puppy just got diagnosed with
kidney stones. Or maybe your llama." Lara's husky
voice interrupted his flow of panicked thoughts. "You
okay?"

"Peachy." He was afraid to look at her, afraid of
what the sight of her, soft and pliant from sex, would
do to the storm going on inside him. "Are you okay? I
didn't get too intense, did I?"

"Hmm. Well, I don't know for sure. I guess we could
try it again so I can judge properly."

A quick look in her direction confirmed all his fears.
Her dark honey eyes, bright as new planets, teased him
from her nest of forest-green fleece. Her bared skin
glowed with a subtle sheen, as if some sculptor had
added a thin layer of gold leaf over his masterpiece.
His mouth actually watered, his tongue longed to be
lapping at her bounty. A sense of weakness seized his
limbs, his breathing hitched, his lungs fluttered.

What the hell was Lara doing to him?

"In case you haven't figured it out, it was Big
Dog that got me so upset that last day in Loveless. I
shouldn't have left like that." Her gracefully etched
eyebrows drew together in a frown.

"I figured that's what happened." He smoothed one
thumb over the fine hairs. When had he ever cared

about anyone's eyebrows before now? Lara had a way of owning up to her faults that he found incredibly endearing. And at the moment, he couldn't see that she had any faults at all, not really.

But he couldn't very well tell Lara that something had changed, in some confusing way that he didn't even understand yet. He couldn't very well tell her that he was beginning to wonder, in some freaked-out corner of his mind, if this was what "being in love" felt like.

He took a long, steadying breath. No need to go overboard here. No need to rappel off the helicopter until he had all his gear properly fastened and safety-checked.

Instead, he changed the subject. "I hope we don't scare the crap out of Liam by showing up out of the blue. He doesn't do well with surprises."

She sat up, pulling the fleece blanket around her. The wild tumble of her hair made his heart hurt. "Well, I texted to warn him, but he doesn't always get his texts. Cell service comes and goes down there. But I think it'll be okay. I wouldn't do this if I didn't think so."

He nodded, trying like hell to look serious rather than consumed with adoration. "I appreciate it." Unable to help himself, he reached for a tendril of her hair and wrapped it around his finger. A smile ghosted across her luxuriously curved lips. Another of those unsettling pangs roiled his gut.

He decided to blame it on plain old hunger.

"Let's hit the road and see if we can find some *huevos rancheros*."

"Sounds good, especially since I missed my 'purple feast' last night."

He released her hair and sat bolt upright, nearly

bonking his head on the roof of the Hulk. "About that guy."

"That guy? You mean Adam, my chief resident and friend?"

He liked the fact that she used the word "friend." That was a good sign, although "gay friend" would have been even better. "So you haven't slept with him?"

"Why is everyone asking me who I'm having sex with?"

"Excuse me." He pulled her close, feeling a growl build in his chest. "Since we *are* having sex, I think I have a right to know."

She blinked up at him. "*Having* sex?"

"Yeah, having sex. We had sex, are having sex, will have sex. You're not the only one who can parse verbs. Want me to conjugate it some more? Would have had sex, should have had sex, will have had sex, will be having sex as soon as possible . . ."

"Okay, okay, Princeton. Are you having sex with anyone else?"

He gave her an appalled look. "Of course not."

"Of *course* not?"

With a sense of shock, he snapped his mouth shut. In the past, he hadn't given much thought to exclusivity in sex. As long as both partners were protected and willing—and on the same page—what was the big deal? But once Lara had entered his life, the idea of sex with another woman seemed . . . unthinkable.

What was going on?

"Well, I'm not either."

Her words slowly penetrated the buzzing in his ears. He gave her a distracted look and a brisk nod. "All right, then." For a long, strange moment they locked gazes. Crammed into such a small space, surrounded by duffel bags and rumpled bedding, a slight smell of gas and stale coffee hovering around them, Patrick suddenly had the disorienting sense that nothing else existed outside this moment. He cleared his throat. "We should get going."

As they drove south, the sun climbed above the horizon like a particularly festive, bright orange piñata. Lara watched it in quick glimpses. Risking retinal damage seemed more appealing than watching Patrick's impassive face.

Something was going on behind those restless blue eyes, but the hell if she could figure out what. It seemed to her that things had been going along nicely. They'd both declared they weren't sleeping with anyone else. They'd agreed—well, he'd declared, and she hadn't denied it—that they would have sex again in the future. This was all good, right? No heavy commitment or anything like that. Just pure, straightforward sexual satisfaction. The Goddesses would be so proud of her.

Or would they?

A quote from Annabella's workshop on Ten Ways to Deepen Your Soul Connection drifted through her mind. "Emotional harmony is the basis for a truly satisfactory sex life. To achieve this, you must be prepared to expose your flaws and cultivate humility."

Well, maybe Annabella didn't know everything. Lara had never felt so satisfied, but she hadn't exposed any flaws. Then again, Patrick already knew her flaws. He knew about her awkward years, her embarrassing Haven history, her rebellious, sarcastic side. She'd never even bothered to hide any of that from him, the way she had from Adam.

They passed a sombrero-wearing farmer hunched

over a motor scooter, putt-putting along the side of the highway. Patrick raised a hand in greeting, and he waved back.

"Have you been to Mexico before?" she asked.

"Couple times." He lapsed back into silence.

So much for that topic of conversation. Lara turned back to the panorama of sunrise-tinted canyonlands unfurling out the window. If Patrick didn't want to talk, so be it. This wasn't a "date." She didn't have to entertain him. She could go back to thinking about the delicious experiences she'd shared so far with him.

Maybe she could rewrite Annabella's workshop for her now that she had a little more practical experience. She'd include a special section on sex in unconventional locations. *Make sure you always bring a clean blanket with you for those moments of spontaneous lust.*

Smiling to herself, she caught Patrick's puzzled glance, then realized he'd just said something to her. "Sorry, what?"

"If it's too personal a question, you don't have to answer."

"No, I just . . . missed it. What was the question?"

"Your parents. What happened to them? Why did you grow up at the Haven?"

"Liam never told you?" The death of her parents had been such a crucial part of her life it seemed impossible that he didn't know about it.

"No. It never came up, I guess."

"Well. They were killed." She felt, more than saw, his shock. "In a car accident on the way home from a dinner party."

"Where? When?"

"We lived in Houston, Texas, back then. People have been known to drive too fast there." Was it her imagination, or did Patrick ease his foot off the gas pedal just a hair? "My father was a notorious speed demon. He was training to be an astronaut, you know."

"I didn't."

Of course he didn't. How would he know that? She never talked about that time. The earth had cratered under her feet one humid night, and nothing was ever the same again. "I was eleven when it happened. At first I stayed with my father's parents in Texas, but that was a disaster. I was a wreck, and they were old. They had no idea what to do with me. Then my grandmother got sick, and they just couldn't keep me anymore. Aunt Tam showed up out of the blue with a letter my father had sent her years ago, saying he wanted her to be my guardian if anything should ever happen. Next thing I knew, I was living in a brothel in Loveless, Nevada."

Patrick made a *tsking* sound. "It's not a brothel. Everyone in town knows that."

She couldn't help laughing. "You know, in some ways it would have been easier if it *was* still a brothel. People understand brothels. But a Center for Sexual and Spiritual Healing? I was doomed to freakhood before I even stepped onto school grounds."

"That's when you met Liam?"

"Yep. We were outcasts together. Although he didn't mind being a misfit the way I did."

"He didn't mind once you came along. At least he had a friend. It made all the difference."

"For me, too. I would have been miserable if we hadn't become friends. We bonded during science class. I think it was the unit on mealworms. He couldn't bear to touch them, so I had to do all the icky work."

Patrick laughed as he passed a rattletrap truck loaded with crates of avocadoes. "He was a lucky guy. I never had any girl friends in school."

She pulled a face. "You had girls coming out of your ears, the way I remember it."

"But none of them were *friends*. Did you ever think Liam might have a crush on you?"

"What?" Her mouth fell open. "No way. It was never like that."

"Maybe it was but he didn't ever tell you."

She shifted uncomfortably on the seat. She'd never been interested in Liam that way. Wouldn't he have said something? What if she had hurt his feelings, completely unintentionally? She didn't like that thought one bit. "Did he ever mention anything like that?"

"No, no. I just wonder." She continued to stare at him, until he added, "How could he have spent so much time with you and not have a crush on you?" He said it casually, as if wondering how Liam could have stayed out in the sun and not gotten sunburned.

A slow wave of heat crawled up her cheeks. "That's a pretty sweet thing to say."

"Yeah, I'm such a sweet-talker. All the guys at the firehouse say so."

She smiled, then pointed to a sign up ahead. "We're supposed to take that road, then go another sixty miles."

"*Muy bueno.*"

When they reached the first town of any size, they stopped at a *panadería* that had just opened its doors for the morning. The heavenly scent of freshly baked pastries poured from the steamy glass storefront. An old woman with twinkling eyes gave them a smiling, bowing *buenas días*. They bought sugarcoated twists of dough and thick, dark coffee served in paper cups. Lara laughed at the way Patrick downed his doughnuts in quick succession, like popping M&M's down his throat as they walked back to the Hulk.

"I guess you don't worry much about calories."

"I'm a guy. If there's food, I eat it. Anyway, I make up for it." He told her about his addiction to triathlons, rock-climbing, and other feats of extreme sports. Then there were his other skills, the kind that enabled him to hurtle into fires and come out alive.

Back in the truck, Patrick placed his coffee cup in the rickety cup holder, which he'd rigged with a foam sleeve to keep his drinks warm. Lara imagined lots of sleepless nights and moonlit road trips. The thought made her shiver.

"So do you like being a firefighter?" she asked when they were back on the road. "It's not something you ever mentioned in high school. Not that I remember, anyway."

"Love it. To tell you the truth, I'd probably be in jail by now if I hadn't gotten a job on the force. All that pissed-off young maleness—I didn't know what to do with myself. I did all kinds of crazy shit, but my bro's at the firehouse kept me from getting too out of line. I'm really good at firefighting. I studied my ass off for that exam—scored at the top of my class. They couldn't throw enough training at me. I always wanted more. I built myself up, got really strong and fast and smart. Stupid sometimes too, I'll admit. But nothing too serious. I didn't want to get kicked out, or screw up at a fire." He maneuvered his coffee cup out of the sleeve and took a deep swallow. "Turns out, if you save enough lives, you start thinking maybe your existence is worth something after all."

She glanced at him sharply. "You doubted?"

"After the accident? What do you think?"

She went quiet. Truth to tell, she hadn't spared a thought for what Patrick might have gone through. She'd been too worried about Liam. "You know what, Patrick?"

"Hm," he said, through another sip of coffee.

"I really admire you. If you'd gone back to Princeton and resumed your previously arranged life, I'd probably detest you, just like I did back then."

"You *detested* me?"

"Well, in between feeling kind of . . . attracted to you. Not that I'd ever admit it."

He pointed a finger at her triumphantly. "You just did. I heard you. Hey everybody, guess what Lara just confessed?" He honked the horn, which sounded like a sick goose. A family stared at him from an old yellow car in the next lane.

"Oh, shut up," she muttered. "The point is, I like you much more now than I would have if things had happened the way they were supposed to. Turn right!" She pointed wildly at the turnoff they'd almost missed. Patrick yanked the wheel and steered them onto the tiny dirt road marked by a sign that read A LA PLAYA.

"He lives at the beach?"

"Close to the beach, I think." She checked the text message on her phone that held the directions, which were as precise as everything Liam did. "He said it's a little bungalow."

As they hurtled down the narrow, twisting road, between scrubby grass-covered dunes, they both fell silent. All the teasing from a few moments ago still echoed between them, like some haunting melody. And under that lay the confidences he'd shared. Those they'd *both* shared. But for now, all that was forgotten as they focused on the moment ten years in the making.

As the road neared the ocean it veered southward, so it ran along the beach. Straggling pinyon trees studded the terrain. To the right Lara saw flashes of deep sapphire blue, which must be the ocean flirting through the trees, like a peacock shy about unfurling its feathers. She rolled the window down and took deep breaths of fresh, salt-spangled air.

"I wish I'd brought my swimming suit."

Patrick grunted. Glancing at him, she saw deep tension etched across his face. She herself hadn't seen Liam in about five years. But for Patrick it had been twice as long, and their separation took place under the worst possible circumstances. Impulsively she put a hand on his thigh.

"It'll be okay."

He didn't answer. She bit her lip, wishing she could take back the platitude. Wasn't that one of those meaningless statements that didn't help anyway? The kind of thing she never said to her patients?

"Never mind. It'll be what it'll be."

He gave a pained laugh. "I think I like the first one better. But don't worry. I'm fine. I'm a big boy. Whatever happens, I'm glad I came. Glad *we* came. Is this it?"

They pulled up outside a small, squat, one-room bungalow made from weathered planks of wood that still contained a few remnants of flamingo pink paint.

"I think so. He said it's called Casita Rosa."

"Pink house. That's creative."

"You must be nervous if you're critiquing whoever named the house. I don't blame you, I'm kind of nervous too. Who names houses anyway? I never bothered to name my condo, although I bet I could come up with something really cute. 'The Doctor's Pad,' maybe. Hey, that's actually not bad . . ."

"Lara."

A warm hand was gripping hers tight. "Please stop talking so we can get out and see if Liam's here."

"Yeah. Sorry."

She took a deep breath to calm herself. They shared one last glance, then, as if on cue, both opened their doors and stepped out.

The screen door of the Casita Rosa opened with a screech of rusty hinges. And there, framed in the doorway, as slight as ever, but twice as tanned, stood Liam.

Chapter Twenty-Four

*P*atrick froze. His eyes catalogued differences in his brother even while the rest of the world seemed to briefly disappear. Liam looked older, of course. The sun had had a field day with his skin; not only was he tanned, but new lines fanned from the corner of his eyes. His hair, which had always been a few shades lighter than Patrick's, was bleached nearly white blond now.

Was he taller? Unconsciously, Patrick straightened to his full height. He'd always had a couple inches on his brother, but after ten years, who knew? They'd long ago stopped making those pencil marks on the door-jamb.

He raised his hand in a lame hello wave, then signed a greeting instead.

Liam didn't smile. How could he not smile? Liam used to have such a goofy smile, one that popped out at the oddest moments. But this grown-up version of

Liam looked wary and not particularly happy to see them. His gaze slid from Patrick to Lara.

"What are you doing here?" he signed.

"Don't be mad," answered Lara. "Your brother wanted to see you. I thought it was time."

"Why?" Liam had always known how to cut through the crap.

"Because he misses you and he has things he wants to say to you."

Watching Lara's nimble hands form the signs, Patrick felt deeply grateful that she'd come with him. She stood a few steps away, the ocean breeze lifting her hair back from her face. The early morning sun burnished her skin to the color of precious living gold. She glanced at him in a signal to jump in.

"Can we come in?" Patrick signed. "Looks like you have a great place here."

Liam took a long moment to answer, looking back and forth between the two of them several times. Patrick wondered if he could tell they'd recently been making love in the back of the Hulk. Liam had always had a freakishly acute sense of smell, which apparently went along with his autistic tendencies.

Finally, his brother nodded, then vanished inside the little bungalow. After exchanging a quick glance, he and Lara followed. It was like stepping inside the inside of a seashell that still smelled of the ocean. All the colors were soft, some version of delicate beige or soothing silvery gray. A carefully made bed took up one corner, a tiny kitchenette another. A low daybed, covered with a silky crocheted throw, sat under a picture window with a view of the beach. Everything seemed to have its place, from the frying pans hanging in order of size on hooks above the sink to the books marching in perfect formation on a homemade shelf.

The tiny, tidy cottage exuded an atmosphere of peace. For someone like Liam, who craved order, it must be perfect.

It couldn't be more different from the Callahan Ranch, with its mounted animal horns and rawhide rugs.

But one thing was utterly familiar. Patrick breathed in the scent of chamomile tea and fried bacon, the aroma that meant morning back home, where Liam had eaten the same breakfast every day of his life.

Liam offered water, which they both accepted. He gestured to the daybed while he crossed to the tiny kitchenette. An orange water cooler sat next to the sink. He filled two mason jars from the spigot, then carefully brought them to Patrick and Lara.

"How did you find this place?" Patrick asked.

"My girlfriend found it."

Patrick nearly choked on a mouthful of water. "*Girlfriend*?"

A concerned smile skimmed across Liam's face. "Are you okay?"

"Yeah. Sorry. I just didn't know. Where is your girlfriend?"

Liam sat down on the edge of the bed. "She's at work right now. Do you have a girlfriend?"

Patrick shot a quick look at Lara, who shrugged uselessly. "Uh . . . sort of, I suppose."

"Sort of?" Liam's frown reminded Patrick of how meticulous he'd always been about defining things. He didn't like gray areas. He needed everything to be clearly one way or another way. How could Liam understand his confusing relationship with Lara when he didn't understand it himself?

"I haven't asked her about it," he signed, "but I see her as my girlfriend. I hope she sees me that way too."

He was careful not to mention that he was talking about Lara. He wasn't quite ready to reveal that much.

"When are you going to ask her?"

"Very soon."

Liam finally looked satisfied. He sat back, rubbing both hands on his knees in another very familiar gesture. Then he spoke out loud. "Give me some news about yourself." Since he'd gone deaf at the age of eleven, he could still speak, although sometimes his phrasing could be odd, especially as time went on. The specialists had told the Callahans this was normal, since sign language required a different way of communicating concepts. The more he adapted to signing, the less comfortable he felt speaking English.

"Well, I live in a city called San Gabriel, in California. I'm a firefighter."

Liam looked mildly curious. "You fight fires?"

"Sometimes. I also help people at accident scenes. We get a lot of medical calls."

Lara jumped in. "He came back to Loveless to help fight a huge wildfire. He rappelled out of a helicopter. And he rescued a llama."

"My shining moment," signed Patrick.

Liam laughed. The sound sent happy chills all the way to the soles of Patrick's feet. Even as a little kid, he'd loved making Liam laugh, because it was such a happy, no-holds-barred, childlike sound. Before he could fully enjoy the moment, Liam sobered, and signed, "Did you see Big Dog and Mom?"

"Yes. They're fine, but Big Dog's meaner than ever."

A shadow fell over Liam's face. "Because of me?"

"No. I don't know. It's probably because of me. Liam . . . I wanted to—"

But before he could get any further, Liam rose to his feet. "It's time for me to go surfing. You can come if you want. It only takes sixteen seconds to walk to the beach from here."

Patrick looked at Lara, who offered him an encouraging gesture.

"Yes," he signed to Liam.

"I'm going to take a little nap," signed Lara. "We didn't get a lot of sleep last night."

Patrick tried not to react to that comment, though he couldn't avoid the sudden mental image of Lara's half-nude body writhing beneath his. God, he was a beast. Lara was trying to give him time alone with his brother, and he was thinking about getting her naked. Freaking animal, that's what he was.

As she stretched out on the couch, the two brothers headed for the front door. Before they stepped outside, Liam put on sports sunglasses with a head strap to keep them in place. Bright light had always been a problem for him.

A tiny path wound its way past scruffy beach grass and over a low sand dune. When they cleared the small rise, Patrick let out a sharp breath at the sight of the pristine, virtually empty white sand beach spread out before them. Sparkles danced on the ocean waves, as if the sun was sprinkling bright confetti for a party.

"Nice place," signed Patrick. "You got your own private beach?"

"I let other people use it sometimes."

Patrick chuckled. "You did good, brother. Really good."

The praise sent a rush of red to Liam's cheeks. "Thanks, brother."

And all of a sudden, Patrick was sure he was going to cry. Liam had called him "brother." He wouldn't do that if he hated him, right? His throat tightened, his eyes prickled. With every fiber of his being he fought against the disaster of tears. Not that men couldn't cry. He'd seen lots of masculine tears at fire scenes, when someone was still trapped inside or when their dog was rescued. Fear, relief, anguish—they all brought tears.

He'd even seen tears from firefighters after an especially emotional rescue, or a failed rescue attempt. Captain Brody encouraged the guys to talk about what they'd seen and experienced during tough calls, and often that meant tears.

But not from him. No fucking way. Not in front of the guys at the firehouse and not in front of his little brother.

"The wind really blows the spray around," he signed, after wiping a drop of moisture from the corner of his eye.

Liam didn't notice anything odd; he tended to miss emotions unfurling right in front of him. "The surfing's good too."

"You surf?"

"Yes. You want to go? See who stays up longest?"

"Surfing?" He'd never surfed in his life, having never lived anywhere near an ocean. But he'd snowboarded and skateboarded, and surely that was close enough so he could fake it. He shoved aside the thought that he was supposed to be hashing things out with Liam, not picking up a new sports obsession. "You're on."

Liam gave a little hop of excitement, which reminded Patrick of Goldie. "I bet I'll beat your ass, big brother."

"Only one way to find out."

He followed Liam to a small grass-thatched hut that sheltered several battered old surfboards in a meticulously ordered pile. Liam sorted through them, finally presenting him with a yellow longboard.

"This one's for studs," signed Liam. "I hope you can handle it."

He looked at it with deep skepticism. It was a helluva lot longer than a snowboard, and it didn't have any fastenings for your boots. *Of course not, you ass, surfers go barefoot.*

He followed Liam's lead, kicking off his shoes and stripping down to his boxers. "Really, we're doing this in our underwear?"

"Right here, right now," declared Liam, whose chest looked a lot more sculpted than it had at seventeen. "Just like old times." He found a set of ear plugs dangling from a nail and inserted them in his ears. Ever since his disastrous ear infection, Liam had to be careful not to get water in his ears.

Again that treacherous avalanche threatened in Patrick's chest. In the old days he and Liam had invented a million ways to compete. First to the end of the driveway on their skateboards. First to the garbage can with their bags of garbage. Highest on the trampoline. It was how they connected, and neither cared who won. In fact, Patrick preferred it when Liam won; maybe Liam had felt the same way.

They hadn't been officially competing the night of the accident. But they were always competing; it was understood. Liam had been first to the RV, first to veer away, first to go flying through the air.

Fuck.

Patrick jammed the surfboard under his arm and followed his brother to the edge of the ocean. Warm water lapped at his toes. Liam settled himself belly first onto his board and began paddling out, dipping under the first wave to get his head wet. Patrick followed, wobbling from side to side as he tried to get the

hang of it. Something told him he was about to get his
ass handed to him.

He gritted his teeth and flailed at the water. Damn
it, he wouldn't go down without a fight.

When they passed the point where the waves were
breaking, Liam stopped paddling and hauled himself into a sitting position, dangling his hands in the
water to keep the board pointed the right way. Patrick
mimicked him, feeling about as graceful as a whale.
For a time they drifted like that, Liam gazing intently
at the swells coming in. It was mid-morning by now,
and the sun beat down on their heads and shoulders.
A few other surfers were staking out an area farther
down the beach, where ominous rocks protruded like
shark's teeth.

At least Liam hadn't picked that spot; his intention
apparently wasn't to drown his uninvited brother.

A gesture from Liam made him snap to attention.
He watched carefully as Liam gauged the wave, paddled furiously, then pulled himself into a standing position. The wave pushed him forward on its creamy,
curling edge. Liam balanced with a sort of awkward
grace, knees bent, arms stretched to the sides, body
loose and easy. He could have ridden all the way to
shore, but instead dove into the water just before the
wave crashed into sparkling smithereens.

"Whoo-hoo!" Patrick yelled, making big splashes of
celebration as a visual reinforcement. Liam surfaced
with a wide grin, then gestured at him to take the next
wave. He took a deep breath. His little brother had
made it look so easy. He was older, stronger, fitter, and
he'd always been able to beat Liam at just about everything. Why should this be any different? Piece of cake.

The wave loomed behind him. He paddled the
way Liam had, then grabbed the board in both hands,

hauled himself up—and went tumbling head over heels in a chaotic maelstrom of white foam and swirling saltwater. He surfaced, gasping, to the sight of Liam's amused face.

When he'd managed to mount the surfboard again, Patrick signed, "It's harder than it looks." Good thing the board was tethered to his ankle, or that would have been the last he'd seen of it.

A few attempts later he was wishing he never had to see the damn board again. The thing was slippery as a freaking eel—a flat, hard eel that kept bonking him on the head, the knees, and the shoulder. The board seemed to have no mercy. Neither did Liam, who clearly found the whole thing hilarious. By the time Patrick gave up and stalked out of the water, a thin line of blood ran from a cut on his knee, his upper back was scorched, and his body felt like one big bruise.

Liam walked, cheerful and completely bruise-free. "It takes a while to learn," he signed. "It took me fifty-two tries before I could stand up. Don't worry, you did good."

Patrick smiled through gritted teeth. "I did lousy. You won big, brother. Is there a mountain nearby? Snowboarding's more my thing."

"No mountain. But we could do a dune race."

"You have dune buggies around here?"

"No. A foot race. Running up and down the sand dunes is good exercise."

Since Liam didn't even look winded, Patrick supposed it made sense that he wanted more exercise. Then again, he hadn't been wrestling with a vengeful fiberglass murder weapon.

He started to beg off, but the determined look on Liam's face stopped him. Liam wanted to race. The hell if he'd deny his brother. "Sure. Foot race. I'm in."

They ran across sand that was beginning to radiate the sun's heat directly into the soles of their feet. Liam practically danced over the dunes, zipping right and left to avoid scratchy beach grass, a few sharp pebbles, and even a stray crab claw. Patrick, meanwhile, managed to trip over a beer can, stumble into someone's abandoned fire ring, and nearly sprain his ankle trying to avoid a dead jellyfish.

Worst of all, he didn't actually avoid the jellyfish.

"I give up," he signed to Liam, who leaned over him as he lay flat on his back, his right foot covered in disgusting jellyfish goo. "You win. I preemptively admit defeat in any competition that takes place in Mexico."

The laughter dropped from Liam's face, leaving something that looked very much like hurt. "What else?" he signed.

"What else?" Patrick stared up at him. The hot sand grated against his sunburned shoulders. His knee throbbed. "Okay. What else. The accident. My fault."

Liam slowly shook his head. "No. *My* accident," he said out loud, emphatically thumping his fist against his chest. "Mine."

"You're right. Sorry."

But Liam was still waiting, implacable, his head and upper body blocking the sun.

Patrick drew in a deep breath. "I shouldn't have left you. I should have stayed after it happened, no matter what Big Dog said. That was wrong."

Liam tilted his head just a bit, so a sliver of sun flared at the edge of Patrick's vision. He shaded his eyes with one hand while continuing to sign with the other.

"You want more? All right, more." He thought hard, thought of everything that had happened since he'd last seen Liam, and everything he'd missed. "Here it is. I'm an arrogant prick and you did just fine without me, brother. I'm proud of you."

At that, Liam reached out his hand and grasped Patrick's. He scrambled to his feet and for a long moment the two brothers looked each other in the eye. Hugging had never been their thing; Liam didn't really like it. Instead, Patrick crossed his wrists and hugged them to his chest. The sign for love.

Liam took it in with a slight frown, as if he didn't know why "love" needed stating. He pinched his thumb and middle finger together and drew a string outward from his chest, then made Lara's name sign. Did he like Lara?

Patrick nodded. Even to Liam, who tended to shy away from emotional conversations, it must be obvious.

Liam looked thoughtful as he picked up his surfboard and led the way back to the hut. "There's an outdoor shower at my house. Let's race."

"It's all yours. Enjoy your shower. I'll see you in a few." Patrick gingerly pulled on his lizard T-shirt, wincing as it clung to his newly scorched skin.

Liam gave him the good-bye sign and ambled away. Patrick watched him go. His little brother had totally, absolutely schooled him. Put him through his paces, humiliated him in the realms of surfing and sand-dune-racing, and forced him to issue the *right* apology.

All this time, what had he been picturing? To be honest, he'd imagined his mother tending Liam, Big Dog calling in the best therapists. He'd pictured his brother as nearly helpless, the way he'd been right after the accident. Logically, he'd known that Liam must have recovered, at least to some extent. He'd figured their parents would spare no expense, that his brother would be coddled and treated like a prince as he worked his way back to health.

The idea that Liam would have seized his independence, made his own life for himself, taught himself how to surf, found a *girlfriend*?

He stole a glance around the beach, but saw no one except a few surfers still floating out to sea. Closer, a sandpiper poked his long bill at the wet sand at the ocean's edge. A little pink crab scuttled sideways into a clump of grass. A hummingbird swooped past, hovering like an animated jewel before whisking its wings and disappearing in a blurry flash of ruby red.

Blurry because now that he was alone, Patrick did nothing to stop the tears that seemed to well from the very deepest part of his being—a place that hadn't seen the sun in a very long time.

Chapter Twenty-Five

Lara woke to an unexpected sight: two sculpted, sun-tousled men. They smiled down at her, one from eyes of fierce cobalt, the other's sunny blue. Both looked grubby and salt-streaked and ready for a long soak in a hot tub, or at least a shower. The smell of sun, ocean, and sweat permeated the air.

She promptly leaned over the edge of the couch and threw up.

Liam backed away in horror. He'd never been comfortable with bodily functions. Patrick crouched next to her, swiping her hair away from her face as she retched miserably. "Don't worry about it, sweetheart," he murmured. "Get it all out."

Her stomach clenched, over and over again, as the contents spilled to the floor. When she was done, she kept her head where it was, hanging over the edge, so she didn't have to meet anyone's eyes.

"Don't move. I'll be right back."

Patrick disappeared, and a second later a damp cloth was pressed against her face. Shaking, she moved it across her mouth. "I'm so sorry," she croaked.

Patrick used the towel to dab a spot that she'd missed. "Don't worry about it, honey. Just lie back and take it easy."

She did as he said, a little startled by his use of the word "honey." Opening her eyes a crack, she raised an eyebrow at Patrick.

"He asked me and I told him," he said in a husky voice, wiping her hair off her damp forehead.

She groaned. "What a mess."

"Actually, he's fine with it."

"No, I mean the floor. Just let me catch my breath and I'll clean it up."

"No way. Stay where you are. I got this."

Lara finally dared to lift her head. "Where's Liam?"

Liam was nowhere to be seen. "I guess you scared him off," said Patrick with a wink. "Don't take it personally."

As he rose to his feet, she noticed a trickle of dried blood on his shin. "What happened?"

"Manly stuff. Brotherly bond stuff. You wouldn't understand."

She struggled to sit up. "Did you fight? I should have known you guys would get into trouble if I wasn't there. I should never have left you alone."

He gently pushed her back down, then went into the kitchenette to rummage for rags. "No fights, at least not with blows. Or words," he explained over his shoulder. "You have to speak man language to get it. He told me what he thought of me abandoning him to the tender loving care of Big Dog Callahan. I apologized and told him I was proud of him."

"So you had a conversation?"

"Hell no. Well, a little bit, at the end."

"At the end of *what*?"

Patrick reappeared with a stainless steel mixing bowl and a pile of torn T-shirts. "At the end of the Callahan Brothers Truth and Reconciliation Olympics. I guess you had to be there."

He knelt down and began mopping up the mess. Lara covered her face with one arm; even the sight of it was making her nauseous again. "I'm supposed to be back at work on Monday. I hope this is done by then."

"If you're not better by tomorrow we're not going anywhere. But these things usually pass quickly, as you know, Doc."

She groaned. "I don't think this is food poisoning. There's a stomach flu going around in San Diego. I think I picked it up at the hospital."

"How long does it last?"

"A few days, usually. I'll need fluids. Liam better have some bottled water. I'm not taking any chances."

"I have a case of water in the Hulk." Patrick finished cleaning the floor and went to the sink to wring out the rags. "Keep that bowl close in case it hits you again. I'm going to go hang these up and check on Liam. My brother might be able to beat me on a surfboard, but when it comes to cleaning up after my girl, I'm undefeated."

"Yay for you," she said weakly. The words "my girl" made her insides go warm and squishy, or maybe that was . . . She steeled herself, fighting a new wave of nausea. This one passed over without any new disaster. "I think I'm just going to lie here perfectly still until further notice."

"Good plan. If you feel like napping, that works too. Sleep's a cure for everything, right? At least that's what they're always telling me whenever I break a bone. Which happens a lot." He came to her side and passed a light hand over her forehead. "No fever."

"You're playing doctor?"

"Hey, I do more than dangle out of helicopters. I'm a trained paramedic, you know. Most of us are."

"Right. Forgot." Her eyes drifted shut. "Thanks, Patrick. I owe you. I don't know what, but something."

"I'll mark it down. We'll think of something good."

The next couple of days passed in a blur of dry heaves and vertiginously spinning rooms. She clung to the couch as if it were a lifeboat, only leaving when she had to stagger to the bathroom. On Sunday she borrowed Liam's phone—neither hers nor Patrick's had reception—to call the hospital. As soon as they heard she'd contracted the dreaded stomach flu making the rounds, they told her to take the whole week off. She also had to call the clinic and reschedule her interview.

If not for Patrick she would have lost her mind along with every trace of food in her system. He was . . . well, perfect. He tended to her with a sort of brisk practicality that was exactly what she needed. He brought her bottled water, Gatorade, crackers, and miso soup, which he claimed worked better than chicken soup. The sound of his voice always made her perk up, no matter how deeply queasy she was feeling. The rest of life went on without her. Liam kept his distance, only speaking to her from the other side of the room. Liam and Patrick seemed to spend a lot of time surfing. She was vaguely aware when Liam's girlfriend came home, and some sort of uproar ensued.

But mostly she slept and sipped her fluids. And lived for the moments when Patrick would come rub her neck or give her a discreet sponge bath. Or drop a kiss on her head. Those were the only moments she felt like an actual human with a future that didn't involve mixing bowls. The thought crossed her mind that she might be pregnant, except she quickly realized it wasn't possible. Pregnant by Patrick . . . the idea ought to have alarmed her. But it didn't. It made something spark to life, like a beacon on some distant horizon.

The thought capsized under a wave of nausea. When she surfaced, when Patrick had rinsed out the bowl and brought it back, skimming a tender hand across her forehead, another stunning truth occurred to her.

I love you.

The words arose from the depths of her queasiness, quite naturally, as if they had been there all along.

But they couldn't have been. *Love Patrick?* Impossible. She would have known something like that. Stomach bugs did funny things to your brain, that was all.

"You ran away with the housekeeper?" Patrick couldn't get over it. Soledad Ramirez had worked for the Callahans for years. She had to be fifteen years older than Liam. She was pretty enough, he supposed, but his general impression had always been one of a dark-haired whirlwind of hard work. She used to tear through the ranch house like a hurricane of Ajax. They'd all been surprised when she learned sign language faster than any of them, and used it to insist that Liam put his dirty socks in the hamper and stop making careful piles of midnight snack plates in his room.

"Soledad is a wonderful person, for a hearie," he signed. "I trust her. She's very capable and she doesn't let anyone push her around. And she's not a housekeeper anymore. She cleans houses for vacation rentals now. I do the cleaning here so she doesn't have to. Except for vomit. I don't clean up vomit."

"No, clearly that's my job around here."

"Dad fired her. He shouldn't have done that," Liam signed.

They were floating on their surfboards, taking advantage of a relatively calm day to give him a chance to practice surfing without nearly drowning. So far, so good. "He fired her because of you?"

"No, he fired her because he started firing everyone. That's not right. And he shouldn't have made you leave."

Of course that would have upset Liam. Liam lived by rules and one of the Callahan family rules was that you stuck together. "No, he shouldn't have. Is that why you left, because he fired Soledad?"

"Yes. It wasn't right. He was changing things around. Why can't I go in the barn? That doesn't make sense."

Patrick could imagine how upsetting Big Dog's unpredictable behavior must have been for Liam. He'd always relied on his routines.

"Are you ever going to back to Loveless?"

Liam shielded his eyes from the sun as he watched the oncoming swells. "Soledad and I will discuss it after we get married."

"Married?"

"Of course. You're supposed to be married if you live together. Here comes a good one."

He leaped onto his board and skimmed toward the shore. Patrick was so shocked that the wave caught him with one foot on the board, the other sticking out behind him as if he were attempting some kind of oceangoing pirouette.

He crashed into the churning foam for the hundredth time since coming to Baja.

Married? His younger, developmentally challenged, deaf brother was getting married before him?

He surfaced and discovered his ankle tether had come undone and his surfboard was bouncing on the waves a short distance away. Liam was shouting and pointing at it. He gave his brother a wave of acknowledgment and paddled over to the board. Resting his arms on it, he kicked his way toward shore. He was thirty years old, which meant Liam was twenty-eight. Plenty old enough for marriage. And it made sense that he'd see marriage as a requirement of living together as a couple. Liam might be his little brother, but he was a grown man perfectly capable of deciding what he wanted, and going after it.

In some ways, Liam had things more together than he did. The realization was just as humbling as this whole surfing fiasco.

By midweek Lara was feeling well enough to sit down for dinner at the outdoor table behind the bungalow. A red and white striped beach umbrella sheltered them from the late day sun. Soledad brought out brightly colored bowls filled with a fish stew she swore would strengthen Lara's digestion. Some tortillas, a few bottles of *cerveza*, and they had themselves a feast. Liam wore his hearing aid headset for the occasion, though he could only use it for a short time until his head began to ache.

A paler, thinner Lara took a careful sip of broth, then set down her spoon. "I want to thank all of you and apologize for being the worst houseguest ever. It's not every day someone shows up uninvited, throws up all over your living room floor, then refuses to leave the couch for the next week."

"It hasn't been a week," pointed out the always literal Liam.

"It hasn't? It sure feels like it." She inhaled the steam rising from her spoonful of soup, as if trying to acclimate her stomach to it in advance. "Anyway, I'm really sorry. If any of you is ever feeling sick, there's a couch waiting for you up in San Diego. Open invitation."

Patrick raised his bottle of Corona and clicked it against Soledad's. "Same goes for San Gabriel, although my couch isn't much to speak of." In fact, he could barely summon an image of his lonely apartment. It felt like a million years since he'd been there.

"San Gabriel?" Soledad brightened. "You're one of the bachelors, no? The ones on TV? The sexy, single firefighters that all the girls go crazy for? But there's a *maledicto*, what is it . . . a curse?" She crossed herself.

"That's a huge exaggeration." Patrick stuffed a chunk of whitefish in his mouth to avoid further comment. He felt Lara's teasing gaze on him.

"There is no curse?"

Congratulating himself on his forethought, Patrick pointed to his mouth and chewed earnestly at his fish.

"I don't know," said Lara. "If Patrick Callahan IV, the handsome, dynamic, heroic, partially college-educated fireman can't find anyone to marry him, I think this curse might need looking into."

"You won't marry him?" Liam asked, looking seriously from one to the other of them. "Why not? He's not a bad guy, overall."

Lara choked on her spoonful of soup. Patrick, fighting to keep a straight face, pounded her on the back. She gagged, and Liam scrambled away from the table. Patrick swung her chair around so if she threw up she'd be pointed away from the table.

"How is it possible for one person to produce so

much vomit?" Liam murmured to Soledad with complete seriousness. He had no concept of sarcasm.

Lara's shoulders quaked—from laughter, Patrick hoped. Was she laughing at Liam's comment or at the thought of marrying him? Was the idea really so ludicrous? Not that he was thinking about marriage. But surely once a guy had taken care of a girl while she was sick, that girl ought to put him in the category of potential life partner.

Really, she shouldn't be laughing quite so hard.

He put an arm around her while her ribs quaked. Finally she straightened up. "I'm okay. I'm okay. False alarm," she told the other two with a bright smile. "That'll teach you to surprise me with crazy talk. So. Soledad and Liam. When exactly did the sparks begin to fly between you two?"

The rest of the meal was devoted to getting to know Soledad—the more Patrick saw, the more he liked her down-to-earth, devoted style—and sharing stories from the firehouse.

Crazy talk. The phrase stuck in his mind and mocked him the rest of the night.

The next day, he and Lara packed their things into the Hulk. Soledad loaded them up with avocadoes and oranges. Liam gave them a letter to deliver to their parents. A last round of hugs, then they waved good-bye to Liam and Soledad and left the Casita Rosa.

The vehicle lurched down the gravel beach road. Patrick split his attention between keeping the wheels on the ground and making sure Lara was okay. She looked a little green but waved him off.

"Don't worry about me. Just get us to the main road in one piece."

As he steered the Hulk from one rut to the next, he remembered the accident that had killed her parents.

"I know I might seem like a reckless driver," he said, swinging the wheel to avoid a jackrabbit bouncing across the road. "But I've never even gotten a ticket."

"Is that because the cops never caught up with you?"

"Haha. Quite the comedienne. No, it's because I'm an outstanding driver, and if I were to break a traffic rule, they'd be so in awe of my technique they'd forget about giving me a ticket and simply applaud my expertise."

"Wow. I'm about to give you a ticket for arrogance."

He smiled, then turned serious. "What I mean to say is, you're safe with me. I might take risks when it really matters, if it would save someone's life. But I never take risks without a good reason."

She gave him an odd look. "The funny thing is, I never even thought to be nervous. I know what a great driver you are. I've seen you on a dirt bike, remember?"

Patrick was about to point out that his dirt bike skills weren't the best example, having landed him in the hospital, when both their phones beeped. "We finally got service, I guess."

Lara was already checking her messages. "Megan called. Did she call you too?"

"I don't know." He tossed his phone to her. "You look. I don't want to make an ass out of myself after just ranting about my safe driving record."

But she was listening to the message. Her eyes went wide. "Listen." She put the phone on speaker and played the message again. Megan had left it the day before.

"Lara, I'm trying to find Patrick. Have you seen him? If you're with him, tell him another wildfire broke out and this one's a lot closer. It's headed in our direction.

The firefighters came out and told us to evacuate, but Dad thinks he can handle it by himself. When are you coming back? Please call as soon as you get this message. Or tell Patrick to call. I'm really scared and Dad won't listen to anything I say."

Adrenaline sizzled through every nerve of his body. He slammed the accelerator down and the Hulk hurtled across a rut, briefly going airborne.

"Sorry," he said grimly, putting a hand to Lara's torso, making sure her seat belt was nice and tight.

"No worries. Drive as fast as you need to."

"I'll drop you off in San Diego, then—"

"No. There's a quicker way, through Arizona. The border crossing is faster. It'll save us at least two hours. And you know what Southern California traffic is like. We're much better off going through Nogales."

"But you have to get back to work."

"Not until Monday. And anyway, you were stuck down here because of me. I'm coming with you, and that's final. I might be able to help. Have you forgotten I'm a doctor?"

"No. I'd forgotten—" He hadn't really forgotten anything, but every thought other than the ranch had fled like a flight of panicked swallows. "I'd forgotten you're you. Thank you."

And he stepped on it.

Chapter Twenty-Six

*F*or most of the drive they watched the dry, sun-baked Mexican landscape pass by in concentrated silence. Lara didn't want to break into Patrick's single-minded focus on the road with anything less than earth-shattering news. He seemed to be wrapped up in some kind of deep communion with the highway.

His driving was a thing of beauty. The way he maneuvered through the twisting curves in the rugged mountain passes took her breath away. He passed slower vehicles with meticulous precision, never reckless, never out of control. For the first time in many years she thought about her parents making that last, fatal drive. The police had said it wasn't her father's fault, but she'd looked it up. He'd been driving ten miles above the speed limit, not unusual for him. But maybe he could have reacted more quickly to that drunk driver if he'd been going the limit. He'd always been a larger-than-life, cocky daredevil of a man—a male version of his sister Tam.

In her mind, she'd blamed him. And maybe some of that blame had carried over to Patrick after the dirt bike accident.

She gave him a sidelong look, taking in his intent scowl, the set of his jaw, the firm contours of his lips. Patrick had carried a lot of blame over the last ten years. But he hadn't let it destroy him. Instead, he'd done something with it. Found a purpose. Saved lives. Then he'd faced his worst accuser, his own father, so he could help his family, whether they wanted it or not. Her respect for him rose another few notches. Really, she couldn't imagine it getting much higher.

For so long she'd blamed him for running away when Liam was in the hospital, but what about her? Hadn't she run from Loveless and never looked back, until forced to? All those years she'd spent rejecting Aunt Tam, wanting nothing to do with the Haven, wanting no one to take the place of her lost family. She still remembered the first time she walked into the Haven and nearly gagged at the scent of sandalwood. Right away she'd turned against the place. She'd stuck to her silly black clothes and made fun of everything there and fled as soon as possible.

What if everything she'd done, from adopting a goth girl persona and even pursuing a medical degree, had been to reject her eccentric, free-spirited, bigger-than-life aunt and her madcap existence? The aunt who'd done nothing but love her and accept her and support her in whatever she chose to do. The aunt who was the closest person she'd had to a family.

Deep in her own thoughts, she barely noticed as they passed the ten kilometers to *la frontera* sign.

Things were moving so fast, as they had ever since Patrick came back into her life. Another few minutes and they'd be in the United States again, back to reality. Back to hospitals and fires.

"I tried calling Megan, but she isn't answering her phone," said Patrick grimly. "I'd call the firehouse but they probably have their hands full."

"Do you want me to call the Haven? Maybe your mother can do something."

He ran a hand across the back of his neck. "Why didn't I think of that? Yes, that would be great. If Big Dog listens to anyone, it's Mom."

She dialed the number as Patrick maneuvered them into the line at the border control. After a few rings Romaine answered.

"Romaine, thank goodness! This is Lara. Is Candy Callahan still there?"

"Candy went back to her ranch. Where are you?"

"Mexico."

"Mexico?"

"Long story. Does Candy know about the fire?"

"Of course she knows about the fire. The whole town is covered in ash again. You wouldn't recognize the Cadillac. It looks like a hearse."

Lara gripped the phone so hard she inadvertently pressed a few buttons, which gave a scolding beep. Was the Haven in danger too? Not the Haven. Not all those pillows and wall hangings and hokey hand-painted sayings. Not her last link to her childhood. "Is . . . uh . . . what about you guys, the Haven . . ."

"We're fine so far. The fire isn't headed in our direction. But the whole town is covered with flying cinders. We're all supposed to stay inside. The Callahans and other people out that way are in the worst trouble.

They're supposed to evacuate, but you know how Big Dog is. That's why Candy went back. Janey went with her. Everyone does what Janey says."

Not Big Dog. Romaine was too new to Loveless to know that, but Lara decided not to mention it.

"Can you get in touch with Candy and see if she got him out? We're headed to the ranch now, and it would help if we knew what was going on."

"I'll try. I'll give you a call back if I hear anything."

"Thanks, Romaine."

Lara clicked off the phone. The Mexican police, armed with automatic weapons, were waving them across the border.

"Did you hear all that?"

"Yes." If possible, Patrick looked even grimmer. "I wish Janey hadn't gone. He hates her, especially now that my mom's staying at the Haven. If anything's guaranteed to make him dig in his heels, it's Janey trying to boss him around."

Lara's heart sank at the memory of the animosity Big Dog had for the Haven and everyone associated with it. "He hates all of us. I'm at the top of that list. Maybe I shouldn't go either. I don't want to make things worse."

"I don't care what Big Dog thinks, but if there's an active fire, I don't want you anywhere close."

"Hey. I did okay at the Waller Canyon Fire."

"That's not the point. I just . . ." He gripped the steering wheel until his knuckles turned white. "I don't want you in danger."

Lara shivered at the intensity in his voice. She fought against that weak feeling, the one that made her want to curl up against Patrick's side and let him take care of everything. She was a grown, independent woman who was perfectly capable of taking care of herself. "Doctors face danger all the time too. Crazy patients, bacteria, staph infections, viruses—"

"Okay, okay." Patrick looked a little pale. "I'm not questioning your courage. But if something happened to you at a fire on *my ranch*, I'd want to kill someone."

"Kill someone? Geez, 'Psycho.' That's a little extreme, don't you think?"

Expressions chased each other across his face like summer lightning: fury, fear, determination. "I don't know. Maybe I'm an extreme kind of guy. I'm just telling you how I feel."

"Well, it's sweet that you're so concerned about my safety—"

"Why'd you call it crazy talk?" He tossed the abrupt question like a hand grenade.

"What?" This conversation was giving her more whiplash than all those hairpin curves in the canyons.

"When Liam started asking about marriage. You said it was crazy talk. I want to know why. What's so crazy about it?"

She had a sudden impulse to put her hand to his forehead and check his temperature. "Patrick, what the hell has gotten into you? Are you worried about the ranch? The fire department is probably handling things just fine."

A muscle jumped in his jaw. "Answer the question." He forced the words through tightly gritted teeth.

Okay, so maybe he was serious. Maybe she'd hurt his feelings with her casual dismissal of marriage. "Well . . . we . . . I mean . . . how would we . . . " The problem was, off the top of her head she couldn't come up with any objections, though she knew there had to be a million. "I've never really thought that much about marriage," she finally said. "It always seemed like something for the future. A 'someday' sort of thing."

He drummed his fingers on the steering wheel. "That's a good way to put it. 'Someday.' But when do you know when 'someday' comes? What if it's now? You and me?"

Holy crap. Was this some kind of cockeyed marriage proposal? But he hadn't said he wanted to marry *her*. He hadn't even said he loved her. This was just Patrick being Patrick, knocking her off balance when she least expected it. How did he always do this to her? She used her most authoritative doctor voice. "I don't think this is the right time to talk about something like this. It makes no sense. We don't even live in the same place."

A brusque wave of his hand dismissed that objection. "I'm not tied to San Gabriel forever. I've thought about joining a hotshot crew or one of those private firefighter-for-hire groups that gets called to the really tough wildfires. Or I could transfer. I don't think I'll ever have trouble finding work."

Was he seriously thinking about this? Her irritation grew. "Your family hates me."

"Donkey's balls, to quote my dad. Liam and Megan love you. My mom likes you just fine. She's living at your property, remember? And Big Dog's insane. I'm done making decisions based on Big Dog."

Lara dug her fingernails into her palms. They zoomed up the perfectly ordinary highway that now felt like a direct route to crazyland. When she pictured marriage, she'd always imagined something safe and comforting. She'd imagined coming home after a long day's work to a foot rub and a glass of wine. Calm conversations about where they should spend Christmas. Gentle laughter about the upstairs neighbor or the annoying dog across the street. She'd pictured marriage as a sort of warm bath.

Life with Patrick would be more like whitewater rafting. He was the man who always kept her guessing, who pushed her headlong into her own sexuality, who made her laugh and, in the next moment, made her more furious than anyone else on the planet.

Just look at how he was approaching this whole conversation. If he really wanted to propose, where was the ring? Where was the bended knee?

"I don't even know why you're talking about this," she hissed. "Because we've had sex? I'm not some girl in a Regency romance."

"A what?"

"You know, back when sex automatically meant marriage, unless you were a rake. A cad."

He shot her a look. "A 'cad.' Oh my. Say it ain't so."

"Of course you aren't a cad. That's my whole point. You won't be a cad if you don't marry me just because we're having sex." She inhaled a deep breath, trying to summon one of Aunt Tam's meditation mottos. *Return to your center. Ground yourself in your inner truth.*

"But that's just it. I *am* saying, marry me."

So much for returning to her center. "You aren't *really* saying it, Patrick. You're just being crazy."

"You keep saying that. But what's so crazy about it? So far your objections are geography and Big Dog. Neither of them matters one bit."

She put her hand to her head, wishing everything would stop spinning.

"Are you okay?"

"Can we please stop talking about this?"

"Sure." He winked, that teasing, vivid flash of blue that had tormented her since she was twelve. "For now."

"Patrick!"

He closed his lips with a zipping gesture and they both fell silent. Alongside the road, telephone poles flashed by in a steady pattern. Lara rolled down the window and let the flow of air cool her face. They zipped through one tiny town, then another, eating up the miles to the ranch.

Lara stewed over everything Patrick had said. The closer they got to the ranch, the more angry she got. They passed from Arizona to Nevada, then turned onto the highway that would take them to Loveless. If Patrick was serious, then he'd delivered the worst proposal in the history of mankind. If he wasn't serious, then why had he brought it up? What was he really up to?

It finally clicked about fifty miles from Loveless. *I'm done making decisions based on Big Dog.* But was he? "I know what you're doing."

"What do you mean?"

"As always, you're trying to find the thing most likely to piss off your father. It worked when you invited me to dinner, so why not up the ante? Why not tell him we're getting married? You'd guarantee yourself a rant. He already gave me one. He said no Callahan would ever marry someone like me."

Patrick whipped his head around, spearing her with blue fire. "That's fucked up. I don't care what Big Dog says, thinks, or does. I make my own decisions."

"But that's just words, Patrick. I know I'm right. What other explanation is there? You've been trying to tick off your dad your entire life."

"What 'other explanation'?" She could practically see the steam coming out of his ears as he passed a trundling RV going about ten miles under the speed limit. "What about the fact that we're good together? No, *great* together? What about the fact that I want to be with you all the time, and I think waking up next to you for the rest of my life would be pretty freaking amazing?"

Lara's hair chose that moment to whip itself out of its shaky knot. She gathered it off her face and wrapped it around her hand while she rolled the window back up. The sudden quiet gave his words even more significance. Was he actually, really proposing, and not in the most backward way imaginable? "Are you seriously saying you're serious?"

"I'm saying I could be serious. I'm saying we should give it serious consideration. I'm saying I don't see why we shouldn't think about it."

"*Patrick!*"

"What?"

She struggled to get a grip on her storm of emotions, but failed utterly. "If you're really proposing, you're doing a horrible job. Like epically, ridiculously horrible. If you ever decide to do it for real, think back to this moment and do everything the opposite."

He shot her a stunned look, opened and closed his mouth a few times, then directed his attention back to the road, jaw clenched, eyes narrowed to a squint.

Okay, so he had said a few nice things in there. But they'd been buried underneath a bunch of confusing statements, none of which translated to "I love you." He had said that thing about "waking up next to her," which was pretty darn romantic. And being "great together."

But what about love?

"Holy mother of God," Patrick murmured. "Just look at that."

Huge billows of ominous black smoke roiled on the horizon. It looked like a thunderstorm lit with lightning flashes of demonic orange.

"Wow," she breathed.

"Good thing is, I'd say that's still a few miles from the ranch. We should have time. But not a helluva lot. Hang on."

He put the accelerator to the floorboards. Lara gripped the door handle as the Hulk rocked and rolled at top speed down the highway.

Patrick barreled through Loveless, where the streets were nearly empty and everything was coated with a light dusting of pale ash. So he'd made an ass out of himself with Lara. What else was new? She'd shot him down, even though he didn't even know exactly what he was trying to say. The whole thing sat in his gut like a bad fishburger. But he couldn't think about it anymore now. That fire was calling his name.

Smoky air filtered through the dashboard vents. He opened his glove compartment, brushing against Lara's bare knee in the process. With savage satisfaction he noted the goose bumps that rose on her skin at his touch. Her khaki shorts stopped at mid-thigh, and her smooth skin had been distracting him the whole trip. Maybe that's why he'd fucked everything up.

He pulled two particle masks from his glove compartment and handed one to her. Using his knees to steer, he snapped one of them around his mouth, then gestured for her to do the same. Efficiently, she did so, then put all her hair back in a twist, anchoring it with a clip.

He nodded and gave her a thumbs-up. They both faced forward, the lower half of their faces shielded by the thin white filters.

At least they couldn't talk anymore. He couldn't make a fool of himself, and she couldn't hurt his pride.

Lights flashed behind them. A Loveless fire engine,

sirens sounding, zoomed past. Patrick recognized Pedro in the front seat and waved. The firefighter beckoned to him to follow close.

Drafting off a fire engine—not something any fire department normally encouraged. Patrick took it as either a sign of confidence or of how bad things stood at the ranch. Either way, he'd take them up on it. He fell in line behind the engine. Both vehicles flew down the last stretch of the main road. Together they took the sharp turn onto the long gravel driveway to the ranch house.

Just past the perimeter of the Callahan acreage, the wildfire squatted like a giant, belching toad. Even with the windows rolled up they could hear it roaring like a monster throwing a tantrum.

"I'm way ahead of you, asshole," Patrick shouted, forgetting where he was for a moment. All those hours he'd spent knocking down brush had paid off. There was no doubt in his mind that if he hadn't done it, the ranch house and all the outbuildings would be toast. At the very least, he'd bought them some time.

"Is it okay?" Lara shouted through her mask.

He shook his head. Hell no, it wasn't okay. He'd slowed the fire down, but with flames the height of the Space Needle, it wouldn't take much for them to jump to the nearest clump of brush, or the nearest outbuilding.

"Maybe, but we should get everyone out."

"What about him?"

She pointed at the ranch house roof. A large figure kneeled on the asphalt shingles, braced at a precarious angle. He held a garden hose, which he sprayed across the roof, splashing himself as much as the asphalt.

"Lord love a duck," breathed Patrick. "He's even crazier than I thought."

Chapter Twenty-Seven

*P*atrick brought the Hulk to a screeching halt a short distance from the fire engine. He jumped out and ran to intercept Farris, who was the first to descend from the rig.

"I'll get my father off that roof."

Farris didn't look happy. "We shouldn't even be here. I convinced the captain to swing by on our way out there." He gestured to the smoking, billowing fire line. "Can't let Big Dog Callahan do himself in, even if he's making a damn good effort."

"I got it from here. You guys do what you have to do."

"You sure?"

"Yes. I'll bring him down if it kills us both. Two fewer Callahans for you to worry about." He winked with the bravado of a longtime firefighter.

"Your sister will be glad you're here. She's been going crazy." He pointed across the yard to Megan, who was being comforted by the young firefighter

Pedro. Patrick's heart clenched at how terrified she looked. "You have your King, right?"

"Yes, sir." His work radio was stashed in his rig.

Farris gave him the tactical frequency they were using. "Keep us posted. I don't like the way that fire looks."

"It looks hungry, that's what." Patrick shook his hand. "Appreciate the help. You may be hearing from me yet, but I'll do all I can from this end."

Farris clapped him on the shoulder, called to Pedro, and a minute later the fire engine pulled out.

From the roof, Big Dog yelled, "Go on, then, you yellow-bellied sons of bitches!"

Oh, Christ. His father was in a full-throttle rage. Patrick ran to Megan and gave her a quick hug, trying to infuse his strength into her. "It's all right, Meggie. I'm on it. Where's Mom?"

Tears had left a trail of dirty streaks across Megan's freckled face. "She's around. She's with that really tall woman, Janey? I think they decided to get the animals out of the barn and stables just in case."

"That's a great idea. Why don't you go help them?" A horrible thought struck him. "Where's Goldie?"

"I don't know." Megan looked around helplessly. "I've been so worried about Dad I haven't paid attention to anything else."

"Well, you did the right thing. You did great, Megan, don't worry about Dad. I'll take care of it. Go help Mom and Janey." He beckoned to Lara, who was shading her eyes to look up at his father, who had forgotten about the hose and was still brandishing his fist at the departing fire engine.

"Lara, can you help Megan find Goldie and get the other animals out?"

She nodded and jogged toward them. Patrick saw

the exact moment she switched into doctor mode and swept Megan with an assessing look. Taking his sister by the arm, she murmured, "First things first. Let's get some water going out here. We can't let anyone get dehydrated. Megan, can you point me to some bottled water?"

Lara put an arm around his sister and firmly steered her toward the house. Patrick let out a sigh of relief. It was nice to know a smart, capable, compassionate doctor was on his side. Even if she did laugh at the very thought of marrying him.

He hurried to the ladder his father had used to climb to the roof. It was wildly askew, with one leg barely on the ground. He corrected it, made sure it was securely anchored, and scrambled to the roof. A blast of water hit him right in the face.

"Aim it somewhere else, Dad!" he shouted.

"Donkey's balls! I'm tired of everyone telling me what to do!" He swished the stream of water back and forth across Patrick's face.

Oh Lord. Big Dog had totally lost it. Patrick hurried back down the ladder, located the spigot and turned it off. As the water stopped flowing, he heard a bellow of outrage from the roof. He raced back up the ladder. At the top, Big Dog balanced precariously, fists ready to let fly, completely oblivious to the fact that he was one wrong half step from tumbling to the ground.

He had to get his dad to come down before Big Dog killed one or both of them.

"Truce, Dad! I'm on your side. We don't need to wet down the house yet. The sun will just dry it out. It's better to save the water for when the fire's on top of us."

A look of deep-seated suspicion creased Big Dog's face. "Save the water?"

"Yes, save it for when, or if, the fire gets this far. If the power goes out, we won't have any well water. We need to fill some buckets up."

Big Dog still refused to budge. "The firemen told me to evacuate. Not going to leave my property undefended. And there ain't no law that can make me."

"You're right. There isn't. And I'm right here with you, Dad. Come down and help me get ready."

Big Dog squinted at him, almost as if struggling to recognize his own son. "What are you up to?" he asked in an ugly voice. "Some kind of sabotage?" His foot slipped on the slippery roof and he staggered.

"Dad, I've got no hidden agenda. I want to help you save the place. But you can't do it if you go splat. Now, come on." He reached up a hand, only to have it swatted away with the end of the hose.

Damn it to hell. If he got his father any more upset, anything could happen. Maybe he should just climb back down the ladder and start filling buckets himself. Without water, his father wouldn't have much to do on the roof. He'd seen plenty of crazy behavior on fire scenes, but something about Big Dog seemed off. Had he been drinking? Smoked the wrong kind of cigar?

"Okay, Dad. I'm going down. Join in whenever you're ready. We'll take care of this thing, all right?" He took a step backward down the ladder.

An uncertain look crossed his father's face. God, he looked old. So old. And, for one crucial second, confused.

Then he slipped, as if on a banana peel.

The hose snaked up into the air, then came whipping past the ladder. The metal fitting at the end slashed across Patrick's cheek. He felt blood but didn't have time to worry about it because his father came next, skidding down the roof, windmilling his arms and legs.

Patrick lunged to the side, managing to wedge his body under his father's. He wrapped one arm around Big Dog's chest and dragged him sideways, so the ladder took both their weights. The thin aluminum shook beneath him but stayed steady. Big Dog twisted one way, then another; he seemed completely disoriented.

Patrick's arm muscles burned and shook with the effort of keeping a 200-plus pound man propped in midair. "Dad! Calm down. I can't keep hold of you if you keep squirming around like that."

"Patrick? Is that you?"

"Yes, I'm here." Sweat poured off his face. "We have a little situation here, but I'm not going to let you go. I'm a firefighter, remember? I do this kind of thing all the time. You're going to be fine, but you have to do exactly what I say. Understand?"

He took his father's short grunt as an affirmative.

"I want you to try to get one foot onto the ladder." With the way his father's legs were swinging back and forth, he had a very good chance of knocking both of them off the ladder. "Do you think you can do that?"

"I don't know. Don't let me go."

Patrick's heart skittered at the frightened tone of his father's voice. Though he'd phrased it more as an order, the undertone of panic was loud and clear. "I got you, Dad. I promise. If you can get at least one leg hooked onto the ladder, you'll feel a lot better. Try the left leg. Nice and easy."

Slowly, in short fits of movement, Big Dog slid his foot toward the ladder. It hit a rung with a clang that seemed to startle him.

"That's good, Dad. Just like that. Now make sure

you're on it, good and steady." Patrick shifted his head and took a gulp of smoky air. His father stank of fear and sweat, and with his big body crowding close to the ladder, there was no escape. He hadn't been this close to his father in twenty years.

Big Dog grunted. "Got my foot."

"Way to go. Now, nice and slow, shift your weight onto the ladder. That's right. You're doing great, Dad. You'd never know you weren't a fireman yourself. Now I'm going to help you turn so you can get your hands on the ladder." He shifted his own body to the side to give his father room. Big Dog inched over. Patrick guided his father's left hand onto the side of the ladder. He latched onto it with a desperate lunge.

"Perfect. Are you ready for me to let you go? I'm going to climb down a few rungs, then you can turn your body to face the ladder and come after me. Got it?"

Big Dog nodded.

"I'm letting go on three. One . . . two . . . three." He released his grip on his father but kept his hands hovering close until he was sure Big Dog wasn't going to somersault off the ladder. Then he slowly extracted himself and took the next rung, then the next. As soon as his father had made his way down the ladder, Patrick slumped against the warm aluminum, the release from tension nearly capsizing him.

Images shot through his mind: his father landing on his back on the gravel, his head splitting open, the life draining out of his eyes. His father *could have died*. He gave a silent prayer of thanks that he'd been quick enough to stop his tumble.

A shout of terror roused him. Someone was running from the direction of the barn. Lara.

"The barn's on fire! The hayloft is smoking!"

Patrick scrambled down a few more steps, then jumped the rest of the way to the ground. He grabbed the hose and dashed toward the barn. But the hose only reached halfway. He flung it aside.

"I think there's a spigot in the barn, but it might not be working. Just in case I can't get to it, get some buckets from that shed and fill them at the hose," he ordered Lara, who was right on his heels.

"What about your father?"

He looked over his shoulder to see Big Dog reach the ground. "If he'll help you, great. See if you can keep him out of my way."

"I'll do what I can. Oh, wait, Patrick! Your father has barrels of drinking water in the barn. The spigot in there must be working."

She turned away, but he grabbed her hand and swung her close to him for a fast, hard kiss on the lips. "You're a gem. Thanks for being here. Get the buckets anyway, it can't hurt." Then he ran toward the smoking building.

He knows what he's doing, Lara told herself sternly as she watched Patrick disappear inside the barn. *He does this sort of thing all the time. He's a stud. An expert. Don't freak out.* But still, it scared the crap out of her to realize he planned to tackle the smoking hayloft with no gear and no backup other than a few civilians and a llama.

She jogged toward Big Dog. He was swinging his head from side to side with a disoriented expression. Something about the way he held himself, a little jerky, a little threatening, jogged something in her memory. One of her patients, maybe?

Dismissing the thought, she stepped in front of him. "Mr. Callahan, Patrick asked if we'd fill some buckets with water. Can you help me?"

It took a moment for his eyes to focus on her. "What are *you* doing here?"

"I'm here to help with the fire," she said, enunciating every word clearly, the way she did with her elderly patients. Big Dog wasn't quite that old, but he was acting so strange at the moment. Maybe he was suffering from post-traumatic shock. She decided to keep a close eye on him. "We need all the hands we can get. Just like the old days, we're going to do a bucket brigade."

"Bucket brigade?"

"Yes. You with me?"

A shout from the direction of the barn made her swing around. A flock of chickens came charging out, followed by Janey, shooing them with big sweeps of her arms. From the stables beyond the barn, Candy Callahan led a lively piebald mustang by a rope halter. The horse reared nervously against the restraint of the rope. Candy whispered to him and stroked his neck.

Along with her came Megan, dragging an extremely reluctant Goldie by a collar around her neck. The white llama kept digging her heels into the dirt, trying desperately to stop their forward progress. Megan shouted, "Patrick's fine! He wants you to leave, you dumb llama! Why are you so stubborn?"

Lara ran forward to help her. "Obviously she and Patrick are a match made in heaven."

Megan was on the verge of tears—or maybe way beyond tears. "Do you have the buckets? Where are the buckets?"

"I was with your father. I'll get them."

Then two things happened in quick succession. Goldie yanked the collar out of Megan's grasp and wheeled around, quickly following Patrick inside the barn. And, like a gaseous Jack-in-the-box, a flame popped from the old structure's roof.

A slow smolder had transformed into a live blaze.

Megan turned to chase down Goldie, but Lara grabbed her arm. "No. We have to get water, remember? *Water.*"

"But Patrick's inside there."

"Where he needs water. Never mind. Stay with your father, okay? He's acting strange. I'll get the buckets."

Candy and Janey were now running back to the stables. Lara dashed into the toolshed and grabbed a pile of plastic five-gallon buckets. She dumped them next to the end of the hose, then ran to open the spigot.

"Start filling those buckets," she shouted to Megan and Big Dog. They did as she said—surprise, surprise—Big Dog aiming the hose at the bucket, Megan holding it steady. When it was nearly filled, Lara yelled, "That's enough. Don't make it too heavy." They filled another one, then she and Megan each took one and ran across the yard with them.

"Patrick?" she called into the interior of the barn, where smoke swirled in a wild gray hurricane. "Are you in here?"

"Don't come in!" he yelled from deep inside the barn.

"We brought water!"

"Put it down next to the door, then go." As her eyes adjusted to the crazy whirlwind of smoke, she saw him in the middle of the barn, aiming a stream of water at the hayloft. He must have found the spigot. An ominous crackling emanated from above, the sound a campfire makes when it finally catches. Goldie cowered behind Patrick, whimpering and quivering.

"Grab Goldie too." With the back of his hand, he swiped sweat off his forehead. "What kind of llama trots right back into a burning building?"

Lara and Megan left the buckets at the entrance to the barn, where the big double doors stood wide open, and hurried past an old tractor and stacks of hay bales. Patrick kept a hose aimed squarely on the hayloft while he spoke over his shoulder. "Quick as you can. If she won't go, she won't go. I don't want you guys in here."

Megan wrapped Goldie's leash around her wrist and began coaxing her toward the barn door.

Lara tugged at Patrick's arm. "Did you call the firemen?"

"Yeah. They're on their way."

"Then you should get out too. This whole place could blow up."

"I'm keeping an eye on it. The structure's still sound. There's plenty of ventilation thanks to all the holes in the roof. If I don't keep some water on it, it's going to go fast." He glanced back at Megan and Goldie. "Can you get them the fuck out of here, like, now? This is making me nervous."

"How do you think I feel? Come on, Patrick, please." She put her arm around his waist, as if he was a stubborn llama digging in his heels. "Don't be crazy."

He turned flinty blue eyes on her. In that moment he looked so commanding, so utterly in charge of himself and his surroundings, that she felt a moment of pure awe. "I'm not. Now get them out."

Lara opened her mouth, shut it again. If he was going to be so pigheaded as to stay inside a burning barn that might collapse at any moment, there was something she wanted to say. Something so important, so significant, that she couldn't get it out of her mouth. Then Goldie bleated, a panicked sound that sent intense fear welling through her. She pushed it away before it swamped her. She had to stay strong for Megan, for Patrick. "Promise you'll come out if it gets worse," she ordered him, silencing the other thought that drummed through her mind.

At his nod, Lara ran to help Megan. Goldie had reached a state of advanced anxiety. Her eyes were rolling back in her head, her entire body a mass of trembles. If only she had a tranquilizer pen with her, but no such luck. "How about if we just lift her up and carry her?"

"She'll kick us or spit at us," Megan said.

"What if we each bind together two of her legs and just lift her up?"

"Are you kidding?"

"You know what? She's a llama, not a mule. I bet if we just start walking out of here, she'll come. She knows fire's bad." Lara jumped to her feet and stalked toward the daylight outside the barn. "If she wants to stay here with the scary fire, maybe that's her choice."

Megan skipped up beside her. "If she doesn't come, Patrick's going to be mad."

"Would you guys just go?" he roared at them over the sound of rushing water and snapping sparks.

"He wants us to leave. Anyway, Goldie's coming." A huge swell of relief swamped her as Goldie trotted past them. "She might be scared, but she's no dummy."

Patrick's voice came roaring after them. "Run!"

Then something exploded and the fires of hell rained down.

Chapter Twenty-Eight

*F*lames raced along both side walls of the barn, like the inside of an incinerator. A loud crash sounded, followed by a long, ominous creaking noise. Lara's ears rang and nothing seemed to sound right.

"Run," she yelled in Megan's direction. When no one answered, she looked back. Megan was sprawled on the floor, one leg bent under her. Something had fallen on her leg; it looked like a chunk of metal. She ran back, crouched by Megan's side, felt her pulse.

Still alive. Thank God.

"Megan, can you hear me? Are you awake?"

A low moan sent a shot of relief through her. Then she realized she couldn't see Patrick in the wild confusion of smoke and flames.

"Patrick!" she screamed.

Megan stirred. "Patrick? Where is he?"

"Patrick!" Lara tried again, in the grip of sheer, blinding fear. He was somewhere in that crazy morass of lethal flame, armed with nothing but a garden hose and his own skills. "Patrick!"

"Get . . . out!" His voice came to her faintly from somewhere on the floor. "Get . . . Megan . . . out."

Lara's thoughts spun in a wild kaleidoscope. *Get Megan out?* Yes, of course that's what she had to do. Megan needed her. If she didn't help the girl, she'd burn to death in this barn. But what about Patrick? She couldn't just leave him. She couldn't.

"I . . . Patrick, please!" Her voice broke.

"I'm . . . coming. Promise. Get Megan. Love. You." His voice came in short, breathless gasps, so she wasn't sure if she'd heard right. He was hurt. She knew it with every fiber of her being. She had to go to him, see if she could help him. But she couldn't, she had to do as he asked and help Megan.

She crouched next to Megan's face. The smoke was lighter down there. She took off her particle mask, which she'd pushed on top of her head earlier, and fastened it on Megan's face. Above it the girl's eyes were huge with fear. Lara spotted one of Megan's blue paisley bandannas sticking out of her pocket. She plucked it out and tied it around her own mouth. It gave her less breathing room than the face mask had, but she couldn't have Megan passing out.

She kept her voice brisk and businesslike. "I'm going to roll that metal thing off your leg, then I'm going to help you get up and we're going to get the hell out. You understand?"

Megan nodded. Lara crawled to the lower part of her body and shoved at the metal. The chunk of steel looked something like an old tool, or maybe a pump handle. It was warm to the touch but not hot enough to burn. Logic told her the piece of metal hadn't exploded, just rolled from somewhere. When she pushed it off Megan's leg, she saw a giant bruise on the girl's skin.

"I think you might have a fracture," Lara told her. "We have to get you out of here. Bend your good leg and get your foot under you, then I'll lift you up."

She put her hands under Megan's arms and heaved her upward. Megan cried out as her injured leg dragged along the floor. Lara wished she could stop and tend to her, but the flames licking at the walls were roaring loader than ever, and a hot wind chased after them. *Get out, get out*, it seemed to be saying—as if it spoke for Patrick.

She gave one last, desperate glance into the depths of the barn but saw no sign of him.

"Put your arm around my neck and let's go," she yelled to Megan. They limped toward the door one agonizing step at a time. It was so close, only a few yards away, but if felt like an impossible distance, with Megan moaning in pain. Lara cursed the fire, the smoke, the distance from Patrick.

She hadn't told him that she loved him.

She did it now, into the constant, roaring cacophony, every word snatched away by hot wind. "I love you. Get out. Please."

Something hot landed on her leg. She bent down to brush it away, and burned her hand. *Stupid.* Another cinder flew against her arm. Shit. They were going to burn to death in this place, she and Megan, their poor human skin and flesh no match for this vicious whirlwind of flame. She wrapped her arms around Megan, determined to take the worst of it.

Just then, when they were still at least two yards from the big barn door, a crowd of figures stormed in. Lara blinked at them, eyes stinging, sure she was hallucinating one more bizarre happening in this surreal stream of events. What were they, these helmeted, masked, padded people emerging from the gray and orange swirl? Whatever they were, they took charge immediately. One of them broke away from the others and ran toward her and Megan.

Lara snapped out of her smoke-induced trance. She tried to say something but all she could do was cough. *Firefighters.* Of course.

The firefighter—she thought it might be Pedro—picked up Megan, one arm under her back, the other under her knees.

"Her leg might be broken," Lara finally managed to say. Her throat felt raw from the smoke. He nodded. "Patrick Callahan's back in there somewhere."

Another nod, and a thumbs-up. He gave her a push toward the door, obviously wanting her to go ahead. She resisted. "I have to see if Patrick's okay!"

"We're on it," he yelled through his face mask. "He's holding up a broken post."

"What?"

He prodded her again. "Just go. We got Patrick. We're not going to let anything happen to him." He shifted Megan in his arms and jerked his head at Lara. "She's going to need your help, no paramedics on the scene yet."

Lara nodded and ran after him, through the cinders clutching at her with sharp, fiery fingers, through the choking smoke, away from death and terror and . . . the other part of herself.

My God, that's what it was. Somehow, Patrick had woven himself into her heart, her body, her soul. Or maybe he'd been there all along, waiting for her to discover his daring, his unexpected kindness, everything that made him Patrick, precious, irreplaceable Patrick, who was now single-handedly keeping a barn from collapsing on them all.

She burst into the open air, where more firefighters were hauling a heavy hose toward the barn. One firefighter, axe in hand, headed up a ladder toward the roof.

"Don't you dare chop up my barn!" Big Dog yelled from the ground. Candy was with him, hanging desperately onto one of his arms. Lara caught her eye and pointed to the firefighter still carrying Megan. Candy screamed and pulled away from Big Dog.

When Pedro had carefully settled Megan onto a patch of grass, Lara knelt next to her. The girl's face was a white mask of pain, her lips trembling. "You're doing great, Megan."

Pedro pushed up his face mask. "There's a medical kit in the engine. You got her from here?"

"Yes. Thank you."

He hesitated, clearly reluctant to leave Megan's side.

Lara lost it. She screamed at him. "Go back in and get Patrick! What the fuck are you waiting for?"

Candy, who had just knelt at Megan's side, glanced up. "Patrick? What do you mean, get Patrick? Where is he?"

Pedro gave Lara an angry look, snapped his face mask down and plunged back toward the barn.

Candy grabbed at Lara. "Where's Patrick?"

"The firefighters are getting him out." Lara's voice shook. It better be true. It had to be true. "He'll be fine." But how could it be true? How could he be fine when he was stuck inside the heart of a volcano?

She forced herself to focus on Megan. "I'm going to feel your leg, see if there's an obvious break. Ready?"

As soon as Lara touched her, Megan gasped and

Candy burst into tears. Lara pushed her hair out of her eyes. "Candy." She waved a hand in front of her face. "I need your help. Can you go to that fire engine and find their medical kit? It should be obvious. It'll have either an X or a cross on it. Can you do that for me?"

Candy took a deep, gasping breath, then nodded tightly. "I can do that. I'll be okay. I'll be right back."

Lara felt Megan's pulse, noted her shallow breathing. The girl was probably going into shock. She needed to get to a hospital as quickly as possible. In the calmest voice she could manage, she said, "Sweetie, I need you to stay still. Just relax and let me do my thing. I promise you I'm very good at it. The firefighters are good at what they do too, so don't worry about Patrick. Just focus on me and do exactly what I say, okay?"

Megan's drifting gaze homed in on Lara's, and after a moment she nodded.

"Okay, first thing, stay calm. Have you ever seen those T-shirts? 'Stay calm and sleep with a firefighter'? 'Stay calm and read a book'? That sort of thing?"

A smile ghosted across Megan's pale lips. Good sign.

"Great. Stay calm and do what Lara says."

Assessing Megan's purpling leg, she saw lots of swelling but no break in the skin. Judging by the amount of pain and swelling, she'd probably sustained a simple fracture.

"I don't think it's a major break," she told Megan, taking the opportunity to check the girl's alertness. She could have some other, hidden injury, blood secretly pouring into her abdominal cavity. "I'm going to immobilize it so it doesn't hurt as much, then we'll get you to the hospital and they'll splint it properly. Sound good?"

Megan nodded as Candy reappeared, hauling a

heavy, soft-sided orange saddlebag with an X and First Aid written on it in Sharpie. Lara looked inside and found plenty of material for a makeshift splint, including a flat tongue depressor and some Ace bandages.

"Candy, I'm going to need your help. I want you to hold her ankle and keep a tiny bit of a tug on it while I set this splint." She demonstrated, taking gentle hold of Megan's ankle and applying a steady traction. Megan bit her lip to stop the moan of pain.

"That doesn't hurt her?" Candy cried.

"It'll hurt a little, but once we get that leg immobilized, she'll feel a lot better. You okay, Megan?"

"Yes," she gasped.

"What the hell's going on here?" The booming voice of Big Dog startled them. Candy, who had just taken hold of Megan's foot, jarred it against her thigh, making Megan cry out. He stepped so close to Lara that she felt his pants leg brush her arm. Too close for comfort. Whether he was still in shock or not, the man was unpredictable. She couldn't allow him to interfere.

Lara gave him a stern warning look as she wrapped the Ace bandage into a pad. "I'm splinting her leg. Please back away."

"Get your hands off my daughter."

"Daddy! Stop it!" Megan was getting agitated, which was the absolute worst thing that could happen.

She had to get him away from Megan. The splint would have to wait. Scrambling to her feet, she spread her arms wide, as if to shield Megan from his presence. "Mr. Callahan, you'd better back up, right now. You're causing more harm than good."

"Who asked you to play doctor?"

"Go away, Cal," Candy urged from her position at Megan's feet. "Please, just go. Have you forgotten? Lara *is* a doctor, and she's helping Megan."

Big Dog made a wild gesture with his arm, barely missing Lara. "I'm not leaving my own daughter in *her* hands."

"Would you stop with that stupid attitude?" Candy wailed. "I'm so sick of it I could cry!"

But Lara had had enough. "Don't let her move that leg, Candy," she ordered Mrs. Callahan. "And you, Mr. Callahan, you might not like me, but you'd better get used to me. I'm not going anywhere." She moved forward, forcing him to retreat one step at a time. "And if you don't let me do my job, I'll get those firefighters to remove you from the premises."

She'd used that line a few times at the hospital with unruly family members, but had no idea if it would work on someone's private property. But it did its job; it caught his attention. He drew his head back as if building up a head of steam. And then—

"You don't call the shots around here!" he bellowed, planting his feet so she'd have to bump into him. "I do. If I don't want you here, you better get out."

"Oh yeah? Well, I won't! Not until Megan's leg is set and Patrick's safe!"

"Patrick? What's he got to do with it?" He tried to bully past her.

She had to do something, say something so crazy and extreme he'd forget about bothering Megan. Something that would grab his attention once and for all.

"We're getting married, that's what!"

It worked. He stopped dead, his jaw falling open.

"So you can put that in your cigar and smoke it!" Which didn't even make sense, but was worth it just to see the look on Big Dog's face.

"Did you guys hear that?"

The raspy, hoarse voice made her swing around. Patrick, supported by a firefighter she didn't recognize, was looking at her with a look of wicked glee. He was covered in soot and bits of hay. In his sweaty, sooty face, his eyes glittered like blue jewels catching the sun.

"Did you just say . . ."

She flung herself at him, only checking herself at the last possible moment in case he had injuries. "Are you okay?"

"I'm fine, thanks to these guys. They're making me go to the hospital, but I'm not worried. I've been through worse."

"He has multiple abrasions and a possible hematoma," said the other firefighter dryly. "Probably a hernia and a cracked rib or two. That tends to happen when you're holding up a barn with your back. Fire's under control now."

"Thank God," said Lara. Big Dog grumbled something behind her.

A siren announced the paramedics' arrival. "Rescue ambulance is here. We gotta get this guy out of here," said one of the firefighters.

"Do they have room for two patients?" Lara asked. "I have a simple fracture and a possible shock victim over here."

"Megan?" Patrick swung around to look at his sister.

"She's fine, but it's a lot of trauma. And the circumstances aren't exactly conducive to proper field care." She deliberately ignored Big Dog's grumbling. "She needs a hospital."

Paramedics jogged toward them with a gurney. Patrick pointed at Megan. "There's the patient. She's got a broken leg, so be careful."

They veered past him and went to collect Megan. "Patrick, you need to go too," Lara said.

"Someone can drive me. I don't need an ambulance. Broken leg's worse."

"You're so pumped full of adrenaline right now you're not feeling the pain. But you could have internal bleeding or other damage." She called to the paramedics. "You can handle two patients, right? Abrasions, hematoma, possible cracked ribs, possible internal bleeding."

"The firefighter from the barn?" The paramedic barely looked up from his quick, efficient field-splinting of Megan's leg.

"That's the one."

"Sure, we can handle two, as long as he can use a jump seat. Stay right where you are, mister. We'll be back in a minute." They rolled Megan onto the gurney and trotted with it toward the ambulance. Candy ran alongside, while Megan gave them a brave wave.

"We'll see you at the hospital, Megan," called Lara.

She turned back to face Patrick. "You'd better do exactly what that paramedic said. Don't even think about moving."

"Why would I want to go anywhere when I can just stand here and gaze at my beautiful fiancée?" He winked, a flash of vibrant blue in his weary face. The firefighter still supporting him smirked.

Lara's face heated. Before she could explain her reckless announcement of their nonexistent marriage plans, Big Dog shouldered her aside. He looked more agitated than ever.

"Weren't you supposed to be keeping the place safe from fire?" he thundered at Patrick.

Lara gave an outraged gasp.

"We were doing just fine before you came back," Big Dog said. "Soon as you showed up, another wildfire hits. Then the barn catches fire. I don't know what kind of firefighter you are, but that's not what I call a good record."

Patrick's jaw went tight as a drum. Lara knew he was fighting not to rise to the bait. He must be exhausted and hurting, and now to have his father dump his usual harsh blame on him—it was too much.

If he wouldn't respond, she would.

"You take that back," she ordered Big Dog. "Megan would have died if Patrick hadn't been in that barn. It would have collapsed on top of us. Right?" she appealed to the other firefighter.

"Quite likely." he nodded, with that dry manner of his. "That's why he stayed back."

"It wouldn't have been on fire in the first place if not for Patrick," growled Big Dog.

"I suppose he's responsible for the weather?" Her anger rose, and her voice along with it. "No rain in eight months, that's his fault? He started that wildfire, that's what you're saying? Even though he was in *Mexico*? Do you blame everything on Patrick, by default? Just like with Liam. The accident *wasn't* Patrick's fault. This fire wasn't his fault. None of it was his fault! Ever! It's unfair and it's wrong and you should take it all back, right now." Her voice rang through the yard, warring with the sounds of the firefighters gathering up their gear and the paramedics getting Megan settled into the ambulance. "Your son is incredibly brave and tough and caring. He's a real-life hero, and if you aren't proud as hell of him, you're completely insane."

She fixed her gaze on Big Dog's reddening face, sparing a moment to worry if she was inciting a stroke. Would the rescue ambulance have room for three Callahans? What the hell. It was time someone told Big Dog the truth.

Big Dog swung his face down to hers. "What's it to you, little hippie chick?"

She refused to back down, meeting him practically nose-to-nose. "I'm a *doctor*, not a hippie chick. And you know what? I know you're trying to insult me, but it's not working. I'm proud of the Goddesses. At least they're nice to people. They're even helping *you*." She gestured wildly at Janey, who was across the yard, chanting to the three frightened mustangs tied to a tree. "And what's it to me?" She poked him in the chest, hard. "I love Patrick, that's what!"

Chapter Twenty-Nine

*F*ortunately, no one had much time to react to Lara's spontaneous declaration, as the paramedics chose that moment to help Patrick into the ambulance. He was either exhausted or simply stunned by her reckless words; he accepted the ride to the hospital without complaint. The paramedics bundled him into the van, the other firefighter ran to help his crewmates with the cleanup, and Lara was left to face Big Dog Callahan on her own.

But he seemed distracted, scratching his head and staring after the ambulance. "Everyone left?"

Lara gazed at him, puzzled. His rage had subsided, replaced by the same confusion she'd seen earlier. Surreptitiously she checked his breathing; it seemed fine. "Your wife went with Megan and Patrick to the hospital."

"And Liam?"

Liam? How was she supposed to answer that one?

Shouldn't Patrick be the one to tell Big Dog they'd seen his younger son, and that he was living in sinful bliss with the family's former housekeeper in a ramshackle cottage in Baja?

Choosing her words carefully, she said, "Liam's doing well. We saw him. He sent you a letter. Patrick will give it to you when he's back from the hospital."

Big Dog nodded, his gaze drifting to the buzzing activity around the barn. The firefighters were gathering up their ladders and hoses. Janey was tending to the still terrified horses.

After all the drama, Mr. Callahan looked like a confused old man. Guilt tugged at her conscience. Maybe she shouldn't have yelled at him, despite the awful things he'd said to her.

"Would you like a ride to the hospital?" she asked him softly. "I'm headed that way."

"*No.* No. You can't make me go to the hospital. No one can make me do anything." As he took a stumbling step backward, his expression of pure, cornered dread rang a bell in Lara's mind. She'd seen that look before. On Mr. Kline's face when his family first brought him in. And suddenly everything came clear.

Big Dog's weathered face held the terror of a man who knew he was losing his grip on reality.

She ran through the symptoms of early stage dementia. Change in personality, or, more often, a strengthening of preexisting personality traits. Confusion about time and place. Memory loss. Challenges in solving problems. Agitation. All of them amplified by his forceful personality. She hadn't spent enough time with Big Dog to know firsthand if he had all or most of the symptoms, but she'd bet if she talked to Candy and Megan, the diagnosis would be clear. She should have recognized it long ago, but her history with him had gotten in the way.

She put her hand on his arm, half-amazed that he allowed it. "You're right, Mr. Callahan. But Patrick and Megan might like to see you."

He focused briefly on her, as if not quite sure he recognized her. More bits of information cascaded through her mind. *Firing the servants.* He probably didn't want anyone to witness his confusion. *Anger.* For a powerful man like Big Dog, loss of control must have been infuriating.

What should she do now? He ought to be evaluated, but she was probably the last person he'd trust to do it.

A firefighter came toward them, removing his helmet as he walked. Lara recognized him from the barbecue as Farris. "Barn's a loss," he told them. "Unsafe to enter. I don't know how Patrick managed to get that beam wedged in there, but it should hold for now. Best to tear it down as soon as possible."

"What happened?" Lara asked him. "There was some sort of explosion."

"Yeah, there was. Pedro thought he got a whiff of cigar smoke. If someone left a cigar in there, it could have started a slow smolder and eventually ignited one of the gas cans. There were a few stored in the back, looks like. Not the best way to stockpile gasoline."

Lara stole a glance at Big Dog, who got a hunted look. He was the only one who smoked cigars. That would mean that Big Dog himself had started the fire. And why was he keeping gasoline cans in a barn? Some kind of paranoia?

"So you're saying this fire had nothing to do with the wildfire?"

"No. Someone did a heckuva job clearing the brush.

Looks like the wildfire's going to miss this place entirely."

"Patrick." Lara wanted it on the record, before witnesses. "Patrick's been here clearing brush for a few weeks."

"Tell him he did a good job."

"We'll do that."

Big Dog was frowning again, looking at the ground and kicking at a rock. "Where'd Patrick go?"

"He went to the hospital. We should go too, Mr. Callahan. I'm sure Megan and Patrick would love to see you. And your wife needs you."

Surrendering, he allowed her to lead him to Patrick's truck. She noticed that his shirt was still damp from his time on the roof, but it didn't seem to bother him. Her patient, Mr. Kline, was often oblivious to his own personal hygiene. She added that to her running mental tally of the symptoms she'd noticed. Fatigue made dementia symptoms worse, and the poor man was definitely exhausted.

She helped him into the passenger seat, wondering at her own choice of words. *Poor man?* Was she really feeling sorry for Big Dog Callahan, terror of the state of Nevada and his own family? Now that she suspected dementia, she could only look at him as a patient. Whether he liked it or not.

He fell asleep on the way to the hospital, his body shaking with long, loud snores. It took her a while to get used to the Hulk's stiff clutch and oversensitive brakes. She couldn't wait to tell Patrick that his vehicle was just like him, stubborn and hard to handle. Smiling at the thought, she placed a call to Adam, who'd started in the neurology program before switching to family medicine. In a low voice, she quickly ran through what she knew about Mr. Callahan's recent behavior. "Sounds pretty classic," he said. "No one in the family has suspected something like this?"

"No. I think they're too afraid of him. He's a very . . . well, domineering type of person."

"Kind of like his son?"

"Cheap shot, Adam."

"Sorry. Do you want me to ask around about neurologists in Nevada?"

"That'd be great."

When she hung up, Big Dog was awake. "Something's wrong with me," he said, with perfect lucidity.

Drat. She should have waited until he couldn't overhear. "Possibly. But if we catch it early enough, there is medication that can slow it down. I was just talking to a doctor in San Diego, where I work. He's going to ask around and find someone local for you."

He laid his head back against the seat. In profile, his resemblance to Patrick stood out more. Same strong nose, same cheekbones. Same stubborn jawline. "Comes and goes, you know. Like walking on quicksand."

Lara's breath caught. Was he actually confiding in her . . . trusting her? She chose her words carefully. "I've heard others say the same thing. You're not alone in this, Mr. Callahan. It's important to get evaluated as soon as possible. You can learn to manage the symptoms, and doctors can help with treatment. But your family's going to need to know what's going on."

"Not your business," he barked.

Lara tightened her grip on the steering wheel of the Hulk and tried to channel Patrick's strength. Brave, tenacious Patrick, who'd kept an entire barn from crashing down on them. This difficult, short-tempered man, was his father, and he deserved her absolute best.

"They need to know, sir."

He rubbed his hands on his pants, which made her wonder if they were sweaty, and if he was nervous. What would it be like for someone so powerful to admit to something as terrifying as dementia symptoms? He must have felt so alone. Her heart went out to him. She knew all too well what being alone felt like. More than anything, he needed someone he could trust.

"But I won't do anything until you're ready," she said.

That seemed to calm him, though he said nothing else until they reached the hospital.

In the hospital parking lot, Lara took his arm since he still seemed shaky. He didn't object to her support, which gratified her. Had he forgotten she was the hated hippie chick from the Haven? Had she finally crossed over in his mind to legitimate citizen or even medical professional?

Or perhaps he knew he needed her at the moment.

Candy met them in the lobby. She didn't seem to notice anything odd about the sight of her husband arm in arm with the girl he'd wanted to ban from the property.

"Patrick's asleep," she told them. "They treated him for dehydration and cracked ribs, but they found no internal bleeding."

Lara hid her overwhelming relief behind a professional nod. No need for the Callahan family to have any more part in her personal drama with Patrick. "And Megan?"

"She's awake. Six weeks in a cast, but overall she was lucky. You all were."

Big Dog pulled his arm from Lara's and announced, "I'm going to see Megan. Candy, you stay here and listen to Lara." He shot Lara a meaningful scowl.

"No, Mr. Callahan—"

"Please," he barked. She'd never heard him say "please" before. "You spoke your mind the last time. Do it again now." He trundled off in the direction Candy had come from.

Lara gaped after him. After treating her like crap all these years, now he wanted *her* to break his news to his wife? It had to be done, and she was happy he realized that, but surely it would be better coming from him, or his doctor. But as she met Candy's questioning gaze, she realized that she was exactly the right person.

Like it or not, she held a unique place in the Callahan family.

"Is there somewhere we can talk in private, Mrs. Callahan?"

"You look exhausted, my dear. When's the last time you ate?"

Lara tried to remember; it must have been in Mexico, a lifetime ago. "Let's see what the cafeteria is like."

The hospital cafeteria's atmosphere and food smells instantly made Lara feel at home. Going for comfort food, she piled her tray with french fries and chocolate milk while she gathered her thoughts. She picked a table in the corner where she and Candy could have privacy.

"Mr. Callahan," began Lara, when they were seated. "Well, he wants me to tell you something."

"I already heard the firefighters talking about it. You and Patrick are getting married. I must say I'm very pleased to hear it."

"No, that's not— What? You're pleased?" That was impossible. She stuck a fry in her mouth. Nothing like a french fry to smooth over moments of confusion.

"I think you're adorable together. He's clearly crazy about you. I just hope you appreciate him. The Callahan men are notoriously difficult, you might say. But they're worth it, for the most part." Candy stabbed her fork into her chopped salad. "Breaks are sometimes needed, of course."

"Mrs. Callahan—"

"Candy, please. You can't call your mother-in-law Missus. It's too confusing."

Lara groaned silently. What impossible tangle had she set into motion with her reckless confrontation of Big Dog? "Nothing's exactly set in stone as far as that goes. What I really wanted to talk to you about is your husband."

Candy paused, fork halfway to her mouth. "Cal?"

"I wish I'd picked up on this sooner, but I think his personality change . . . well, not so much change as . . ." How to put it?

"Worsening?"

"If you will. It may actually be a sign of something neurological. I suspect it might be early stage," God, this was hard, "dementia."

Candy's fork clattered to the table. She covered her mouth with her hand.

"This is not a diagnosis," Lara said quickly. "All I'm saying is that he should be assessed by a specialist. They'll do a thorough physical and neurological examination. Let's not jump to any conclusions yet, but if that is what's going on, there are a few treatments to try. They can give him medication to slow down the process, and anti-depressants that can help his mood. The important thing is to see a good doctor as soon as possible. Early diagnosis is extremely helpful. I should have a referral soon." Since Candy still seemed to be in shock, she kept talking, trying to keep her tone calm and reassuring. "I know some excellent neurologists in San Diego, and they're going to get some names for me. I know this is a shock, but if there is an identifi-able neurological change under way, that can actually help all of you learn to cope with it better. Not that you haven't been coping, but—"

"Shh." With quiet dignity, Candy put her hand over Lara's. "Thank you. Really, thank you. It's better to know. I learned that with Liam."

For a moment neither of them spoke. Lara felt over-whelmed with sympathy for the other woman. Two of her children in the hospital, the other far away, and now this bombshell about her husband.

"I knew something was wrong, but I didn't know what to do." Candy shook her head. "There was noth-ing I *could* do, the way he was acting. But if he's willing to see a doctor . . . ."

"He may still fight it," Lara warned. "He's terrified. He might change his mind about all this, and I expect he'll blame me. You know, the hippie chick who sold him out." She could just imagine the fireworks. They'd make his rooftop standoff with the fire department look tame.

Candy was watching her with a look that made Lara self-conscious. She busied herself with her mini-carton of chocolate milk.

"You're very brave, aren't you?" Candy said.

"Me?" Lara thought that description fit Patrick far more than it did her.

"After Liam's accident, you were the only one who dared to tell Big Dog that he wasn't being fair to Pat-rick."

"Well, he wasn't."

"Of course he wasn't. But you were the only one who said it out loud. You kept saying Patrick should be allowed to see Liam."

"I knew how close they were. I thought it would

help Liam to have him nearby. And Patrick was going out of his mind."

"You care about people. You take care of them, and you say the things that need to be said. It's a rare quality. No wonder Patrick's so taken with you. You're quite similar, I believe."

"Hardly. Tough firefighter, pale-faced doctor."

"Nonsense. You're beautiful. I always thought so, even when I only saw you in black. Patrick's a lucky man. You must love him, to get involved in our problems like this."

Lara felt a deep blush sweep across her face. She took a long drink of her milk, hoping the carton would block her embarrassment. "Well," she said, "I'm happy to help the family in any way I can. I'll be back in San Diego, but I'll make sure you have my cell number. Big Dog may forget that we had a temporary truce, but I won't."

Candy gave her a knowing smile. "Of course you won't. Brave, like I said."

"Honestly, Mrs. Callahan, I think you're pretty brave yourself."

"Comes in handy when you're with a Callahan man." She gave a quick wink, as evanescent as a snowflake.

Before leaving the hospital, Lara snuck into Patrick's room. He was deeply asleep, his face peppered with cuts, including a big gash on his cheek. His legs were tangled in a white sheet; it looked as if he'd been fighting with it. She checked the nurses' notations on the board, then gingerly lay down next to him, relaxing into the heat radiating from his body. She put her hand on his chest, feeling it rise and fall.

"Biggest heart in the world," she whispered. "How did I never see it before?"

He answered with a soft snore.

"Thank you for getting out alive. I couldn't have . . . borne it if you hadn't. And sorry about that whole marriage thing in front of Big Dog. I don't know what came over me. I couldn't stand how he was talking to you. But I've explained to your mother that we aren't actually getting married. You'd better not feel obligated. Maybe I should leave you a note about it."

Tracing her finger along his hard chest muscles, she tried to imagine what such a note would say. *Please forgive my heat-of-the-moment craziness. Pretend the word "married" never came out of my mouth, though to be perfectly honest, the idea doesn't seem so crazy now. I'm sorry that I scoffed at it. I'd be honored and happy to marry you, but don't take that as any sort of obligation, despite what I blurted out in front of your father. He probably won't remember anyway.* She broke off that train of thought before it got too ridiculous.

"I can't believe how mixed-up everything has gotten. When I came to Loveless, I was so sure I wouldn't let the chaos get to me." She snorted. "Guess I'm no match for two fires, a missing brother, a former governor losing his marbles, and a bunch of hippie goddesses . . . not to mention the llama. I have to go back to San Diego. If I'm not back at work on Monday, they might fire me. And then where would I be?"

No mystery there. Any hope of order and control in her life would be gone. She couldn't let that happen. She had to go home.

Oh, but it hurt to leave Patrick. How was she going to do without him? She breathed deeply, inhaling the scent of him through the overlay of antiseptic and bandages. "Please get better really soon. Here's a huge secret, Patrick. I said the part about getting married to shock Big Dog, but the rest of it is true. I really do love you. Crazy, isn't it? I wonder if there's some kind of cure."

She let out a long sigh and hugged him as tightly as she could without endangering his cracked ribs. "Please get better soon. I want my wild, daredevil Patrick back. All right?"

A soft wheeze made her go still. Had he been awake that whole time? Carefully, she extracted herself from his side. Whew. He was still asleep. His dark eyelashes fanned across his cheeks, his mouth slightly open. She longed to press her lips against his one more time, to taste that quintessential Patrick Callahan flavor.

But if she did that, she might never be able to leave. Instead, she ran from the hospital room without looking back.

Patrick woke up from the most bizarre dreams of his life. He was carrying an elephant, on which rode his entire family. Lara was leading the way, dancing with a series of transparent veils and whispering things he couldn't hear. When he finally opened his eyes, his heart was pounding and his entire body ached.

Bit by bit his world rebuilt itself around him. The fire. The explosion in the barn. Megan. Big Dog's harsh accusations. Lara's shocker of an announcement. The hospital. His mother. Where was everyone? How long had he been asleep? He raised himself into a sitting position, his ribs groaning in protest. A plastic dish filled with the contents of his pockets sat on the tray table to the side. He pulled it over and fished out his cell phone.

Five-thirty in the morning. Two days later. He'd been asleep for *two days*? Did that qualify as a coma? He hadn't even had a concussion; he'd been perfectly alert in the ambulance and during the doctor's exams.

Maybe they'd given him some kind of drug to make him sleep.

Amazingly, he felt great, considering he'd wedged his body between a cracked beam and the old tractor for what had felt like hours. Maybe that hadn't been such a good idea, but it was all he could think of at the time. And hell—he was fine and everyone had survived. He'd done his job, no matter what his father said.

Honestly, it barely bothered him anymore. Lara's defense of him made it all worth it.

Two messages on his cell. Might as well listen to them, since it seemed far too early to wake up the nurses and ask for breakfast.

The first message was from Lara. "I'm on my way back to San Diego. If I'm lucky I'll still have a job. Don't worry about . . . well, what I said to your father. I was just trying to freak him out. It seemed to work. Anyway, we'll talk soon. Call me when you're conscious and feeling up to it. I . . . Get better soon! Oh— the Hulk is in the parking garage and the keys are under the mat. Talk to you soon."

He nearly threw the cell phone across the room. What kind of a message was that? It sounded like a blow-off.

Then the captain called.

"Psycho, it's Brody. I need you in San Gabriel as soon as possible. Melissa went off to some island for a goddamn story and I need to go after her. That leaves the station short-handed unless you get your ass back here. Call me as soon as you get this."

Chapter Thirty

The firefighters of San Gabriel Fire Station 1 barely had time to clap Patrick on the shoulder and tease him about the state of his face before he was back in the thick of things. Captain Brody had already taken off. Apparently Melissa had gone to Santa Lucia Island to interview a scandal-ridden senator who was holing up at an exclusive estate. A storm had struck the island hard, cutting off ferry service. More storms were in the forecast, and Brody wasn't waiting around another moment. He'd already taken off, leaving an SOD captain in charge.

A fire at a pizza joint, three freeway accidents, and a heart attack kept Patrick busy his first shift back. No stranger to pain on the job, he kept his ribs tightly wrapped as he worked. It only hurt when he bumped into something, and even then the pain didn't bother him. It felt strange to be back—familiar, yet distant, as if everything happening in San Gabriel was a pale shadow of what really mattered. He kept wondering how Megan was adjusting to her crutches, and if his father had seen the neurologist yet, and if Lara ever thought about him. These were things he couldn't text them about while lying awake in the middle of the night.

He probably could text Lara—she worked crazy hours too. But he didn't. It hurt him that she'd left before he woke up. What kind of way was that to treat a guy? Announce that you were marrying him, then take off? It wasn't right. Especially after that guy had spilled his guts and told her he loved her.

Of course, that happened in the heat of the moment, when he thought he might die. And quite possibly she hadn't even heard him. But he'd said "I love you" with all the sincerity in his heart, with the knowledge that those could very well be his last words, since the barn was threatening to collapse.

She should have at least stuck around long enough for him to repeat the words in a quiet, flame-free environment.

The other guys noticed his moodiness. After his second twenty-four-hour shift, he met Ryan and Vader at Lucio's, the restaurant now owned by former Chief Roman. Ryan was taking care of Danielle, Brody's five-year-old, while Brody chased after Melissa. Danielle immediately ran into the kitchen to flirt with Roman, with whom she'd conceived an instant infatuation the first time he'd swung her onto his gigantic, sky-high shoulders.

As they tucked into plates of veal piccata, Vader pointed his fork at Patrick. "Your head isn't in the game, dude. Something happened to you in Nevada."

"Yeah, I cracked two ribs and got my pretty face cut to ribbons."

Vader shook his head and spoke through a mouthful of meat. "No, it's something deeper than abrasions."

"Right, I forgot you're Mr. Sensitive now. They do fine work, the Haven Goddesses."

Ryan squinted back and forth between the two of them. "You guys speaking in some kind of code? Did I hear 'Vader' and 'sensitive' in the same sentence?"

"Yo, I can outsensitive Psycho any day," Vader boasted, flexing his pecs. "I've been trained by the best."

Patrick flicked his chest. "What do your pecs have to do with your massive new sensitivity?"

"What do you mean?"

"You did that thing with your pecs."

Vader planted his elbows on the table and fixed Patrick with a penetrating look. "I see what's going on here. You've decided that mocking me will distract me so I won't notice that something changed while you were in Nevada. You might as well just cut the crap and share your feelings."

Patrick blinked, shook his head, blinked again. But Vader was still giving him that earnest, *sensitive* look. "Only if you bring back the old Vader."

"Fine." Vader made his pecs jump again. "Now talk."

Patrick drew in a deep breath. It occurred to him that he'd spent enough time in exile fighting battles with himself, by himself. These guys were his brothers in every way except by blood. He could trust them. He counted off, as if he was about to launch off a chopper, then spoke.

"I might have brought up the idea of marriage with Lara. She laughed in my face, more or less. But then later she told my father that we were getting married. Unfortunately, I was about to get shoved into an ambulance at the time and didn't get a chance to nail her down. Then I passed out for two days and when I woke up she was gone. And Brody wanted me back. So I'm here. Fighting fires. She's in San Diego doctoring people. End of story."

"End of story?" Ryan shook red pepper flakes over his plate of food. "If that's the end, it's not much of a story. Why don't you go see her?"

"I can't. I've been taking a lot of time off work."

"Then call her."

"So she can dump me over the phone?"

"Dude." Vader shook his head sadly. "She told your father you were getting married. Chicks don't do that if they don't mean it on some level."

Patrick gave Ryan a *Who the hell is this guy?* look. Ryan, who looked like he was about to crack up, shrugged. "Vader makes a good point. Maybe she's embarrassed because she said that to your father. Now she's waiting for you to make your move."

"Waiting for me?"

"You *are* the man, even if you are acting like a sulky little girl." Vader stabbed a chunk of veal onto his fork.

"He doesn't mean that," said Ryan quickly, before Patrick could take offense. "He means that sometimes, when it comes to women, you just have to eat your pride and lay it all on the line."

Patrick slumped back in his chair. Lay it all on the line. He hadn't done that, had he? He'd danced around the idea of marriage, not really proposing, not really saying anything. And he'd left out the most important part of the whole thing, that little detail called love. "What if I've already irredeemably fucked it up?"

"That's what I love about you, Psycho." Ryan play-punched him on the shoulder. "You've got a killer vocabulary. Irredeemably? I bet she eats that up. She's a doctor, right?"

"Yes. A great doctor. She's smart and gutsy and says what she thinks. She cares, you know? No one's more loyal or standup than Lara Nelson."

"You left out her hotness," said Vader. "She's got knockout—"

Like lightning, Patrick reached out and grabbed him by the throat. "Watch it, bud."

"Eyelashes, I was going to say," Vader squeaked, rubbing his throat after Patrick released him. "It's like they've been dipped in gold."

Ryan snorted. "Seems like you better do something about this, Psycho. Someone else could be checking out her eyelashes down there in San Diego. Besides, who says you have to stay in San Gabriel? San Diego's a great place to live. You could pick up surfing."

Patrick winced. "Pass on that one. But you have a point. I've been thinking about joining a hotshot crew. I bet there's one based in San Diego. But . . ." He trailed off, not wanting to say what he feared most, that she didn't want him in San Diego, that she was perfectly fine with her condo and her job at the hospital and her chief resident "friend."

For ten years you figured your family was perfectly fine without you, some part of him whispered. *You decided they didn't want you, and were better off that way. You abandoned Liam. Just walked away.*

"Screw it." He balled up his napkin and tossed it on the table. "If she thinks she doesn't want me, I'll just have to change her mind. I know how to wear people down. I know how to get under people's skin until they either give in or want to shoot me."

"Hell yeah, you do," Vader agreed, a little too vigorously, Patrick thought—but he let it slide.

"I've got four days off coming up. Four days to talk her into giving me a chance."

"It won't take you more than four minutes, my man. You're the Mighty Psycho, dude! And the Goddesses all say she's head over heels for you."

Patrick gave Vader a hard stare. "You couldn't have mentioned that before?"

"You don't need external validation, dude. You need to believe it in your heart." He thumped his chest.

Ryan choked with laughter, while Patrick just shook his head and tossed some bills on the table.

As he was leaving, Roman emerged from the kitchen, with Danielle swinging from one of his arms as if it were a tree branch.

"Great meal, Chief," said Patrick with a mock salute. "Wish I could stay for dessert, but I have a girl to win over."

Roman stuck out his hand. "Going up against the curse? Good luck to you. Hope you make it back in time for the wedding. Mine," he added, when Patrick started to explain that his marriage plans weren't exactly a sure thing.

A few hours later he was on a plane to San Diego.

"Are you sure about this?" The clinic administrator didn't seem to believe anything Lara was telling him.

Of course she wasn't sure. In fact, she was terrified. But it had taken only one day back in her familiar, lonely, orderly routine in San Diego to realize she'd already made the choice.

It had taken her overly stubborn brain a while to catch up with her heart.

"Absolutely. I really appreciate the opportunity, but I have things I need to take care of back home."

"In Loveless, Nevada."

"In Loveless, Nevada. Twenty-three thousand people without a women's health clinic, imagine that.

It cries out for an enterprising young doctor who happens to own her own building, don't you think?"

"If you say so."

Adam had an even more skeptical reaction when she gave him the news during a pharmaceutical luncheon. As the sales rep droned on about a new fertility drug, he whispered, *"Live* in Loveless? Have you really thought this through?"

"I'll take my boards in Nevada instead of California. I even have a built-in staff."

"Those what-did-you-call-them? The Goddesses?"

"Yeah. Romaine wants to help out, and so does Janey. I don't see why a clinic can't also offer healing massage and maybe a few workshops on emotional and mental health topics."

Adam pretended to scrawl some notes on the sales rep's pitch. No one else even bothered. "You said you hated Loveless."

"My family's there." Her heart warmed as she said the words out loud for the first time. "And it's not such a bad place. The town has finally warmed up to me."

"And that psychotic maniac has nothing to do with this?"

She hesitated, then decided there was no reason to hide the truth, no matter what happened next with Patrick. "Well, yes. I'm in love with him."

"In love!" Heads swiveled, and the sales rep on the stage glared at them. "I didn't know that was on the agenda."

"It wasn't, believe me. Not in the plan, not on the radar, and I have no idea what's going to come of it. I don't even know what I *want* to come of it. Except . . ."

She hesitated. Into the gap came the voice of the sales rep. "With our product's fewer side effects and lower cost profile, more couples will be able to afford to make their dream of having children come true."

"Children." A lightbulb went off, suddenly illumi-
nating her entire world. The same thought had surfaced
briefly during her bout of stomach flu in Mexico. Now
the full truth shone with a bright, steady light. Why else
had she gone into family medicine? Why else did she
cherish the time she spent with her youngest patients?
Why else had she taken Liam under her wing? "I want
a family. I want children. Wild ones, the kind who ride
dirt bikes and howl at the moon. The kind who watch
out for each other and love their families so much they
stay inside burning buildings to save their sisters. Or
brothers."

"I have no idea what you're talking about."

"You aren't very close to your family, are you?"

"Sure. I see them every Christmas. That's close
enough for me."

"Well, I wasn't even sure I had a family until I went
back to Loveless. It turns out that I have two. One of
them just doesn't know it yet. But I think they'll come
around."

Even Big Dog would, if she was stubborn enough
about it. And she would be.

But Adam was now eyeing a fresh-faced intern who
was taking nearly as many notes as he was pretending
to. "What was that?"

"Nothing. Thanks for being such a good friend."

When Lara got home, the dark silhouette of a man leaning against her patio railing gave her a fright, until she
caught the faint scent of smoke and the indefinable es-
sence of Patrick. She pushed aside a dangling vine to
flick on the outdoor light. It was Patrick, all right. The
cuts on his face, along with the tension in his body,
made him look more dangerous than ever.

She took a deep breath of sweet jasmine-scented air. "How are you feeling? You aren't in pain, are you?"

He ignored the part about pain. "I'm feeling confused."

"Oh." She swallowed.

"Yeah. One minute I'm getting the good news that I'm engaged to be married, the next I'm on my ass in a hospital bed and my alleged fiancée is nowhere around. Makes it hard for a guy to know where he stands." He shoved his hands in the pockets of his jeans. The muscles of his forearms rippled in the most distracting way.

Three steps separated her from him. She took the first step. Her skin tingled. She felt light-headed, as if she might float the rest of the way. "Where does a guy want to stand?"

He stilled. His electric blue gaze locked onto her. It seemed to pull her forward like a tractor beam.

She took the next step up.

"I can't speak for other guys, but this one wants to be standing as close as possible to you."

The third step must have vanished, because suddenly he was so close the heat of his body reached out and embraced her. She felt surrounded by blue fire— the true blue flame that burned deep in Patrick's soul. She couldn't speak, just moved next to him, to the spot that felt like destiny.

"I want to stand by you, stand up for you, stand next to you, in whatever way you want." His low voice ricocheted through her heart. "If you're not ready to stand in front of some judge yet and make it official, I'll wait. But I want that too. I want you, Lara. It doesn't matter where, or when, or who doesn't like it. We're meant to be together. If you don't see that as clearly as I do, I'll just have to move down here and wear you down," he cupped her cheek, "kiss by kiss, stroke by stroke, touch by touch . . ."

Her knees very nearly gave way beneath her. "What are you saying?"

He gripped her chin so she couldn't look away. "If we could go inside, I could show you." Those fierce blue eyes promised bliss beyond imagining. "But it comes down to this. I love you. I want you. I trust you more than anyone I know. I admire you. I respect you. And I can't keep my hands off you. To me, that adds up to spending my life with you. But if you aren't there yet, I'll wait. Not patiently, though. I'll be the kid in the backseat going, 'Are we there yet, are we there yet?' "

A smile spread across her face. It felt so deliriously good to be with him again. The passion and love in his eyes had the power to make her cry if she let it. She fought back the tears, needing to get a few things settled first.

"What about that? Kids, I mean."

Sheer emotion flashed across his face. "I'm for them."

"They make things kind of crazy and chaotic."

He shot her that vital, megawatt, daring grin. "Yeah. Just the way I like it."

She surrendered to that magnetic pull, losing herself in the vivid light of his eyes. They made her think of the sunlight dancing on the waves in Mexico, the endless horizon promising all the wonders of the world. Complete, absolute love swamped her.

"We can probably handle it."

"Honey, I'm pretty sure if I'm with you, I can handle anything."

And then she was in his arms and she knew with

every particle of her being that everything was going to be all right.

"*I love you* too," she told him, after they'd made it to the bedroom, stripped naked, and attacked each other like hungry wildcats. "I told you so in the hospital."

"You mean when I was unconscious."

She giggled in a way that made her seem sixteen again. "I might not be as brave as you seem to believe. I think I'm the one in the habit of running, not you. But I'm not doing that anymore."

"Oh, you're brave, all right," he said. "You think being with me isn't brave? You have the heart of a lion, my sweetest love."

The endearment made her glow. Patrick made a mental note to say sweet words more often, just so he could enjoy the tender curve of her lips. She ran her foot up and down his shin. He exulted in the feel of her bare skin against his.

"I should probably mention that I'm going back to Loveless. I'm going to turn the Haven into a women's health clinic."

He gave a soundless whistle. "Now that *is* brave."

"Yeah. I don't know how it's going to work out. The town can use a clinic like that, but it's still a risk. A lot of people still hate the Haven and everything to do with it."

"Not a lot. Might be a few diehards, but they'll get over it. And if they say anything, they'll have to deal with me. I intend to wield the Callahan name like a sword. Might as well do some good with it."

"But you . . . you aren't going to be in Loveless, are you?"

"Oh, I'll be there, especially if you are. There's a hotshot crew based in Nevada. I'm pretty sure I can get a spot on it. Hotshot crews travel a lot during wildfire season. But when I come home, I promise I'll make up for lost time."

"Are you really okay with leaving San Gabriel?"

"Yeah. It's time. The family needs me. Mom's going to need help with Big Dog, and it's not fair to dump it all on Megan. I might even try to convince Liam to visit now and then. I'll still get my adrenaline fix when wildfire season rolls around."

She was doing something with her hands, some maddening, muscle-tracing, chest-hair-curling thing. It made his train of thought go right off the rails.

In a sudden move, he crouched over her and pinned her arms to the bed. "You know what a hotshot crew is?"

"Whatever it is, it sounds like you'll fit right in." She sounded a little breathless.

As he spoke, he kissed his way down her delectable throat. "They're elite, specially trained, very physically fit firefighters who tackle the most dangerous," he tugged her nipple with his mouth, "hottest part of the fire."

"The hottest part?" She wrapped her hand around his cock. He closed his eyes at the sheer delight of her touch.

"Yes, the fastest-moving, most dangerous, hottest part. It's called the 'head.'"

She burst out laughing and moved her hand along the length of his shaft. "You're joking, right?"

Smiling through his blood-pounding arousal, Patrick wondered if it was always going to be this way with them—laughter mixed with ferocious want. And underneath it all, bone-deep happiness.

Suddenly overcome, he dropped his forehead to

touch hers. "You're the love of my life, you know that?" he whispered.

A tear ran down her cheek, then another. She didn't try to hide them or wipe them away. She let them flow. During all the things she'd been through—being a misfit in Loveless, Liam's accident, the barn fire, even getting sick in Mexico—he'd never seen her cry. Tenderly, he used his thumb to absorb her tears.

"Don't be sad," he murmured.

"I'm not. I'm just too happy not to cry."

"That might be a problem." He ran his hand possessively down her torso, to the heat below. "Because I intend to make you so happy, you might never stop crying."

She gave a gurgle of laughter. His toes curled. "Show me."

"It's going to take a while."

"We have a saying at the Haven. 'The longest journey starts with a single stroke.' " She lifted her hips to guide him into her entrance, where the hottest part of the fire awaited.

"Goddesses know best." And he sank into her, sank into the rest of his life . . . sank into home.